Crime Files

Series Editor
Clive Bloom, Middlesex University, London, UK

Since its invention in the nineteenth century, detective fiction has never been more popular. In novels, short stories and films, on the radio, on television and now in computer games, private detectives and psychopaths, poisoners and overworked cops, tommy gun gangsters and cocaine criminals are the very stuff of modern imagination, and their creators a mainstay of popular consciousness. Crime Files is a ground-breaking series offering scholars, students and discerning readers a comprehensive set of guides to the world of crime and detective fiction. Every aspect of crime writing, from detective fiction to the gangster movie, true-crime exposé, police procedural and post-colonial investigation, is explored through clear and informative texts offering comprehensive coverage and theoretical sophistication.

More information about this series at
http://www.palgrave.com/gp/series/14927

Lucy Andrew · Samuel Saunders
Editors

The Detective's Companion in Crime Fiction

A Study in Sidekicks

palgrave
macmillan

Editors
Lucy Andrew
University Centre Shrewsbury
University of Chester
Chester, UK

Samuel Saunders
University Centre Reaseheath
University of Chester
Chester, UK

Crime Files
ISBN 978-3-030-74988-0 ISBN 978-3-030-74989-7 (eBook)
https://doi.org/10.1007/978-3-030-74989-7

Cover credit: Pictorial Press Ltd/Alamy Stock Photo

This Palgrave Macmillan imprint is published by the registered company Springer Nature Switzerland AG
The registered company address is: Gewerbestrasse 11, 6330 Cham, Switzerland

For mum, from Lucy

For Emma, from Sam

Praise for *The Detective's Companion in Crime Fiction*

"The detective's sidekick is an intriguing and fascinating character in crime fiction. However, although this complex and evolving character raises many critical questions in regards to gender, genre and the politics of representation, the sidekick has hitherto been relatively underresearched by critics. Samuel Saunders' and Lucy Andrew's ground-breaking volume addresses this absence, offering rich, original and highly readable chapters on one of crime fiction's most well-loved yet at times elusive figures. Ranging from historical contextualisation to the most recent portrayals in the genre, and encompassing fiction as well as adaptation, the essays in this companion are certain to appeal to a wide range of readers and interests. Students, academics and researchers of crime fiction and popular culture will want to add this book to their list of essential reading."

—Charlotte Beyer, *Senior Lecturer in English Studies, University of Gloucestershire, UK*

"*The Detective's Companion in Crime Fiction: A Study in Sidekicks* provides a welcome and long overdue corrective to the lack of high-quality and detailed scholarship on the complex and changing figure of the detective's sidekick. With impressive breadth and scope, this collection of essays is essential reading for anyone interested in the figure of the sidekick in crime writing from the nineteenth century to the present day."

—Clare Clarke, *Assistant Professor of English, Trinity College Dublin, Ireland*

Contents

Notes on Contributors

Oriah Amit is a Ph.D. candidate at the University of California, Los Angeles. Her dissertation examines the relationship between narrative, futurity, and the expansion of the security state in late Victorian and Edwardian novels.

Lucy Andrew is a Senior Lecturer in English Literature and Programme Leader of B.A. (Hons) English at University Centre Shrewsbury, part of the University of Chester, where she researches children's and young adult fiction, crime fiction, and popular culture. She is the author of *The Boy Detective in Early British Children's Literature: Patrolling the Borders Between Boyhood and Manhood* (Palgrave, 2017) and co-editor of *Crime Fiction in the City: Capital Crimes* (UWP, 2013) with Catherine Phelps.

Nathan Ashman is a Lecturer in Crime Writing at the University of East Anglia and the author of *James Ellroy and Voyeur Fiction* (Lexington Books, 2018). His research spans the fields of crime fiction, contemporary American fiction, and ecocriticism, with a particular specialism in the works of James Ellroy.

Sally Beresford-Sheridan is a Ph.D. Candidate at the University of Waterloo. Her research focuses on women's British detective fiction of the interwar years. She examines how the language of these 'middlebrow' texts, in conjunction with advertising and publication history, created reading communities amenable to cultural change in Dorothy L. Sayers and Agatha Christie.

J. C. Bernthal holds a Ph.D. in queer literary analysis from the University of Exeter and has taught at the Universities of Cambridge, Exeter, Bristol, and Middlesex. He is the author of *Queering Agatha Christie* (Palgrave, 2016) and, most recently, co-editor with Rebecca Mills of *Agatha Christie Goes to War* (Routledge, 2019).

David Bishop is a Programme Leader for Creative Writing at Edinburgh Napier University in Scotland. A Robert Louis Stevenson Fellow in 2017, he writes the Cesare Aldo historical mystery novels, published by Pan Macmillan. His non-fiction publications include *Endeavour: The Complete Inspector Morse*, which analyses Colin Dexter's novels and their adaptations.

Dominique Gracia conducts research that focuses on Victorian poetry and short fiction, media history, and the reuse and recurrence of the Victorian in twenty-first-century television. Recent publications consider the utility of Friedrich Kittler's media history for literary studies, and the relationships between aesthetics, ethics, and friendship in NBC series *Hannibal*.

Alexander N. Howe is Professor of English at the University of the District of Columbia where he offers classes on American Literature, Literary Theory, and Film. He is the author of *It Didn't Mean Anything: A Psychoanalytic Reading of American Detective Fiction* (McFarland, 2008) and numerous articles on genre fiction and film.

Michelle D. Miranda is a tenured Associate Professor with the State University of New York. She has a Ph.D. in criminal justice, forensic science concentration, from the Graduate Center of the City University of New York. Dr. Miranda is the author of the book *Forensic Analysis of Tattoos and Tattoo Inks* (CRC Press, 2015) and the article "Reasoning Through Madness: The Detective in Gothic Crime Fiction" (Palgrave Communications, 2017).

Alice Nuttall completed her Ph.D. in English Literature at Oxford Brookes University, studying postcolonialism, the Gothic, and children's literature, with a particular focus on the representation of Native American characters in YA fiction. She is now a children's writer and independent researcher, and loves reading crime novels and middle-grade fiction.

Samuel Saunders is a researcher of nineteenth-century crime and detective fiction, popular fiction and print culture, and is currently HE

Teaching and Learning Coach at University Centre Reaseheath, University of Chester, UK. His first monograph, on Victorian periodicals and detective fiction, was published in 2021.

Kwasu Tembo is a Ph.D. graduate from the University of Edinburgh's Language, Literatures, and Cultures department. He currently lectures at Ashesi University in Accra, Ghana. His research interests include comics studies, literary theory and criticism, and philosophy. He has published widely on contemporary issues and debates concerning popular, visual, and digital culture in various international publications and collected editions.

Annette Wren obtained her doctorate in December 2019. Titled *'Now Watson, the Fair Sex Is Your Department': Gender and Sexuality in Post-2010 Sherlock Holmes Adaptations*, she examines gender and sexuality in post-2010 adaptations of Sherlock Holmes. She teaches a variety of courses focused on crime fiction, adaptation, and Victorian studies.

CHAPTER 1

Introduction: Step Forward, Sidekicks

Samuel Saunders and Lucy Andrew

A surprisingly troublesome aspect of putting together this collection of essays on the figure of the sidekick in popular crime fiction was deciding on its main title. Both editors were relatively pleased with the subtitle, *A Study in Sidekicks*, but *The Detective's Companion in Crime Fiction* turned out to be far more challenging to construct. Originally it read *The Detective's Assistant in Crime Fiction*, a title that we decided on perfectly naturally and largely instinctively. However, we eventually came to realise that our unquestioning use of the term 'assistant' was quietly highlighting the exact prevalent prejudices surrounding the sidekick that was the very inspiration for the collection's creation. The sidekick has historically been relegated to the simple position of the assistant, 'stupid friend', incompetent helper or overly enamoured biographer of a given text's hero-detective (Knox 1929), and this is, in fact, the precise attitude which the present collection is designed to challenge.

S. Saunders (✉)
University Centre Reaseheath, University of Chester, Chester, UK

L. Andrew
University Centre Shrewsbury, University of Chester, Chester, UK

L. Andrew and S. Saunders (eds.), *The Detective's Companion in Crime Fiction*, Crime Files, https://doi.org/10.1007/978-3-030-74989-7_1

'Assistant', then, was an insufficient term, as we argue that the 'sidekick' is almost always far more than simply the detective's assistant. Yet a replacement term for our title proved elusive. Indeed, a lengthy discussion surrounding what we could use as a more appropriate descriptor began to raise the very questions which this collection purports to answer. What exactly is the nature of this relationship between the hero-detective and sidekick? What does it mean to be a sidekick? What are the various purposes of the character, and why have they largely been forgotten in favour of a prevailing ideology that sidekicks simply exist to assist or accentuate other, supposedly more important characters? Are they indeed something more than a mere assistant to the detective? If so, then what precisely are they? And what kind of hierarchical relationship does the sidekick have with other characters in the narrative?

Just about the only constant feature that we could satisfactorily identify across innumerable popular crime series was that, despite the varying degrees of complexity that often exists within it across different cultural productions, there is always at least some form of a significant relationship between the sidekick and the hero-detective. The word 'companion', we therefore feel, works rather more effectively than 'assistant', as it better highlights how hero and sidekick often rely on each other and implies a far greater degree of narrative equality between the two characters. There is a distinction to be drawn at this point, however, between 'companion' and *friend*. Indeed, Margaret Kinsman points towards a 'rudimentary friendship' between the detective and his sidekick in early forms of detective fiction such as the *Sherlock Holmes* stories, and argues that 'modern crime and mystery fiction writers have modified this generic convention to present increasingly diverse configurations of friendship, exploring that mysterious and universal dynamic that unites people across barriers of age, race, class, distance and experience' (2000: 153). Whilst it is true that many of the detective/sidekick relationships explored in this collection could be described as friendships, we have deliberately opted for the slightly vaguer moniker of 'companion', as it covers a broader range of relationship types—hierarchical, professional and familial or even occasionally antagonistic—in addition to traditional friendships. In essence, the deliberate use of 'detective's companion', rather than 'detective's assistant', accurately summarises the opening argument of our collection: that the sidekick is an integral and crucial part of crime fiction with far greater significance, responsibility and narrative complexity within the genre than has hitherto been recognised. We aim to redress the prevailing attitude that the sidekick is simply the detective's biographer, assistant and 'stupid friend', by demonstrating how the sidekick is a necessary, often enriching and, crucially, universal presence in the genre across a number of different textual forms, from globally recognised detective fiction to more obscure cultural productions.

The original idea to produce a volume of essays on the subject of the sidekick in crime fiction first emerged through a conversation between the two editors at the fourth annual conference of the International Crime Fiction Association (formerly known as the Captivating Criminality Network), which took place at Bath Spa University in June 2017. A discussion surrounding the fact that crime fiction has been rather comprehensively examined from a variety of scholarly perspectives, and how those working on it are often forced to dig relatively deeply to find new ways of exploring the genre, naturally turned to what these understudied areas might be. The sidekick, it quickly emerged, is one such aspect of crime fiction, as a figure present in almost all of the different incarnations of the crime genre since its creation, yet almost continuously overlooked (or in some cases completely ignored) in scholarly examinations of it. Indeed, the word sidekick itself rather unfortunately echoes the word sidelined, and much of the scholarship has hitherto naturally aligned itself in favour of examining the eponymous detective of detective fiction (or, indeed, the crime of crime fiction).

Within established discourse, there is a general consensus that the sidekick exists only for several predefined purposes. The first, and perhaps most obvious, is that the sidekick is a bumbling and inefficient figure present only to accentuate the hero's or detective's supreme abilities, often (though not always) through their own intellectual deficiency. This certainly echoes Ronald Knox's idea that the 'Watson' figure of classic crime fiction is little more than the detective's 'stupid friend'; Antoine Dechêne, for example, characterises the sidekick as 'dull' and 'plodding' (Dechêne 2018: 127), whilst Stephen Knight refers to the sidekick as archetypically representing a 'baffled and threatened populace' always relegated to looking up to the detective's sheer intellectual brilliance against which their own pales in comparison (Knight 2004: 67).

This idea of the sidekick 'looking up' at the detective's proficiency is a trope that appears quite consistently across scholarship concerning crime fiction, and it is seen to consistently exist since the genre's generally accepted inception. Martin Priestman, for example, argues that crime fiction that appeared after the Second World War continued an already well-established

> line of *superior* detectives going back to Poe's Dupin, with a cultured rapport with his well-bred suspects offsetting his scientific sharpness, an effortless ascendancy over local police, a largely inviolate private life, and a *series of upward-gazing sidekicks*. [all our emphasis] (Priestman 2003: 200)

Maurice Lee echoes Priestman's argument, when he suggests that the 'astonished sidekick' is a recognisable convention in detective fiction that stretches as far back as Edgar Allan Poe's Dupin short stories (Lee 2010: 370). Similarly, Susan Rowland, in her analysis of Anna Katharine Green's *The Leavenworth Case* (1878) as a precursor to the clue-puzzle form of detective fiction which characterised its supposed 'golden age',[1] argues that the 'less astute sidekick' was, and remains, an 'enduring trope' of the genre (Rowland 2010: 117). She also, perhaps a little harshly, refers to the sidekick as, simply, 'dimmer' than the detective, and thus unworthy of dedicated critical examination (Rowland 2010: 119).

The sidekick as the upwardly-gazing, intellectually inferior character is therefore quite a common image. However, some have recognised this line of thinking as slightly unfair; in his widely cited monograph *Detective Fiction* (2005), for example, Charles Rzepka briefly explores the infamous companion to Sherlock Holmes, Dr John Watson, as an embodiment of the traditional sidekick, and correctly argues that '[f]ew scholars of the Holmes canon appreciate the strokes of genius evident in Doyle's creation of Watson' (Rzepka 2005: 122). Rzepka contends that Watson's character is, in fact, deliberately crafted to be both intellectually inferior to Holmes, but still a proficient enough scientist to justify his position as Holmes's constant companion (Rzepka 2005: 122–123). In fact, one might develop this slightly by arguing that Watson's position as a medical doctor actually codifies him as extremely intelligent, which helps to accentuate Holmes's abilities more effectively than if Watson were brainless. Simply put, it would not highlight a particularly 'superior' intellect if Holmes were to be simply more intelligent than a 'stupid' friend. Indeed, as a number of our own chapters argue, the extant popular conception of Watson as dull-witted stems not from the original Sherlock Holmes stories, but largely from the 1930s and 40s film adaptations starring Basil Rathbone as Sherlock Holmes and Nigel Bruce as Watson. Martin Kayman also adds a further layer of complexity to the idea that the literary sidekick is intellectually deficient to the hero-detective by suggesting that the sidekick's cognitive deficiency is designed not only to accentuate the detective's intelligence, but also to reassure the reader that they are, at least, smarter than the detective's 'stupid friend'. He goes on to argue that this is a way for the reader to realise that they are not supposed to feel challenged by the detective's prowess but are instead meant to simply trust it in much the same way as the sidekick (Kayman 2003: 69).

It should also be noted that the apparent cognitive superiority of the hero-detective, relative to the supposedly poor intelligence of the sidekick, is a phenomenon which seems to be relatively isolated to crime fiction, and that outside of the genre, the sidekick already occupies a position of greater complexity that has been widely recognised both within and outside of academic scholarship. In short, the sidekick is not simply always intellectually inferior to the hero-protagonist, but instead often exists to manifest qualities which the protagonist does not possess. These qualities vary across different forms of popular culture; as Bronwyn T. Williams argues, heroes from popular action films such as *Van Helsing* (2004) or *Independence Day* (1996), often embody characteristics other than intellectual proficiency, such as 'physical strength, calmness under pressure, stoicism and so on' and thus sidekick figures (for example, Jeff Goldbum's character David Levinson from *Independence Day*) are there to provide the characteristics that the action-hero (in this case, Will Smith's Captain Steven Hiller) does not possess, but requires in order to succeed (Williams 2007: 683). Other examples of this in action could include the character Q from the *James Bond* series of novels and films, Ron Weasley and Hermione Granger from the world-famous *Harry Potter* novels, or even Spock from the original *Star Trek* television series. Consequently, outside of crime fiction the sidekick actually often manifests those characteristics that are leftover from the hero-protagonist, in this case, the capacity to be 'bookish and nerdy', or in other words, to be their intellectual superior (Williams 2007: 683).

Back in the world of crime fiction, Kayman also gestures towards another common ideology surrounding the sidekick, when he suggests that Dr. Watson, who again is used to manifest a typical sidekick, 'mediates our attitudes towards the hero' by acting as the narrator (Kayman 2003: 69). In short, the sidekick often provides the narrative voice in detective fiction, and therefore is designed to act as an intermediary between the reader and the detective, and to translate the detective's activities into something the reader can understand (Rowland 2010: 117). Rzepka also muses on this idea, when he suggests that the most important narrative device for detective fiction is for it to somehow control the flow of the reader's access to information, and that it is the sidekick who is usually brought in to fulfil this function as a textual representative of 'average' intelligence (Rzepka 2005: 20). Rzepka's argument thus echoes Knight's suggestion that the sidekick represents a 'baffled and threatened populace', whilst Heather Worthington concurs and highlights how this phenomenon stemmed directly from the earliest incarnations of the detective genre. She argues that Edgar Allan Poe's narrator figure, the first incarnation of the recognisable sidekick in detective fiction, 'renders Dupin and his methods comprehensible to the reader, a device that Dr. Watson and later detective assistants will further develop' (Worthington 2010: 22).

One might be forgiven for assuming that the importance placed on the sidekick to act as both the narrator and (subsequently) mediator in a significant amount of popular crime fiction would afford the figure a significant place in scholarly analysis of the genre. But, in fact, it often proves oddly reductive, as the sidekick's position as the narrative voice tends to obscure exploration of any other purposes they might potentially have. Sonya Freeman Loftis, for example, explores the various connections between Sherlock Holmes and his perception as autistic, yet she labels Watson, as the narrator, simply the 'neurotypical sidekick', who manifests wider typical social attitudes towards psychological difference. In essence, Loftis argues that Watson as the sidekick is designed to represent the often closed-minded and misunderstanding attitudes of the wider public through his narration, which would mirror the reader's own thoughts, were they in Watson's position: 'Watson's invisible, default position as neurotypical narrator mirrors the assumed norm of the majority perspective in our society at large' (Freeman Loftis 2014: n.p.). Perhaps even more unfortunately for the sidekick, some have argued that they are ineffective even in their mandate as the texts' narrative voice. The late celebrated author of crime fiction P. D. James, for example, argues that Watson's narration of the Sherlock Holmes stories, whilst highly detailed, does not allow the reader to gain a true insight into the 'core of the man' which always remains elusive (James 2009: 11). Thus, Watson fails in his purpose of providing us with clear narration, even though the purpose of the character is to regulate the amount of information readers receive at any one time. James therefore suggests that we would probably be 'unwise to accept Watson's partial view of the measurement of [Holmes's] talent', and instead to view him distrustfully (James 2009: 11).

For the most part, then, the sidekick has hitherto received only cursory glances in academic scholarship, and many of these have tended to be reductive, dismissive, and often repetitive and largely underdeveloped. However, perhaps the most significant problem with current scholarly discourse on the sidekick is the fact that the majority of critical analyses of the character assume that they are only worth studying in terms of their relationship to the primary hero-detective or main protagonist. Even Bronwyn T. Williams's excellent reading of the sidekick as embodying missing characteristics, including intellectual superiority over the hero in various forms of popular culture, still only implies that the sidekick simply exists to manifest those characteristics which the hero does not possess, even if these qualities are largely positive. However, there has been at least some progress in sidekick scholarship in recent years. Kristen L. Geaman's edited essay collection *Dick Grayson, Boy Wonder: Scholars and Creators on 75 Years of Robin, Nightwing and Batman* (2015), for example, is the first academic book to focus predominantly on one of the most famous sidekicks of all time: Robin. Whilst Batman himself necessarily has a place in this collection, he consistently plays second fiddle to Dick Grayson, the first character to take on the Robin mantle back in 1940. Additionally, Lucy Andrew's *The Boy Detective in Early British Children's Literature: Patrolling the Borders between Boyhood and Manhood* (2017) spends considerable time focusing on boy sidekicks to adult detectives in late-nineteenth- and early-twentieth-century boys' story papers, identifying characters such as Sexton Blake's Tinker and Nelson Lee's Nipper as partial inspiration for the longer-lasting adult superhero/boy sidekick tradition inaugurated by the Batman/Robin pairing. Most recently, Stephen M. Zimmerly's *The Sidekick Comes of Age: How Young Adult Literature is Shifting the Sidekick Paradigm* (2019) offers a detailed exploration of the adolescent sidekick in a range of genres of young adult fiction, including dystopian fiction, fantasy, detective fiction and superhero narratives, and explores four key roles that the sidekick frequently plays, all of which can be recognised in various sidekicks to detective protagonists. Zimmerly identifies these sidekick roles as:

> 'narrative gateway[s]' through which the reader can better understand an enigmatic protagonist; as a 'devil's advocate' to provide conflicting views;

as 'comic relief' to an otherwise serious hero; or as a 'foil' to contrast with the protagonist. (Zimmerly 2019: 2)

All of these recent studies bring into focus the sidekick character, who is more commonly relegated to the background in the vast majority of crime fiction scholarship. Significantly, they also address the role and representation of the detective's sidekick in forms of fiction that are often omitted from the traditional history of crime fiction, such as comics and graphic novels, children's literature and young adult fiction.[2] It is telling that it is at the fringes of crime fiction research—particularly in scholarship that deals with young and potentially disempowered figures—where the sidekick is starting to emerge as a more centralised figure. The first of these forms—comics and graphic novels—is the most commonly omitted, despite the success of a number of popular graphic novel crime narratives such as Alan Moore's *From Hell* (1989–1998), Frank Miller's *Sin City* (1991–2000) and Max Allan Collins' *Road to Perdition* (1998), all of which have been adapted for the big screen. Whilst superhero narratives dominate the comics market, and admittedly not all superheroes fit comfortably in the genre of crime fiction, Neil Shyminsky observes that '[a]s a crime fighter, the typical superhero is a reactionary whose concern is the maintenance of the law and the status quo' (2011: 289), a definition which also fits with most detective protagonists in more traditional forms of crime fiction. Of all the famous superheroes, it is Batman, oft-cited as 'the world's greatest detective', who perhaps has the strongest ties to the crime fiction tradition and, more specifically, the detective fiction tradition, drawing on both American dime novels and British story-paper detective fiction for inspiration (Andrew 2017: 4, 63).[3] It is in superhero comics, too, that the term 'sidekick' is most prominently adopted and, of all the superhero sidekicks, Robin, the Boy Wonder, is by far the best known and is thus an important aspect of this study. Our collection therefore not only seeks to analyse the significance of the overlooked sidekick figure, but also to increase the range of narrative forms that we consider as crime fiction and to broaden the scope of our analysis of the history and development of the genre.

Alongside superhero comics and graphic novels, our contributors also focus on children's literature, young adult fiction and a range of television series—not merely adaptations of well-known texts, but also those that significantly reimagine famous characters, as well as original series which develop new traditions and sidekick variations. In addition to these forms, of course, we examine some of the staples of crime fiction: the short stories of Edgar Allan Poe and Arthur Conan Doyle; the clue-puzzle series of Agatha Christie and Dorothy L. Sayers; the police procedural novels of Colin Dexter. Yet, there are some more surprising subgenres here, too, that are not commonly associated with the sidekick tradition, such as sensation fiction, Victorian police memoirs and hard-boiled detective fiction. That the sidekick can be traced across all of these varied forms suggests that they are indeed a figure of significance, and worthy of critical attention. Our commitment to diversity in our analysis of the sidekick figure expands beyond form and subgenre. In its exploration of the sidekick, this collection aims to enter into discussions around race, class, age, gender, sexuality and neurodiversity and to examine sidekick characters who occupy different points along these various spectra. In fact, several of our contributors examine how their chosen sidekicks use their invisibility and their status as marginal or 'other' to their advantage and, in so doing, emphasise the worth of figures who are frequently overlooked, underestimated and, invariably, taken for granted by fictional detectives and real-life readers alike.

In short, we seek to begin to rectify multifarious scholarly oversights and add to the new sidekick narrative which is beginning to emerge at the margins of crime fiction studies as the sidekick in popular crime fiction, we suggest, is worth a substantial critical study of its own. As much as various pieces of scholarship have dismissed the sidekick as simply the genre's narrative voice, the fact that the sidekick is indeed the reader's window into the world of the detective, whether we trust it or not, should place the sidekick in a position of scholarly interest. In fact, whether we trust the sidekick's narration in crime fiction or not is in and of itself an interesting conversation, which has not yet been had, and studying the sidekick therefore affords us the opportunity to have it. Our opening chapter to the collection, Michelle D. Miranda's 'One Fixed Point in a Changing Age' revisits two of the most famous sidekicks in detective fiction and systematically demonstrates how they are far more than simply the 'stupid friend'. Miranda simultaneously explores the idea that the sidekick exists as the reader's insight into crime fiction, that the sidekick offers a 'practical functionality' to the narrative, and ultimately argues that the 'intellectual inferiority' of the sidekick is actually a necessity of the genre, rather than a character flaw.

Similarly, the general scholarly assertion that the sidekick's presence stretches back to the very earliest incarnations of popular detective is broadly true. However, we disagree with the academic consensus that the sidekick has existed from the very beginning simply to accentuate or highlight the detective's superiority. This point of contention has allowed us to return to some of the earliest periods in the genre's history, as well as to revisit some widely studied and globally loved texts with a view to challenging this idea. Indeed, Miranda's chapter examines the position of the 'narrator' in Edgar Allan Poe's 'Dupin' short stories from the 1840s, widely acknowledged to be a seminal moment in the evolution of the genre, and essays such as Oriah Amit's chapter on the marginal and seemingly invisible Victorian 'street urchin sidekicks' and *The Moonstone* (1868) and Samuel Saunders's essay on mid-nineteenth-century police fiction and 'reader sidekicks' both highlight how the sidekick occupies a more complex literary space in detective fiction than simply the detective's, for want of a better term, 'cheerleader'. Indeed, Saunders's essay also highlights how the sidekick is particularly conspicuous when absent, and argues that the figure is sorely missed in the apparent 'interregnum' period of detective fiction that existed between approximately 1840 and 1880 (Kayman 1992: 105). Furthermore, Annette Wren's chapter on the new incarnations of Dr. John Watson in contemporary adaptations of Arthur Conan Doyle's Sherlock Holmes stories—specifically, the television series *Elementary* and Brittany Cavallaro's young adult *Charlotte Holmes* series—revisits perhaps the best-known sidekick in popular detective fiction, and explores how the Watson character has evolved since his appearance in the late-Victorian era. These early chapters in the collection therefore take us back to some of the genre's most recognisable nineteenth-century roots, to perform various purposes. They explore how the purpose and presence of the detective's sidekick are deeply rooted in some of the genre's best-known examples, and thus highlight how the sidekick tradition has just as long a history as crime fiction itself. Crucially, however, these chapters also argue that the sidekick's position in widely known Victorian crime fiction occupies a far more complex and crucial position than has previously been recognised.

Moving into the twentieth century, this collection also explores how the sidekick has had a far greater impact on Golden Age crime fiction than has hitherto been accepted. J. C. Bernthal's chapter on the different sidekicks to Agatha Christie's famous Belgian detective Hercule Poirot explores how Christie played with the sidekick convention for various effects, and how she also used the character to explore ideas of metatextuality by inserting herself into the narrative through a sidekick character.

Bernthal brings his chapter up to date by focusing on the creation of new sidekick identities in Sophie Hannah's Poirot continuation novels. Similarly, Sally Beresford-Sheridan's chapter on the female sidekick in Dorothy L. Sayers's Lord Peter Wimsey novels gives a greater focus to the connections between Alexandra Katherine Climpson and Harriet Vane, their relationship with Wimsey himself, and looks at both female sidekicks' evolutions throughout the series of novels. Additionally, Alexander Howe's chapter on sidekicks to Philip Marlowe also explores the idea of the specifically female sidekick, arguing that they had a far more complex position in the hard-boiled tradition manifested by the Marlowe novels than has hitherto been recognised.

Subsequent essays in the collection bring the volume's exploration of the sidekick tradition firmly into the contemporary era. These chapters simultaneously complete an extensive chronology of the figure's evolution from the nineteenth century to the present day, highlight how it has remained integral to the fabric of the genre's construction since the very beginning, and perhaps most interestingly demonstrate how the label of sidekick is often difficult to pin down and has the ability to shift in unexpected ways. Some of these chapters centre on sidekick figures who do not fit the somewhat benign model of the sidekick found in earlier texts, but instead interrogate the assumed morality of the sidekick figure and uncover ruptures in the relationship between the detective and the sidekick. Nathan Ashman's chapter on the *Ezekiel 'Easy' Rawlins* mysteries interrogates the position of the sidekick in relation to the detective, arguing that the psychopathic sidekick figure Raymond 'Mouse' Alexander loudly manifests qualities that the detective, 'Easy' Rawlins himself, consciously chooses to ignore, particularly those that surround Easy's relationship with his own perceptions of his race. Mouse is a violent, criminalised figure who simultaneously performs the protective role of the Watsonian sidekick whilst also posing a threat to Easy's new life as a respectable and fairly prosperous member of the community through his detective work. Kwasu Tembo's chapter on *Batman: A Death in the Family*focuses on another troubled sidekick, Jason Todd, the second boy to take on the mantle of Robin to Bruce Wayne's Batman. Tembo's chapter explores how Jason's role as a 'bad' sidekick leads to his demise and, like Bernthal's chapter on Christie's sidekicks, explores how the sidekick figure can develop ideas of metatextuality, examining the effects of the public vote on Robin's death in the *Batman* comic. Similarly, Lucy Andrew's chapter on Frank Miller's *All Star Batman &*

Robin (2005–2008) explores another damaged incarnation of the Boy Wonder in a dark and violent retelling of Dick Grayson's Robin origin story from 1940. Andrew contends that Miller's narrative interrogates and problematises the adult detective/boy sidekick relationship, uncovering its not-so-innocent roots and heralding the dawn of an era in which the boy sidekick is 'the ultimate problem child'.

The final section of this collection examines the instability of the sidekick role and of the detective/sidekick relationship through analysis of texts in which the traditional detective/sidekick hierarchy is destabilised and where the sidekick has a greater mobility and flexibility within the narrative. For example, David Bishop's essay on sidekicks in Colin Dexter's *Inspector Morse* novels and the accompanying televised series *Inspector Morse*, *Lewis* and *Endeavour*, demonstrates how the position of sidekick is in and of itself difficult to identify, as Morse himself functions as both protagonist *and* sidekick at various points across the character's evolution and across different forms of media. Elsewhere, Alice Nuttall's paper on Robin Stevens' *Wells and Wong* series of children's historical detective fiction, inspired by Golden Age clue puzzles, explores character relationships against a diverse set of cultural backgrounds, and also highlights how the sidekick position is often changeable given the literary context of the text itself. Whilst quintessential English schoolgirl Daisy Wells self-identifies as the detective heroine at the beginning of the series, her trusty sidekick Hazel Wong, a Chinese immigrant and hence an obvious outsider in a British boarding school in the 1930s, transforms and repositions herself as the series progresses, leading to a more complex relationship between the two young investigators. In a similar fashion, Dominique Gracia's chapter looks at the role of what she terms the 'extraordinary sidekick' character in a variety of televised forms of crime fiction, such as *The Mentalist*, *Lucifer* and *Hannibal*, to question how the character can be simultaneously a sidekick and yet also the protagonist of the series whom the viewer follows and sees most frequently and who is imbued with the 'extraordinary' talents more commonly associated with the lead detective.

In summary, then, this collection is designed to perform a number of important functions. We seek to bring the position of the sidekick to the forefront of scholarly consciousness, by highlighting how the character has been unfairly characterised as a stereotypical and formulaic role, and simultaneously showing how this, simply, is actually not the case. We also seek to demonstrate how the sidekick has been a constant and complex presence in popular crime fiction since its earliest inception from the early nineteenth century, and also how the figure of the sidekick has transcended traditional crime writing and has broken new ground in contemporary or experimental forms of the genre. This, we argue, should cement the sidekick's place as a fundamental part of crime fiction which continues to move across generic boundaries and evolutions. Finally, the completion of this collection has raised even further questions that warrant exploration in future scholarly studies. Indeed, the tension in the sidekick's position as somehow invisible in their narration, yet also as a character that can (and does) use their narrative voice to interrogate themselves, their background and their personality, is just one example of a question that certainly needs working out in further research (see, for example, the tension between the ingenious invisibility of Poe's unnamed Narrator as pointed out by Alexander Howe, vs. the vocal internalised exploration of Hazel Wong's character and cultural position in the *Wells and Wong* series of novels noted by Alice Nuttall). However, for now, we are content to say that this initial exploration into the figure of the sidekick necessarily allows the character to step up and into the limelight.

Notes

1. 'Golden Age' is defined here as the 1920s and 1930s, using a definition purported by Julian Symons in his 1972 monograph *Bloody Murder: From the Detective Story to the Crime Novel.*
2. Notably, Charles J. Rzepka and Lee Horsley's edited collection *A Companion to Crime Fiction* (2010) attempts to rectify these omissions through the inclusion of Christopher Routledge's chapter 'Crime and Detective Literature for Young Readers' and Arthur Friend's chapter on 'Crime in Comics and the Graphic Novel'.
3. Andrew identifies the adult detective/boy assistant pairings in British boys' series such as *Sexton Blake* and *Nelson Lee* as the inspiration for the Batman/Robin relationship, drawing parallels between the origin stories of the Robins and various boy sidekicks in the British boys' story papers and positing that the tradition may have influenced the *Batman* comics via dime-novel detective Nick Carter and his sidekick, Chick. The publisher of the Nick Carter stories, Street & Smith, had an agreement with the British Amalgamated Press which enabled them to re-use published Sexton Blake stories, replacing the names of Blake and his sidekick, Tinker, with those of Nick and Chick Carter (Andrew 2017: 63, 198n).

Reference Lists

Andrew, Lucy. 2017. *The Boy Detective in Early British Children's Literature: Patrolling the Borders between Boyhood and Manhood*. Basingstoke: Palgrave Macmillan.

Dechêne, Antoine. 2018. *Detective Fiction and the Problem of Knowledge: Perspectives on the Metacognitive Mystery Tale*. Basingstoke: Palgrave Macmillan.

Freeman Loftis, Sonya. 2014. The Autistic Detective: Sherlock Holmes and his Legacy. *Disability Studies Quarterly* 34.4: n.p.

Geaman, Kristen L. (ed.). 2015. *Dick Grayson, Boy Wonder: Scholars and Creators on 75 Years of Robin, Nightwing and Batman*. Jefferson, NC: McFarland & Company, Inc., Publishers.

James, P.D. 2009. *Talking About Detective Fiction*. London: Knopf Doubleday.

Kayman, Martin. 1992. *From Bow Street to Baker Street: Mystery, Detection and Narrative*. Basingstoke: Palgrave Macmillan.

———. 2003. The Short Story from Poe to Chesterton. In *The Cambridge Companion to Crime Fiction*, ed. M. Priestman. Cambridge: Cambridge University Press.

Kinsman, Margaret. 2000. A Band of Sisters. In *The Art of Detective Fiction*, ed. Warren Chernaik, Martin Swales, and Robert Vilain, 153–169. Basingstoke: Palgrave Macmillan.

Knight, Stephen. 2004. *Crime Fiction 1800–2000: Detection, Death, Diversity*. Basingstoke: Palgrave.

Knox, Ronald. 1929. *The Best Detective Stories of the Year 1928*. London: Faber and Faber.

Lee, Maurice S. 2010. Edgar Allan Poe (1809–1849). In *A Companion to Crime Fiction*, ed. C. Rzepka and L. Horsley. Chichester: Wiley Blackwell.

Priestman, Martin. 2003. Post-war British crime fiction. In *The Cambridge Companion to Crime Fiction*, ed. M. Priestman. Cambridge: Cambridge University Press.

Rowland, Susan. 2010. The "Classical" Model of the Golden Age. In *A Companion to Crime Fiction*, ed. C. Rzepka and L. Horsley. Chichester: Wiley Blackwell.

Rzepka, Charles. 2005. *Detective Fiction*. Cambridge: Polity.

Shyminsky, Neil. 2011. "Gay" Sidekicks: Queer Anxiety and the Narrative Straightening of the Superhero. *Men and Masculinities* 14.3: 288–308.

Symons, Julian. 1972. *Bloody Murder: From the Detective Story to the Crime Novel*. London: Faber and Faber.

Williams, Bronwyn T. 2007. Action Heroes and Literate Sidekicks: Literacy and Identity in Popular Culture. *Journal of Adolescent and Adult Literacy* 50.8: 680–685.

Worthington, Heather. 2005. *The Rise of the Detective in Early Nineteenth Century Popular Fiction*. Basingstoke: Palgrave Macmillan.

———. 2010. From The Newgate Calendar to Sherlock Holmes. In *A Companion to Crime Fiction*, ed. C. Rzepka and L. Horsley. Chichester: Wiley Blackwell.

Zimmerly, Stephen M. 2019. *The Sidekick Comes of Age: How Young Adult Literature is Shifting the Sidekick Paradigm*. Lanham, MD: Lexington Books.

CHAPTER 2

'One Fixed Point in a Changing Age': Reframing the Sidekick

Michelle D. Miranda

Introduction: The Sidekick and the Detective Story

Le Chevalier C. Auguste Dupin. Consulting detective Sherlock Holmes. Everything we know about these detective heroes, we know because of their sidekicks. The nameless narrator and companion of C. Auguste Dupin featured in Edgar Allan Poe's series of short detective stories from 1841 to 1844, and Dr. John H. Watson, the devout friend of the famous consulting detective Sherlock Holmes featured in Sir Arthur Conan Doyle's detective stories that appeared from 1887 to 1927, played critical roles in conveying the extraordinary analytical skills of their friend

"Good old Watson! You are the one fixed point in a changing age" (Doyle [1917] 1967. His Last Bow. In *The Annotated Sherlock Holmes*. Vol. II, ed. William Baring-Gould, 792–803. New York: Clarkson N. Potter, p. 803).

M. D. Miranda (✉)
State University of New York, Farmingdale, USA
e-mail: michelle.miranda@farmingdale.edu

L. Andrew and S. Saunders (eds.), *The Detective's Companion in Crime Fiction*, Crime Files, https://doi.org/10.1007/978-3-030-74989-7_2

to the reader. The sidekick has traditionally allowed the detective to appear superhuman simply by standing in amazement, and has served to chronicle the accomplishments of a brilliant thinker and problem solver. As the fictional detective has varied in prowess and technique since Dupin and Holmes, so too has the sidekick varied in presence, purpose, and necessity since the nameless Narrator and Watson. Complex in character and crucial to unravelling mysteries, these two sidekicks feature prominently in detective fiction, lending themselves to setting a benchmark against which other sidekicks can be compared and contrasted. By exploring exactly how Poe and Doyle 'set the standard' for the sidekick from which others have evolved (or perhaps devolved), we can thus establish a concrete basis against which all subsequent sidekicks can be measured.

Both critics and authors of detective fiction have weighed in on the debate surrounding the sidekick's position—with some less forgiving than others, especially when it comes to Dr. Watson. In 1929, Ronald Knox famously addressed the role of the sidekick in detective fiction, asserting:

> The stupid friend of the detective, the Watson, must not conceal any thoughts which pass through his mind; his intelligence must be slightly, but very slightly, below that of the average reader. This is a rule of perfection; it is not of the esse of the detective story to have a Watson at all. But if he does exist, he exists for the purpose of letting the reader have a sparring partner, as it were, against whom he can pit his brains. 'I may have been a fool,' he says to himself as he puts the book down, 'but at least I wasn't such a doddering fool as poor old Watson'. (15)

Similarly, in a 1929 essay, Dorothy L. Sayers described the three benefits to the presence of the sidekick, referencing the overall 'formula of the eccentric brilliant detective whose doings are chronicled by an admiring, thick-headed friend' (13). Sayers first references the convenience of such an arrangement, as the presence of the sidekick allows for the utterance of 'expressions of eulogy which would be unbecoming in the mouth of the [detective], gaping at his own colossal intellect', and then proceeds with a more direct jab at the sidekick's intellectual prowess—'the reader [...] is usually more ingenious than [the sidekick] [...] for though the reader likes to be mystified, he also likes to say "I told you so"' (1929: 14). Sayers finally adds, 'by describing the clues as presented to the dim eyes and bemused mind of Watson, the author is enabled to preserve a spurious appearance of frankness, while keeping to himself the special knowledge on which the interpretation of those clues depends' (1929: 14). More recently, in a 1990 critique of sidekicks that have transitioned from novel to screen, Walter Goodman writes:

> [The sidekicks] tend to be stolid rather than imaginative [...] when they do attempt a leap, it is likely to be in the direction of the obvious so that they can be set to rights by the boss, whom they nevertheless follow with undeviating loyalty [...] Should it come to any sort of violent encounter [...] these subordinates can be useful companions. (27)

Alas, if the detective can (and does) solve the mysteries alone and the sidekick is not up to the intellectual task of crime solving, one is faced with the challenge of reconciling the role of the sidekick. Simply stated, the detective/sidekick convention adds a duality to crime solving, a duality that can be described as one in which the detective detects while the sidekick narrates. But this duality is more complex than it initially seems. There is a practical functionality to the sidekick, too, namely that of companion, protector, narrator and sounding board for the detective.

Perhaps the sidekick's most notable role is that of the narrator and chronicler of the detective's actions for the benefit of the reader. The sidekick is meant to be an observer, or more correctly a 'see-er', and to accurately record the actions and assessments of the detective. The sidekick tells the tale through their own eyes (which is meant to transition seamlessly to reader visualization) and serves to watch, listen and report. The sidekick thus provides a baseline for the intellectually ordinary; detective stories are structured around the narrator's 'frustrated desire to behold and comprehend that detecting' (Krasner 1997: 425). This is necessary; the partners must not be equal with respect to powers of observation and drawing inferences from those observations, lest the sidekick's narration becomes too informative to the reader who must be kept in the dark. The sidekick thus exhibits a degree of intelligence that is *necessarily* surpassed by the detective hero, rendering the latter figure extraordinary. The detective is able to observe the minutiae that are often overlooked by the eager sidekick, and the detective demonstrates his above-average intellect using superior analytical reasoning skills to describe to the mystified sidekick the significance of those observed trifles. This difference in intellectual prowess between the detective and the sidekick, or 'intellectual alienation' (Knight 1980: 44), is of paramount importance to the dynamic of the detective story; the detective and sidekick are meant to be unequal in intellectual skill, specifically with respect to problem-solving and analytical reasoning. Yet the sidekick can also be educated in their own right.[1] The sidekick thus possesses adequate knowledge, but also the inability to apply that general knowledge to the task at hand, which in turn allows the reader to follow along with the sidekick and yet still remain astonished by the clues and their significance when detailed by the detective. The sidekick's generalized knowledge, coupled with his lack of specific 'crime-solving' knowledge, provides a balance that serves to acquaint the sidekick with the reader, and thereby facilitates mutual companionship.

The sidekick also serves as the sounding board by listening to the methods applied by the detective and occasionally adding a comment that indicates that the 'obvious' clues were overlooked or their implications were unnoticed or misinterpreted by the sidekick, which further serves to highlight the differences between the ordinary sidekick and his extraordinary companion. The sidekick's help in solving cases and locating clues is often negligible (if not detrimental), but his surprise and amazement at the denouement is grand, a sentiment that is designed to be passed on to the reader. The relationship between the sidekick and reader is, therefore, perhaps more important than that between the sidekick and the detective. The sidekick must form a kinship with a reader, such that the relationship between the two is that of a longstanding, mutual friendship. As a companion to the reader, the sidekick acts as a consistent, recurring element of the story that is both familiar and comfortable. Furthermore, the sidekick is the reason these stories are being told—without Watson (or any other narrator in detective fiction), the reader would never know the adventures of Holmes or the ways in which Holmes solved the cases. In addition to highlighting superhuman qualities, the sidekick also serves to point out the lack of social skills of the detective so as to relate to the reader when contempt for the overachieving, sometimes arrogant detective may enter into the mind of the reader. The sidekick is thus the intermediary—the glue that holds together the fragile relationship between the reader and the detective. One could imagine that Holmes is so busy solving the crime that he would be far too busy to recount his adventures in a palatable way for the reader of 'average intelligence', and would be unlikely to do so as he often does not see the point of the exercise at all.[2]

The sidekick therefore fulfils a complex and multifarious role as the detective's loyal companion, protector and sounding board, as well as the narrator and intermediary between the detective and the reader. As the character evolves in Poe's and Doyle's writings, the sidekick has become more meaningful to the detective story and more important to both the detective hero who wishes to remain in the spotlight, and the reader who relies on the sidekick's accurate retelling of the event. In short, while the detective stands omnipotent in detective fiction, his very existence is because of, and not in spite of, the sidekick.

Upon Closer Inspection: Detailing the Sidekicks

The Narrator

Poe's nameless narrator comes to Dupin on a chance encounter in an obscure library in Paris, when both were looking for a book even more obscure than the library itself. Upon meeting, the Narrator describes fierce admiration for his new companion: 'I felt my soul enkindled within me by the wild fervor [sic] and the vivid freshness of his imagination [...] I felt that the society of such a man would be to me a treasure beyond price' (Poe [1841] 1994: 77). His latter assertion alludes to why the Narrator felt it necessary to document Dupin's unravelling of mysteries and share these exploits with the public. When the Narrator first experiences Dupin's peculiar analytical ability, there is an expression of amazement along with a hint of intellectual inferiority, with the Narrator remarking '[m]y astonishment was profound [...] It was beyond my comprehension' (Poe [1841] 1994: 79). This perpetual sense of wonder and lack of understanding would become the cornerstone of the detective/sidekick dichotomy, namely the disparity in intellect, which becomes more pronounced as the story progresses as the sidekick himself regularly draws attention to his inability to think like Dupin.

In the early stages of 'The Murders in the Rue Morgue' (1841), the Narrator is firmly placed on equal footing with the public when contemplating the material presented in the newspaper articles regarding the deaths of Madame L'Espanaye and her daughter, Mademoiselle L'Espanaye: 'I could merely agree with all Paris in considering them an insoluble mystery. I saw no means by which it would be possible to trace the murderer' (Poe [1841] 1994: 85). This statement, and others like it, serves to remind the reader that their knowledge base or data set is equivalent to that of the narrator, and that this information (or lack thereof) would be used by both the sidekick and the reader to assess the task at hand. Establishing the relationship and comparable intellect between the sidekick and the reader serves to keep them at the same pace in the investigation, while at the same time sets them apart from the detective.

Upon examination of the crime scene, it soon becomes clear that the Narrator does not share Dupin's observation and analytical skills, as the Narrator describes to the reader: 'I saw nothing beyond what had been stated in [the newspaper]. Dupin scrutinized everything' (Poe [1841] 1994: 86). The Narrator serves to describe the scene to the reader, providing access to a normally inaccessible place and serving as the reader's eyes and ears to situate the reader within the scene. But the reader quickly learns that while the Narrator is providing the details needed to engage the reader, the Narrator still overlooks the trifles that define Dupin's investigation, which further demonstrates the intellectual stratification among the detective, reader and narrator. When asked by Dupin about his evaluation and interpretation of the scene, the Narrator remarks that he observed 'nothing peculiar [...] nothing more than we both saw stated in the paper' (Poe [1841] 1994: 87), to which Dupin replies, 'You have observed nothing distinctive. Yet there was something to be observed' (Poe [1841] 1994: 88). Even upon examination of the crime scene, the Narrator does not gain any new insight and is therefore no closer to solving the crime, and after Dupin provides a reconstruction of events, the Narrator is still unable to fully 'see' what Dupin observed and understand how such observations led to Dupin's inferences. The Narrator states: 'I seemed to be on the verge of comprehension, without power to comprehend' (Poe [1841] 1994: 92). Upon the denouement, the Narrator then informs the reader that: 'I understood the full horrors of the murder at once [...] But I cannot possibly comprehend the particulars of this frightful mystery' (Poe [1841] 1994: 94). Here, it becomes apparent that the Narrator lacks not only the observational and analytical reasoning skills, but also the general knowledge and experience (and Poe might add the imagination) to consider the significance of the data in a manner that produces a comprehensive reconstruction of events as they occurred. These revelations of bewilderment, even in light of a detailed and precise explanation of events based on minute details, not only lay the foundation for the dynamic between the detective and sidekick that characterizes later detective stories, but also serve to convey the sidekick's inferior intellectual prowess and observational oversight. Crucially, however, it also helps the reader to not feel like an outsider having missed the obvious—after all, the sidekick was there and missed it all too.

The second story in the Dupin series, 'The Mystery of Marie Rogêt' (1842), presents an interesting approach to detective fiction, as the case was based on the real-life, still-unsolved death of Mary Rogers on the border of New York and New Jersey in 1841. The tale presents Poe's attempt to apply himself to crime solving utilizing the detection skills he had introduced through Dupin in the 'The Murders in the Rue Morgue' and simultaneously, Poe uses the tale as a critical assessment of the methods of investigative policing, media (newspaper) reporting, and interpretation of ongoing forensic investigations in the nineteenth century.[3] In this particular mystery involving the suspicious death of Marie Rogêt, the Narrator takes on an interesting role as what could best be described as a research assistant, tasked with reviewing media accounts of an event in order to extract critical information and relay it to Dupin for analysis: 'I procured [...] a full report of all the evidence elicited and [...] a copy of every paper in which, from first to last, had published any decisive information in regard to the sad affair' (Poe [1841] 1994: 489). As the story progresses, the intellectual difference between the Narrator and Dupin becomes apparent, and the Narrator's inability to apply Dupin's methods to extract meaningful information from the documentary record presented is exposed. Dupin indirectly criticizes the Narrator by challenging the reliability of the information in the newspapers that the Narrator believed provided reliable clues to the mystery of Marie Rogêt's death. As seen in 'The Murders in the Rue Morgue', the Narrator is once again on equal footing with the wider public in believing the material presented in the newspaper articles, with Dupin pointing out 'You have observed, in your notes [...] the most general opinion [...] the popular opinion' (Poe [1842] 1994: 509). Upon perusing the Narrator's notes, Dupin systematically picks apart each argument presented by the journal, remarking, 'it is the object of our newspapers rather to create a sensation – to make a point – than to further the cause of truth' (Poe [1842] 1994: 496). The Narrator becomes exasperated when Dupin demonstrates the flaws in each reporter's news account of events concerning the death of Marie Rogêt, with Dupin cautioning the Narrator against accepting the suggestions in one news story, adding that other news sources have merely accepted the first story as true and reiterated the material. Dupin indicates that the assertions are built on assumptions and later states that the news sources are ignorant of the facts, disingenuous and persistent in error. This criticism of news and its presentation of false or incomplete data serves not only as an important lesson in caution and ratiocination being taught by the detective, but also establishes that the sidekick is more closely aligned with the public—and therefore more closely aligned with the reader.

The Narrator overlooks important clues in the text and at the same time blindly accepts data presented—data that Dupin systematically discredits through his knowledge and experience. It is only after picking apart the obvious features of the case that Dupin draws attention to the importance of trifles, proposing that in order to effectively ascertain the circumstances surrounding Marie Rogêt's death, Dupin and the Narrator should discard the obvious aspects of the case, focus on the ancillary details, and, in essence, question everything: 'We must occupy ourselves with other investigations [...] [There are] important questions utterly untouched by the evidence; and there are others of equal moment, which have met with no attention. We must endeavour to satisfy ourselves by personal inquiry' (Poe [1842] 1994: 505). Unhappy with the data presented from the Narrator's research, Dupin relegates the Narrator to reviewing affidavits while Dupin goes through the newspapers for those important ancillary details that the Narrator overlooked. When Dupin presents the Narrator with a new set of critical information from the same material which had been reviewed by the Narrator initially, the Narrator states, 'Upon reading these various extracts, they not only seemed to me irrelevant, but I could perceive no mode in which any one of them could be brought to bear on the matter in hand. I waited for some explanation from Dupin' (Poe [1842] 1994: 508). Once again, the Narrator overlooks the important details that are critical to the investigation and focuses on information that was erroneous, contradictory and in some instances, completely wrong. Without the ability to extract the correct information, the Narrator would never be able to reason analytically and come to a logical conclusion. Throughout 'The Mystery of Marie Rogêt', Poe thus utilizes the Narrator as a manifestation of the public to present all of the reported 'facts' of the case, along with the subsequent interpretations, clarifications and criticisms of those 'facts' by an expert. This is done so that the reader can draw inferences about Rogêt's death (and, more importantly, the mysterious death of Mary Rogers). Poe tries his hand at real criminal detection, utilizing the case of Marie Rogêt as a means to present his attempt at analytical crime solving.

Astounded once again in 'The Purloined Letter' (1844), the Narrator presents a final example of how Dupin's intellect is applied to criminal investigations. The apparent difference in observational skills between the Narrator and Dupin is again highlighted in a brief exchange in which

Dupin asks the Narrator if he has ever noticed the street signs over shop doors, to which the Narrator replies, 'I have never given the matter a thought' (Poe [1844] 1994: 330). In drawing a parallel between the case and the signs, Dupin asserts that evidence 'escape(s) observation by dint of being excessively obvious' and that the investigatory blunder by the Prefect is due to oversight of that which is hiding in plain sight (Poe [1844] 1994: 330). This street-signs exchange between Dupin and the Narrator is similar to the exchange between Holmes and Watson in 'A Scandal in Bohemia' regarding the stairway in their flat. Watson admits, when questioned by Holmes, that although he has seen the steps in 221B Baker Street hundreds of times, he does not know the number of steps that are present. For Holmes, this is because Watson 'sees, but does not observe' (Doyle [1891b] 1967: 349). Holmes also echoes Dupin in *The Hound of Baskervilles*, remarking that 'The world is full of obvious things which nobody by any chance ever observes' (Doyle [1901–2] 1967: 18).

Thus, whether it is in a street scene during a leisurely stroll, a crime scene or a review of a letter or series of news briefs, the Narrator consistently overlooks numerous details that have meaning to his detective counterpart. The interactions between the sidekick and the detective demonstrate their differences with respect to both thought and action, with the latter demonstrated by the detective navigating through a scene and ultimately obtaining far different results. While such interactions serve to augment the analytical contrast between the detective and sidekick, they also serve to strengthen the correlation between the sidekick and the reader. Not only does it place the reader on equal footing with the sidekick, but it also serves to make the denouement grander, effectively elevating the status of the detective as cases are solved. One might ask what the sidekick would gain by expressing their foolishness and oversight to the reader, but therein lies the power and importance of the sidekick—putting aside their ego to convey a lesson in observation and attention to detail. As the most prolific sidekick in the history of detective fiction, John Watson's humility is immeasurable in this regard.

Dr. John H. Watson

Watson is the sidekick extraordinaire. His background and persona are more developed than Poe's Narrator, embracing all of the Narrator's characteristics and also possessing many additional attributes that became the basis for sidekicks that appeared after him. Throughout the stories,

Holmes routinely refers to Watson as his friend, companion, biographer and historian. Upon completion of their first case together, *A Study in Scarlet* (1887), Watson establishes his role in the series by remarking to Holmes, 'Your merits should be publicly recognized. You should publish an account of the case. If you won't, I will for you', to which Holmes simply replies, 'You may do what you like, Doctor' (Doyle [1887] 1967: 233). Watson is loyal—describing himself as obedient[4]—is invaluable to Holmes, and is consistently amazed by the reasoning skills and powers of observation that characterize the detective. Even Holmes is aware of Watson's importance, famously remarking, 'I am lost without my Boswell' (Doyle [1891b] 1967: 351). Enamoured with Holmes, Watson informs the reader that he 'had no keener pleasure than in following Holmes in his professional investigations, and in admiring the rapid deductions, as swift as intuitions, and yet always founded on a logical basis, with which he unravelled the problems which were submitted to him' (Doyle [1892b] 1967: 244). For years, Watson chronicles Holmes's investigative skills, and his role becomes not only preparing and cataloguing dramatic accounts of Holmes's adventures, but also deciding which accounts should be written and presented to the public:

> When one considers that Mr. Sherlock Holmes was in active practice for twenty-three years and that during seventeen of these I was allowed to cooperate with him and keep notes of his doings, it will be clear that I have a mass of material at my command. The problem has always been, not to find, but to choose. (Doyle [1927] 1967: 453)

While some stories are published with Holmes's reluctant permission and others remain withheld due to their sensitive nature (usually due to the status of the client), it is often Watson who uses his discretion when it comes to producing stories for public consumption.[5] Watson is even tasked with clearing up the occasional rumour or providing the true account of a historical event that was enveloped in some degree of mystery.

In a departure from the Narrator's technique of recounting the rigid, analytical nature of Dupin, Watson serves to tell more of a story by adding elements of character and scene development to Holmes's investigative adventures. Watson's descriptive narrative portrays a world 'crowded with solid, mundane material objects [...] and physical comforts' that serve to situate the reader and make the reader feel safe (Krasner 1997: 426).

The faithful reader of Holmes's adventures soon learns that Watson's accounts are not always recorded systematically without extraneous flourishes and drama, establishing Watson's role as a storyteller rather than solely a biographer. Indeed, Sayers argues:

> Holmes [...] does not always play fair with the reader. He picks up or pounces upon a minute object and draws a brilliant deduction from it, but the reader, however brilliant, cannot himself anticipate that deduction because he is not told what the small object is. It is Watson's fault, of course – Holmes indeed remonstrated with him on at least one occasion about his unscientific methods of narration. (Sayers 1929: 32)

Indeed, on several occasions Holmes himself comments on Watson's writing style, remarking in one instance: 'Detection is, or ought to be, an exact science [...] You have attempted to tinge it with romanticism, which produces much the same effect as if you worked a love story or elopement into the fifth proposition of Euclid' to which Watson replies to Holmes, 'But the romance was there [...] I could not tamper with the facts' (Doyle [1890] 1867: 611). A frustrated Watson then addresses the reader in a bid for sympathy, adding, 'I was annoyed at this criticism of a work which had been specially designed to please him' (Doyle 1890] 1867: 611). Such personal statements directed towards the reader allow for the bond between the reader and Watson to exist and develop throughout the Sherlock Holmes series.

Holmes occasionally points out his displeasure with the way Watson presents his case:

> [Y]ou have erred, perhaps, in attempting to put colour and life into each of your statements, instead of confining yourself to the task of placing upon record that severe reasoning from cause to effect which is really the only notable feature [...] Crime is common. Logic is rare. Therefore it is upon the logic rather than upon the crime that you should dwell. You have degraded what should have been a course of lectures into a series of tales. (Doyle [1892c] 1967: 114)

In another instance, Holmes remarks,

> Your fatal habit of looking at everything from the point of view of a story instead of as a scientific exercise has ruined what might have been an instructive and even classical series of demonstrations. You slur over work

> of the utmost finesse and delicacy in order to dwell upon sensational details which may excite, but cannot possibly instruct, the reader. (Doyle [1904] 1967: 491)

It therefore becomes apparent that Watson is a storyteller, not an investigator writing academic treatises. During one exchange between Holmes and Watson, Holmes dismisses Watson's spurious attention to irrelevant details:

> 'The Haven is the name of Mr. Josiah Amberley's house,' I explained. 'I think it would interest you, Holmes. It is like some penurious patrician who has sunk into the company of his inferiors. You know that particular quarter, the monotonous brick streets, the weary suburban highways. Right in the middle of them, a little island of ancient culture and comfort, lies this old home, surrounded by a high sun-baked wall mottled with lichens and topped with moss, the sort of wall—.' 'Cut out the poetry, Watson,' said Holmes, severely. 'I note that it was a high brick wall'. (Doyle [1926b] 1967: 547)

Holmes further points out those instances when Watson has been wrong in his recounting of events and details. One specific example Holmes targets was Watson's report of his apparent 'death' at the hands of Moriarty:

> There I was stretched when you, my dear Watson, and all your following were investigating in the most sympathetic and inefficient manner the circumstances of my death [...] At last, when you had all formed your inevitable and totally erroneous conclusions, you departed for the hotel and I was left alone. (Doyle [1903a] 1967: 336)

Yet, in those stories narrated by Holmes, he laments not having Watson's 'ejaculations of wonder' (or 'exaggerated estimates' of Holmes's skills embedded in the story (Doyle [1926a] 1967: 707, 720). Holmes needs Watson, and despite his embellishments, inaccuracies and poetic musings, Watson is the only one able to tell the public about Sherlock Holmes in a way that maintains the integrity of Holmes's abilities and at the same time conveys them to the interested reader. Indeed, Pasquale Accardo remarks regarding the competing scientific versus romantic narrative construction, 'If Watson had been able to comply with Holmes's wishes, he would have produced nonadventures [sic] as tediously dull and pretentious as the literary reconstruction of Mary Rogers's murder' (1987: 48).

In a more macabre exchange demonstrating the dichotomy between Holmes's abstract, 'cursed' mind and Watson's optimistic, romantic outlook (and one that further solidifies the importance of Watson as storyteller), the duo discuss their interpretations of the countryside passing in the distance during a train ride:

> [Y]ou look at these scattered houses and you are impressed by their beauty. I look at them and the only thought which comes to me is a feeling of their isolation and of the impunity with which crime may be committed there. (Doyle [1892c] 1967: 121)

Horrifying Watson with references to tortured children and murderous blows to man, it becomes clear that Watson is essential to serve as an intermediary between the detective and reader. Watson effectively softens the analytical, abstract persona and methodology of Holmes by adding the extraneous details and personal flourishes that humanize Holmes and infuse elements of reality into the stories. Watson details features and mannerisms of a client to convey a sense of humanity while Holmes sits back with his eyes closed to listen to the facts; includes moments in time filled with conversations that have no apparent bearing on an investigation to demonstrate companionship and trust between the detective and sidekick; highlights picturesque scenes in London to add elements of familiarity and atmosphere; and occasionally remarks on his own curiosity with respect to Holmes and his habits in an effort to remind the reader of the contrast between him and his extraordinarily clever friend. All of these extraneous elements serve to make the reader feel as if they are accompanying Holmes and Watson on their adventures.

In further demonstration of his role as a storyteller, Watson intensifies Holmes's powers by pointing out the ineptitude of others, such as extant law enforcement (Inspectors Gregson, Lestrade, and other investigators encountered throughout the memoirs are often subjected to Holmes's frustrations concerning the investigative oversight of the police) and also himself. On several occasions, Watson is sent out alone to 'observe and report' in an effort to 'simply report facts in the fullest possible manner to [Holmes], and leave [Holmes] to do the theorizing' (Doyle [1901–2] 1967: 35). Watson is not always successful, with Holmes stating quite bluntly, 'Your hiding place my dear Watson, was very faulty [...] You really have done remarkably badly' (Doyle [1903b] 1967: 389). Watson also demonstrates his inability to recognize his close friend, roommate and companion when he is in disguise (as a priest in 'The Adventure of the Final Problem' and as an elderly book collector in 'The Adventure of the Empty House').

In spite of Watson's investigatory blunders, Holmes is rarely, if ever, set on the wrong path. In fact, Watson's errors are useful to Holmes in the form of a new line of inquiry and reasoning. As a sounding board, Watson often presents alternate hypotheses, or scenarios, which Holmes systematically rules out. Watson asks questions that a novice detective (i.e. the reader) might ask, which not only demonstrates Holmes's problem-solving skills but allows the reader to stay connected to the plot. This plays out in 'The Adventure of the Bruce-Partington Plans' when Holmes and Watson are considering the placement of the body on the roof of the train. Watson blurts out a series of questions and statements of incredulity which enables Holmes to work through his reasoning in between the seemingly rapid-fire interrogation: 'Could it not have been dropped from the bridge? [...] How could he be placed there? [...] It seems improbable [...] Oh, that was it, was it?' and finally exultation, 'Splendid Holmes, you have got it!' (Doyle [1908a] 1967: 447). Such an exchange supports the role of Watson as a sounding board, allowing Holmes to work out his reasoning, all while demonstrating the intellectual discrepancy between detective and sidekick. As Umberto Eco points out: 'Watson (narratively) exists just to verify [Holmes's] hypothesis. Watson represents the unquestionable guarantee that Holmes's hypothesis cannot be any longer falsified' (Eco 1983: 219). While Watson often overlooks the significance of what he sees or misses clues entirely, he serves to direct Holmes to the truth. In 'The Adventure of the Retired Colourman', Sherlock sharply remarks to Watson: 'It is true that in your mission you have missed everything of importance, yet even those things which have obtruded themselves upon your notice give rise to serious thought' (Doyle [1926b] 1967: 550) and in *The Hound of the Baskervilles*, Holmes explains how Watson's reports provided the investigatory leads that led Holmes to various clues (Doyle [1901–2] 1967: 83). At the same time, Watson effectively serves as a voice for the reader, presenting possible scenarios that may have crossed the mind of those following along on the adventure.

One does not need to search for very long to find an instance in which Watson attempts to problem-solve like Sherlock Holmes. Such instances often lead the reader to conclude that Watson does not possess Holmes's power of observation, or that Watson is unable to draw the proper inferences from his observations. In many cases, Watson is forthcoming with both Holmes and the reader, admitting that he is unable to follow the line of reasoning employed so effortlessly by Holmes.[6] In 'A Scandal in Bohemia', Watson and Holmes have a conversation that becomes a fairly common exchange between the two:

> I could not help laughing at the ease with which he explained his process of deduction. 'When I hear you give your reasons,' I remarked, 'the thing always appears to me to be so ridiculously simple that I could easily do it myself, though at each successive instance of your reasoning I am baffled until you explain your process. And yet I believe that my eyes are as good as yours.'
> 'Quite so,' he answered [.. .] 'You see, but you do not observe. The distinction is clear.' (Doyle [1891b] 1967: 349)

In 'The Adventure of the Blue Carbuncle', Watson asserts, 'I can see nothing', to which Holmes replies, 'On the contrary, Watson, you can see everything. You fail, however, to reason from what you see. You are too timid in drawing your inferences' (Doyle [1892a] 1967: 453).

Based on these repeated exchanges between Holmes and Watson, one might notice that while Watson's education and skills as a medical practitioner enable him to detect and observe symptoms to diagnose a patient, he is unable to use similar methods to conduct investigations and solve crimes. Perhaps this is due to Watson's inability to consider an infinite number of possibilities when it comes to crime and criminal motivations. Or, it may be due to Watson's lack of imagination, which has been described by Poe and others as being a critical skill of the analytical mind.[7] However, what Watson is *actually* capable of doing is observing and reporting on those eccentric characteristics which humanize the abstract, analytical man that is Sherlock Holmes. In essence, Watson has spent a substantial portion of his time reporting on the disposition of his most notable longstanding 'patient'. As such, Watson is a Sherlock Holmes scholar. This fact is almost always overlooked, and while Watson is often criticized for his lack of observational skills and powers of deduction with regard to unravelling mysteries, his life's work has in actual fact been to study Holmes and disseminate his research to the public in the form of short stories and novels that chronicle Holmes's unique skill set. Watson is not stupid, thick-headed or dim-witted; he is in fact the world's foremost expert on Sherlock Holmes. In a subtle exchange between Watson and Stamford, the man who had just prior introduced Watson and Holmes for the first time in *A Study in Scarlet*, Watson states 'The proper study of mankind is man, you know', to which Stamford replies, 'you must study him then' (Doyle [1887] 1967: 152). Without Watson, we would not know 221B Baker Street or the object in which Holmes keeps his tobacco, what musical instrument Holmes plays to parallel his moods, or, most importantly, how Holmes is so clever and extraordinary.

During their first encounter, Watson states, 'I eagerly hailed the little mystery which hung around my companion, and spent much of my time in endeavouring to unravel it' (Doyle [1887] 1967: 153). In their seventeen years together, Watson learns to read Holmes's expressions from paying attention to and studying Holmes's actions and inactions. Subtle observations include Watson's keen observation that Holmes 'was sensitive to flattery on the score of his art as any girl could be of her beauty' (Doyle [1887] 1967: 174). Watson is also able to extract valuable information about Holmes at those rare moments when Holmes was willing to share details about his life's work.[8] Similarly, Watson remarks in 'A Scandal in Bohemia', 'There was something in his masterly grasp of a situation, and his keen, incisive reasoning, which made it a pleasure to me to study his system of work, and to follow the quick, subtle methods by which he disentangled the most inextricable mysteries' (Doyle [1891b] 1967: 356). In 'The Resident Patient', Watson confesses, 'I was sufficiently conversant with Holmes's methods to be able to follow his reasoning' (Doyle [1893] 1967: 267). On the matter of Watson and method, Holmes even remarks, 'It is true that you have missed everything of importance, but you have hit upon the method' (Doyle [1891a] 1967: 411). Contrary to these statements by Watson and Holmes, in her criticism of Watson, Sayers states, 'The beauty of Watson was that after thirty years he still did not know Holmes's methods' (1929: 43). Perhaps this is not necessarily the case—or even the point.

In many instances, Watson is capable of detecting when Holmes is engrossed in an unsolved problem and could anticipate Holmes's subsequent behaviour, whether it be prolonged periods of sitting in silence, profound restlessness, reckless behaviour,[9] or, in times of inactivity, drug mania.[10] Watson could read those intense physical expressions and behaviours that indicated Holmes was hot on a clue:

> I could tell by numerous subtle signs, which might have been lost upon anyone but myself, that Holmes was on a hot scent. As impassive as ever to the casual observer, there were none the less a subdued eagerness and suggestion of tension in his brightened eyes and brisker manner which assured me that the game was afoot. (Doyle [1908b] 1967: 249)[11]

In these intimate descriptions of Holmes shared with the reader, Watson is drawing the proper inferences from his observations of Holmes, which are based on physical trifles and signs that are overlooked by others. Watson is harnessing on his own experiences as well as his education to interpret Holmes's behaviour relative to the status of the investigation.

Watson's role as companion and narrator is thus much deeper than that of simple biographer. Towards the end of the Sherlock Holmes series, in an adventure published in 1923, 'The Adventure of the Creeping Man', Watson summarizes his role, describing an evolving, dynamic relationship between him and Holmes:

> The relations between us in those latter days were peculiar. He was a man of habits, narrow and concentrated habits, and I had become one of them. As an institution I was like the violin, the shag tobacco, the old black pipe, the index books, and others perhaps less excusable. When it was a case of active work and a comrade was needed upon whose nerve he could place some reliance, my role was obvious. But apart from this I had uses. I was a whetstone for his mind. I stimulated him. He liked to think aloud in my presence. His remarks could hardly be said to be made to me – many of them would have been as appropriately addressed to his bedstead – but none the less, having formed the habit, it had become in some way helpful that I should register and interject. If I irritated him by a certain methodical slowness in my mentality, that irritation served only to make his own flame-like intuitions and impressions flash up the more vividly and swiftly. Such was my humble role in our alliance. (Doyle [1923] 1967: 751)

In this passage, Watson provides insight into his function, specifically highlighting his status as Holmes's sounding board. Watson's tone may be interpreted as one of resignation that downplays his importance to Holmes and, more importantly, to the reader. For Watson may be part of Holmes's habit and routine, but his assertion of being a humble role is misplaced. Perhaps, without Watson's presence, Holmes's intuitions would not be so apparent and his investigative drive would deteriorate.

As the detective's companion and admiring friend, the sidekick remains faithful and loyal through the investigation and even during periods of inactivity. The sidekick routinely demonstrates their loyalty by protecting the detective and accompanying them without reluctance during perilous adventures. The Narrator in Poe's 'The Murders in the Rue Morgue' (1841) is ready with a pistol when awaiting the arrival of the owner of the ourang-outang, who is to be confronted by Dupin about the events surrounding the deaths of Madame and Mademoiselle L'Espanaye. Similarly, on several occasions, Holmes asks Watson if he has a pistol on hand, and Watson is always prepared for danger even when little is known of Holmes's plans.[12] On top of carrying a pistol when necessary, Watson accompanies Holmes even when Holmes is concerned about danger due to breaking laws or seeking out a dangerous criminal mastermind.[13] Described by Holmes as 'born to be a man of action' (Doyle [1901–2] 1967: 89), as a comrade with nerve, Watson's characteristic traits of loyalty and bravery are likely due to his position as a military veteran and middle-class Victorian. Watson appears to successfully balance the necessity of his firearm with his own moral obligations, following Holmes into dangerous situations at the ready to protect his companion in the name of societal justice. Unlike the sidekick-as-hired-thug (as exemplified, for example, by author Margery Allingham's Magersfontein Lugg, sidekick to fictional detective Albert Campion), the educated Dr. Watson has neither links to the criminal underground nor a drive to resort to violence. But, just as Watson does not shy away from accompanying Holmes on his adventures, Watson always remains ready to confront a suspect with a pistol by his side or even join Holmes on a chase for a savage, spectral beast. In *The Hound of the Baskervilles*, when the baronet comments to Holmes, 'You look like a general who is planning a battle with his chief of staff', Holmes replies, 'That is the exact situation. Watson was asking for orders' (Doyle [1901–2] 1967: 93). Holmes knows that he can rely on Watson's bravery and restraint in tense situations. Whether as a sounding board or an armed companion, it is clear that, without Watson, the stories of the greatest consulting detective of all time would have never been told.

Conclusion: A Long and Patient Study

Sidekicks have served as companions to several great literary detectives throughout the history of crime fiction. However, Poe's nameless Narrator and Doyle's Dr. John Watson are far more than inferior sidekicks to their detective-hero counterparts. These sidekicks serve several practical functions for both the detective and the reader, most notably presenting the reader with the unique methods and extraordinary skills used by these detectives to solve crimes, specifically the powers of observation and reasoning. The sidekick serves a critical role by serving as a sounding board to the detective when outlining the process of reasoning that becomes central to crime solving. Methods of reasoning, such as Dupin's ratiocination or Holmes's deduction, are described to the companion by the detective as the clues are observed and interpretations are generated, which is in turn narrated to the reader by the companion. Amid the keen observation skills and logical reasoning methods employed by the detective, the sidekick often stands in stark contrast—routinely overlooking or misinterpreting clues that later become remarkably obvious to the companion (and the reader), allowing the detective to appear extraordinary. The sidekick acts as an intermediary, allowing the detective to convey superhuman status through his enigmatic methods, all while retaining commonality and kinship with the reader. Such an approach renders the sidekick an essential component of detective fiction. Most importantly, the sidekick has evolved to serve as a storyteller, adding the details and flourishes that, while not relevant to solving the apparent crime, allow the reader to obtain a sense of reality allowing them to engage and form a kinship with the sidekick in an effort to connect with the omnipotent detective. The sidekick provides the reader with privileged information—insight into the thoughts and reasoning of the detective—as well as exclusive access to the crime scene and traces observed therein. Acting as the inimitable conduit, the sidekick must faithfully recount events and, at the same time, maintain the bond between the reader and the detective. All of these seemingly extraneous elements serve to make the reader feel as if they are accompanying the detective and sidekick on their adventures, which is not only necessary to maintain reader interest, but further contributes to the longstanding legacy of detective fiction, and the clever detectives that allow their stories to be told by their loyal, often overlooked, sidekicks. As historical elements, the Narrator and Dr. John Watson can be firmly and sensibly placed in the foundation of detective fiction for which all detective fiction can be measured. Writers of detective fiction have experimented with the sidekick in their works—from intellectual prowess to gender to removing the sidekick altogether—but echoes of Poe's nameless Narrator and Doyle's Watson can frequently be heard in those iterations and reincarnations. As a result, the bond between the reader and the sidekick contributes to the impact and continued allure of the fictional detective story.

Notes

1. As Sydney Roberts argues: 'Watson's alertness as a medical man is immediately evident. His deduction of the solubility in water of the famous pill was quick and accurate, nor did he fail to diagnose an aortic aneurism in Jefferson Hope' (Roberts 1953: 79). Watson is a physician who lends his expertise to the first investigation alongside Holmes in *A Study in Scarlet*. When asked to comment on the nature of pills recovered from the death scene of Joseph Strangerson, Watson remarks 'from their lightness and transparency, I shall imagine that they are soluble in water' to which Holmes responds, 'Precisely so'. Holmes then places the pill in a wine glass containing 'a teaspoonful of water', adds milk to make it 'palatable' and gives the contents to the landlady's ill terrier (Doyle [1887] 1967: 193).
2. That said, in 'The Adventure of the Blanched Soldier', one of only two stories narrated by Holmes himself, Holmes concedes that Watson's manner of establishing reader interest is a necessity.
3. For more detailed coverage of Poe and the Mary Rogers case, see: Walsh, John. 1968. *Poe the Detective: The Curious Circumstances Behind 'The Mystery of Marie Rogêt'*. New Brunswick: Rutgers University Press; Paul, Raymond. 1971. *Who Murdered Mary Rogers?* Englewood Cliffs: Prentice Hall; and Arntfield, Michael. 2016. *Gothic Forensics: Criminal Investigative Procedure in Victorian Horror & Mystery*. New York: Palgrave Macmillin (specifically Chapter 5: 'The Mystery of Marie Rogêt': Holdback Evidence and the Copycat Effect).
4. See, for example, 'The Adventure of the Illustrious Client'; 'The Adventure of the Dying Detective'.
5. See, for example, 'The Adventure of the Veiled Lodger'; 'The Adventure of the Second Stain'; 'The Resident Patient'; 'The Five Orange Pips'; 'The Adventure of the Golden Pince-Nez'.
6. See, for example, 'The Resident Patient'; 'A Case of Identity'; *The Sign of the Four*; 'The Adventure of the Three Gables'; 'The Stockbroker's Clerk'; *A Study in Scarlet*; 'The Adventure of the Speckled Band'; 'Silver Blaze'; 'The Adventure of the Empty House'.
7. For a discussion on imagination and its role in reasoning, see Miranda (2017).
8. See, for example, 'The Gloria Scott'; *The Hound of the Baskervilles*.
9. See, for example, 'The Man with the Twisted Lip'; *The Sign of the Four*; 'The Problem of Thor Bridge'; *The Hound of the Baskervilles*;

'The Adventure of the Beryl Coronet'; 'The Adventure of the Norwood Builder'.
10. See, for example, 'The Adventure of the Missing Three-Quarter'.
11. See also 'The Boscombe Valley Mystery'; 'The Adventure of the Bruce-Partington Plans'; 'The Adventure of the Norwood Builder'; 'The Adventure of the Priory School'; 'The Adventure of the Devil's Foot'; 'The Adventure of the Dancing Man'; 'The Naval Treaty'; 'Silver Blaze'; 'The Adventure of the Golden Pince-Nez'.
12. See, for example, *A Study in Scarlet*; *The Hound of the Baskervilles*.
13. See, for example, 'The Adventure of the Speckled Band'; 'A Scandal in Bohemia'; 'The Adventure of Charles Augustus Milverton'; 'The Final Problem'; 'The Adventure of the Norwood Builder'.

References

Accardo, Pasquale. 1987. *Diagnosis and Detention: The Medical Iconography of Sherlock Holmes*. Rutherford: Fairleigh Dickinson University Press.

Doyle, Arthur Conan. (1887) 1967. *A Study in Scarlet*. In *The Annotated Sherlock Holmes*, vol. I, ed. William Baring-Gould, 143–234. New York: Clarkson N. Potter.

———. (1890) 1967. *The Sign of the Four*. In *The Annotated Sherlock Holmes*, vol. I, ed. William Baring-Gould, 610–688. New York: Clarkson N. Potter.

———. (1891a) 1967. A Case of Identity. In *The Annotated Sherlock Holmes*, vol. I, ed. William Baring-Gould, 404–417. New York: Clarkson N. Potter.

———. (1891b) 1967. A Scandal in Bohemia. In *The Annotated Sherlock Holmes*, vol. I, ed. William Baring-Gould, 346–367. New York: Clarkson N. Potter.

———. (1892a) 1967. The Adventure of the Blue Carbuncle. In *The Annotated Sherlock Holmes*, vol. I, ed. William Baring-Gould, 451–467. New York: Clarkson N. Potter.

———. (1892b) 1967. The Adventure of the Specked Band. In *The Annotated Sherlock Holmes*, vol. I, ed. William Baring-Gould, 243–262. New York: Clarkson N. Potter.

———. (1892c) 1967. The Adventure of the Copper Beeches. In *The Annotated Sherlock Holmes*, vol. II, ed. William Baring-Gould, 114–132. New York: Clarkson N. Potter.

———. (1893) 1967. The Adventure of the Resident Patient. In *The Annotated Sherlock Holmes*, vol. I, ed. William Baring-Gould, 267–280. New York: Clarkson N. Potter.

———. (1901–2) 1967. *The Hound of the Baskervilles*. In *The Annotated Sherlock Holmes*, vol. II, ed. William Baring-Gould, 3–113. New York: Clarkson N. Potter.

———. (1903a) 1967. The Adventure of the Empty House. In *The Annotated Sherlock Holmes*, vol. II, ed. William Baring-Gould, 329–349. New York: Clarkson N. Potter.

———. (1903b) 1967. The Adventure of the Solitary Cyclist. In *The Annotated Sherlock Holmes*. vol. II, ed. William Baring-Gould, 383–397. New York: Clarkson N. Potter.

———. (1904) 1967. The Adventure of the Abbey Grange. In *The Annotated Sherlock Holmes*, vol. II, ed. William Baring-Gould, 491–507. New York: Clarkson N. Potter.

———. (1908a) 1967. The Adventure of the Bruce-Partington Plans. In *The Annotated Sherlock Holmes*, vol. II, ed. William Baring-Gould, 432–452. New York: Clarkson N. Potter.

———. (1908b) 1967. The Adventure of Wisteria Lodge. In *The Annotated Sherlock Holmes*, vol. II, ed. William Baring-Gould, 238–259. New York: Clarkson N. Potter.

———. (1923) 1967. The Adventure of the Creeping Man. In *The Annotated Sherlock Holmes*, vol. II, ed. William Baring-Gould, 751–765. New York: Clarkson N. Potter.

———. (1926a) 1967. The Adventure of the Blanched Soldier. In *The Annotated Sherlock Holmes*, vol. II, ed. William Baring-Gould, 707–721. New York: Clarkson N. Potter.

———. (1926b) 1967. The Adventure of the Retired Colourman. In *The Annotated Sherlock Holmes*, vol. II, ed. William Baring-Gould, 546–557. New York: Clarkson N. Potter.

———. (1927) 1967. The Adventure of the Veiled Lodger. In *The Annotated Sherlock Holmes*, vol. II, ed. William Baring-Gould, 453–461. New York: Clarkson N. Potter.

Eco, Umberto. 1983. Horns, Hooves, Insteps: Some Hypotheses on Three Types of Abduction. In *Dupin, Holmes, Peirce: The Sign of Three*, ed. Umberto Eco and Thomas Sebeok, 198–220. Bloomington: Indiana University Press.

Goodman, Walter. 1990. Sidekicks: Dimmer than the Stars, Yet… *The New York Times*, May 6.

Knight, Stephen. 1980. *Form & Ideology in Crime Fiction*. Bloomington: Indiana University Press.

Knox, Ronald. 1929. *The Best English Detective Stories of 1928*. New York: Liveright.

Krasner, James. 1997. Watson Falls Asleep: Narrative Frustration and Sherlock Holmes. *English Literature in Transition* 1880–1920 (40): 424–436.

Miranda, Michelle D. 2017. Reasoning Through Madness: The Detective in Gothic Crime Fiction, *Palgrave Communications*, 3. http://www.palgrave-journals.com/articles/palcomms201745.

Poe, Edgar Allan. (1841) 1994. The Murders in the Rue Morgue. In *The Complete Illustrated Stories and Poems*, 75–102. London: Chancellor Press.

———. (1842) 1994. The Mystery of Marie Rogêt. In *The Complete Illustrated Stories and Poems*, 485–522. London: Chancellor Press.

———. (1844) 1994. The Purloined Letter. In *The Complete Illustrated Stories and Poems*, 319–333. London: Chancellor Press.

Roberts, Sydney Castle. (1953) 2018. *Holmes and Watson: A Miscellany*. Reprint. London: The British Library.

Sayers, Dorothy L. 1929. *The Omnibus of Crime*. New York: Payson and Clarke Ltd.

CHAPTER 3

'Passed by Unnoticed': Surveillance and the Street Urchin in Wilkie Collins's *The Moonstone*

Oriah Amit

Introduction

The diamond thief at the centre of Wilkie Collins's 1868 novel *The Moonstone* is traced not by a detective, but by a street urchin. Readers encounter this minor character towards the end of the narrative, when Franklin Blake—serving as the emissary to recover his family's missing moonstone diamond—describes his associate, the lawyer Matthew Bruff, being 'accosted' at a train station (Collins 1868: 208). There, Blake and Bruff encounter 'a small boy, dressed in a jacket and trousers of thread-bare black cloth, and personally remarkable in virtue of the extraordinary prominence of his eyes.' 'They projected so far,' Blake says, 'and they rolled about so loosely, that you wondered uneasily why they remained in their sockets' (Collins 1868: 208). This remarkable figure turns out to be a working-class boy known as 'Gooseberry,' who is employed to run

O. Amit (✉)
University of California, Los Angeles, CA, USA

L. Andrew and S. Saunders (eds.), *The Detective's Companion in Crime Fiction*, Crime Files, https://doi.org/10.1007/978-3-030-74989-7_3

errands for Bruff. The boy's nickname refers to the unnerving protrusion of his eyes, but over the course of the following pages, it is precisely those organs that become crucial to locating the thief of the eponymous moonstone.

Gooseberry's entrance into the novel foreshadows the way in which he will blur the line between detection and delinquency. Although the small boy in threadbare clothes might easily be confused for a miscreant rather than a capable sidekick when he 'accost[s]' Blake and Bruff at the train terminus, Collins quickly redirects his unprepossessing exterior to the maintenance of social order. Within the next few lines, Gooseberry is seated in the driver's box of a cab, navigating Blake and Bruff through London to recover the missing diamond. As I will argue, it is Gooseberry's identity as a street urchin—an urban figure who attracts negative attention, if he attracts it at all—that makes him particularly useful as a sidekick. In a number of key moments, Gooseberry proves that he is able to manoeuvre through certain spaces, covertly collect information, and observe minute details with more success than either Blake or Bruff. But Collins's representation of Gooseberry's superior observational abilities also calls attention to the ethical dimensions of involving children in professions that expose them to physical or moral danger. In this chapter, I examine Gooseberry through discourses surrounding child labour in social journalism of the mid-nineteenth century in order to demonstrate that Collins mediates between, on the one hand, an understanding of the extraordinary potential of the working child and, on the other, the possibilities for their exploitation.

Gooseberry's Covert Urban Surveillance

In *The Moonstone*, Gooseberry becomes the sidekick of Sergeant Cuff, the detective called in to solve the case, because of his ability to go places and observe things that other characters cannot. His age and class status largely enable his mobility in a wide variety of urban spaces, in some of which the adult, middle-class Bruff, Blake, and even Sergeant Cuff would otherwise attract unwanted attention. Over the course of his sleuthing, Gooseberry follows the diamond thief from a bank on Lombard Street, the financial district of the City, to the Tower Wharf, an area populated largely by dock-workers and sailors, and he makes stops at several public houses in between. His presence goes ignored by the suspects he trails through each of these locations, although their populations vary widely in class backgrounds and professions. Cuff offers perhaps the most concise explanation for Gooseberry's chameleon-like ability to disappear into these different urban backgrounds: 'The boy—*being* a boy—passed unnoticed' (Collins 1868: 211). Cuff hits on the notion that a criminal would more likely be on guard for an adult detective, while Gooseberry, as a child, can slip past his observation. But boys were also an especially conspicuous sight in London in the latter half of the nineteenth century, which paradoxically meant that they would be even less likely to attract the attention of observers. As Gareth Stedman Jones contends, there was a large pool of unskilled juvenile labour in the period preceding the passage of the 1870 Education Act, which set the framework for schooling all children between the ages of five and twelve (Jones 1971: 71–72). In 1861, an 'overwhelming proportion' of unskilled labourers aged ten to twenty were employed as messengers, inn-servants, and, by the end of the century, as van boys (Jones 1971: 68). These careers involved a high degree of circulation through various areas of London, making working boys ubiquitous in locations similar to the ones through which Gooseberry travels.

It is not only Gooseberry's ability to circulate unobserved through spaces where other characters cannot that sets him apart, however; it is also his perception of visual details that go unnoticed by them. As Chris Otter observes in *The Victorian Eye*, '*Who* could see *what*, *whom*, *when*, *where*, and *how* was, and remains, an integral dimension of the everyday operation and experience of power' (Otter 2008: 1). In discerning clues that elude Blake, Bruff, and even Sergeant Cuff, Gooseberry gains access to knowledge that grants him a degree of power over these men, despite his socially marginalised position.[1] His ability to wield this power in subtle ways is clear in a scene late in the novel, when Gooseberry, Bruff, and Blake arrive at the bank to which they believe they have traced the missing diamond. As Bruff and Blake prepare to enter, Gooseberry looks 'longingly at his master,' communicating his desire to follow them with his eyes rather than in words (Collins 1868: 208). As if he were addressing a dog rather than a junior employee, Bruff instructs him: 'Come in then, and keep at my heels till further orders' (Collins 1868: 208). While the exchange might seem to suggest Gooseberry's subordinate status, it actually reveals a tactful manipulation. Gooseberry's fluent use of emotive communication is strategically performative, and allows him to appear to have subjected himself to his employer's wishes while at the same time eliciting Bruff's sympathetic acquiescence to his request.

The scene demonstrates that Gooseberry is equally savvy in manoeuvring through social interactions and urban spaces. Moreover, it serves as a blueprint for his ability to leverage his disenfranchised social position as a tactical form of influence. By the end of the scene, Bruff and Blake have trailed an innocent man into a local chemist's shop. Only Gooseberry, as Bruff suggests, 'has [his] eyes about [him]' (Collins 1868: 209). It soon becomes clear that he has followed the right suspect out of the bank, expressly disobeying his employer's command to stay close and wait for orders. Two details respecting Gooseberry's aptitude for detection are clear in this episode. First, it arises from his body—it is physical and instinctual; and secondly, it is superior to that of the adults around him. If we follow Michel Foucault's explication of subjugated knowledges, we might classify Gooseberry's spatial and sensory abilities as 'a whole set of knowledges that have been disqualified [...] naive knowledges, located low down on the hierarchy' (Foucault 1980: 82). Seen through this lens, Gooseberry can be included in a list of socially marginal figures who take on important investigative roles in the fiction of this period: the masculine heroine Marian Halcombe of Collins's earlier novel *The Woman in White* (1859–60), the mute investigator Joseph Peters of Mary Elizabeth Braddon's *The Trail of the Serpent* (1860), and Ezra Jennings, Dr. Candy's racially outcast assistant who discovers how a draught of opium led Blake to remove the moonstone from his cousin's room. Like these other characters, Gooseberry uses the traits that might ordinarily be perceived as limiting his social influence—in his case, his age and his class—to his advantage in gaining information that is inaccessible to others. The quality that differentiates Gooseberry from Halcombe, Peters, and Jennings is the confluence of his seamless integration into the urban environment of London with his preternatural perceptive faculties. These traits are often associated with the detective himself rather than with the sidekick: Inspector Bucket of Charles Dickens's *Bleak House* and Arthur Conan Doyle's Sherlock Holmes are two famous examples who are equally savvy in their knowledge of urban space and their ability to navigate it. When these capabilities are paired with Gooseberry's socially inferior status as a labouring child, however, they urge a reconsideration of both the origins of visual surveillance in the urban environment and of the supreme authority of the detective in Victorian fiction.

As Clare Clarke argues, 'it has become something of a critical orthodoxy' in studies of nineteenth-century detective fiction to emphasise the investigator's primacy of sight as his means of obtaining knowledge'

(Clarke 2014: 36). Inspector Bucket appears 'to possess an unlimited number of eyes,' and his insistent forefinger directs other characters to '[l]ook again' and see the clues that they have missed (Dickens 1853: 222, 223). Likewise, in *A Study in Scarlet,* Sherlock Holmes describes his process of deduction as follows: 'I have to bustle about and see things with my own eyes [...] Observation with me is second nature' (Doyle [1887] 1892: 30). Critical inquiries into the genre of detective fiction have similarly focused on vision and sight as the primary skills of the inspector, especially in light of D. A. Miller's foundational study *The Novel and the Police* (1988). Drawing on Foucault's *Discipline and Punish,* Miller suggests that visual surveillance is both the primary apparatus of police discipline and the ultimate goal of detective fiction. The genre, he argues, links 'the detective's brilliant *super-vision* and the police *supervision* that it embodies,' a move that brings 'the entire world of the narrative' under surveillance (Miller 1988: 35). If, however, we shift the focus from the detective to his sidekick, we see that surveillance is not always the privileged activity of the investigator, but is often undertaken by the lowest members of society. In *Bleak House,* it is the lowly chimney sweep Jo who 'silently notices' the small, white hands of a disguised Lady Dedlock, a clue that becomes central to revealing her tarnished past (Dickens 1853: 160). In *A Study in Scarlet* and later in *The Sign of Four*, Holmes is aided by the Baker Street Irregulars: a band of six 'ragged street Arabs' who, he says, can 'go everywhere, see everything, and overhear everyone' (Doyle 1900: 88). Like Gooseberry, these minor characters utilise local, urban knowledge in order to collect information that passes below the reach of the police and the detective inspector. As the character of Gooseberry suggests, however, their observational potential is not always entirely contained within the model of disciplinary surveillance.

In *The Moonstone*, Collins is particularly attuned to the troubling moral difficulties involved in bringing children into proximity with crime, even when those children are employed in apprehending the offenders. The moral danger of an early exposure to violence is evident in a scene where Cuff and Blake discover the strangled body of Godfrey Ablewhite, the philanthropist who is finally revealed to be the diamond thief. Cuff instructs Gooseberry not to follow them into the room, but Gooseberry again disobeys a direct command, unable to suppress his desire to see what is hidden inside. When Blake discovers the boy in the room several lines later, he reprimands him before attempting to physically remove him: 'There was something so hideous in the boy's enjoyment of the horror of the scene,' Blake says, 'that I took him by the two shoulders and put him out of the room' (Collins 1868: 213). Gooseberry, however, refuses to be ejected, and he soon reappears with a chair, onto which he climbs to get a better view of the corpse. Blake calls particular attention to the boy's unruly gaze, describing how his eyes 'rolled frightfully—not in terror, but in exultation' of the violence before him (Collins 1868: 213). In the grisly aftermath of the crime, Gooseberry's 'irrepressible' (Collins 1868: 213) gaze becomes not only unnecessary, but also indecent, and even delinquent. The ocular tools that had earlier enabled the disciplinary arm of the law to reach into previously inaccessible corners of the urban environment are here in need of discipline themselves.

It is curious that despite his instrumental role in solving the crime at the centre of *The Moonstone*, Gooseberry has not been studied as much more than an example of Collins's flair for adding local colour to his plots. Ross Murfin dismisses him as an accessory to the 'silliness' of Sergeant Cuff's unveiling of Ablewhite's identity (Murfin 1982: 659). Sue Lonoff, by comparison, suggests that he becomes a bodily repository for the excessive sensationalism called up by the horrific scene of discovery at the end of the novel, and contends that his rolling eyes reveal him as an 'uncouth' and 'gloating' foil to Blake, the 'reluctant witness' of the gruesome event (Lonoff 1982: 124–125). To characterise Gooseberry either as a comic throwaway character or as a repository for the novel's excessive sensationalism, however, is to overlook his distinctive capacity for observation. His rolling eyes, ridiculous as they may appear, are a bodily representation of his unbounded, highly kinetic vision. They form a sharp contrast to Cuff's more disciplined, 'immovable eyes' (Collins 1868: 58), but they also enable Gooseberry to see things that Cuff cannot. Yet, as the scene above reveals, there are permissible social limits to Gooseberry's observation. Although his surveillance of crime is sanctioned when it serves the purpose of detection, his observation of the scene of the crime is, in itself, forbidden. What turns Gooseberry's eyes 'hideous' (Collins 1868: 213) in this episode is not simply the pleasure he takes in looking (as readers, we too take a grim pleasure in Cuff stripping away Ablewhite's disguise); rather it is his underage status. Despite Gooseberry's proficiency in detecting crime, his supervisors realise—apparently too late—that because he is a child, he should be prevented from witnessing it.

Boy Labour and the Origins of the Street Urchin as Sidekick

In order to contextualise the ambivalent responses of Blake, Bruff, and Cuff to Gooseberry's observation of crime, it is illuminating to situate *The Moonstone* alongside a history of social journalism focusing on the welfare of labouring children. One of the primary aims of Henry Mayhew's *London Labour and the London Poor*, published in 1851, was to provide an account of the education and employment of street children in London. The study emphasises boyhood as the period of life in which future habits and behaviours would be cemented, and thus it places a strong emphasis on the moral dangers of early recruitment into the labour market. In a chapter titled 'Of the Education of the Coster-Lads,' Mayhew cautions: 'It is idle to imagine that these lads, possessed of a mental acuteness almost wonderful, will not educate themselves in vice, if we neglect to train them to virtue' (Mayhew 1851: 35–36). The precarious position of the working child is echoed in the writing of one of Mayhew's contemporaries: the social and educational reformer Mary Carpenter. In her 1853 study, *Juvenile Delinquents, Their Condition and Treatment*, Carpenter suggests that children born into poverty, 'of which there will always be multitudes, will and must lapse from poverty to vice, unless they are cared for' (Carpenter 1853: 28). Carpenter argues that these children are 'passed by unnoticed,' and thus are 'actually driven into crime' by a lack of state resources or guidance (Carpenter 1853: 28). Here it seems no accident that Collins and Carpenter employ the same language in reference to the working-class boy: passing unnoticed in the urban environment and being passed by unnoticed for governmental assistance are intertwined.

The Moonstone also builds on an established tradition of fictional and socio-historical Victorian writings that feature the street urchin. One of his most famous roles is as the eponymous reformed orphan of Charles Dickens's *Oliver Twist*, serialised between 1837 and 1839.[2] Street urchins make other frequent appearances in didactic popular fiction, including James Greenwood's *The True History of a Little Ragamuffin* (1866), Hesba Stretton's *Jessica's First Prayer* ([1867] 1897), and Silas K. Hocking's *Her Benny* ([1879] 1890). As John Sutherland notes, these latter stories belong to a genealogy of morally improving fiction, and their plots centre on the ways in which the street urchin may triumph over his or her circumstances by avoiding vice and crime (Sutherland 2014: 335). In addition to the social journalism that Mayhew and Carpenter conducted, the Ragged School Union also began, in January 1849, its own quarterly publication to report on the condition, need, and improvement of the children it served.[3]

But how did the street urchin, who formed a primary object of observation in mid-Victorian social journalism, become a figure involved in the surveillance of others in detective fiction? The answer lies partially in the prominence of observation and its attendant technologies in the mid-Victorian period. Otter contends that recent scholarship on the historical relationship of visual observation to power in the Victorian period has drawn most heavily on the Benthamite Panopticon and the flâneur as tools for analysis (Otter 2008: 3). Nowhere is this more evident than in studies of the detective novel, where the police detective appears to combine elements of both forms of visual observation to become an urban, mobile state apparatus of surveillance and control. Certainly, both the flâneur (the urban pedestrian that Charles Baudelaire outlines as an aesthete of the asphalt) and the Benthamite Panopticon (a model for optimal carceral efficiency) find their echoes in *The Moonstone*. Like the flâneur, in whom Walter Benjamin suggests that 'the joy of watching prevails over all' (Benjamin 1973: 98), Gooseberry takes an obvious visceral pleasure in the observation of others. His perception, like that of the pedestrian observer that Benjamin describes, is markedly labile and ambulatory. Likewise, when Gooseberry stands upon his chair and looms over Bruff, Cuff, and Blake to survey Ablewhite's disguised body, he bears a striking resemblance to the Panoptic watchtower. In his close observation of Cuff's removal of Ablewhite's wig, false beard, and face paint, Gooseberry also seems to take on the role of Foucault's 'inspector [...] at the centre of the Panopticon' who can 'judge at a glance, without anything being concealed from him, how the entire establishment is functioning' (Foucault 1975: 204).

Yet, despite the characteristics he shares with these established models of visual observation, Gooseberry is backed by neither the bourgeois freedom of the flâneur nor the disciplinary power of the Panopticon. His role is more clearly illuminated when we re-evaluate the role of the observer in the nineteenth century. As Jonathan Crary remarks, the observer is not simply one who sees, but 'more importantly one who sees within a prescribed set of possibilities, one who is embedded in a system of conventions and limitations' (Crary 1992: 6). It might seem counterintuitive that within the systemic strictures of *The Moonstone*, Gooseberry has the clearest view of the operations taking place around him. As I suggest, it is precisely the prescribed social and novelistic limitations in which he circulates that enable his more complete view of his environment. In other words, it is Gooseberry's position as a sidekick—one whose age, station, and minor narrative role make him inferior to nearly every other character in the novel—that enables him to watch others while remaining unobserved. The central question is thus not how, but rather why the figure of the street urchin is appropriated by this text for the purposes of surveillance, and in what ways he is influenced by his recruitment into that function.

The social journalism of Mayhew and Carpenter urges a redirection of the potential of the labouring boy from crime to formal education, and then to productive labour. Inherent to their studies is an understanding of working boys as particularly susceptible to the influence of delinquency, as well as a sense that they have been wronged by their environment. Carpenter identifies a profound contradiction in the state's treatment of the working boy: when he needs financial support, as we have noted, he is 'passed by unnoticed,' but as she suggests in a later chapter, the state is waiting to punish him whenever he transgresses. In the character of Gooseberry, Collins mediates between discourses of the street urchin as a semi-criminal figure in need of discipline and one whose productive potential is exploited under a governmental system that ignores his wellbeing. As a type of native informant, Gooseberry negotiates the interchange between the policing mechanisms of the law and the criminals that populate London's streets. His particular form of employment demands that he move in and among what Lynda Nead refers to as 'unruly' spaces—the docks, terminals, and taverns that can sometimes elude the surveillance of the police (Nead 2005: 198). Yet in the startling visual pleasure that Gooseberry derives from Ablewhite's strangled corpse, Collins also suggests the consequences of such an early exposure to crime.

Susan Zieger suggests that Gooseberry's rolling eyes add a touch of sensational 'pleasure, zaniness, and mayhem' to *The Moonstone* by 'overflowing their function of registering and conveying information' (Zieger 2018: 111). Certainly, their excess recalls Collins's background as an author of primarily sensation fiction. But the boy's eyes also represent the novelist's attempt to square Gooseberry's potential as a young detective with the dangers that such a career might pose. When Blake 'wonders uneasily' how Gooseberry's eyes manage to 'remain in their sockets,' we are given a morbid sense that the various parts of the boy's body are only tenuously held together (Collins 1868: 208). As Zieger suggests, the potential detachability of Gooseberry's eyes foreshadows the development of new surveillance technologies at the end of the nineteenth century, notably the handheld 'detective' camera that would be introduced in the 1880s. His eyes also suggest, however, that there is something harmful to the human body in the work that Gooseberry performs so well. When Gooseberry's 'irrepressible' gaze oversteps its bounds, Collins asks us to consider whether this is not the natural consequence of ignoring the marginalised subjects and minor characters whose labour enables the satisfying resolution of the detective plot (Collins 1868: 213).

Colonial Doubles

Readers will recall that Gooseberry is not the only street urchin figure with acute perceptive abilities to appear in *The Moonstone*. Earlier in the novel, we are introduced to an unnamed young English boy who serves as the travelling companion of three Brahmins who have made their way to England to return the moonstone diamond to India.[4] Like Gooseberry, this boy is employed in the work of surveillance, but he also appears to possess a prescient ability that expands his field of vision beyond even Gooseberry's. His so-called clairvoyance is described by Penelope, a maid who watches from behind a hedge as the Brahmins pour a black, inky substance into the reticent boy's palm and instruct him: 'Look' (Collins 1868: 17). He resists at first, saying that 'he didn't like it,' but he complies when the chief Brahmin asks 'whether he would like to be sent back to London, and left where they had found him … a hungry, ragged, and forsaken little boy' (Collins 1868: 17). After 'making signs' in the air above the boy's head, the Brahmins direct his gaze in order to ascertain the whereabouts of Blake, who is at that moment on his way to deliver the diamond to his cousin, Rachel Verinder:

> [T]he chief Indian said these words to the boy; 'See the English gentleman from foreign parts.' The boy said, 'I see him.' The Indian said, 'Is it on the road to this house, and on no other, that the English gentleman will travel to-day?' The boy said, 'It is on the road to this house, and on no other, that the English gentleman will travel to-day.' The Indian put a second question – after waiting a little first. He said: 'Has the English gentleman got It about him?' The boy answered – also, after waiting a little first – 'Yes.' (Collins 1868: 17)

When a third question is put to the boy, he ends the ritual, saying, 'I am tired ... I can see no more today' (Collins 1868: 17).

The scene depicts the practice of ink-gazing, which Zieger notes was 'a pastime of wealthy tourists to Cairo in the 1830s and ' 40s'; later, it became a popular parlour trick, which appeared in a number of mid-Victorian writings (Zieger 2018: 88). Collins's description bears a striking resemblance to an incident of the practice recorded in 1836 by the Orientalist Edward William Lane in *An Account of the Manners and Customs of the Modern Egyptians*, in which a famed Cairo magician chooses a child of eight or nine 'from among some boys in the street' (Lane [1836] 1890: 369) and questions him about the location and appearance of a number of figures until his sight grows too dim to continue (Lane [1836] 1890: 370–74).[5] Several similar experiments are conducted on other Egyptian street boys, some chosen by the magician and some others by Lane himself. According to the magician, only prepubescent boys, pregnant women, virgins, and black female slaves possess the ability to see images in ink, although boys feature as the overwhelming vehicle of choice in Lane's account (Lane [1836] 1890: 369). The 'Magician at Cairo' that Harriet Martineau describes in her 1848 account *Eastern Life: Present and Past* also employs young male subjects in his ink-gazing ritual, especially those that have been 'picked up in the street' (Martineau 1848: 139). Martineau does not speculate as to why these boys are the chosen vessels for clairvoyant sight, but her narrative makes clear the performative quality conveyed by the 'quivering' eyelids of the small child 'crouched' before an aged magician, who rests 'the tips of his fingers firmly on the crown of [his] head' (Martineau 1848: 138).

While Lane and Martineau present ink-gazing, in part, as an Orientalist spectacle performed for the entertainment of wealthy Western tourists, Collins's description of the practice is markedly different. The Brahmins seem to be entirely unaware of their white audience hiding in the hedge, and the ink-gazing ritual is taken on not as a performance but in an earnest desire to collect information. More importantly, however, Collins centralises the imperial gaze by exchanging the Eastern street boy for an English one. Like Gooseberry, this boy's sidekick is recruited for his local knowledge—he must draw upon his familiarity with the geography of his home country in order to identify the road by which Blake will travel in the account he gives to the Brahmins (17). Unlike Gooseberry, however, this boy's role as a native informant is coerced; the Brahmins remove him from his abject condition as 'a hungry, ragged and forsaken little boy' sleeping in a basket in a London market, and they threaten to return him to that condition if he fails to cooperate with their requests (Collins 1868: 17). Penelope, the lady's maid who watches the ritual from behind the hedge, perceives this disciplinary measure as unduly harsh, and suggests that the boy is 'ill-used by the foreigners' (Collins 1868: 17) when she relates what she has seen to her father, the butler Gabriel Betteredge. It is significant to note, however, that the Brahmins only threaten the boy with the indifference of his own home government to his plight.

By refashioning state neglect as a coercive measure that the Brahmins use as leverage against their nameless boy assistant, *The Moonstone* might seem to transfer the social injustice of his circumstances onto a colonial source. Penelope's concern for his treatment at the hands of the Brahmins is particularly damning when considered in light of the fact that his plight seems to have been ignored before the Brahmins found him. Moreover, the narrative itself seems unconcerned with the future of this apparently kidnapped English boy, and what will become of him once the moonstone is recovered and his native knowledge of England is no longer useful to the Brahmins remains unclear. Aligning the boy's fate not with the state but with its colonial subjects might be considered a strategic displacement on Collins's part, and an example of what Stephen Arata terms reverse colonisation: a literary strategy that allows Victorian fictions to 'rid themselves of figures who disrupt or trouble the domestic order, or who simply find no suitable place within established hierarchies' (Arata 1996: 107). But the narrative evacuation of this earlier character doesn't rid the novel of the troublesome figure of the street urchin; instead, it amplifies the significance of Gooseberry's absolute refusal to be either ejected or repressed at the close of the novel. When Gooseberry elevates himself above the heads of his superiors to survey the crime scene in Ablewhite's room, he can no longer be ignored—he oversteps the role of the sidekick to become surveillance personified. The scene recalls an earlier one from *Bleak House*, in which a group of curious boys termed 'outposts of the army of observation' skirt around the policeman stationed in front of Mr Krook's door to get a glimpse of Nemo's lifeless body inside (Dickens 1853: 101). Unlike this group of boys, who 'quail and fall back' before the 'tower' of the policeman guarding the scene (Dickens 1853: 101), Gooseberry fashions himself into a tower of observation, his gaze penetrating into the dark corners of the novel to suggest that no event can escape his view.

When Gooseberry's sweeping gaze is paired with the clairvoyant vision of his unnamed double, it is clear that street urchins command the greatest mastery of sight in *The Moonstone*. Despite the enormous positive potential of these variegated visual forms, however, there remains a constant threat that the category of the street urchin will slip into that of the criminal. The travelling companion of the Brahmins participates in thwarting the work of Sergeant Cuff and the London police by helping to locate and transport the diamond back to its native home. In the process, he also becomes an accessory to murder. Gooseberry, by contrast, is initially recruited as an assistant of the law. Nevertheless, his repeated subversions of the orders he is given by his superiors and the visual pleasure he takes in the discovery of Ablewhite's body bode ill for his continued role as an agent of social order, despite Cuff's assertion that 'one of these days…that boy will do great things' in the role of a detective sergeant (Collins 1868: 211).

In *The Moonstone*, therefore, the street urchin is portrayed as a figure with enormous potential either to aid or thwart the work of the police. The merging of these two qualities aligns Gooseberry with the delinquent boy protagonists of another literary form that became popular in the 1860s: the 'penny dreadful.' The young working-class heroes of this genre, which was aimed at a similarly young and working-class audience, 'move from a position of submission to adult rules […] towards one of quasi-adult independence unchecked by moral, legal and social codes' (Andrew 2017: 14). Although Gooseberry uses his special detecting abilities to uphold rather than break the law, his evasion of adult authority and supervision at key moments in the novel reveals this as a personal choice. In his depiction of Gooseberry deciding whether he will submit to moral and social discipline or not, Collins presents the labouring boy as a complex figure who is, at least in some respects, in control of his own destiny.

Conclusion

Gooseberry is not the first example of the street urchin as the detective's sidekick in Victorian fiction, but he represents a particularly influential precedent for what would become a stock figure by the end of the century. He has a probable origin in Tom, the boy assistant who features in Collins's earlier short story 'The Fourth Poor Traveller,' an interpolated tale included in Charles Dickens's *The Seven Poor Travellers* and published in a special 1854 Christmas edition of *Household Words*. He also shares a number of similarities with Sloshy, the orphan boy who is adopted by a police detective and trained in the skill of sleuthing in Mary Elizabeth Braddon's 1860 novel *The Trail of the Serpent*. The critical and commercial success of *The Moonstone,* however, positions Gooseberry as the character who had the most lasting influence on later and more famous iterations of the boy's sidekick. Robert S. Paul, Sally Mitchell, and Leslie Haynsworth have suggested that Gooseberry was a probable origin for Sherlock Holmes's working-class boy assistants who appear collectively as the Baker Street Irregulars, and later as the lone boy assistant Cartwright in *The Hound of the Baskervilles* (1902). Crucially, Doyle's sidekicks are largely anonymous, existing as nonspecific parts of a larger matrix of urban knowledge rather than as individuals with distinct skills or characteristics. As such, Zieger classifies them alongside 'the fast new transportation and information networks' upon which Holmes relies (Zieger 2018: 70). They might also be categorised as contract labourers with a rigidly capitalistic relationship to their employer Holmes. In one of only three lines of dialogue that he speaks in *The Sign of Four*, Wiggins—the leader and only named member of the Baker Street Irregulars—requests '[t]hree bob and a tanner' from Holmes for travel expenses (Doyle 1900: 155). Later, after Holmes provides the boys with instructions to locate a boat belonging to one of his suspects, he offers them 'the old scale of pay': a set wage of one shilling for each of them, with a bonus of one guinea to the boy who successfully completes the task (Doyle 1900: 155). The relationship of these boys to the work of observation is not constructed as one of pleasure or even interest, as Gooseberry's is, but purely of labour for monetary compensation.

A similarly commercial relationship is established between detectives and their sidekicks in the boys' story papers popular from the 1890s to the 1930s. In 'A Dead Man's Secret,' the first Nelson Lee mystery written by Maxwell Scott (the pen name of Dr. John Staniforth), Lee is aided in his investigations by a delinquent street urchin called Nipper and, at the end of the narrative, invites the boy to become his assistant. As the series grew in popularity, Nipper gained a permanent role as Lee's sidekick and employee, and was soon joined by Tinker, the boy assistant to fictional detective Sexton Blake in another set of long-running mystery stories aimed at boy readers.[6] The status of Nipper and Tinker as permanent employees, as well as companions and even surrogate sons to the detectives with which they work, differentiates them from the largely anonymous Baker Street Irregulars, whose role is more closely aligned with that of contract labourers with uncertain job security. Monetary compensation also separates the depictions of Nipper, Tinker, and the Baker Street Irregulars from that of Gooseberry, whose less-defined relationship to the tasks he performs allows Collins to draw attention to the ethical problems attached to exposing a child to crime through participation in the work of detection.

To account for Collins's markedly different characterisation of the street urchin assistant, we might turn to Henry Mansel's notorious condemnation of sensation novels. In his article, Mansel contends that 'excitement, even when harmless in kind, cannot be continually produced without becoming morbid in degree' (Mansel 1863: 482). Collins, who was certainly aware of Mansel's denunciation, implicitly addressed this critique through his depiction of Gooseberry. In terming his visual interest in crime 'hideous' (Collins 1868: 213), Collins suggests not only Blake's over-delicate scrupulousness, but also a larger concern that young people are shaped by their exposure to what Mansel might call 'excitement' (Mansel 1863: 482). The novel's ambivalence towards Gooseberry, evinced by Cuff's encouragement of his observation and Blake's antipathy towards him, mediate between, on the one hand, an understanding that the working child possesses an abundance of resources and imaginative skill, and on the other hand, lacks the maturity to contend fully with everything he sees. In response to new forms of visual observation that emerged at the start of the nineteenth century, Crary poses two related questions: 'How is the body, including the observing body, becoming a component of new machines, economies, apparatuses ...? In what ways is subjectivity becoming a precarious condition of interface between rationalised systems of exchange and networks of information?' (Crary 1992: 2). Collins's depictions of Gooseberry and the nameless assistant to the Brahmins in *The Moonstone* suggest the various modes by which the marginalised boy subject is forgotten and passed over when he is recruited into the work of surveillance. Differentiating his examination of the street urchin from that of social journalists like Mayhew and Carpenter, whose writing casts working-class children as objects of institutional and behavioural observation, Collins instead addresses the ways by which vision itself became a mode of work with its own particular forms of discipline for boys in Victorian England.

Notes

1. The fact that Gooseberry derives his superior observational ability from his socially marginal position closely aligns with a similar trend that can be traced in mid-Victorian female detectives. Two clear cases are Mrs. Paschal of William Stephens Hayward's 1864 *Revelations of a Lady Detective* and Miss Gladden of Andrew Forrester's 1864 *The Female Detective,* who both suggest that it is their social marginalisation as women that affords them greater perceptive abilities than their male counterparts.
2. Dickens also wrote a number of investigative reports on the condition of pauper children, including 'London Pauper Children' in the August 31 1850 issue of *Household Words*and 'Little Pauper Boarders' in the August 28 1869 issue of *All the Year Round*.
3. Although it was begun with the purpose of documenting the impoverished circumstances of its students, *The Ragged School Union Magazine* also became involved in social journalism concerning poverty and its connection with criminality more broadly in the mid-Victorian period. See 'The Low Haunts of London' (1851) and 'Haunts of Crime' (1869) for two examples of articles it published in this vein.
4. The diamond was stolen by Rachel Verinder's uncle, John Herncastle, during the storming of Seringapatam described in the novel's prologue.
5. As both Jenny Bourne Taylor and Alison Winter observe, Collins was greatly interested in mesmerism, a pseudoscientific practice popular in Britain in the mid-nineteenth century which was said to grant subjects clairvoyant sight (59, 124). Martineau linked ink-gazing with mesmerism in 1848, suggesting that the former was simply an Eastern variant of the latter (140). The well-travelled Mr. Murthwaite echoes the notion in *The Moonstone*, but he discredits both ink-gazing and mesmerism in his theory that the 'boy is certainly a sensitive subject to the mesmeric influence—and, under that influence, he has no doubt reflected what was already in the mind of the person mesmerizing him' (143).
6. For more on the characters of Nipper and Tinker and their role in shaping the formation of the juvenile detective tradition, see 'Taming the Beast: Adolescence, Empire, and the Detective's Boy Assistant' in Lucy Andrew's *The Boy Detective in Early British Children's Literature: Patrolling the Borders between Boyhood and Manhood.*

Reference Lists

Andrew, Lucy. 2017. *The Boy Detective in Early British Children's Literature: Patrolling the Borders between Boyhood and Manhood*. Basingstoke: Palgrave Macmillan.

Anon. 1851. The Low Haunts of London. *Ragged School Union Magazine*, 3, December, 200–205.

———. 1869. Haunts of Crime. *Ragged School Union Magazine*. May, 104–107.

Arata, Stephen. 1996. *Fictions of Loss in the Victorian Fin de Siècle: Identity and Empire*. Cambridge: Cambridge University Press.

Benjamin, Walter. 1973. *Charles Baudelaire: A Lyric Poet in the Era of High Capitalism*, trans. Harry Zohn. London: NLB.

Carpenter, Mary. 1853. *Juvenile Delinquents, Their Condition and Treatment*. London: W. & F.G. Cash.

Clarke, Clare. 2014. *Late Victorian Crime Fiction in the Shadows of Sherlock*. Basingstoke: Palgrave Macmillan.

Collins, Wilkie. 1868. *The Moonstone*. New York, NY: Harper & Brothers.

Crary, Jonathan. 1992. *Techniques of the Observer: On Vision and Modernity in the Nineteenth Century*. Cambridge: MIT Press.

Dickens, Charles. 1850. London Pauper Children. *Household Words*. 1.23, August 31, 549–552.

———. 1853. *Bleak House*. London: Bradbury and Evans.

———. 1869. Little Pauper Boarders. *All the Year Round*. 2.39, August 28, 301–305.

Doyle, Arthur Conan. (1887) 1892. *A Study in Scarlet*. London: Ward, Lock, Bowden, and Co.

———. 1900. *The Sign of Four*. London: G. Newnes.

Forrester, Andrew. (1864) 2016. *The Female Detective*. Scottsdale, AZ: Poisoned Pen Press.

Foucault, Michel. 1975. *Discipline and Punish: The Birth of the Prison*, trans. Alan Sheridan. New York, NY: Vintage Books.

———. 1980. *Power/Knowledge: Selected Interviews and Other Writings, 1972–1977*, trans. Colin Gordon, Leo Marshall, John Mepham, and Kate Soper. New York, NY: Pantheon Books.

Greenwood, James. 1866. *The True History of a Little Ragamuffin*. New York, NY: Harper & Bros.

Haynsworth, Leslie. 2001. 'Sensational Adventures: Sherlock Holmes and His Generic Past.' *English Literature in Transition, 1880–1920* 44 (4): 459–85.

Hayward, William Stephens. 1864. *Revelations of a Lady Detective*. London: George Vickers.

Hocking, Silas K. (1879) 1890. *Her Benny*. London: F. Warne and Co.

Jones, Gareth Stedman. 1971. *Outcast London: A Study in the Relationship Between Classes in Victorian Society*. New York, NY: Pantheon Books.

Lane, Edward William. (1836) 1890. *An Account of the Manners and Customs of the Modern Egyptians*. London: Ward, Lock, and Co.

Lonoff, Sue. 1982. *Wilkie Collins and His Victorian Readers: A Study in the Rhetoric of Authorship*. New York, NY: AMS Press.

Mansel, Henry. 1863. Sensation Novels. *Quarterly Review* 113 (226): 481–514.

Martineau, Harriet. 1848. *Eastern Life: Present and Past*. London: Edward Moxon.

Mayhew, Henry. 1851. *London Labour and the London Poor: A Cyclopaedia of the Condition and Earnings of Those That Will Work, Those That Cannot Work, and Those That Will Not Work*. London: George Woodfall.

Miller, D.A. 1988. *The Novel and the Police*. Berkeley, CA: University of California Press.

Mitchell, Sally. 2012. *Victorian Britain: An Encyclopedia*. London: Routledge.

Murfin, Ross C. 1982. The Art of Representation: Collins' *The Moonstone* and Dickens' Example. *ELH* 49 (3): 653–672. https://doi.org/10.2307/2872759.

Nead, Lynda. 2005. *Victorian Babylon: People, Streets and Images in Nineteenth-Century London*. New Haven, CT: Yale University Press.

Otter, Chris. 2008. *The Victorian Eye: A Political History of Light and Vision in Britain, 1800–1910*. Chicago, IL: University of Chicago Press.

Paul, Robert S. 1991. *Whatever Happened to Sherlock Holmes: Detective Fiction, Popular Theology, and Society*. Carbondale, IL: Southern Illinois University Press.

Scott, Maxwell. 1894. A Dead Man's Secret. *Halfpenny Marvel*, 46, September 18, 1–15.

Stretton, Hesba. (1867) 1897. *Jessica's First Prayer and Jessica's Mother*. Philadelphia, PA: Henry Altemus.

Sutherland, John. 2014. *The Longman Companion to Victorian Fiction*. London: Routledge.

Taylor, Jenny Bourne. 1988. *In the Secret Theatre of Home: Wilkie Collins, Sensation Narrative, and Nineteenth-Century Psychology*. London: Routledge.

Vlock, Deborah. 1998. *Dickens, Novel Reading, and the Victorian Popular Theatre*. Cambridge: Cambridge University Press.

Winter, Alison. 2000. *Mesmerized: Powers of Mind in Victorian Britain*. Chicago, IL: University of Chicago Press.

Zieger, Susan. 2018. *The Mediated Mind: Affect, Ephemera, and Consumerism in the Nineteenth Century*. New York, NY: Fordham University Press.

CHAPTER 4

'…Always with the Inspector': The Reader as Sidekick in Mid-Victorian 'Detective Literature', 1845–1887

Samuel Saunders

Introduction: The Mid-Victorian 'Gap'

The concept of the 'sidekick' as a character present to only perform a limited set of functions, such as to accentuate the detective's sleuthing abilities, validate certain pieces of information and/or, in many cases, narrate the story to the reader, has been well-established by a widely recognised literary tradition in popular detective fiction. Figures such as Edgar Allan Poe's unnamed narrator, Arthur Conan Doyle's Dr. John Watson, Agatha Christie's Captain Arthur Hastings, Dorothy L. Sayers's Mervyn Bunter or even Margery Allingham's Magersfontein Lugg all perform specific and largely similar tasks in their respective narratives, a fact that has helped create a stereotypical and widely accepted image of the 'sidekick' as little more than the 'stupid friend' of the detective (Knox 1929). Each of these characters famously acts as the foil to the detective, and they have been largely perceived as designed to merely assist the

S. Saunders (✉)
University Centre Reaseheath, University of Chester, Chester, UK

L. Andrew and S. Saunders (eds.), *The Detective's Companion in Crime Fiction*, Crime Files, https://doi.org/10.1007/978-3-030-74989-7_4

sleuth in their endeavours, confirm pre-existing information and (in the cases of Poe's narrator, Doyle's Watson, and Christie's Hastings) relate the narrative to the reader in their own words, acting as the detective's pseudo-biographer.[1]

However, this well-established image of the archetypical sidekick neglects to cater for a substantial gap in the generally accepted chronology of the detective genre itself. It has historically been notoriously difficult to establish exactly what constituted detective fiction across the mid-Victorian era, defined here as the years between the final appearance of Edgar Allan Poe's narrator (1845) and the first appearance of Dr. Watson (1887). Indeed, when musing on Sherlock Holmes's consciously made (and rejected) connections between himself and Poe's fictional detective, C. Auguste Dupin in the early stages of the first Holmes novel, *A Study in Scarlet* (1887), Martin Kayman succinctly (and rather rhetorically) asks:

> [H]ow are we to explain that it took forty years for Dupin to find his inheritor? What was happening in the meantime, merely inadequate attempts to develop the genre 'invented' by Poe, which, barring a largely isolated attempt by Wilkie Collins some twenty years later, had to await the genius of Conan Doyle to get it right? (Kayman 1992: 105)

Naturally, there have been extensive scholarly efforts to resolve this problem. A number of critics, such as Stephen Knight, Charles Rzepka and John Scaggs, take Kayman's allusion to Wilkie Collins's writing and develop it outwards, favouring mid-Victorian sensation fiction as largely carrying the evolutionary chronology of the detective genre across this supposed 'interregnum' period. As such, many of the stereotypical elements of the detective story are often deliberately and retrospectively identified in a variety of examples of this genre, including the fictional detective and the fictional sidekick (Priestman [1998] 2013: 37). Multiple characters from different examples of sensation fiction have been labelled amateur 'detectives', including but not limited to Walter Hartright from Collins's novel *The Woman in White* (1861), Franklin Blake from *The Moonstone* (1868) and Robert Audley from Mary Elizabeth Braddon's *Lady Audley's Secret* (1862) (Priestman [1998] 2013: 37). Predictably, the literary counterparts to each of these characters have been naturally positioned as 'sidekicks' in one form or another. Characters such as Marian Halcombe from *The Woman in White*, George Talboys from *Lady Audley's Secret* or even Gabriel Betteredge or Ezra Jennings from *The*

Moonstone have all been dubbed sidekicks to their respective detectives, largely due to the functions they perform that seemingly conform to the accepted conception of the sidekick's role. Betteredge, for example, both aids Sergeant Cuff and Franklin Blake in their endeavours to discover the thief of the eponymous moonstone and relates the story directly to the reader at various points throughout the novel.[2]

It is the purpose of this chapter to add a much-needed layer of complexity to this narrative by looking at mid-Victorian detective literature from an alternative perspective, and by doing so to shed new light on the concept of the literary sidekick. It does this by exploring the influence of popular mid-century journalism on the development of detective fiction, and challenges the position of sensation fiction as the standard iteration of the detective genre in this period. The chapter argues that mid-Victorian detective fiction was *also* represented by the influx of memoir-styled fiction marketed as the true recollections and experiences of (usually retired) police officers and detectives (Saunders 2018: 76–90). Memoirs marketed in this way, as the chapter will explore, were contemporarily viewed as a form of detective fiction, and examining them can help create an alternative perception of the position of the sidekick, because in this kind of writing many of the duties of the character were actually performed by the *reader*.

The Journalist as Sidekick

The position of the reader as the sidekick in mid-Victorian crime fiction is inherently connected to contemporary forms of popular journalism, and so it is here where this chapter begins its exploration. The police received extensive criticism in the pages of mid-Victorian periodicals, especially after the passage of the 1856 County and Borough Police Act that made the establishment of police forces mandatory across Britain. A significant number of commentators were curious as to the socio-economic and political implications of the new concept of nationwide law enforcement, and partisan divisions quickly opened up (Saunders 2019a: n.p.). Magazines such as the largely conservative *Quarterly Review* often viewed the police as trusted protectors of the social and capitalist status quo,[3] whilst those of a more progressive persuasion tended to contend that the police were inept, too expensive and socially oppressive (Morphet 2009: 522). In April 1870, for example, the particularly militant *Saturday Review* argued, in a slightly alarmist fashion, that certain areas of London had almost descended into a state of complete lawlessness due to the police's apparent inability to keep the peace ('Inefficiency of the London Police' 1870: 575).

However, on a more universal scale, numerous journalists quickly noticed that police officers regularly patrolled dangerous or supposedly criminalised areas of inner-cities, and realised that they could reveal the hidden details of these spaces if they were asked about their experiences or even accompanied on their beats. Consequently, police officers began to appear in articles dedicated to the exploration and description of usually inaccessible or otherwise dangerous urban locations, and thus the journalist becomes our first visible sidekick figure as they frequently tagged along as police officers performed their duties and documented their actions for the benefit of readers in an almost proto-Watsonian form.

The interest in producing writing that explored inaccessible realms of criminality was built on a long and well-established literary tradition dating back to the early eighteenth century. Daniel Defoe's *The History of the Press Yard* (1717), for example, provided curious readers with a colourful description of the interior of the infamous condemned ward of Newgate Prison. Over a century later, Pierce Egan's *Life in London* (1821) included a remarkably similar scene from inside Newgate, where the protagonists, Corinthian Tom, Jerry Hawthorn and Bob Logic, witnessed several prisoners being prepared for the gallows (Egan 1821: 314–315). Even a young Charles Dickens produced examples of this kind of writing, with pieces such as 'A Visit to Newgate' and 'Criminal Courts' appearing in the collected group of essays today known as *Sketches by Boz* (1833–6), while G. W. M. Reynolds's popular penny blood *The Mysteries of London* (1844–5) additionally included a chapter describing the interior of Coldbath Fields. However, the steady progress of urban expansion across the mid-Victorian era changed the way that crime-exploration writing was produced and presented. Urban spaces grew alarmingly quickly throughout this period, and journalists became increasingly interested in exploring the chaos and hidden criminality of complex street-level activity (Saunders 2019b: 102). As Christopher Pittard contends, in an echo of Michel de Certeau's famous argument regarding the 'blind' pedestrian, the street-walker's perspective of the city was undisciplined, and at street-level the supposedly ordered world of law enforcement quickly gave way to a subterranean, hidden and disordered world of criminality (de Certeau 1984: 93 and Pittard 2007: 4). Thus, writing that was designed to help readers comprehend the city in which they lived, and to help them observe and understand its criminal element, grew exponentially alongside the city itself and came to share the metropolis's chaotic and random qualities (Fyfe 2009: 2–5). In 1861, for example, *Blackwood's Edinburgh Magazine* published an article discussing the case of Eliza Fenning, which opened with a highly detailed description of a part of London that, it assumed, its readers would have naturally avoided in reality and of which they probably had little knowledge:

> Immediately adjoining to High Holborn, and parallel with the southern side of Red Lion Square runs a long, narrow gloomy lane, called Eagle Street. Sickly children dabble in the gutters [...] Vendors of tripe and cat's-meat, rag and bottle dealers, marine-store keepers, merchants who hold out temptations in prose and verse, adorned with apoplectic numerals, to cooks and housemaids to purloin dripping, kitchen-stuff, and old wearing apparel, barbers who 'shave well for a penny,' shoe vampers, fried fish sellers, a coal and potato dealer, and a bird-stuffer, share the rest of the street, with lodging-houses of the filthiest description. (Paget 1861: 236)

As awareness of the police spread, authors realised that officers could help them perform the task of penetrating and revealing street-level criminal activity more effectively by providing both specialist knowledge of the city and physical and social protection. Journalists thus began to directly accompany police officers on their patrols; in the early 1850s, for example, Charles Dickens famously followed two police inspectors—Charles Frederick Field (1805–1874) and Jonathan Whicher (1814–1881)—on their nightly rounds, and published widely cited accounts of his adventures alongside them in his magazine, *Household Words*. An extract from one of these pieces, titled 'On Duty with Inspector Field', highlights Dickens's interest in entering and revealing the realms of criminals to the reader in the protective company of the police:

> We stoop low, and creep down a precipitous flight of steps into a dark close cellar. There is a fire. There is a long deal table. There are benches. The cellar is full of company, chiefly very young men in various conditions of dirt and raggedness. Some are eating supper. There are no girls or women present. Welcome to the Rat's Castle, gentlemen, and to this company of noted thieves! (Dickens 1851: 266)

The line '[w]elcome to the Rat's Castle, gentlemen, and to this company of noted thieves!' is particularly noteworthy here. On one level, it acts as Field speaking to Dickens, welcoming him to the first port of call on their nightly patrol and cementing him as Dickens's guide and protector. However, it simultaneously acts as Dickens speaking directly to the *reader*, demonstrating how he is consciously positioned as the conduit through which the reader observes the police officer in action. This, I suggest, codifies Dickens as Field's sidekick and (consequently) ties this kind of writing to later iterations of crime fiction where the sidekick performed a similar task of mediating between the reader and the detective by relating the activities of the latter directly to the former in a controlled way (Rzepka 2005: 20).

The concept of journalists using the police as a source of knowledge and protection when delving into the subterranean world of urban crime appeared in numerous articles published throughout the mid-Victorian era. In 1865, for example, *Temple Bar* produced a piece where the author stated how their urban explorations had been in the constant company of an inspector who had, essentially, showed him around the criminal neighbourhood:

> From Stepney police-station, again, I have started – always with the Inspector – to go the round of cheap gaffs, squalid saloons, small music-halls, dancing taverns, and concert rooms of the Ratcliffe Highway and Whitechapel. [...] where the shottishe [sic] is danced by foreign gentlemen and ladies [...] habitually carry knives, and occasionally use them. ('On Duty with the Inspector' 1865: 349)

Again, the journalist is presented as the conduit through which the reader observes the interaction between the police and criminality, providing the reader with a privileged view into the 'squalid saloons, small music-halls, dancing taverns and concert rooms' contained in areas of the city that were usually deemed to be too dangerous to explore alone. A further example appeared in the May 1869 issue of the *Ragged School Union Magazine*, which included a piece written by a journalist who states that they had explored particularly 'low' areas of London in the constant company of a police officer who had, once again, provided specialist knowledge and had ensured their safety:

> In company with detectives, he has visited beershops, lodging-houses for travellers, and dolly shops in Tiger Bay, Kent Street, the Mint, and the

> other favourite haunts of our criminal classes. ('Haunts of Crime' 1869: 104)

Finally, in 1851 the *Ragged School Union Magazine* produced a particularly interesting piece that described how a police officer provided escort to an entire group of determined journalists who had travelled from Scotland specifically to see London's supposed 'criminal underworld'. In this, the officer is directly described as both a guide and protector, and the author argues that:

> Without the protection of the police such an enterprise would of course have been impossible; but on presenting a letter which we had brought from Scotland, we found the authorities ready to afford every facility, and as the best method of accomplishing our object, we were intrusted [sic] to the guidance of [...] an officer of the detective force. ('The Low Haunts of London' 1851: 200)

As we can see, then, in periodical journalism designed to explore the hidden criminality of the city at street-level, journalists were continually (and sometimes consciously) positioned as sidekicks to the necessarily-present police officer, who provided them with both specialist knowledge and protection in physical and social terms. They moved in the police's constant company, observed and documented their behaviour and interactions with criminals, and (perhaps most importantly) occupied a familiar mediating position between the reader and the detective, providing the literary window for the reader to observe the detective in action. Indeed, this pre-empts the exact same mediating position that the sidekick of classic detective fiction is, even today, often seen to occupy (Rowland 2010: 117). The journalist occupied the same shocked, often slightly ignorant layman position as later sidekicks from popular detective fiction who are designed to provide the reader with a figure with which to identify. Dr John Watson, for example, famously makes frequent exclamations of astonishment at Sherlock Holmes's deductive abilities, which mirror the reader's own bewilderment (or at the very least are designed to help instil it).[4] Thus, while Watson acts as the reader's window into Holmes's world, in mid-Victorian urban exploration journalism the reader's connection into the text's universe was the journalist, who acted as the go-between between the reader and the police officer.

Police Memoirs and Reader Sidekicks

However, the journalistic interest in using the police as a protective force in order to explore and reveal criminal activity in the urban city actually sparked the production of a fictional genre that, rather conversely, *removed* the journalist from their position as sidekick, mediator and storyteller. This was 'police memoir' fiction, a form of writing contemporarily (though tentatively) labelled 'detective literature' in 1862 by the journalist William Russell, who was perhaps the most prolific author of police memoirs of the nineteenth century (Saunders 2018: 84). These texts can be thematically connected to urban exploration journalism, in that they were similarly targeted at readers who were interested in experiencing the world of crime as closely as possible but without having to go to the trouble of becoming a criminal themselves. They were thus designed to use the experiences of a supposedly real police officer or detective to allow readers figurative access into the criminal underworld lurking beneath the surface of their own existence and, as they offered quite cheap and sensationalised thrills, they were exceedingly popular across the mid-Victorian era (Saunders 2018: 83–84).

Despite the fact that both urban exploration journalism and police memoir fiction were designed to reveal concealed criminality in the city-space through relating the experiences of police officers, there is a clear difference between the two forms of writing—the presence of a figure that occupied a literary space between the detective and the reader, and that mediated between them. While authors of journalism dedicated to exploring urban criminality had depicted themselves as accompanying a police officer on their patrols, police memoir fiction had no such character. Instead, the narrative voice was almost always that of the police officer speaking directly to the reader, and there was rarely, if ever, a secondary character that accompanied the detective and who related the narrative. As a result, I suggest that the readers themselves became the sole, complete and manifest sidekick of the detective in this genre, occupying the stereotypical sidekick 'character space' (Woloch 2009: 14).

This repositioning occurred for a number of reasons, but perhaps the most important to highlight here is that one of the sole points of the police memoir genre was to allow the police officer a voice to relate their own experiences, and to permit the reader to directly accompany them on their adventures from a place of complete safety. In other words, one of the overall purposes of police memoir fiction was to allow the reader to effectively become the detective's sidekick. As the job of narrating the story to the reader was left to the detective, the presence of a character who acts as the detective's companion, biographer and who performs mediation between the detective and the reader became unnecessary, and thus the *reader* moved into the sidekick 'character-space' to act as the detective's companion, accompanying them in their exploits and gazing upwardly at their prowess (Priestman [1998] 2003: 200).

Russell's best-known police memoir, titled 'Recollections of a Police Officer', can help to effectively demonstrate this in action. The text was published in 12 instalments in *Chambers's Edinburgh Journal* throughout 1849, and told the adventures of an anonymous detective known only as 'Waters'. Waters operates alone in each of the individual stories, flitting up and down the country and in and out of usually inaccessible criminalised locations across different urban environments. As he goes, he relates his experiences directly to the reader, who thus comes to share in them alongside him, and he makes it clear in the opening instalment that his sole purpose was to penetrate the private realms of criminality and for the reader to essentially 'come along for the ride':

> 'Here is a written description of the persons of this gang of blacklegs, swindlers and forgers,' concluded the commissioner, summing up his instructions. 'It will be your object to *discover their private haunts*, and secure legal evidence of their nefarious practices [...].' [my emphasis] (Russell 1849: 55–56)

Thus, as the stories are related by Waters himself, the usual dichotomy of characters typically present in detective fiction, the detective and the sidekick, initially seems to be missing. However, it does still exist in an amended form. The sidekick figure, acting as the detective's companion, is a position occupied in these narratives by the reader themselves, to whom the detective speaks as the adventures progress, and who is afforded a privileged insight into the operational methodologies of the police. This is evidenced later in the narrative when Waters is working on a case, in a scene where he gains access to a house where a group of criminals are hiding out. As yet unknown as a detective in London, Waters passes inside unnoticed, and the reader follows in his wake, witnessing everything that Waters does by receiving information from him in his own words:

> We soon arrived before the door of a quiet, respectable-looking house in one of the streets leading from the Strand: a low, peculiar knock, given by Sandford, was promptly answered; then a password, which I did not catch, was whispered by him through the key-hole, and we passed in. [...] We proceeded up stairs to the first floor, the shutters of which were carefully closed, so that no intimation of what was going in could possibly reach the street. [...] a roulette table and dice and cards were in full activity: wine and liquors of all varieties were profusely paraded. (Russell 1849: 57)

I have deliberately chosen this scene to illustrate this point, as the juxtaposition between this and that presented in Dickens's 'On Duty with Inspector Field' is somewhat remarkable. While this moment itself bears a curious similarity to when Dickens and Field first enter the 'Rat's Castle' den of thieves, quoted earlier, the narrative voice here is far different. In Dickens's piece, Dickens himself acted as the mediator between the reader and the detective, and drew attention to this by consistently addressing the reader himself. However, in 'Recollections of a Police Officer', the reader instead accompanies the sleuth directly and receives the narrative from them first hand. This, I argue, cements the reader as the detective's companion, observer and (thus) as their sidekick.

Russell penned a significant number of other police memoirs that similarly retold the exploits of a detective figure first hand, thus consistently positioning the reader as the sidekick. These included a novelised reprint of 'Recollections of a Police Officer', which appeared in 1856 under the title *Recollections of a Detective Police Officer*, as well as *Experiences of a Real Detective* (1862) and *Autobiography of an English Detective* (1863), among many others. Elsewhere, Russell was also not the only author to capitalise on the popularity of relating the police experience. Other texts published throughout the mid-Victorian era included, but were not limited to, Charles Martel's *Diary of an Ex-Detective* (1860), 'Recollections of a New York Detective' from *Twice a Week* (1862), 'An Australian Detective's Story' from *Once a Week* (1864), Andrew Forrester's *Secret Service; or, Recollections of a City Detective* (1864), 'From a Detective's Note-Book from the *Argosy* (1872) and 'My Detective Experiences' published in *Chambers's Edinburgh Journal* (1886), all of which positioned the reader as the sidekick or companion to the protagonist-detective.

Finally, in 1864, two further police memoirs appeared that, again, situated the reader as the sidekick figure, but which are worth briefly mentioning specifically before this chapter moves on: Andrew Forrester's *The Female Detective* and William S. Hayward's *Revelations of a Lady Detective*. These texts are often explored in relation to the development of detective fiction and its connection with femininity, as they both (relatively unprecedentedly) depicted female detective protagonists.[5] However, they were also attempts to create a new and innovative form of text within a genre market already saturated with examples of itself (Saunders 2018: 88). In both novels, again, the reader directly accompanied the detective in their activities against criminals, but using *female* detectives was particularly useful this time as it allowed readers to access an even greater variety of inaccessible spaces than simply urban criminality. For example, in *Revelations of a Lady Detective* the protagonist-detective character, Mrs. Paschal, is required to infiltrate a convent, and the reader, acting as her companion, naturally comes along with her:

> At the expiration of a week, I entered the convent as a lay-sister, and was much struck by the calm inoffensive piety displayed by those with whom I came into contact. The nuns were exceedingly kind to me, but I fancied that their amiability was somewhat studied and forced [...] I assumed a harmless character, which recommended me to the nuns. I was always docile and very obedient. I would run about the house for them and bring them books from the library [...] The prevailing sin of the sisters I found was listlessness and laziness, including a disinclination to work. (Hayward [1864] 2013: 148–149)

Thus, not only were police memoirs helpful to allow readers an insight into supposedly criminal spaces across the cityscape, they were also useful to allow readers an insight into a much wider *variety* of usually restricted locations by accompanying the privileged detective as their sidekick-companion. Indeed, another example from *Revelations of a Lady Detective* depicted Paschal infiltrating a domestic space in disguise as a maidservant, providing the reader with an unusual insight into servant-class life within an upper middle-class domestic home. (see the story titled 'The Mysterious Countess' (Hayward [1864] 2013: 17–48).

There are numerous other examples of this kind of writing from which I could quote to continue highlighting how the police memoir genre repeatedly positioned the reader as the detective's figurative companion, and so an initial conclusion can be drawn at this point. While contemporary journalism interested in urban exploration positioned the journalist as the reader's window into the world of the detective, the purpose of the police memoir—a genre that had evolved *out* of this journalistic interest—was to actually give the police officer a voice of their own. This effectively removed the sidekick character from the narrative, in order to allow the officer to speak for themselves. However, this did not have the effect of obliterating the *concept* of the sidekick, as the sidekick mantle was simply passed onto the reader, who came to occupy the position of the detective's companion that observed their actions and gazed in wonder at their prowess.

Reader Sidekicks and Sensation Fiction

At this stage, however, it is important to point out that this idea that the reader occupied the character space of the sidekick was also transposed into other kinds of fiction than simply the police memoir. As mentioned in this chapter's introduction, the mid-Victorian era (and, indeed, the development of the detective novel) is frequently characterised by the popularity of sensation fiction—novels designed to depict scandal, murder, death, detection and crime in order to provide readers with a thrill, and which caused a substantial (and occasionally vitriolic) reader reaction at the time they were published (Knight 2004: 39). Interestingly, this kind of writing was actually seen by at least some contemporary commentators to have evolved directly *out* of the police memoir. In 1863, the *London Review* argued:

> It is now some years since the name of 'Waters' first became familiar and welcome to readers in railway trains. [...] the policeman line of writing was found to possess an interest often sadly wanting to more decorous publications. [...] Accordingly the criminal novel is now the *mode*. The crime is, of course, a mystery; and the plot is the statement of the means by which the mystery is detected. Mr. Wilkie Collins was perhaps the first to adopt this fashion. ('The Last Sensation Novel' 1862: 481)

Thus, police memoirs, for this article at least, had directly spawned sensation fiction, which used many of the same structural tropes—detectives and detection, criminals and crime, and (in particular) the desire to explore and reveal locations that were often inaccessible to readers (though in the case of sensation fiction this was frequently the domestic arrangements of the bourgeoisie, rather than the hidden criminality of the urban city [Pykett 2003: 32]). The trope of the police officer's ability to penetrate anywhere, with the reader acting as their would-be sidekick as they did so, was naturally also transposed into sensation fiction from the police memoir, albeit in a less immediately obvious form. Charles Dickens's *Bleak House* ([1853] 1988) for example, a novel today seen as one of the earliest sensation novels (Pykett 2003: 33–4), depicts the detective, Mr Bucket, traversing the length and breadth of London and conversing with characters from all walks of life and from all social backgrounds with ease. Bucket's connection to the forms of writing discussed so far in this chapter is clear; he was famously based directly on Dickens's own adventures alongside inspectors Field and Whicher, quoted earlier on, and like his counterparts, repeatedly inserts himself, chameleon-like, into any situation and observes others without being observed himself.

Conversely, however, Bucket is not the strongest character-connection to the concept of the reader *sidekick* in sensation fiction, as the reader does not receive the narrative directly from him throughout the novel, and is not privy to his thoughts and methodologies as he works through the case. It is with Mary Elizabeth Braddon, one of the best-known authors of sensation fiction, where we find a stronger example of a sensation text where the detective penetrates usually restricted areas and the reader occupies the position of their sidekick as they do so. Her first novel, *Three Times Dead, or, the Secret of the Heath* ([1860] 1866), republished as *The Trail of the Serpent* in 1861, was based on both Dickens's writing and that of G. W. M. Reynolds (Braddon 1893: 25), and positions the reader as the figurative companion of a mute detective. Perhaps most interestingly, in the first edition of the novel, this character was named *Waters*, in an apparent (or perhaps coincidental) connection to William Russell's fictional detective. However, he was rechristened 'Peters' in subsequent editions.

Peters's abilities as a detective are actually augmented by the fact that he cannot verbally communicate, as it makes him a natural at keeping secrets from other characters while simultaneously revealing them to the reader sidekick. Like Bucket, Peters possesses the ability to go wherever he pleases, unseen and unremarked, and the reader directly accompanies him as he goes. A scene that demonstrates this particularly well appears when he overhears a conversation in a public house between the novel's villain and his lover:

> But in I walks, past the bar; and straight afore me I sees a door as leads into the parlour – the passage was jolly dark; and this 'ere door was ajar; and inside I hears voices. [...] so I listens. (Braddon [1861] 1866: 275)

Peters walks confidently into the scene to overhear the conversation better and, as in police memoir fiction, the reader sidekick follows in his wake. Peters then actually uses his muteness to his advantage, as once his quarry learns of it, he simply assumes that he is not a threat:

> [I]n I walks, very quiet and quite unbeknownst. He was a-sittin' with his back to the door, and the young woman he was a-talkin' to was standin' lookin' out of the winder; so neither of 'em saw me. [...] He turned round and looked at me. [...] I says to myself, if ever there was anything certain in this world since it was begun, I've come across the right 'un: so I sits down and takes up a newspaper. I signified to him that I was dumb, and he took it for granted I was deaf as well [...] so he went on a-talking to the girl. (Braddon [1861] 1866: 276–277)

Additionally, Braddon's most famous novel, *Lady Audley's Secret* ([1862] 1997), is also relevant to this idea of the detective penetrating an inaccessible location and the reader acting as their would-be sidekick figure. This novel depicts the amateur detective, Robert Audley, investigating the disappearance of his friend, George Talboys. Robert correctly suspects Lady Audley, who in reality is Talboys's supposedly dead wife Helen, of murdering him, and sets out to prove it. Talboys himself is frequently viewed as the sidekick figure in this novel; however, I argue that his disappearance early on actually causes the reader to directly take his place as Robert's companion as he searches for the required evidence. Through accompanying Robert, the reader is thus again permitted to access usually inaccessible places, both through Robert's authority as pseudo-detective and his position as a legitimate member of the family unit. This is a position that Lady Audley herself does not occupy, codifying her as an external threat to the safety and sanctity of the middle-class home. The reader therefore accompanies Robert into locations that they would ordinarily not be able to view, including Lady Audley's private dressing room, which is accessed specifically through the use of a secret passageway of which she had no knowledge and thus signalling his legitimacy as a member of the family (Braddon [1862] 1997: 55–56).

These are just a small sample of a large number of sensation novels that were connected to police memoir fiction in that they placed the reader in the position of the sidekick or companion to an apparent detective who could penetrate a usually inaccessible location. Indeed, even some contemporary reviews of sensation novels highlighted the idea that the reader directly followed the usually-present detective figure as their would-be observer and sidekick. In 1863, for example, Margaret Oliphant, writing in *Blackwood's Edinburgh Magazine*, suggested that the central pillar of a number of genres of popular mid-Victorian fiction (not solely sensation fiction) lay in how they utilised a police officer to track down a criminal, though she was apparently not particularly enthused about this idea:

> Murder is our *cheval de bataille* [...] The horrors of our novels are crimes against life and property. The policeman is the Fate who stalks relentless, or flies with lightning steps after our favourite villain. (Oliphant 1863: 168)

Overall therefore, I suggest that the mid-Victorian era was a period when the traditionally recognised figure of the sidekick in various forms of crime fiction was largely invisible, almost completely submerged in alternative forms of writing that focused on placing the reader within the story for themselves. Rather than present a character designed to represent the reader within the text, mid-Victorian crime fiction often attempted to relay the story directly to the reader, and thus positioned them within it for themselves as the supposed detective's companion, observer and admirer. Thus, Edgar Allan Poe's unnamed narrator in the Dupin short stories, often cited as an influence over the construction of the sidekick figure in later iterations of detective fiction was, I suggest, an anomaly not to be replicated until the late-Victorian era, particularly the emergence of Dr. John Watson in the Sherlock Holmes stories written by Arthur Conan Doyle. This, I contend, contributes to why the mid-Victorian era, where the dichotomy between the detective and sidekick is far less immediately obvious, is still commonly codified as a generic interregnum even today.

Conclusions: The End of the Reader-Sidekick

There is a final issue that needs to be addressed, however, before this chapter concludes. Why did the relationship between fictional detective and reader sidekick, so prominent and popular in various forms of mid-Victorian detective fiction, disappear relatively quickly as the nineteenth century approached its end? Why did figures such as Doyle's Dr. Watson once more come to occupy such a prominent mediating, buffering position between the reader and the detective, when preceding forms of fiction did not construct themselves in this way? Indeed, why is it that we recognise and accept this form of detective fiction, where the sidekick arbitrates between the reader and the sleuth, as a standard way of constructing the genre over any other kind of form?

There are two potential answers to these questions. The first lies within broader changes that took place within the detective genre itself as a consequence of a number of significant and widely publicised events that damaged the reputation of the police across the late-Victorian era. The relationship between the detective and reader sidekick (or indeed between the detective and the journalist performing urban exploration) had been largely reliant on a sense of trust existing between these figures. Journalists, readers and, by extension, the wider public were required to have faith in the police to perform their duties adequately and honestly, so that they could accompany them safely. This had seemingly been the case—up to a point. As Clive Emsley asserts, mid-Victorians had been, on the whole, 'proud of their police', and journalistic commentary in any guise (supportive or otherwise) had most definitely helped to cement the police as a necessary and intrinsic part of the social fabric of mid-Victorian society (Emsley 1999: 30).

However, this position of trust began to destabilise as the era approached the 1870s and 80s as a result of a sequence of terrible failures on the part of the police, all of which were reported widely in the press, damaging their reputation. These included, but were not limited to, the Clerkenwell Prison bombing in 1867, the Hyde Park riots (also in 1867) and, perhaps most notably of all, the 1877 'turf fraud' scandal, where three detective inspectors from the Metropolitan Police's 'detective department' were convicted of corruption and collusion with convicted criminals (Rzepka 2005: 111). Things were only to get worse across the 1880s, as the sustained bombing campaign across Britain by the Irish Republican Brotherhood, the 'Bloody Sunday' riots of 1887, and as the mismanaged and still-unsolved 1888 Whitechapel murders committed by Jack the Ripper largely prevented the police from recovering their reputation. Consequently, the loss of trust in the police meant that they were no longer able to act as trustworthy guides and protectors into the criminal underworld supposedly lurking beneath society's surface. As they were now seen as inept, corrupt and inefficient (and in some cases, even as part of the criminal world themselves), police officers were no longer a respectable source of information—and were certainly no longer figures that respectable authors or journalists would wish to accompany on their exploits. Throughout the 1880s, therefore, there was a corresponding increase in interest in the concept and use of fictional private detectives, amateur sleuths and officers for hire, as well as an increase in the depictions of largely useless and occasionally corrupt official police officers that were juxtaposed against them. The necessity for a narrator and biographer character to occupy the space of the sidekick, and to act as a buffer character between reader and detective protagonist, largely resurfaced, as detective narratives now required a trustworthy figure with which they could identify. The most famous example of this was, quite obviously, the infamous Sherlock Holmes and his faithful narrator-companion, Dr Watson.

The second answer, quite simply, stems from the fact that both Holmesian and supposed 'Golden Age' detective fiction, characterised by authors such as Christie, Sayers, Allingham and Patricia Wentworth, had a renewed focus on the puzzle element of the story that required the reader to attempt to solve the mystery at the same time as the sleuth (Knight 2004: 87). Earlier police memoir fiction had been structured in a largely procedural fashion, where the focus was on relating the adventures of the police as they fought crime and simply observing them in action, and not on encouraging the reader to solve a mystery in direct competition with the detective themselves. However, to structure a text where the reader was required to attempt to solve the puzzle for themselves naturally necessitated a renewed mediating, buffer presence between themselves and the detective, so that the reader did not always know what the detective was thinking or calculating. Thus, the Watsonian sidekick necessarily reappeared, to act as a window into the activities of the sleuth, but whose own incompetence naturally withheld information from the reader that would, in effect, spoil the solution to the puzzle if it were to be revealed to them too quickly by the detective's own voice.

Overall, then, I suggest that the construction of mid-Victorian detective fiction was constantly influenced by simultaneously produced popular journalism, in particular that which was interested in crime and law enforcement, and that this helped to both create and destroy the concept of the reader sidekick in mid-Victorian detective fiction. A number of journalistic forms, such as crime reporting, police criticism and (crucially) urban exploration journalism had initially painted the new police as a trustworthy and largely necessary social institution that occupied a rapidly growing space between the general public and the criminal underworld, and could help those without knowledge or expertise to access this underworld more effectively. This was naturally transposed into various kinds of popular fiction that sought to provide readers with the thrill of exploring criminality from a place of complete safety, particularly including popular police memoirs that depicted officers speaking directly to a reader who accompanied them on their duties in their protective company. As a result, the reader themselves came to occupy the literary character space of the stereotypical sidekick, and this positioning of the reader as the detective's companion was also evident in various other kinds of mid-Victorian fiction. Popular sensation fiction, for example, the works by Mary Elizabeth Braddon, Wilkie Collins and even Charles Dickens, also show evidence of how the police penetrated the private, and how reader occupied a literary space usually filled by the sidekick.

However, these kinds of fiction were predicated on the maintenance of a level of public trust in the police and detective forces. The police had enjoyed mostly universal support across the mid-Victorian era (despite some disagreement about their political implications and remit). This was, however, to fundamentally change as the Victorian era approached its end, and a series of damaging scandals, and how they were reported in the press, changed the way that the police were used in fiction and fundamentally affected the construction of detective fiction itself. The police were no longer viewed as trustworthy figures that could be accompanied on their duties, but were instead seen to be at best incompetent and slightly foolish, and at worst almost criminals themselves. Thus, the rise of the private or amateur detective in late-Victorian fiction, designed to compete with the reader to solve a puzzling mystery, both mirrors this ideological shift, and also hails the end of the reader as sidekick in nineteenth-century detective fiction.

Notes

1. This is occasionally consciously recognised by the detective protagonist—Sherlock Holmes, in particular, is aware of his friend Watson's position as his biographer, especially when Holmes himself, on rare occasion, narrates the stories directly to the reader. In 'The Adventure of the Blanched Soldier' ([1926a] 2009), for example, Holmes states that he underestimated how difficult it is to present the story in an interesting fashion to the

reader. Similarly, in 'The Adventure of the Lion's Mane' ([1926b] 2009]), Holmes remarks that he 'must act as [his] own chronicler' for once.

2. There have also been, naturally, numerous more complex readings of sidekick characters in sensation fiction than this: see Oriah Amit's chapter on the street-urchin figure in *The Moonstone*, contained in this collection, for a good example.
3. See 'Judicial Statistics', *Quarterly Review*, July 1870, p. 90 as a representative example of this attitude. This example is by no means the only incident of a politically or socially conservative magazine supporting the police in this open fashion, but it is usefully representative.
4. A good and quite famous example of this is Watson's famous exclamation from 'A Scandal in Bohemia' (1891), where he states '[m]y dear Holmes [...] this is too much. You would certainly have been burned had you lived a few centuries ago' (Doyle [1891] 2009: 260).
5. See, for example, Joseph Kestner's *Sherlock's Sisters: The British Female Detective, 1864–1913.*

Reference Lists

Anon. 1851. The Low Haunts of London. *Ragged School Union Magazine*, January, 200–205.

———. 1862. The Last Sensation Novel. *London Review*, November, 481–482.

———. 1869. Haunts of Crime. *Ragged School Union Magazine*, May, 104–107.

———. 1870. Inefficiency of the London Police. *Saturday Review*, April 30, 574–575.

Braddon, Mary Elizabeth. (1862) 1997. *Lady Audley's Secret*. London: William Tinsley. Reprint, Ware: Wordsworth Editions.

———. 1893. 'My First Novel. The Trail of the Serpent.' *Idler*, July, 19–30.

———. (1860) 1866. *Three Times Dead, or, The Secret of the Heath*. London: Ward, Lock and Tyler.

Conan Doyle, Arthur. (1887) 2009. *A Study in Scarlet. Beeton's Christmas Annual*. Reprint, *The Complete Illustrated Sherlock Holmes*, London: CRW.

———. (1891) 2009. A Scandal in Bohemia. *Strand Magazine*, June. Reprint, *The Complete Illustrated Sherlock Holmes*, London: CRW.

———. (1926a) 2009. The Adventure of the Blanched Solider. *Liberty Magazine*, October. Reprint, *The Complete Illustrated Sherlock Holmes*, London: CRW.

———. (1926b) 2009. The Adventure of the Lion's Mane. *Liberty Magazine*, November. Reprint, *The Complete Illustrated Sherlock Holmes*. London: CRW.

de Certeau, Michel. 1984. *The Practice of Everyday Life*, trans. Steven Rendall. Berkeley, CA and Los Angeles, CA: University of California Press.

Dickens, Charles. 1851. On Duty with Inspector Field. *Household Words*, June 14, 265–270.
———. (1853) 1988. *Bleak House*. London: Bradbury and Evans. Reprint, London: Penguin Classics.
Egan, Pierce. 1821. *Life in London*. London: Chatto and Windus.
Emsley, Clive. 1999. A Typology of Nineteenth-Century Police. *Crime, Histoire Et Sociétés/crime, History and Societies* 3 (1): 29–44.
Fyfe, Paul. 2009. The Random Selection of Victorian New Media. *Victorian Periodicals Review* 42 (1): 1–23.
Hayward, William Stephens. (1864) 2013. *Revelations of a Lady Detective*. London: George Vickers. Reprint, London: British Library.
Kayman, Martin. 1992. *From Bow Street to Baker Street: Mystery, Detection and Narrative*. Basingstoke: Palgrave Macmillan.
Kestner, Joseph. 2003. *Sherlock's Sisters: The British Female Detective, 1864–1913*. London: Routledge.
Knight, Stephen. 2004. *Crime Fiction 1800–2000: Detection, Death, Diversity*. Basingstoke: Palgrave Macmillan.
Knox, Ronald. 1929. *The Best Detective Stories of the Year 1928*. London: Faber and Faber.
Morphet, David Ian. 2009. *Quarterly Review* (1809–1967). In *Dictionary of Nineteenth Century Journalism*, ed. Laurel Brake and Marysa Demoor, 522–523. London and Ghent: Academia.
Oliphant, Margaret. 1863. Novels. *Blackwood's Edinburgh Magazine*, August, 168–183.
Paget, John. 1861. Judicial Puzzles—Eliza Fenning. *Blackwood's Edinburgh Magazine*, February, 236–244.
Parkinson, J.C. 1865. On Duty with the Inspector. *Temple Bar*, June, 348–358.
Pittard, Christopher. 2007. Cheap, Healthful Literature: The Strand Magazine, Fictions of Crime and Purified Reading Communities. *Victorian Periodicals Review* 40 (1): 1–23.
Priestman, Martin. (1998) 2013. *Crime Fiction: From Poe to the Present*. Devon: Northcote House. Reprint.
———. 2003. 'Post-War British Crime Fiction'. In *The Cambridge Companion to Crime Fiction*, ed. Martin Priestman. Cambridge: Cambridge University Press.
Pykett, Lyn. 2003. The Newgate Novel and Sensation Fiction, 1830–1868. In *The Cambridge Companion to Crime Fiction*, ed. Martin Priestman. Cambridge: Cambridge University Press.
Rowland, Susan. 2010. The "Classical" Model of the Golden Age. In *A Companion to Crime Fiction*, ed. Charles Rzepka and Lee Horsley. Chichester: Wiley-Blackwell.

Russell, William. 1849. Recollections of a Police Officer. *Chambers's Edinburgh Journal*, July 28, 55–59.

———. 1862. Experiences of a Real Detective. *Sixpenny Magazine*, March, 325–334.

Rzepka, Charles. 2005. *Detective Fiction*. Cambridge: Polity.

Saunders, Samuel. 2018. 'To Pry Unnecessarily into Other Men's Secrets': Crime Writing, Private Spaces and the Mid-Victorian Police Memoir. *Law, Crime and History* 8 (1): 76–90.

———. 2019a. 'To Get to the Very Bottom of the Social Fabric': Mid-Victorian Journalism and the Police Officer, c. 1856–1877. *Wilkie Collins Journal* 16.1: n.p. https://wilkiecollinssociety.org/to-get-to-the-very-bottom-of-the-social-fabric-mid-victorian-journalism-and-the-police-officer-c-1856-1877/.

———. 2019b. 'I was Again Passing Along Leicester Square ... With all my Eyes About Me': Mapping Popular 'Police Memoir' Detective Fiction. *Victorian Popular Fictions* 1(2): 100–109.

Woloch, Alex. 2009. *The One vs. The Many*. Princeton, NJ: Princeton University Press.

CHAPTER 5

'You Have a Grand Gift of Silence, Watson': Reinventing Agency in Twenty-First-Century Adaptations of Dr. Watson

Annette Wren

Introduction

'A Scandal in Bohemia' (1891) begins with Sherlock Holmes reassuring Dr. John Watson that he should not leave when the disguised King of Bohemia arrives at 221B Baker Street for a clandestine appointment: 'Stay where you are. I am lost without my Boswell. And this promises to be interesting. It would be a pity to miss it' (Doyle [1891a] 2009: 147). In this quotation, Holmes compares Watson to James Boswell (1740–1795), whom the *Oxford Dictionary of National Biography* identifies as 'lawyer, diarist, and biographer of Samuel Johnson' (Turnbull 2004). A dictionary could use similar descriptors to define John Watson: army doctor, Afghan War veteran, and biographer of Sherlock Holmes. This phrase 'biographer of' implies not subordination but power: Boswell and Watson control how audiences perceive their respective biographical subjects. This reliance naturally extends to readers as well and underscores

A. Wren (✉)
Texas Christian University, Fort Worth, TX, USA

L. Andrew and S. Saunders (eds.), *The Detective's Companion in Crime Fiction*, Crime Files, https://doi.org/10.1007/978-3-030-74989-7_5

a narrator's, and specifically in this case, Watson's, influence. In this spirit of empowering narrators, this chapter examines how Dr. John Watson's role as Sherlock Holmes's sidekick becomes more diverse in two twenty-first-century adaptations: CBS's television series *Elementary* (2012–2019) with Sherlock Holmes (played by Jonny Lee Miller) and Dr. Joan Watson (played by Lucy Liu) and Brittany Cavallaro's first novel in her Charlotte Holmes series, *A Study in Charlotte* (2016), with Jamie (James) Watson and Charlotte Holmes.

These Americanized adaptations produce equal partnerships by creating a new power dynamic between Holmes and Watson. Charlotte and Sherlock are drug addicts that embody their progenitor's high intelligence quotient (IQ) but lack a corresponding emotional quotient (EQ), defined as 'the ability to perceive and express, assimilate, understand and manage emotions' (Bar-On et al. 2000: 1108). Jamie and Joan first foster sobriety in their respective Holmes and this sobriety ensures that Charlotte and Sherlock are stable enough to emotionally and psychologically mature. Second, Jamie and Joan teach the Holmes figures to properly handle EQ because the Watsons possess an overabundance of EQ in the same manner that Charlotte and Sherlock carry too much IQ. These new power dynamics emphasize that the role of a sidekick is not inherently unequal to that of the detective. Instead, the Holmes–Watson relationship is an equal partnership, because the Holmes characters develop from and acknowledge the significance of EQ; in turn, Jamie and Joan increase their IQ while learning from their respective Holmeses. These themes adeptly harmonize with trends in contemporary American popular psychology, which has its roots in the ideology of self-help that developed between the 1930s and 1960s and stresses a positive correlation between building EQ confidence and increasing self-esteem (Illouz 2008: 15). Therefore, these adaptations emphasize that EQ is just as significant as IQ.

For the purposes of this chapter, I examine Cavallaro's first novel in the *Charlotte Holmes* series, *A Study in Charlotte* (2016), and *Elementary*'s Season 1 (2012–2013). This choice underscores the significance of developing character rapport in the 'first' of any textual or visual source. I use the names 'Holmes' and 'Watson' when discussing Doyle's original characters. While Charlotte and Jamie prefer to call themselves 'Holmes' and 'Watson' as well, to avoid confusion I will refer to them by their first names. In *Elementary*, Joan Watson always refers to Sherlock Holmes as 'Sherlock' while he uses 'Watson', but for added clarity I will use 'Sherlock' and 'Joan'.

In Cavallaro's fictional universe, Sherlock Holmes and John Watson were flesh-and-blood men with children, grandchildren, great-grandchildren, etc. Charlotte and her elder brother, Milo, grew up on the Holmes estate in Sussex, United Kingdom. The Holmes descendants have maintained lifestyles similar to that of their progenitor. Charlotte herself solved her first crime, a jewel heist, when she was ten years old (Cavallaro 2016: 10). However, there is a negative space in the Holmes family tree. The Holmes and Watson families have drifted apart[1] and Jamie's life as John Watson's great-great-great grandson stands in stark contrast to Charlotte's life as Sherlock Holmes's progeny. Jamie's father and mother are divorced, and he lives with his mother in London while his father resides in Connecticut in the United States with a new family. Jamie had never met a Holmes until his first day at Sherringford, a private preparatory near his father. *A Study in Charlotte* takes place at Sherringford, where Jamie meets Charlotte and the two quickly bond while investigating the murder of Lee Dobson, Jamie's rugby teammate and Charlotte's rapist.

In CBS's television series, Sherlock Holmes is a recovering drug addict living in New York City. To help his son avoid a relapse, Sherlock's father hires Dr. Joan Watson as Sherlock's 'sober companion' (Joan gave up her career as a surgeon to help addicts during their recovery journeys). Sherlock observes that Joan finds his detective work thrilling and begins to utilize her knowledge and skills when working cases for the New York Police Department (NYPD) and eventually offers her an apprenticeship: she will stay with him and receive a stipend while he teaches her his methods. The first season follows Sherlock and Joan as their relationship shifts from one of addict-and-counsellor to detective-and-apprentice to detective-and-detective. This season culminates in a hunt for the criminal mastermind known only as Moriarty, who, in a provocative twist of fate, is Irene Adler, Sherlock's former lover whose ostensible murder was the impetus for his drug addiction. In the end, Moriarty's capture is only possible because Joan has successfully transitioned into the role of detective.

As discussed above, *Elementary* and *A Study in Charlotte* are Americanized, twenty-first-century adaptations of the Holmes series. Both adaptations work well together in an analysis for two significant reasons. First, neither source directly engages with one of the most iconic elements of the Sherlock Holmes canon: 221B Baker Street. Joan and Sherlock live in a New York brownstone that lacks a specific address; Jamie and Charlotte work in Sciences 442 (coincidentally or purposefully 221 doubled), a large supply closet on the Sherringford campus (Cavallaro 2016). This disengagement with 221B Baker Street symbolizes these adaptations' revisioning of the source material. 221B Baker Street belongs, first and foremost, to the archetypal Sherlock Holmes. Holmes has already picked out 221B as a residence when Stamford introduces him to Watson in *A Study in Scarlet* ([1887] 2009); Holmes always remains at 221B while Watson moves in and out according to his matrimonial status; 221B's parlour is where Holmes greets *his* clients and reveals the solutions to *his* cases. 221B is, consequently, the physical embodiment of Holmes's power. By shifting away from this address, these adaptations signal to viewers and readers that the story is no longer one of Holmes, but of Holmes *and* Watson, thereby performing adaptation's goal to 'highlight often perplexing gaps, absences and silences within the original' text (Sanders 2015: 126). As such, Watson's 'grand gift of silence' (Doyle [1891c] 2009: 215) that Holmes so admires in 'The Man with the Twisted Lip' (1891) transforms into a grand gift of agency. Second, both adaptations avoid a clichéd romance plotline that often arises from a partnership between a heterosexual man and a heterosexual woman (Welch 2015: 138). While Sherlock is a libidinous protagonist, he and Joan never entertain the thought of a sexual relationship. Jamie and Charlotte do tentatively kiss when Dobson's murderer, Nurse Bryony, poisons Jamie. However, this kiss is secondary to Jamie's role in fostering Charlotte's sobriety and EQ development. As Charlotte tells Jamie after the kiss, 'That's all I can do … that's all – it's nearly too much for me to touch anyone, after Dobson, and I – for you, I'm trying' (Cavallaro 2016: 289). Additionally, Jamie's feelings for Charlotte are more complex than simple sexual attraction: 'I had never wanted to be her boyfriend. I wanted something smaller than that, and far, far bigger, something I couldn't yet put into words' (Cavallaro 2016: 18). Jamie describes sex as a 'commonplace kind of complicated' and that nothing 'about Charlotte Holmes was commonplace' (Cavallaro 2016: 108). Instead, *Elementary* and *A Study in Charlotte* explore psychological transformations, a shift that creates more complex narratives focused on fostering EQ progress first, and solving crimes second.

Sherlock Holmes and His 'Boswell'

Peter Conroy (1992) outlines how Dr. John Watson, as Sherlock Holmes's biographer, creates a rigorous order of events for each of Holmes's cases: first, the 'preliminary demonstration', which is 'a remark or action by Holmes [that] provokes Watson's incredulous reaction'; second, the case itself where 'Watson's incredulity reappears and is even reinforced when he is (again) unable to interpret the clues or to elucidate the circumstances of the crime'; and third, the resolution to the case, in which 'Holmes share[s] with Watson the whole deductive process, the chain of reasoning which led to the solution, and thereby restores Watson's faith in him' (42). Conroy's summary emphasizes how Watson's roles as Holmes's foil and biographer create an inequality between detective and doctor. Holmes is always one step ahead of his biographer, and Watson's continuous battle to transition from incredulity to amazement reaffirms Holmes's superiority. And yet, Watson's role is not necessarily artless because the sidekick is an advantageous character in detective fiction. While not always requisite, the sidekick is often indispensable as 'the readers' guide and informant, their eyes and ears' (Krawczyk-Żywko 2015: 134). In other words, Watson's most important contribution to the Sherlock Holmes canon is persuading the reader to believe in Holmes's wondrous and at times almost supernatural deductive abilities. For example, in 'A Scandal in Bohemia' (1891), Holmes quickly deduces that Watson has gained seven-and-a-half pounds, has walked recently through the rain, and has a 'most clumsy and careless' servant (Doyle [1891a] 2009: 146). While Holmes describes these deductions as 'simplicity itself', Watson exclaims that Holmes's skills would certainly have sent him to burn at the stake for witchcraft a few centuries prior (Doyle [1891a] 2009: 146). Similar overtures from Watson pervade the Sherlock Holmes canon. For example, Watson exclaims 'in unfeigned admiration' (Doyle [1891d] 2009: 173) or gives 'a start of astonishment' (Doyle [1905] 2009: 480) when Holmes utilizes his ratiocination to uncover facts about Watson, a client, or a crime scene. However, this bafflement is not a detraction from the good doctor's character. As Dorothy L. Sayers (1946) points out, 'The beauty of Watson was, of course, that after thirty years he still did not know Holmes's methods' (108). This lack of knowledge is advantageous for the reader: if both Holmes and Watson understand the detective's methods, there is no need for an explanation for the reader's benefit. And without that verbal expounding of facts, the reader cannot follow Holmes's deductions. As Conroy emphasizes in his defense of Watson as the biographer, Watson controls the story's narrative and 'eclipses Holmes himself as the distinctive mark of these detective stories' (37). Thus, Watson's narration shapes readers' perceptions of Sherlock Holmes's greatness. Watson's 'hero-worship attitude' towards Holmes (Krawczyk-Żywko 2015: 136) pervades the Sherlock Holmes canon and 'encourages audiences to admire and, as much as possible, understand Holmes's mental processes' (Porter 2016: 51).

Like the reader, Holmes benefits from and relies on Watson's presence. For example, Holmes often requests Watson's attendance on a case, even after the doctor's marriage. In this role Watson frequently acts as the 'muscle' during an investigation, keeping suspects at gunpoint when necessary (as in 'The Boscombe Valley Mystery' [1891b]). While Holmes may not approve of Watson's tendency to romanticize their adventures (see *The Sign of the Four* [1890] for an example of Holmes's displeasure), the detective nevertheless steadfastly considers Watson his 'friend and colleague', a phrase first found in 'A Scandal in Bohemia' (Doyle [Doyle 1891a] 2009: 148). Significantly, in 'The Adventure of the Creeping Man' (1923), Watson describes himself as a 'whetstone' for Holmes's mind: 'I stimulated him. He liked to think aloud in my presence ... His remarks could hardly be said to be made to me – many of them would have been as appropriately addressed to his bedstead – but none the less, having formed the habit, it had become in some way helpful I should register and interject' (Doyle [1923] 2009: 1027). While these instances emphasize Watson's benefit to Holmes, the term 'whetstone' does not imply equality: Watson is a 'friend and colleague', yes, but also a tool to stimulate Holmes's deductive powers.

However, Watson is not without agency. Watson is, for example, vocal in his criticism of Holmes's drug use, which includes a seven-percent solution of cocaine. At the beginning of *The Sign of the Four*, Watson is particularly infuriated with Holmes's cocaine addiction, and confronts the detective: 'Count the cost! Your brain may, as you say, be roused and excited, but it is a pathological and morbid process, which involves increased tissue-change and may at last leave permanent weakness' (Doyle [1890] 2009: 75). By the time of 'The Adventure of the Missing Three-Quarter' (1904), Watson proudly tells his reader that he had weaned Holmes off the 'drug mania' that threatened the detective's career (Doyle [1904] 2009: 589). Watson may pride himself on this victory, but the doctor declines to offer any specific details concerning how he cured

Holmes of his drug habit. This vagueness calls into question the veracity of what could be one of Watson's greatest contributions to Holmes's consulting detective business.

Watson's ambivalent agency is often diminished in adaptation, depicting Holmes's sidekick as a fool. Adrian Conan Doyle, one of Doyle's sons, identified Hollywood as the culprit behind the production of Watson as 'the bumbling ass' (qtd. in Toadvine 2012: 48). Lucyna Krawczyk-Żywko (2015) specifically cites Nigel Bruce's depiction of Watson as a stain on the doctor's reputation (139). Bruce's representation of Watson as a comical stooge is at odds with Doyle's intention as well. Doyle reportedly said that 'those who consider Watson to be a fool are simply admitting that they haven't read the stories attentively' (qtd. in Toadvine 2012: 48). Diminishing Watson's role does not do justice to his place in the Sherlock Holmes canon. And yet, an inequality *does* exist between Holmes and Watson. Watson is, most decidedly, Holmes's sidekick: the willing whetstone, the steadfast biographer. Therefore, while Dr. John Watson is a 'friendly, human, likeable' character (Krawczyk-Żywko 2015: 134), he is *not* Sherlock Holmes's partner.

The Sidekick's Evolution to Partner

Notwithstanding Sherlock Holmes's cultural cache as an independent and often reclusive consulting detective, scholarship has noted John Watson's powerful influence over the detective in recent adaptations.[2] This shift in influence belies a shift in Sherlock Holmes's narrative purpose. In both Doyle's canon and recent adaptations, Sherlock Holmes 'needs to become involved with other people' (Porter 2016: 67). Without this stimulation, Holmes resorts to cocaine. In other words, he both craves and requires the 'mental exaltation' (Doyle [1890] 2009: 76) that comes from detective work, a career that inherently requires human interaction. For Doyle's Holmes, this involvement is fulfilled when he solves a case. However, modern adaptations, such as the BBC's *Sherlock* (2010–2017), Guy Ritchie's *Sherlock Holmes* franchise (2009–), and the two adaptations under discussion here, turn to what Lynnette Porter (2016) identifies as Sherlock Holmes's 'final problem': 'not his ability to store and access data, but to open his mind to the possibility of being vulnerable around his friends and accepting the help of those who love him' (67). Holmes's purpose is no longer to solve crimes, but to solve his defunct emotional literacy. EQ development then operates as a subset to this larger 'final problem'. As equal partners, Jamie and Joan help Charlotte and Sherlock 'solve' their IQ–EQ imbalance.

Encouraging and Managing Sobriety

Unlike Dr. John Watson, who becomes indispensable to Sherlock Holmes through his role as both 'whetstone' and biographer, Jamie and Joan are essential because they foster and support sobriety in their respective Holmeses, the first step in creating an EQ–IQ balance. Simply put: Charlotte and Sherlock cannot perform detective work and use drugs. While Holmes's seven-percent cocaine solution is an occasional indulgence and an eccentric (rather than alarming) habit, Sherlock and Charlotte suffer from crippling, debilitating addictions. Sherlock's drug addiction banished him from Scotland Yard, where he offered his services as a consulting detective. Specifically, Irene Adler's death induced Sherlock's descent into addiction. As Sherlock tells Joan in 'M.' (1.12), before Irene's death his drug use was recreational or an occasional 'boost' in a strenuous investigation. Irene's death sent him careening over the edge into total dependency. Instead of helping Scotland Yard find M. (the man suspected of murdering Irene), Sherlock turned to opiates. Charlotte's drug habit, on the other hand, began at the age of 12. She started with cocaine, and then cycled through morphine between rehabilitation visits before finally settling with OxyContin as her preferred drug (Cavallaro 2016: 251). While Charlotte is sober when she and Jamie meet at Sherringford, her body bears the scars of her addiction (Cavallaro 2016: 38) and she is at a greater risk for a relapse, although she tries to control her hard drug addiction with cigarettes.

While Doyle's Watson simply informs readers that he has cured Holmes of his drug addiction, Jamie and Joan are active, combative agents of sobriety. As an official sober companion, part of Joan's job includes testing Sherlock for drug use, taking him to Narcotics Anonymous meetings, and responding to any addiction triggers. She even threatens to stab Sherlock with a pushpin if he tries to put himself into another trance to avoid interacting with his fellow addicts at their meetings in 'While You Were Sleeping' (1.2). She also helps Sherlock find a permanent sponsor to replace her once her tenure as a sober companion is up (1.8). Joan makes it explicitly clear to viewers that Sherlock's sobriety is her first priority. For example, when Sherlock's former drug dealer, Rhys, comes to the brownstone to beg for Sherlock's help in rescuing his kidnapped daughter in 'A Giant Gun, Filled with Drugs' (1.15), Joan's primary concern is not rescuing Rhys's daughter, but keeping Sherlock away from Rhys's drugs. When she finds Rhys shooting up in the brownstone's bathroom, Joan threatens to call the police. Her work is especially important in this episode because Rhys pressures Sherlock to use drugs when Sherlock runs into a dead end in the case. Sherlock refuses the drugs; and, when he briefly summarizes Rhys's offer to Joan, Sherlock indicates that he wants to save that story for their next NA meeting, so that others 'may find inspiration' (1.15). Sherlock's choice to share the story at an NA meeting is an offering to Joan to show that he is learning to embrace his emotional vulnerability and responding to her attention to his wellbeing.

Jamie's quest to keep Charlotte sober follows a similar pattern. During their investigation into Dobson's murder, Jamie tells the reader, 'We'd reached an unspoken agreement: she'd dump the pill bottles, and I'd stop checking for them. That's how I chose to read the new and constant presence of a lit Lucky Strike in her hand' (Cavallaro 2016: 72). As with Sherlock, Charlotte is respecting Jamie's presence in her life and fighting her addiction. However, unlike Sherlock, Charlotte does relapse. When Jamie discovers a small part of Charlotte's destructive history with her maths tutor, August Moriarty, Charlotte consumes a large amount of oxy to suppress her conflicting emotions. Charlotte on drugs is disturbing, especially considering her age and drug history; when Jamie finds her, she has hidden herself away in the frozen mud like 'a beaten dog' and Jamie notices that her pupils are 'constricted into tiny black dots', her feet 'black with dirt, her hair wild' (Cavallaro 2016: 246). So, Jamie holds Charlotte to keep her warm while she cycles through the oxy. He also helps her come down from the high, forcing water and crackers on her until they resume their investigation (Cavallaro 2016: 258–259). This commitment to their respective Holmeses underscores Jamie and Joan's own 'noncognitive', or EQ, intelligence. This intelligence relies on an individual having emotional, personal, and social skills 'that influence an individual's ability to cope effectively with environmental demands and pressures' (Bar-On et al. 2000: 1108). Joan is a mature, independent woman with a strong sense of self that rarely wavers under Sherlock's combative attitude and withering commentary; while Jamie characterizes himself as a 'violent dickhead' (Cavallaro 2016: 48) at times, he nevertheless possesses a strong sense of self, much like Joan. He is confident in his academic abilities and easily reads Charlotte's moods and reacts to them appropriately. As such, Jamie and Joan exhibit a high level of EQ, which imbues them with the necessary stability to nurture sobriety and EQ intelligence in Charlotte and Sherlock.

Nurturing EQ Development

Sobriety helps Charlotte and Sherlock grow their EQ proficiency. In Charlotte's case, her low EQ stems from her inability to manage her own emotions, which contributes to her drug use. She explains to Jamie that she began drugs to control her feelings: 'I felt everything, and still everything bored me. I was like … like a radio playing five stations at once, all of them static. At first, the coke made me feel bigger' (Cavallaro 2016: 251). Like Jamie, Charlotte is quick to anger. While Jamie's bursts of anger are impulsive and fleeting, Charlotte's actions, on the other hand, are cunning and vindictive, as exemplified in her revenge against August when he denied her romantic advances before she arrived at Sherringford. She convinced August to procure cocaine for her ('he was so scared that, without it, I'd go through withdrawal') and called the police. Her mother fired August and had him expelled from Oxford. August's family subsequently disowned him, and he took up a menial job working for Charlotte's brother. Charlotte was then sent to Sherringford to 'think on what [she'd] done' (Cavallaro 2016: 250–252). What Charlotte lacks here is the EQ component of stress management, or the ability to 'cope with stress and to control strong emotions' (Bar-On et al. 2000: 1108). This lack of control drives Charlotte's guilt over August's fate and her belief that she is 'not a good person' (Cavallaro 2016: 254).

Sherlock's low EQ exhibits itself in his inability to connect emotionally with others and acknowledge that respecting others' feelings can be as significant as solving a murder case. Joan is the most frequent victim of Sherlock's low EQ. When Joan first arrives at the brownstone as a sober companion in the pilot episode, Sherlock calls her 'a glorified helper monkey' and introduces her to Captain Gregson as a personal valet (1.1). Sherlock also constantly breaks into Joan's phone, displaying a lack of respect for her privacy. When doing so in 'The Rat Race' (1.4), he sets Joan up on a date; and in the later episode 'The Leviathan' (1.10), Sherlock sends a text to Joan's brother to set up a Watson family dinner against Joan's wishes. Sherlock even barges into Joan's bedroom on a regular basis with new information on a case. At several points Sherlock rifles through Joan's clothes to pick out her outfits when she takes too long to get out of bed. Joan is often combative with these invasions, giving Sherlock tit-for-tat (as when she comments that he would look great in a jazzercise outfit in 1.3, 'Child Predator') and instructing him in culturally and socially acceptable behaviour (as when she educates Sherlock in proper roommate responsibilities in 1.11, 'Dirty Laundry'). Sherlock's acrimony underscores his inability to find an emotional connection with others, an issue that also epitomizes his approach to sex. Unlike his progenitor, Sherlock indulges in sexual intercourse and explains to Joan that he needs sex to function at an optimal level (1.1). However, 'optimal level' does not equate emotional attachment. Sherlock finds pleasure in sex because the act releases neurochemicals that help him solve cases, as he explains to Irene Adler in 'The Woman' (1.23). His sexual impulses are not emotional connections, but mere tools. Until his relationship with Irene, Sherlock admits that he found sex with a woman to be 'a perfumed and pillowy means to a physiological end' (1.12). As a further complication, the only person Sherlock has ever empathized with, prior to his time with Joan, is Irene, who later reveals herself to be Jamie Moriarty, a criminal mastermind (1.23). Sherlock's EQ dysfunctionality, therefore, ensures that his one emotional connection is a cunning and frequently immoral antagonist.

Additionally, Sherlock struggles to understand the emotional component of trust. Sherlock breaks Captain Gregson's trust in 'M.' (1.12) when he kidnaps Sebastian Moran (the 'M' in the episode's title and the 'M' suspected of murdering Irene Adler) with the intent of torturing and killing the assassin. While Sherlock does not murder Moran, Gregson suspends Sherlock from all police work. Sherlock cannot understand this banishment and insists to Joan that allowances must be made in his case:

> It's true I have wronged Captain Gregson. It was the cost of revenge, and I incurred it willingly. The larger question is, how does my suspension benefit the city? If the role of the public servant is to keep an eye on the greater good, then why keep me from my work? My work is the greater good. (1.13)

Sherlock does not understand that Gregson values his capacity to trust Sherlock more than Sherlock's deductive abilities. As Gregson explains to Joan in 'The Red Team' (1.13), Sherlock's impulse to kill the man who murdered his lover is understandable; however, an NYPD employee 'does not act on those impulses'. Gregson further posits that Sherlock is not sorry for his actions. Gregson, of course, is right. Accordingly, when Gregson accepts Sherlock back as a consultant, Sherlock must learn to appreciate and earn back Gregson's trust.

Jamie and Joan's attention to fostering EQ nurtures results when Charlotte and Sherlock gain increased confidence and sensitivity when interacting with others. This confidence and sensitivity translate into interpersonal skills. Interpersonal skills are a component of EQ often defined as 'the ability to be aware of, understand and to appreciate others' feelings as well as to establish and maintain mutually satisfying and responsible relationships with others' (Bar-On et al. 2000: 1108). This attention to interpersonal communication emphasizes American pop psychology's concern with the private self and takes particular interest in individuals' successful or unsuccessful attempts to create interpersonal relationships (Frost 2011: 119). In Cavallaro's novel, Jamie's admiration of and devotion to Charlotte boosts her self-confidence and that self-confidence leads to acts of reciprocation. Jamie admits that he has dreamt of being Charlotte's 'trusted companion' ever since he heard of the jewel heist case (Cavallaro 2016: 11) and when he finally meets Charlotte, his loyalty to her is instantaneous. When Charlotte recruits Jamie to break into Dobson's dorm room to steal evidence and escape out the window, Jamie describes Charlotte's work as '*brilliant*' and she rewards him with a 'flicker of a smile' (Cavallaro 2016: 32). Jamie also refuses to blame Charlotte for the rape (Cavallaro 2016: 50) and pushes back against Charlotte's self-blame for August's situation, insisting that she needs to accept August's forgiveness because forgiveness 'isn't a sign of weakness' (Cavallaro 2016: 252). In short, Charlotte gains a friend in Jamie, a connection she admits to lacking until their introduction (Cavallaro 2016: 97). As the novel progresses, her 'flicker of a smile' transforms into more tangible, reciprocal acts in appreciation of Jamie's presence, like playing his favourite songs, Nirvana's 'Heart-Shaped Box' and 'Smells Like Teen Spirit', on her violin (Cavallaro 2016: 65). Additionally, just as Jamie ensures that Charlotte eats and sleeps on a semi-regular basis, readers see Charlotte feel confident enough to return those actions: she leaves Jamie a Cadbury Flake (his favourite candy) on his desk and even voluntarily touches him to fix his glasses (Cavallaro 2016: 201). Charlotte enjoys Jamie's wonderment at her abilities because that wonderment is unadulterated and symbolizes that his trust in her comes without an agenda. His sole purpose in their friendship is to, quite literally, be her friend (Cavallaro 2016: 253). She also comes to Jamie's defense when he falls under suspicion for the attempted murder of a freshman girl: 'Jamie Watson [...] is far smarter than you think. He isn't my accomplice.[3] He's no one's accomplice. And he isn't guilty of anything' (Cavallaro 2016: 132). Perhaps most significantly, when Milo enters the Dobson investigation, Charlotte instructs him to answer Jamie's questions because Jamie is her 'friend and colleague' (Cavallaro 2016: 266), echoing word-for-word Holmes's characterization of Watson but in an entirely new context and meaning. Charlotte's statement here indicates that she is learning that she is a person 'of worth' (Justman 2005: 13) and respects Jamie's presence in her life.

As an added complication, Charlotte does possess a close companion before Jamie's arrival: Lena Gupta, her roommate. Lena is the only one to touch Charlotte without an immediate negative reaction and, in their shared dorm room, Jamie notes that the only personal touch on Charlotte's side is a note from Lena, '*luv u girlie xo Lena*' (Cavallaro 2016: 83). Readers learn that Lena enjoys being one of Charlotte's 'test subjects' (Charlotte uses her to expose a possible suspect) (Cavallaro 2016: 181) and helps Charlotte run the illegal poker games at Lawrence Hall simply because Lena knows that Charlotte needs money (Cavallaro 2016: 3). However, Lena is not equipped to foster Charlotte's EQ because Charlotte's eccentricities and combative attitude have no effect on Lena. Instead, Lena is perhaps best described as a pseudo-Baker Street Irregular: willing to help Charlotte but not possessing the tools or inclination to foster EQ development.

Over the course of *Elementary*'s first season, Sherlock learns to appreciate Joan's presence in his life and reciprocate her devotion to his sobriety with acts of kindness. For example, Sherlock defends Joan and her work in front of her family after he observes that they do not understand why Joan gave up her career as a surgeon. As he eloquently tells Joan's mother in 'The Leviathan' (1.10):

> Hard to picture what she does, isn't it? 'Sober companion.' When I first heard that term, I couldn't imagine what it entailed, and I'm an addict. She practices quite a unique specialty, your daughter. She rebuilds lives from the ground up. You can measure her success in careers restored. In my case, criminals caught and lives saved.

His speech brings Joan's mother to the brownstone to admit to her daughter that she does not like Joan's work because it does not make

Joan happy. Sherlock has facilitated this interaction because he utilized his deductive skills not just to identify the tensions between Joan and her mother, but to remove a 'stumbling block' (Justman 2005: 13) to Joan's own self-worth. Sherlock also demonstrates an increased sensitivity towards Joan's personal life in 'Déjà Vu All Over Again' (1.18). Sherlock overhears Joan promising to meet a friend for drinks, but she completely forgets about this commitment during her surveillance work on her first solo case. Sherlock calls Joan to remind her and sends Alfredo, his sponsor, to take over for Joan so that she does not miss her friend. Additionally, as the first season progresses, Sherlock begins to temper his invasive actions and snappish comebacks towards Joan. In 'Details' (1.16), Sherlock voluntarily admits to Joan, 'If anything [happened] to you, I'm not sure I could forgive myself'. These more considerate actions are complemented by the most telling example of Sherlock's increased interpersonal skills: his proposal that Joan stay on with him not as a sober companion but as a partner. In this rare moment of raw emotion, Sherlock admits to Joan, 'I am … better with you, Watson. Um, I'm sharper, I'm more focused. Difficult to say why, exactly. Perhaps, in time, I'll solve that as well' (1.16). Sherlock, therefore, has learned to communicate, a core tenet of self-help in pop psychology.

Joan's most difficult task in fostering greater EQ in Sherlock is repairing Sherlock's relationship with Gregson after the Sebastian Moran incident. To accomplish this goal, Sherlock must see that he can form not just professional *acquaintances* but create real *friendships*. Joan learns in 'The Deductionist' (1.14) that part of Sherlock's trouble making that transition from acquaintance to friendship arises from Kathryn Drummond, a profiler who studied Sherlock and wrote a book about him in which she predicted his struggles with addiction and posited that he would never make a friend. Sherlock informs Joan that because Kathryn was correct regarding his drug use, she must also be right concerning his inability to form friendships. Joan pushes back: *she* is Sherlock's friend and tells him that 'the only thing you can predict about people is that they'll change' (1.14). Joan's commitment to fostering a friendship with Sherlock is rewarded in the later episode 'A Landmark Story' (1.21) when he and Joan uncover another connection between Moran and Irene. Instead of 'going rogue', Sherlock brings all his findings to Gregson, stating that he wishes not to repeat the incident 'that put you and I at odds back then'. Gregson's reply underscores his continued distrust of Sherlock: 'I wish your word meant something more to me'. So, Sherlock provides a character witness: Joan. She is a character witness not because she used to be his sober companion or that she is now Sherlock's detective-in-training, but because Sherlock has admitted to Joan previously in that episode that he will not be murdering anyone because he finds their new partnership 'very rewarding'. In other words, Sherlock now understands that he cannot be a special allowance because his work is for the 'greater good' (as Sherlock asserted in 'The Red Team') and instead relies on Joan's friendship to demonstrate that he does not want to jeopardize his still-tenuous professional relationship with the NYPD.

In short, Jamie and Joan are teaching Charlotte and Sherlock to embody pop psychology's emphasis on empathy as a form of self-control when in a position of management (in the case of these adaptations, the Holmeses and Watsons are managing and fostering their new partnerships). From this perspective, self-control is not a suppression of all emotion, but rather a call to utilize 'positive talk, empathy, enthusiasm, friendliness, and energy' to 'nurture oneself, and to entertain positive thoughts about oneself and others' (Illouz 2008: 81). Readers see this change in EQ manifest itself in *A Study in Charlotte*'s epilogue, narrated by Charlotte. In her reserved syntax she informs the reader:

> A final note on Watson. He flagellates himself rather a lot, as this narrative shows. He shouldn't. He is lovely and warm and quite brave and a bit heedless of his own safety and by any measure the best man I've ever known. I've discovered that I am very clever when it comes to caring about him, and so I will continue to do so'. (Cavallaro 2016: 320–321)

At the end of *Elementary*'s first season, Sherlock demonstrates his appreciation of Joan by naming a hybrid bee after her: Euglassia Watsonia (1.24). These final acts embody pop psychology's belief that people can undergo 'a revolution' as they engage in 'deprogramming and reprogramming themselves' (Justman 2005: 153). Charlotte and Sherlock have learned to navigate not only their drug addictions but also reprogram themselves to foster healthy, emotional connections with their partners.

IQ Development in Joan Watson and Jamie Watson

In addition to mentoring and fostering emotional development in Charlotte and Sherlock, readers and viewers see Jamie and Joan grow their IQ. As Jamie and Charlotte dig deeper into their investigation, Jamie begins to practice Charlotte's techniques. He characterizes his observations of Detective Shepard as 'Holmesian deductions' and he is quite proficient: Jamie notes that the detective has not slept or showered since the previous night and most likely has children of his own based on his willingness to eat dinner with Charlotte, Jamie, and Jamie's father (Cavallaro 2016: 145). Charlotte also informally instructs Jamie in her methods, beginning with how to detect a liar (Cavallaro 2016: 177). However, these lessons are informal and come second to Jamie's other skills, such as his literary talent.

As Sherlock tells Joan in 'Details' (1.16), he wants to train her in the art of deduction. While Sherlock often identifies her as his protégé, she is nevertheless in the role of an apprentice, significantly different than Jamie's role as Charlotte's partner. Jamie picks up on Charlotte's methods and she informally instructs him in the art of reading clues. On the contrary, Joan's role is professional: Sherlock pays Joan for her work and she even begins to take on her own casework, such as her case regarding a missing woman in 'Déjà Vu All Over Again' (1.18). Sherlock assigns Joan various readings, teaches her singlestick, and approaches each case as a teaching opportunity. Sherlock also takes pride in Joan's apprenticeship. For example, in 'Possibility Two' (1.17), Sherlock tells Bell, 'I'm training her to analyze every environment with the keen eye of the true detective'. The result of this apprenticeship is Joan's ability to start her own detective agency at the end of *Elementary*'s second season (and she maintains her independent business for most of the third season). While Jamie's IQ increases with Charlotte's assistance, Joan's IQ grows so much that she becomes *independent of* Sherlock. Therefore, not only do Jamie and Joan mentor their Holmeses in EQ, these Watsons also show great aptitude in IQ, too.

Conclusion

This chapter highlights the complexity in the word 'sidekick'. A sidekick is not simply an assistant or comedic relief and does not deserve this often disparaging and unflattering characterization. Instead, this role is in constant flux as detective and sidekick interact with one another. Jamie is not simply Charlotte's 'whetstone' and Joan is not merely Sherlock's apprentice. Rather, they are diverse, complex characters whose interactions with their detectives create reciprocal relationships. As a final note, the sidekick role itself is underestimated by the antagonists in these two adaptations. Nurse Bryony's and Jamie Moriarty's diabolical plots fail because they play into the stigmas that characterize sidekicks as 'less-than'. Charlotte tells Jamie that Nurse Bryony's first mistake is assuming a sidekick is a lesser-than role (Cavallaro 2016: 286) and Irene Adler/Jamie Moriarty dismisses Joan, labelling her as Sherlock's 'mascot' in 'The Heroine' (1.24). This argument, moreover, is not meant to besmirch the Conan Doyle's Holmes-Watson homosocial relationship. Instead, these two adaptations challenge that relationship and shift the focus of the story to emphasize that IQ is not necessarily superior to EQ. In these adaptations, the Holmes-Watson relationship comes under a fuller investigation, one that emphasizes equality in partnership.

Notes

1. The one exception to this shift in relations between the two families is the friendship between Jamie's father and Leander Holmes, Charlotte's uncle. The two were flatmates at university and keep in touch.
2. For example, see Lynnette Porter's *Who Is Sherlock?* (2016).
3. Charlotte and Jamie are initially framed for Lee Dobson's murder.

References

Bar-On, R., J.M. Brown, B.D. Kirkcaldy, and E.P. Thomé. 2000. Emotional Expression and Implications for Occupational Stress; an Application of the Emotional Quotient Inventory (EQ-i). *Personality and Individual Differences* 28: 1108–1118.

Cavallaro, Brittany. 2016. *A Study in Charlotte*. Katherine Tegen Books.

Conroy, Peter V. 1992. The Importance of Being Watson. In *Critical Essays on Sir Arthur Conan Doyle*, ed. Harold Orel, 36–54. New York: G.K. Hall & Co.

Doyle, Arthur Conan. (1887) 2009. *A Study in Scarlet*. In *The Complete Sherlock Holmes*, ed. Christopher Roden and Barbara Roden, 3–74. New York: Barnes & Noble.

———. (1890) 2009. *The Sign of the Four*. In *The Complete Sherlock Holmes*, ed. Christopher Roden and Barbara Roden, 75–141. New York: Barnes & Noble.

———. (1891a) 2009. A Scandal in Bohemia. In *The Complete Sherlock Holmes*, ed. Christopher Roden and Barbara Roden, 145–158. New York: Barnes & Noble.

———. (1891b) 2009. The Boscombe Valley Mystery. In *The Complete Sherlock Holmes*, ed. Christopher Roden and Barbara Roden, 184–200. New York: Barnes & Noble.

———. (1891c) 2009. The Man with the Twisted Lip. In *The Complete Sherlock Holmes*, ed. Christopher Roden and Barbara Roden, 211–226. New York: Barnes & Noble.

———. (1891d) 2009. The Red-Headed League. In *The Complete Sherlock Holmes*, ed. Christopher Roden and Barbara Roden, 159–173. New York: Barnes & Noble.

———. (1904) 2009. The Adventure of the Missing Three-Quarter. In *The Complete Sherlock Holmes*, ed. Christopher Roden and Barbara Roden, 588–602. New York: Barnes & Noble.

———. (1905) 2009. The Adventure of the Dancing Men. In *The Complete Sherlock Holmes*, ed. Christopher Roden and Barbara Roden, 480–495. New York: Barnes & Noble.

———. (1923) 2009. The Adventure of the Creeping Man. In *The Complete Sherlock Holmes*, ed. Christopher Roden and Barbara Roden, 1027–1039. New York: Barnes & Noble.

Frost, Jennifer. June 2011. Movie Star Suicide, Hollywood Gossip, and Popular Psychology in the 1950s and 1960s. *The Journal of American Culture* 34 (2): 113–123.

Illouz, Eva. 2008. *Saving the Modern Soul: Therapy, Emotions, and the Culture of Self-Help*. Berkeley, CA: University of California Press.

Justman, Stewart. 2005. *Fool's Paradise: The Unreal World of Pop Psychology*. Chicago: Ivan R. Dee.

Krawczyk-Żywko, Lucyna. 2015. 'My Watson to Your Holmes': Rewriting the Sidekick. *Anglica* 24 (1): 133–146.

Porter, Lynnette. 2016. Inside the Mind of Sherlock Holmes. In *Who Is Sherlock? Essays on Identity in Modern Holmes Adaptations*, ed. Lynnette Porter, 48–69. Jefferson: McFarland & Company Inc.

Sanders, Julie. 2015. *Adaptation and Appropriation*, 2nd ed. London: Routledge.

Sayers, Dorothy L. 1946. The Omnibus of Crime. In *The Art of the Mystery Story*, ed. Howard Haycraft, 71–109. New York: Simon and Schuster.

Toadvine, April. 2012. The Watson Effect: Civilizing the Sociopath. In *Sherlock Holmes for the 21st Century*, ed. Lynnette Porter, 48–64. Jefferson: McFarland & Company.

Turnbull, Gordon. Boswell, James (1740–1795), lawyer, diarist, and biographer of Samuel Johnson. 2004. *Oxford Dictionary of National Biography*. Oxford: Oxford University Press. http://www.oxforddnb.com.ezproxy.tcu.edu/view/10.1093/ref:odnb/9780198614128.001.0001/odnb-9780198614128-e-2950. Accessed 6 June 2018.

Welch, Elizabeth. 2015. Joan for John: An Elementary Choice. In *Gender and the Modern Sherlock Holmes*, ed. Nadine Farghaly, 133–145. Jefferson: McFarland & Company Inc.

Televised Material

Doherty, Robert, creator. *Elementary*. CBS, 2012–2018.
1.1, Pilot. 27 September 2012.
1.2, While You Were Sleeping. 4 October 2012.
1.3, Child Predator. 18 October 2012.
1.4, The Rat Race. 25 October 2012.
1.8, The Long Fuse. 29 November 2012.
1.10, The Leviathan. 13 December 2012.
1.11, Dirty Laundry. 3 January 2013.
1.12, M. 10 January 2013.
1.13, The Red Team. 31 January 2013.
1.14, The Deductionist. 3 February 2013.
1.15. A Giant Gun, Filled with Drugs. 7 February 2013.
1.16. Details. 14 February 2013.
1.17. Possibility Two. 21 February 2013.
1.18. Déjà Vu All Over Again. 14 March 2013.
1.21. A Landmark Story. 2 May 2013.
1.23. The Woman. 16 May 2013.
1.24. Heroine. 16 May 2013.

CHAPTER 6

'A Look of Doglike Devotion': Hercule Poirot's Stooges and Foils

J. C. Bernthal

'Mon ami – *what will you? You fix upon me a look of doglike devotion and demand of me a pronouncement* a la *Sherlock Holmes!' (Christie 1936: 56)*

Introduction

Few detectives are as instantly recognisable as Agatha Christie's Hercule Poirot. The star of over one hundred novels, stories and scripts, Poirot is the self-described 'greatest detective in the world' (Christie 1928: 143), with a steady appearance on the bestseller lists between his first appearance in *The Mysterious Affair at Styles* (1920) and his literary death in *Curtain: Poirot's Last Case* (1975), which earned him a front-page obituary in the *New York Times*. Almost as recognisable as Poirot, however, are his various companions—almost invariably English, and always appearing rather more ridiculous, if less eccentric, than the great Belgian detective himself. This chapter considers a variety of sidekicks presented in selected

J. C. Bernthal (✉)
Norwich, UK

L. Andrew and S. Saunders (eds.), *The Detective's Companion in Crime Fiction*, Crime Files, https://doi.org/10.1007/978-3-030-74989-7_6

Poirot novels by Agatha Christie and Sophie Hannah. These characters, to greater or lesser extents, 'played Watson to [Poirot's] Sherlock' (Christie 1926: 169), but with unique approaches, enabling the detective to show his superiority—and relevance—in evolving literary and social contexts.

Poirot's first and most prominent companion is Captain Arthur Hastings, a privately educated, decorated ex-military man who has worked in politics. Despite these impressive credentials, however, Hastings demonstrates remarkable foolishness and an unfortunate tendency to fall in love. By contrasting him to the prissy European Poirot, and having Hastings' ironic voice narrate the bulk of Poirot's early interwar cases, Christie gently satirises concepts of security in English masculinity and national structures. Going further, I suggest that Poirot's real sidekick in *The Murder of Roger Ackroyd* (1926) is not the narrator who fancies he is 'play[ing] Watson' and who turns out to be the murderer, but rather his gossipy sister with whom Poirot spends more time. This moment hails not only the end of generic reassurance—the promise that certain characters are above suspicion—but also the incorporation of overtly female detection methods into Poirot's arsenal. Poirot's next companion, an eccentric crime writer called Ariadne Oliver, allows Christie to indulge in metatextual comedy, as Oliver is overtly presented as a comic self-portrait of Christie herself. The dynamic between a fictional detective and his fictionalised creator provides further generic innovation, as the investigations themselves reveal their artificiality.

Finally, I explore the Poirot continuation novels by Sophie Hannah, which are narrated by a new character, an insecure and apparently homosexual Scotland Yard police inspector. Poirot mentors Inspector Catchpool, allowing him to grow over the course of the series, and granting readers not only a fresh perspective on the character, with conveniently updated moral fibre, but also a dialogue between the old school that Poirot represents and the new school of crime writing embodied in Hannah's original creation.

Arthur Hastings, OBE

In her autobiography, Christie admits to having written, in the first half-decade of her career, 'in the Sherlock Holmes tradition – eccentric detective, stooge assistant, with a Lestrade-type Scotland Yard detective' (Christie 1977: 282). She particularly highlights having felt 'tied to Poirot and his Watson, Captain Hastings' after the success of her first novel,

The Mysterious Affair at Styles, stating, 'I quite enjoyed Captain Hastings. He was a stereotyped creation but he and Poirot represented my idea of a detective team' (282). Throughout her autobiography, Christie projects—deliberately, as will be explored—an image of ingenuousness; she presents herself as an admirer of Arthur Conan Doyle whose own forays into mimicry just happened to be successful. However, from the outset, the Poirot novels interact self-consciously and even subversively with their generic heritage. Before he has appeared in *Styles*, Poirot is established as an anti-Holmes, and much of this has to do with Christie's creative decisions around Hastings' narration.

Before Poirot has been introduced, Hastings confesses to a friend that he has 'a secret hankering to be a detective [along the lines of] Sherlock Holmes' as opposed to 'the real thing' (Christie [1920] 2016: 9). He goes on to describe having known a real detective, whom he had found surprisingly un-Holmes-like ('a funny little man, a great dandy, but wonderfully clever'), and assures the woman he is trying to impress that he has 'progressed significantly' beyond this man's level (9). When the detective he describes, Hercule Poirot, appears in person a few pages later, Hastings is puzzled all over again by the man's 'extraordinary' appearance and the idea that 'this quaint, dandified little man [...] had been in his time one of the most celebrated members of the Belgian police' (23).

A widely quoted line from the first description of Poirot is the observation that, with his prissy neatness, 'a speck of dust would have caused him more pain than a bullet-wound' (23). The observation is comical in itself, but it also sets up a crucial element of the tone of Captain Hastings' character and narrative. *Styles* was written in the second half of the First World War, and published two years after the conflict had concluded (or, three years after, in the United Kingdom). Hastings, whose name evokes a notable military defeat, is a First World War veteran who, as Anne Hart points out, has no right to use his military title of 'Captain' in peacetime (1990: 127). Hastings referring so lightly and so hyperbolically to 'a bullet-wound' suggests that the war will not inform his character in the same way it would come to sculpt, for instance, Dorothy L. Sayers' detective, Lord Peter Wimsey (see Patterson 2017: 3–10). Even the sidekick's prototype, John Watson in the Sherlock Holmes stories by Arthur Conan Doyle, is fundamentally affected by his experiences in military services—although the details of Watson's war wounds are famously hazy, as his role is foremost to showcase the detective's superior abilities (see Wynne 2010: 32). Hastings, then, is not being set up to make a serious contribution either to the investigation or to the philosophy of the novel: his military background is decoration, and his function is that of the observing ally, rather than the hero.

While Poirot's first dialogue is superficial and expository in nature, the reader will already get the impression that he, and not Hastings, is the sophisticated thinker, despite the latter's claims to superiority. It is already clear that he venerates Poirot, whom he describes as 'a celebrity' before launching into a string of anecdotes about 'his exploits and triumphs' (23, 24). The pair's next dialogue, the morning after the inevitable murder, leaves no doubt as to who is in charge and who is the assistant: Poirot has long paragraphs devoted to outlining his methodology ('We will arrange the facts neatly, each in his proper place [...] We examine. We search'), while Hastings' contributions are limited to small objections like 'Y-es—' and ' quail[ing] before' Poirot's 'extravagant gesture[s]' (40). Over the course of *Styles* and in subsequent cases, Hastings becomes, in Howard Haycraft's words, 'the stupidest of all the modern Watsons' (Haycraft [1941] 1964: 139). Part of this has to do with his absolute investment in the Holmes tradition despite living an experience that runs counter to it: Poirot is peeved when, arriving at a crime scene, Hastings expects him to instantly have all the answers, '*a la* Sherlock Holmes' (Christie 1936: 56). Another part of Hastings' stupidity lies in his unerring habit of reading a crime scene or witness testimony un-analytically. While Watson is content to marvel at Holmes's intellect, or in other words to 'see but [...] not observe' (Doyle [1891] 2009: 162), Hastings is never short on observations which, if anything, serve only to mislead the investigation. Poirot damns his friend with faint praise in *Lord Edgware Dies*, complimenting his 'beautifully and perfectly balanced', 'amazingly normal' mind: 'As in a mirror', he explains, 'I see reflected in your mind exactly what the criminal wishes me to believe. That is terrifically helpful and suggestive' (Christie 1933: 127). At this point, Hastings is being decisively duped by a Hollywood bombshell who is using him to secure an alibi for her husband's murder. More pronounced in relation to Hastings' stupidity, though, are his conservative nationalism and his inherited literary role as assistant and chronicler to a great detective.

Sherlock Holmes's sidekick, Watson, often succumbs to the charms of his friend's female clients, and he marries at least one of them. Elsewhere, I have argued that this is an example of what some theorists call homosexual panic; because Watson spends so much time living with and palpably adoring his male companion, he needs a woman—any woman—to fall in love with (Bernthal 2016: 85–86). The generic requirement for romance, something roundly decried but conformed to by Christie and her peers (see, for instance, Christie [1945] 2013: xv; Sayers 1928: 9–47) is mocked in the figure of Hastings, who falls in love far too easily. By the end of the first novel, Hastings has fallen in love with two women. At the start of the second, Poirot is sighing, 'Already you have seen a goddess!' (Christie [1923] 1994: 15), and at the end of that book, Hastings has married one of the suspects—he is never quite sure which one, because he struggles to tell her apart from her sister, so much so that he prefers to call her by a nickname ('Cinderella') in subsequent books; after all, 'I can't call you Bella [the sister's name, which Hastings has mostly been using]. And Dulcie [her real name] seems so unfamiliar. So it's got to be Cinderella' (208). If Watson enacts homosexual panic, Captain Hastings enacts a burlesque of the same.

The absolute Englishness of Hastings serves, of course, to highlight Poirot's foreignness, and therefore the role of otherness in detection. In making Hastings' English respectability the butt of several jokes, Christie highlights insularity in the nationalism that others Poirot in the first place. In *Dumb Witness*, a stern spinster initiates the following exchange with Hastings:

> 'Can you write decent English?'
> 'I hope so.'
> 'H'm – where did you go to school?'
> 'Eton.'
> 'Then you can't.' (Christie 1937: 104)

In *Peril at End House*, Poirot explains the difference between Hastings and himself as something that is inherently tied up in nationality which manifests in education. When Hastings describes a naval commander, who will prove to be a drug dealer, as a 'pukka sahib', Poirot responds that, while the commander must have 'been to what you consider the right school', 'being a foreigner, I am free from these prejudices and can make my investigations unhampered' (Christie [1932] 1993: 47). In the same novel, when Poirot rifles through a lady's stockings and petticoats, discovers some romantic letters, and starts reading them, Hastings objects, 'scandalised', that he 'isn't playing the game', to which Poirot responds, still in a spirit of jocularity, that they are 'not playing a game' but 'investigating a murder', adding that the lady's maid is bound to know the letters 'by heart' (131). Easily convinced, Hastings becomes Poirot's accomplice and the reader can rest assured that similar exchanges will happen in future adventures. There is a comforting clash between their personalities which does not in any way impede the progress of the investigation or narrative.

Hastings' final appearance is in *Curtain: Poirot's Last Case*, a novel written by Christie around 1940 for publication after her death (in fact, it was published in 1975, a year before her death). While some of the old jokes about English reticence resurface, they are tinged with darkness because Poirot here is infirm and wheelchair-bound, making Hastings his puppet—something that ups the stakes of any demurring. As Poirot puts it:

> You will not look through keyholes. You will remain the English gentleman and someone will be killed. It does not matter, that. Honour comes first with an Englishman. Your honour is more important than somebody else's life. *Bien*! It is understood. (Christie 1975: 74)

Hastings does not look through keyholes in *Curtain*, and people do die. Overall, the character, like his narrative style, is more nuanced here than on previous outings. The action of the novel takes place at Styles Court, the country house setting of the very first case, and the narrative opens with Hastings' reflection that, while he thought himself 'already old and mature' at the time of the first investigation, 'life was only then beginning [and] I had been journeying [...] to meet the man whose influence over me was to shape and mould my life' (5).

Although Poirot's health is greatly reduced in *Curtain*, he remains active in the investigation of crime and in Hastings' private life. Readers learn that Hastings' wife, Cinderella, has died, and that he has an adult daughter, Judith, who refers to Poirot as 'Uncle Hercule' (30). Poirot offers Judith marriage advice and encourages Hastings to leave her alone when he grows concerned about her choice of boyfriend (111). The main villain in *Curtain* is an emotionally manipulative man who plays, Iago-like, on people's insecurities and drives them to murder for sheer sadistic pleasure. One of his targets is Hastings, who ends up attempting to kill the man he thinks his daughter wants to marry—of course, Uncle Hercule knows that Judith is interested in someone altogether more suitable, and manages to stop his friend from doing anything drastic.

The final murder in the novel has as its victim the still-unidentified antagonist, Stephen Norton, who is shot through the forehead. Shortly after Norton's death, Poirot suffers a fatal heart attack, and in a written confession reveals not only Norton's guilt but also the fact that Poirot himself shot this villain whom the law could not touch. Once Hastings has read Poirot's confession, including a long meditation on having usurped the prerogatives of 'the *bon Dieu*' by 'tak[ing] the law into his own hands' (220), he speculates: 'I should have known when I saw the bullet hole so symmetrically in the middle of the forehead' (221). Poirot's obsessive neatness, traditionally mocked by Hastings, is here invested with darkness and tragedy. It takes on religious proportions in the final line, when Hastings recalls his previous reactions to '[t]hat mark on Norton's forehead – it was like the brand of Cain...' (221), revealing not only Hastings' idolisation of his friend with religious overtures, but also the idea that, on some level, he had always known that Poirot had this abuse of power within him. *Curtain* draws a curtain on Poirot's and Hastings' relationship, tail-ending the British interwar trust in authority and generic belief in uncomplicated truth that Hastings represents.

The Siblings Shepherd

The decline of Captain Hastings had already begun in 1928, when Dorothy L. Sayers wrote that Christie was among the last writers 'still cling[ing] to the Watson formula' (Sayers 1928: 34). He went on to feature in novels throughout the 1930s before being dropped altogether, but within and beyond this period Poirot enjoyed a variety of companions including a nurse (*Murder in Mesopotamia* [1936]), a female doctor (*Appointment with Death* [1938]), and a marine biologist (*The Clocks* [1963]). However, the first and most celebrated departure from the Captain Hastings formula occurs in the novel that thrust its author into the international limelight, *The Murder of Roger Ackroyd*, published in 1926. In fact, some commentators have argued that *Ackroyd* dealt the death blow to an unproblematised narrator-companion tradition.[1]

As a narrator, Dr. James Shepherd apparently fails to challenge tradition. He shares a courtesy title, albeit a domestic version of it, with Holmes's chronicler, Dr. Watson, and he first meets Poirot in familiar Holmesian territory: the detective has retired to the countryside to grow vegetable marrows, just as Holmes retired to Sussex to keep bees. Shepherd and Poirot are neighbours and, when their mutual friend Roger

Ackroyd is murdered, the doctor accompanies the detective on his investigations. Before the murder, Poirot tells Shepherd that he misses Hastings, with all '[h]is *naïveté*, his honest outlook, the pleasure of surprising him' (Christie 1926: 21) and, later, Shepherd considers himself to have 'played Watson to [Poirot's] Sherlock' (169), establishing a spirit of continuity. Thus, the unsuspecting first-time reader in 1926 might reasonably have expected James Shepherd to be a new and enduring sidekick for Poirot in retirement.

However, Poirot eventually names the narrator as the murderer, and Shepherd playfully chides the reader for taking his own narrative at face value:

> I am rather pleased with myself as a writer. What could be neater, for instance, than the following:-
> *The letters were brought in at twenty minutes to nine. It was just on ten minutes to nine when I left him, the letter still unread. I hesitated with my hand on the door handle, looking back and wondering if there was anything I had left undone.*
> All true, you see. But suppose I had put a row of stars after the first sentence! Would somebody then have wondered what exactly happened in that blank ten minutes? (310, original emphasis)

On one level, the above passage pre-empts critiques that Christie has not 'played fair' in making the narrator, a character traditionally above suspicion, the murderer. On another level, the text interacts with its own artifice, inviting the reader to share in what is, effectively, a break of the fourth wall. Moreover, the confession draws the reader's attention not to misdirection so much as omission—the incomplete truth of any narrative. When we realise this, we can suspect that we have been reading Dr. Shepherd in his own self-image, rather than as Poirot has treated him. Appealing to readers' preconceptions based on the already established formulae of detective fiction—a country house, an amateur detective with a doctor companion, even a foreword describing the 'story' as 'orthodox' (Christie 1926: v), and then undermining these preconceptions with an appeal to reread and rethink, Christie effects a shattering and entirely self-conscious break with the comfort of a traditional narrative set-up.

Rereading *The Murder of Roger Ackroyd* with the solution in mind, it becomes clear that James Shepherd is never actually in Poirot's confidence; all the information the detective imparts to Shepherd is public knowledge at the time it is shared. The only character Poirot does confide in is the doctor's sister, Caroline Shepherd. More often than not, when Poirot and James have a conversation, the former is on his way to visit Caroline, who, with her gossipy network of wives and servants, is a far more useful ally to him. It is Caroline who is able to glean, during a game of Mah Jong, who likes and dislikes whom (195–206). It is Caroline who, through gossiping with a cleaner, is able to help Poirot locate a missing man (292). It is Caroline who acts as the reader's eyes and ears when her brother takes a telephone call, of which we only experience his dialogue, apparently summoning him to the scene of the crime but which he has engineered to mislead her—and therefore simultaneously the reader (49). Caroline introduces a new tool into Poirot's arsenal: gossip as a way of gleaning important information. This is something she has in common with her contemporary Miss Climpson, one of Lord Peter Wimsey's sidekicks in the books by Dorothy L. Sayers (see Sayers 1927).

Christie, who 'liked the part [Caroline] played' in the novel, acknowledged the character as the basis for her detective Miss Marple (Christie 1977: 434). The mid-to-late nineteenth century was awash with examples of fiction featuring women detectives, often using their social invisibility and tools of gossip to their advantage. However, the early twentieth century saw a decided homosocial turn in the genre, with almost universally male detectives and sidekicks in the moulds discussed above (Munt [1994] 2005: 26). Certainly, after being assisted by Caroline, Poirot never turns his back on gossip. In a much later case, *After the Funeral*, he reveals 'a profound belief [...] that if you can induce a person to talk to you for long enough, [they will impart useful information] sooner or later' (Christie 1953: 190). As his sidekick, overshadowed by a male pretender, Caroline represents the exhaustion of a Holmesian template in detective fiction and the stirrings of a stronger role for women and psychological or domestic, as well as physical and outdoorsy investigative, methodologies.

Mrs. Ariadne Oliver

Among Poirot's assemblage of female companions, the only recurring one is Ariadne Oliver, who has been read as taking over from Hastings as Poirot's sidekick-in-chief (Bargainnier 1980: 57). Although she first appears as a minor ally of Mr. Parker Pyne, another Christie detective (Christie 1932), Oliver joins Poirot in *Cards on the Table* (1936). Here she is introduced as 'one of the foremost writers of detective and other sensational stories', infamous among the reading public for her 'hot-headed feminis[m]' and 'chatty, if not particularly grammatical, articles' in magazines (Christie [1936] 1969: 14). Oliver is also 'an earnest believer in woman's intuition' (14) and insists that Poirot (who has no powers of arrest) should arrest suspicious-looking locals because they are probably guilty of something (Christie [1952] 1974: 150). In Poirot's orderly world, Oliver's scattiness provides comic relief and enough contrast to highlight his own superior skills, whilst constituting a completely unthreatening presence.

Part of Oliver's job—and indeed the job of any popular author, including her creator—is to keep up with changing fashions, paying lip service to them without necessarily being invested. This is a key part of her character, evident in her ever-changing hairstyle, which is a long-running joke ('A severe pompadour at one time, then a windswept style, [followed by] tightly arranged curls' [Christie 1972: 7]'), her introducing Poirot to Ribena for shock (Christie 1966: 11), and her identification of Chelsea as the most likely place to find '[b]eatniks and sputniks and squares' in the 1960s ('I don't write about them because I'm so afraid of getting the terms wrong', she adds [Christie 1961: 19]). Just as Q.D. Leavis decried 'popular novelist[s]' in 1932 for depending on editors who 'keep a scientific finger on the public pulse' (Leavis 1939: 42), Oliver insists that her 'sensational novels' are the 'boring' products of 'hard work':

> I always think I've finished and then when I count up I find I've only written thirty thousand words instead of sixty thousand and so then I have to throw in another murder and get the heroine kidnapped again. It's all very boring. (Christie [1936] 1969: 113)

This statement occurs in *Cards on the Table*, shortly before the second murder, and a thrilling chase scene involving a young woman. However, despite the humour, Christie does not cheapen her work through the character, who is often shown unable to handle the 'real' murders she investigates, critiquing them as 'badly constructed' (30) and depending on Poirot to bring order to her thoughts.

The character, however, develops from being a gentle parody of popular conceptions of women writers to becoming a strategic self-portrait of Agatha Christie herself. She grows to share those traits of Christie's that were public knowledge, such as a fondness for apples, publication by Penguin, and a fraught relationship with dramatists. Christie famously grew frustrated with Poirot, introducing a newspaper serialisation of *Appointment with Death* (1938) with a confession of 'coolness between us':

> There are moments when I have felt: 'Why – why – why did I ever invent this detestable, bombastic, tiresome little creature?'
> Eternally straightening things, eternally boasting, eternally twirling his moustache and tilting his egg-shaped head. Anyway, what is an egg-shaped head? [...] Yes, there have been moments when I've disliked M. Hercule Poirot very much indeed, when I have rebelled bitterly against being yoked to him for life (usually at one of these moments that [*sic*] I receive a fan letter saying 'I know you must love your little detective, by the way you write about him'). (Christie [1938] 1990: 32)

As the Oliver character developed, Christie gave her a creation of her own, a quirky Finnish detective called Sven Hjerson. In her second novel-length appearance, Oliver expresses sentiments almost identical to her creator's:

> Why a Finn when I know nothing about Finland? Why a vegetarian? Why all the idiotic mannerisms he's got? These things just *happen*. You try something – and people seem to like it – and then you go on – and before you know where you are you've got someone like that maddening Sven Hjerson tied to you for life. And people even write and say how fond you must be of him. Fond of him? If I met that bony, gangling, vegetable eating Finn in real life, I'd do a better murder than any I've ever invented. (Christie [1952] 1974: 115–116, original emphasis)

The idea that Christie is 'having fun with her fame' through the character (Gill 1991: 93) has become so widespread that many commentators assume that 'when Mrs Oliver speaks we are listening to Agatha Christie' (Curran 2009: 73).

Christie only made Oliver a sidekick-proper several years after the Second World War, when she reintroduced the character as an old friend of Poirot's in the 1952 novel *Mrs. McGinty's Dead*. She goes on to feature prominently in cases throughout the 1950, 1960, and 1970s, and the bulk of Poirot's last-written case, *Elephants Can Remember* (1972), is from her perspective. This post-war Ariadne Oliver, or Mrs. Oliver 2.0, is a more deliberate self-image, and Christie herself encouraged readers to draw connections.[2] There remains, though, the intriguing fact that when Oliver interacts with Poirot, Christie is, apparently, participating in direct dialogue with her own frustrating creation. Poirot, however, does not respond to any of Oliver's criticisms, instead proving his worth as a detective despite his creator-cum-companion's shortcomings. The sense of herself that Christie creates in Oliver is one of 'a lucky woman who had established a happy knack of writing what quite a lot of people wanted to read' (Christie 1972: 13). The character, therefore, discourages anyone from prying into Christie's personal life, because she seems to be offering a window into it, and, ironically, through Mrs. Oliver, Christie was able to keep her private and creative lives separate.

There is a change of tone in the post-Second World War novels; the playful artifice is still there, but more important is the social impact of crime. Christie was very clear that she saw her role as a crime writer, in later life, infused with responsibility to '[h]old up a mirror to [contemporary] England' (Christie 1970: 13) and Ariadne Oliver becomes, increasingly, less an avenue for gentle parody than a window for Christie to express her personal and professional frustrations. As Poirot's sidekick, Oliver is never quite a comfortable 'fit', partly because of her larger than life personality, and partly because, in representing the author, she might be expected to possess a certain narrative authority over the detective—her willing subjugation to his authority is something more commonly explored in postmodern detective fiction.[3] Eventually, as Poirot/and Oliver become more co-detectives than hero-and-sidekick, Oliver is allowed to solve a standalone mystery, without Poirot, in *The Pale Horse* (1961). Oliver and Poirot are the only unmarried collaborators who address each other by Christian names (Hart 1990: 198–199) and they become, towards the end, infirm equals.

In the pair's final outing, although Poirot solves the crime, Oliver does more of the footwork and the significant bulk of the narrative is devoted to her own internal monologues. They inhabit the same uneasily fictional world, and they share a desire to make a difference through their work.

By giving Poirot a stylised version of herself as a companion, Christie was able to control her own public image: a reader expects to identify with a sidekick, as they marvel at the hero, and the character of Ariadne Oliver exploits this traditional way of reading to create an illusion—the same illusion shattered in *Ackroyd*—of absolute knowledge, in this case, knowledge of the author herself. At the same time, Christie highlights the need for a stable, recognisable core amidst changing fashions in literary production.

Inspector Edward Catchpool

In 2014, Sophie Hannah published *The Monogram Murders*, the first Agatha Christie estate-sanctioned continuation novel featuring Hercule Poirot. Other authors had written 'official' Poirot texts—including Charles Osborne, who novelised a play in (1999), and Julian Symons (1981) and Anne Hart (1990), who published short and long biographies respectively—but all had stuck more or less to the Poirot-and-Hastings formula. Hannah, however, created a new sidekick for Poirot in *Monogram*, who returns in her subsequent entries to the canon. Explaining the decision in an interview for Agatha Christie's official website, Hannah writes:

> It seemed sensible to introduce a new narrator, to go with the inevitable change of writing style. Edward Catchpool sees Poirot through his own eyes and lets me write in my own way while staying true to Agatha's wonderful character and period. (An Interview with Sophie Hannah 2016)

The character is an inspector with Scotland Yard, whom Hannah describes as 'Poirot's sidekick' and 'mentee': 'He's clever but nowhere near as talented a detective as Poirot [but] Poirot sees that Catchpool is bright and has potential' (An Interview with Sophie Hannah 2016). Catchpool's police status puts him in line with many contemporary crime fiction protagonists of the twenty-first century, so his collaboration with a private detective creates a sense of continuity between the Golden Age and the police procedural traditions.

Whereas the police force in Christie's novels is often represented by a single hyperactive and inevitably unobservant detective, Catchpool introduces readers (and Poirot) to a more contemporary understanding of hierarchies within the force. He is frequently torn between professional etiquette and Poirot's unorthodox demands for information: in one novel, he has to get a female friend to telephone suspects, asking for alibis, so that he can plausibly deny involvement and avoid disciplinary action (Hannah 2018: 99–101). His presence as a figure learning from Poirot allows Hannah to create an impression that she, too, has learnt from Christie; indeed, in several interviews she has described the original novels as forming a part of her 'literary DNA' (An Interview with Sophie Hannah 2016). Poirot's new sidekick, then, establishes the detective as a still-relevant figure for contemporary readers.

Catchpool evolves over the course of his few appearances, becoming a more confident figure. In *The Monogram Murders*, he insists at the outset that he is not a hero and has 'no hope of ever being one' (Hannah 2014: 17), a sharp contrast to Hastings' delusions of grandeur in *The Mysterious Affair at Styles*. He is, from his first appearance, completely dependent: even before Poirot has taken him under his wing, he has been extensively mothered by his landlady, set up with linens and health remedies (20) and, although he grows increasingly irritated by Poirot's eccentricities, he never seriously doubts the man's status 'among the most intelligent of men' (29). In the second novel, *Closed Casket*, Catchpool introduces himself more forcefully as 'a detective with London's Scotland Yard', although he still describes his own narrative as 'clumsy' (Hannah 2016: 15). The character explores his own reasons for joining the police force in this book, and objects to what he calls the 'Sergeant Halfwit and Inspector Imbecile' trope in mystery fiction (17). There is evidence, then, that he has become comfortable in his own status as a detective in his own right.

Hannah's third Poirot novel, *The Mystery of Three Quarters*, sees Poirot consulting Catchpool, thus establishing the policeman as a part of his network of allies and informants—and therefore among the best of the best. Indeed, he now has the confidence to explicitly disobey his line manager and arrange for suspects to be interviewed as part of a murder investigation which, officially, does not exist. Catchpool has also, at this point, embraced his position as Poirot's chronicler. Whereas he insists that *The Monogram Murders* is being written 'for the benefit of nobody but myself' (Hannah 2014: 18), in *The Mystery of Three Quarters* he introduces the narrative 'for the benefit of future readers' (Hannah 2018: 48).

Catchpool struggles with women, and consistently resents his mother trying to find him, in reverse Mrs. Bennett-style, a wife. Mrs. Catchpool's 'ambition to see her son settled with a nice young lady' (36) is doomed to frustration, becoming a running joke by the beginning of the third book. During *The Monogram Murders*, Catchpool builds up a close friendship with a waitress, Fee Spring, but at the end of that novel he rejects, before anyone has had a chance to raise the possibility, the idea that there might be a romantic link between them (Hannah 2014: 372). Indeed, he refuses 'to inflict myself' upon any female 'specimen' (104), and some fans have speculated that Catchpool might not be heterosexual, writing of 'very oblique homoerotic subtext':

> It is just barely hinted that Catchpool is gay and struggling with the fact: he comments a few times on how he's NOT going to fall for any of various women he's met; and when he meets a character who argues that those in love should act on it regardless of all rules of society, the Church, or even their marriage vows to other people (!), he seems moved in a way that implies HE'S having to choose between love and 'the rules'. (Anonymous 2015; see also Lisle Library District 2016)

In *The Mystery of Three Quarters*, having been mentored by Poirot through two cases, Catchpool has developed both professional confidence and the personal confidence to reject each potential 'wife in waiting' without meeting them. He advocates choosing one's romantic partner for oneself, but dismisses all 'delightful young wom[e]n' without meeting them (Hannah 2018: 121). When his mother starts to think, 'If he won't be persuaded, even for this one...', with a palpable ellipsis, Catchpool seizes the initiative and takes her to the seaside as a kind of consolation prize, 'to lift her spirits' (37–38). He has developed the confidence to take the societal expectation that he should marry into his own hands.

Poirot seems to understand that Catchpool is not interested in female company and, despite being a prolific matchmaker, consistently sympathises with his friend's decision not to pursue a sex life. In Sophie Hannah's Poirot novels, Inspector Catchpool undergoes a professional apprenticeship and a delayed coming out from beneath his mother's grip. The two interwoven journeys in the narrator's life indicate a renegotiation of the appropriate sidekick for a detective who celebrates his own status as an outsider.

Conclusion

Captain Hastings acts as Poirot's stooge and foil, allowing the great detective to showcase not only his brilliance but also his otherness. This works on two levels, as Hastings' comical—often extremely hindering—Englishness and his expectations that as an Englishman he should be the hero of the story serve to highlight Poirot's foreignness and unconventional heroism. The characters of James Shepherd and his sister Caroline serve to pillory and effectively bury any sense of reassurance in formulaic crime fiction. By self-consciously inhabiting the role of sidekick in an apparently super-conventional mystery novel, Shepherd sets the stage for shock when he proves to be the narrative's chief antagonist. Meanwhile, his sister's secret network of knowledge and assistance comes to the forefront only on rereading *The Murder of Roger Ackroyd*, when one realises that she and not her brother is Poirot's ally.

If Hastings and the Shepherds act to cement Poirot's standing as an unorthodox figurehead for innovating generic traditions, it is no wonder that Christie went in a different direction around and following the Second World War. After all, by this time, Poirot had *become* canonical and Christie was the most widely read of all contemporary crime writers (see Haycraft 1964: 129–131). In the character of Ariadne Oliver, creator of a wildly successful quirky European detective, Christie allows the sleuth to dialogue with his own fictional status; at the same time, she exploits the adage that truth is best evidenced in fiction in order to present a strategically unthreatening self-image, discouraging public scrutiny. Oliver allows Poirot and his creator to revel in self-conscious artifice, but also to propel the detective novel itself into a philosophical genre, evaluating its own status in the real world.

Created almost four decades after Christie's death, Edward Catchpool is Poirot's ally in a twenty-first-century vision of his interwar heyday. Demonstrating a greater degree of psychological complexity than any of his predecessors, Catchpool is a figure of contrasts: he needs Poirot to be a hero, but has actively to create that heroism; he learns from the detective as he indulges his otherness without much sensitivity; and he stands for a generic tension at the heart of continuation novels themselves. As possibly homosexual-but-never-to-be-outed man, Catchpool reflects a need for newness in an evolved genre and conservatism in a fresh contribution to an established canon which, after all, cannot upset any preconceptions. Finally, as a policeman, Catchpool allows his creator, Sophie Hannah, to put the genre's past (the Golden Age format) in dialogue with the present (the police procedural). In all, Poirot's companions serve to illuminate his heroic status in shifting ways, as he is subtly renegotiated for a changing literary marketplace over the course of a century.

Notes

1. I survey a variety of critical perspectives on this question in *Queering Agatha Christie: Revisiting the Golden Age of Detective Fiction*, 47–52.
2. See Christie's response to an editorial in *Woman's Day*, housed in the Agatha Christie Business Correspondence Archive at the University of Exeter.
3. See, for instance, Gilbert Adair's 'Evadne Mount' trilogy, beginning with *The Act of Roger Murgatroyd* (2007). I am grateful to Samuel Saunders for raising the point that Ariadne Oliver acts as an author-substitute rather than a reader-substitute, frustrating the usual model for sidekicks and introducing a potential crisis: with whom, exactly, is the reader supposed to identify?

References

Adair, Gilbert. 2007. *The Act of Roger Murgatroyd*. London: Faber.

An Interview with Sophie Hannah. 2016. *The Home of Agatha Christie*. www.agathachristie.com/news/2016/an-interview-with-sophie-hannah. Accessed 8 July 2018.

Anon. 2015. Comment on *Investigating Agatha Christie's Poirot*, 'New Poirot Novel to be Written by Sophie Hannah' [7 Sep. 2013]. http://investigatingpoirot.blogspot.com/2013/09/new-poirot-novel-to-be-written-by.html?showComment=1420418599232#c6939595831494998739. Accessed 8 July 2018.

Bargainnier, Earl F. 1980. *The Gentle Art of Murder: The Detective Fiction of Agatha Christie*. Bowling Green: Bowling Green University Popular Press.

Bernthal, J.C. 2016. *Queering Agatha Christie: Revisiting the Golden Age of Detective Fiction*. Basingstoke: Palgrave Macmillan.

Christie, Agatha. (1920) 2016. *The Mysterious Affair at Styles*. London: HarperCollins.

———. (1923) 1994. *The Murder on the Links*. London: HarperCollins.

———. 1926. *The Murder of Roger Ackroyd*. London: Collins.

———. 1928. *The Mystery of the Blue Train*. London: Collins.

———. 1932. The Case of the Discontented Soldier. *Woman's Pictorial* 614, 15 Oct.

———. (1932) 1993. *Peril at End House*. London: HarperCollins.
———. 1933. *Lord Edgware Dies*. London: Collins.
———. 1936. *The ABC Murders*. London: Collins.
———. (1936) 1969. *Cards on the Table*. Glasgow: Fontana.
———. 1937. *Dumb Witness*. London: Collins.
———. (1938) 1990. Hercule Poirot—Fiction's Greatest Detective *The Agatha Christie Centenary*, ed. Lynn Underwood, 30–32. Glasgow: Collins.
———. (1945) 2013. Detective Writers in England. In The Detection Club (2013). *Ask a Policeman*, xiii–xx. London: Harper.
———. (1952) 1974. *Mrs McGinty's Dead*. London and Glasgow: Fontana.
———. 1953. After the Funeral. London: Collins.
———. 1961. *The Pale Horse*. London: Collins.
———. 1963. The Clocks. London: Collins.
———. 1966. *Third Girl*. London: Collins.
———. 1970. *Passenger to Frankfurt*. London: Collins.
———. 1972. *Elephants Can Remember*. London: Collins.
———. 1975. *Curtain: Poirot's Last Case*. London: Collins.
———. 1977. *An Autobiography*. London: Collins.
Christie, Agatha, and Charles Osborne. 1999. *Black Coffee*. London: HarperCollins.
Curran, John. 2009. *Agatha Christie's Secret Notebooks: Fifty Years of Mysteries in the Making*. London: HarperCollins.
Doyle, Arthur Conan. (1891) 2009. A Scandal in Bohemia, *The Penguin Complete Sherlock Holmes*, 161–176. London: Penguin.
Gill, Gillian. 1991. *Agatha Christie: The Woman and Her Mysteries*. London: Robson.
Hannah, Sophie. 2014. *The Monogram Murders*. London: HarperCollins.
———. 2016. *Closed Casket*. London: HarperCollins.
———. 2018. *The Mystery of Three Quarters*. London: HarperCollins.
Hart, Anne. 1990. *The Life and Times of Hercule Poirot*. London: Pavilion.
Haycraft, Howard. (1941) 1964. *Murder for Pleasure: The Life and Times of the Detective Story*. New York: Biblio and Tannen.
Leavis, Q.D. 1939. *Fiction and the Reading Public*. London: Chatto and Windus.
Lisle Library District. 2016. Our Book Discussion: On "The Monogram Murders" by Sophie Hannah, *Murder Among Friends*. www.lislelibrary.org/murderamongfriends/our-book-discussion-monogram-murders-sophie-hannah. Accessed 8 July 2018.
Munt, Sally R. (1994) 2005. *Murder by the Book? Feminism and the Crime Novel*. London and New York: Routledge.
Patterson, Nancy-Lou. 2017. *Detecting Wimsey: Papers on Dorothy L. Sayers's Detective Fiction* [n.p.]. Valleyhome Books.
Sayers, Dorothy L. 1927. *Unnatural Death*. London: Victor Gollancz.

———. 1928. Introduction. In *An Omnibus of Crime*, 9–47. London: Victor Gollancz.

Symons, Julian. 1981. The Life of Hercule Poirot, Based on the Notes of Captain Arthur Hastings. *The Great Detectives: Seven Original Investigations*, 95–114. London: Orbis.

Wynne, Catherine. 2010. Sherlock Holmes and the Problems of War: Traumatic Detections. *English Literature in Transition, 1880–1920* 53 (1): 29–53.

CHAPTER 7

Finding the Female Sidekick in the Lord Peter Wimsey Novels

Sally Beresford-Sheridan

Introduction

Dorothy L. Sayers's Lord Peter Wimsey novels, written between the two World Wars, are often seen as conservative by various (especially feminist) critics, who lament the ultimate coupling of Wimsey and Sayers's supposedly feminist heroine, Harriet Vane. Laurel Young, for example, names SueEllen Campbell and Laura Krugman Ray as among those who deride Sayers for creating Harriet Vane as an ultimately 'flawed feminist' who shows 'disturbing slips back into [...] traditional thinking' (2005: 40), while Maroula Joannou comments that much of the popular writing from the 1930s, including Sayers's fiction, was mostly conservative and 'traditional in both content and form' (1999: 7–8).

Sayers is far more progressive however, in terms of both content and form. Through her portrayal of a number of strong female characters, she consistently inserts complex discussion of women's roles, benefits and rights in British inter-war society into her writing. Sayers also asks the reader to question her female characters' positions; are they portrayed as

S. Beresford-Sheridan (✉)
University of Waterloo, Waterloo, ON, Canada

L. Andrew and S. Saunders (eds.), *The Detective's Companion in Crime Fiction*, Crime Files, https://doi.org/10.1007/978-3-030-74989-7_7

detective or sidekick, or are they even able to be categorized as either? Do they, in fact, move beyond such specific generic labels, and instead inhabit many facets of the roles of detective and sidekick simultaneously? Sayers thus asks the reader to broadly question how female detectives and sidekicks detect, how their work is respected, and how others in the novels perceive and treat them. She ultimately marries the discussion of the roles of 'sidekick' and 'detective' with that of women's place in society, providing space for the sidekick position to vary and develop alongside the places where women could enter workplace and professional spaces. In doing so, she uses her writing to do as Kathleen Gregory Klein suggests, depicting women who 'work through existing systems to effect change and to expand women's opportunities' (1995: 200). This chapter examines two of the female characters in the Wimsey canon—Miss Climpson and Harriet Vane—to discuss their fluctuating roles as detectives and sidekicks; how do the ways in which they act help to classify them as detectives or sidekicks? Additionally, how does the perception of these characters by others, especially Wimsey, help to clarify their oscillation between the generic labels of either sidekick or detective, and ultimately, paradoxically, give them the potential to inhabit both?

Sayers repeatedly works the conversation of equality between men and women into her writing, particularly asking for women to have the right to work and 'have occupation' without worrying about their marital state (Sayers [1938] 1946: 110). It takes her several novels to fully discuss the 'woman' question, to which she finally offers a conclusion in *Gaudy Night* ([1935] 1949) and *Busman's Honeymoon* ([1937a] 1976). Young states that Sayers 'incorporate[s] into her fiction her interest in the debate over the changing place of women in society' (2005: 39), and that *Gaudy Night* is the 'text in which a female protagonist's negotiation of gender is of equal importance and often bound up with the mystery' (2005: 42). More specifically, Diana Wallace argues that the novels that focus on the 'six-year courtship' between Lord Peter Wimsey and Harriet Vane 'can be read as a meditation on marriage and its possibilities for the educated woman, and as a plea for women to be able to continue the work they do best after marriage' (1999: 68). Vane is naturally one of the key characters whom Sayers uses to discuss women's place in society, and she is found in four of the Wimsey novels: *Strong Poison* ([1930] 1960), *Have His Carcase* ([1932] 1976), *Gaudy Night* ([1935] 1949), and *Busman's Honeymoon* ([1937a] 1976), as well as a short story 'Talboys' ([1942] 1982) which is set seven years after *Busman's Honeymoon*.

However, I argue that Sayers does not *begin* her discussion surrounding women's rights or place in society with Harriet. Instead she starts through her 'spinster' character, Miss Alexandra Katherine Climpson, in *Unnatural Death* ([1927] 1947), who, in her professional position, blurs the boundaries between the role of detective and sidekick.

Alexandra Katherine Climpson [1]

By the time Sayers had introduced Lord Peter Wimsey in *Whose Body* in 1923, several tropes of the detective genre had already solidified. Dr. John Watson, the famous companion to Sherlock Holmes, substantially helped to construct the extant narrative dichotomy between detective and sidekick that authors of detective fiction have emulated ever since the first Holmes story, *A Study in Scarlet* ([1887] 1987). In Sayers's novels, a continuation of this tradition can seemingly be identified; Wimsey is portrayed as the detective while his manservant, Mervyn Bunter, ostensibly represents the sidekick who performs tasks often ascribed to the role, including 'observ[ing], serving as helpers and, more importantly, bear[ing] witness to the detective's brilliance' (Bredesen 2010: xi). Bunter certainly assists Wimsey in his cases, by collecting evidence with a camera, and by generally taking care of Wimsey, especially as Bunter understands Wimsey's occasional lapses into shock from his wartime trauma. Bunter also rescues Wimsey on occasion (as in *Clouds of Witness* ([1926] 1972). However, Bunter's sidekick role is not quite 'stock and trade'. He never narrates the story—in fact, Sayers never utilizes a completely standard sidekick/narrator character in her stories, despite P.G. Wodehouse's declaration that '[a] Watson of some sort to tell the story is unavoidable' (1977: xv–xvi). It is as a manservant that Bunter can in some respects be Wimsey's Holmesian sidekick, but he is also a servant and thus mostly unseen or in the background of the stories. Sayers acknowledges the Holmesian sidekick arrangement within the relationship of Wimsey and Bunter, but their relationship is sufficiently marginal to the stories themselves so that Sayers is able to develop other kinds of sidekick relationships for Wimsey. She has various characters who participate in a sidekick role when needed, asked, or placed there, yet who do not permanently always stay as sidekicks. In having these fluctuating character roles, she recreates and plays with the idea of the function of the sidekick.

Additionally, as Sayers uses the detective genre to discuss women's roles in society, to 'work out her own humanistic scheme for equality among the sexes within her novels' (Trembley 1995: 86), it is fitting that she does so through offering complex representations of specifically female characters that exist in relation to her established detective. Thus, the *female* sidekick/detective is where she actually focuses the bulk of her attention, and she uses these figures to consistently question standard generic labels of detective and sidekick. Miss Climpson, for example, is introduced as an older working woman operating as a subordinate to Wimsey, and in this she consistently blurs the line between detective and sidekick in various ways: in her role as lead investigator of Wimsey's 'Cattery', and as female sidekick to Wimsey for his private cases. Her professional status also highlights how Miss Climpson is designed to explore the position of working women in society, and Sayers thus uses Climpson's character to extensively discuss the right of women to place, space and to work a job at which they are effective, and importantly, a job that they want and enjoy.[2]

The Spinster Detective

Miss Climpson is notably a spinster, and is therefore immediately not in danger of being included in the stories simply as a love interest for Wimsey. Instead, she is a woman with a strong working relationship with him, and by casting her in this light, Sayers highlights both the effectiveness and the necessity of including female detecting skills in the detective fiction canon. Miss Climpson continues a long tradition of spinster-detectives, particularly exemplified by Andrew Forrester Jr's Miss Gladden ([1864] 2010) and later solidified in Agatha Christie's Miss Jane Marple, introduced in *Murder at the Vicarage* in 1930. In *Sherlock's Sisters*, Joseph Kestner traces the origins of the female detective back to the nineteenth century specifically focusing on detective stories with female protagonists such as W.S. Hayward's *Revelations of a Lady Detective* ([1864] 2010) featuring Mrs. Paschal and Andrew Forrester Jr.'s *The Female Detective* ([1864] 2010) with Miss Gladden. In *The Female Detective*, Miss Gladden herself correctly states that 'the woman detective has far greater opportunities than a man of intimate watching, and of keeping her eyes upon the matters near which a man could not conveniently play the eavesdropper' ([1864] 2010: 2). Miss Climpson similarly detects by utilizing key tropes of the elderly woman spinster sleuth, such as not being taken seriously as a threat, participating in local gossip and hearsay, and simply being able to go where a man cannot without being observed.

Her detecting skills are what is important to the story; she is not a potential love interest for the main male detective and thus does not present either a sexual distraction or an emotional hindrance to him in solving his cases. A number of critics including Kathleen Gregory Klein (1995: 67–68, 141–143) discuss the benefits of the spinster detective, one of which is her lack of sexual attraction, while Birgitta Berglund specifically declares that spinster detectives are the best solution to the difficulty of a successful female detective who will not be conflicted by sexual emotional feelings, nor by the social expectations of settling down, marrying, and raising a family (2000: 144). By having Miss Climpson as a professionally paid and unsexual 'spinster' female detective/sidekick, Lord Peter does not violate, complicate, nor infringe upon his professional relationship with her.

This tradition of the spinster-detective is one which Sayers specifically makes use of, both for discussion on social change and status of women, but also in playing with the detective genre's labels of what it means to be a detective and/or sidekick. Chapter three of *Unnatural Death*, is entitled 'A Use for Spinsters', and opens with a quotation from Gilbert Frankau, who states: 'There are two million more females than males in England and Wales: And this is an awe-inspiring circumstance' (Sayers [1927] 1947: 23). This chapter is designed to raise questions in the reader about, as Wimsey himself later remarks, supposedly 'superfluous women' who do not end up married. The chapter title, 'A Use for Spinsters', is significant, as the label of 'spinster' had a number of unfortunate contemporary connotations. Jane Lewis begins her book, *Women in England 1870–1950* (1984), by stating: 'For all women marriage conferred a higher status than spinsterhood, which connoted failure' (1984: 3). Though Lewis argues that this was more particularly the case prior to World War I, even afterwards marriage was viewed as the more 'successful' option for women, and the alternative was usually a life of poverty and loneliness unless the woman had her own means of living since the wage for women workers was below 'subsistence level' (Lewis 1984: 3). Maroula Joannou gives context to the derogatory term 'spinster' when she notes that approximately one-third of women between the two World Wars who had not married by age 29 did not marry in their 'reproductive years'. She goes on to state that:

> The meaning of spinsterhood became a site of contestation between those who wished to objectify the spinster and others who saw her as a person with needs, desires, and potential of her own. [...] the terms 'superfluous

> woman' and 'spinster' became interchangeable and 'spinster' [began] to be widely used as a pejorative term. (1995: 77–78)

Wimsey is mindful of these connotations and in offering Miss Climpson detecting jobs, demonstrates his awareness of how a spinster-detective has certain advantages, despite her outcast position in society. Indeed, Miss Climpson's detective work is enhanced by both her femininity and her spinster status. She is cognizant of the social expectations and opinions of the spinster and, much in the same way as Gladden and Paschal, Miss Climpson actively uses this to her advantage:

> At length a really brilliant notion occurred to her. She was (she did not attempt to hide it from herself) precisely the type and build of person one associates with the collection of subscriptions. [...] What more natural than that she should try a little house-to-house visiting in a wealthy quarter? (Sayers [1927] 1947: 173)

Her unobtrusive presence also allows others to speak openly around her, something they likely would not do in the presence of either Lord Peter or the police, which is precisely why Wimsey offers her investigating work. As Wimsey explains to Detective Inspector Parker:

> Just think. People want questions asked. Whom do they send? [...] I send a lady with a long, woolly jumper on knitting-needles and jingly things round her neck. Of course she asks questions – everyone expects it. Nobody is surprised. Nobody is alarmed. (Sayers [1927] 1947: 30)

Miss Climpson is all too aware of social stereotypes and expectations and uses this to her advantage. She is able to blend in with her surroundings of tea and social chatter, and thus pick up on pieces of information that are both useful and pertinent to her investigation.

Therefore the spinster detective is an effective detective, and also important for making the social commentary which Sayers inserts into her fiction as to the need for expanded roles for women in professions. When Lord Peter describes his new enterprise, initially providing Miss Climpson with detecting work and setting up the 'Cattery' detecting agency staffed entirely by women, he is conscious of the social discriminations faced by these so-called 'superfluous' spinster figures. He comments several times at the unjustness of a society that merely 'makes fun of them' instead of trying to offer them dignity and respect (Sayers [1927] 1947: 26), and sees through the stereotypes to openly recognize the merits of these 'superfluous' women who are, in fact, well-suited to detection:

> 'Miss Climpson', said Lord Peter, 'is a manifestation of the wasteful way in which this country is run. [...] their magnificent gossip-powers and units of inquisitiveness are allowed to dissipate themselves or even become harmful to the community, while the ratepayers' money is spent on getting work for which these women are providentially fitted, inefficiently carried out by ill-equipped policemen like you'. [...]
> You mean that Miss Climpson is a kind of inquiry agent for you.
> She is my ears and tongue [...] and especially my nose. She asks questions which a young man could not put without a blush. She is the angel that rushes in where fools get a clump on the head. She can smell a rat in the dark. In fact, she is the cat's whiskers. (Sayers [1927] 1947: 30)

Laurel Young references Catherine Kenney, who states that Lord Peter creating this agency is 'not just an act of charity toward [the women] but a service to society'. Young continues that 'Their energy and intelligence suit them well for private inquiry work' (2005: 43).

This inquiry work is directed by Miss Climpson as the leader of an organization started by Wimsey and eventually referred to as his 'Cattery'. More fully described in *Strong Poison*, the Cattery gives work to all sorts of women known by society as 'superfluous'—for example those married and deserted, those widowed, or spinsters (Sayers [1930] 1960: 40). Although again Sayers writes within the framework of the spinster sleuth there is a clear distinction of authority given to Miss Climpson and those working at the Cattery through Miss Climpson's professional relationship with Wimsey. Agatha Christie's Miss Marple, perhaps the most famous of these female spinster sleuths, at first has no clear authority or recognition of her abilities; indeed, in *Murder at the Vicarage* when she is introduced, Marple's detecting abilities only give her the epithet as the 'worst cat in the village' who 'always knows every single thing that happens—and draws the worst inferences from it' (Christie [1930] 1976: 178). Marple is thus not given the same authority as Miss Climpson, and she does not work directly under the protection of a recognized male detective. Contrastingly, in *Strong Poison*, the reader learns that 'Miss Climpson's office boasted a private telephone line to Scotland Yard' ([1930] 1960: 41).

Detective or Sidekick?

So far, however, the argument seems to be that Miss Climpson is an effective spinster *detective*, participating in the spinster-sleuth tradition while at the same time allowing Sayers to insert social commentary of women in the professional sphere rather than being an effective *sidekick* to Lord Peter Wimsey. Yet what separates Miss Climpson from other spinster detectives is her professional oscillation between being an independent detective and sidekick while *employed* by Lord Peter. She is specifically and privately hired (and thus paid) by Lord Peter Wimsey to both be a sidekick and assist him in his cases which he is investigating and to additionally run his 'Cattery' as a detective. It is the distinction of these two separate roles, both of which she is uniquely suited for, where Sayers shows the importance of including Miss Climpson, a spinster, into the professional sphere. Miss Climpson is portrayed throughout the series as working *for* Wimsey. With his own personal cases, Wimsey makes it clear that he is not a client asking Miss Climpson for help (such as often with Misses Gladden and Marple), but rather he specifically sends her on 'inquiries' (Sayers [1927] 1947: 28) for the cases that *he* is investigating, that *he* is interested in. For this, as Wimsey declares to Detective Inspector Parker, is 'where [Miss Climpson's] remarkable tact and shrewdness are going to be so *helpful to us*' (my emphasis, Sayers [1927] 1947: 28).

When Lord Peter Wimsey brings his friend Detective Inspector Parker to meet Miss Climpson, the reader could, like Parker, assume that Lord Peter is referring to a mistress that he has installed in an apartment for his and her convenience. To Parker's great surprise, a woman is introduced who bears no resemblance to a fashionable mistress. Indeed, Miss Climpson moves rapidly in this section from being thought of as a fashionable mistress, to demonstrating her abilities as a detective, to being called upon as Wimsey's sidekick. While the fashionable mistress suggestion offers levity to the story, the important nuance of Miss Climpson's detective and sidekick role is given prominence when she is first introduced.

Miss Climpson immediately starts going into her cases which she has been investigating and explains to Wimsey:

> I have gone *very* carefully into all these cases [...] Dear me! such *sad* stories some of these poor women had to tell me! But I have investigated most

> fully [...] and I feel sure that in the majority of these cases your assistance will be *well bestowed*. If you would like to go through—
> Not at the moment, Miss Climpson,' interrupted Lord Peter, hurriedly. [...] 'Just now, Miss Climpson, we want your help on something quite different.
> Miss Climpson produced a business-like notebook and sat at attention.
> 'The inquiry divides itself into two parts,' said Lord Peter. (original emphasis [1927] 1947: 27)

Thus in this moment, Miss Climpson moves from being the lead investigator of cases for the 'Cattery', to being called upon by Wimsey as his sidekick, making inquiries that will benefit both him and Parker in their own case. Miss Climpson leaves aside her own work to be Lord Peter's sidekick whenever he asks for her.

Sayers highlights the abilities of Miss Climpson, who does prove herself to be the 'cat's whiskers'. While undercover for Lord Peter in *Unnatural Death*, she installs herself in the village to try and determine if Mary Whittaker's infirm aunt was killed by Mary herself. In chapter sixteen, 'A Cast-Iron Alibi', Lord Peter sends instructions to Miss Climpson to find information to break the alibi of the main suspect: Mary Whittaker. Miss Climpson tries to obtain this from Mary's close friend Vera Findlater, and Sayers writes: 'Miss Climpson, most faithful of sleuths, and *carrying Lord Peter's letter of instruction in the pocket of her skirt like a talisman*, had asked the youngest Miss Findlater to tea' (my emphasis, [1927] 1947: 121). And then, while Vera is giving her heartfelt confidences to Miss Climpson, Sayers notes: 'Miss Climpson did not smile. She was accustomed to the role of confidante' ([1927] 1947: 124).

This detection that Miss Climpson performs under the direction of Wimsey is subsequently contrasted to that completed by Lord Peter and Detective Inspector Parker. By doing so, Sayers shows that the case is solved, ultimately, by the detecting skills of all *three*, each thriving in their own particular form of detection. What Miss Climpson offers the trio is precisely what Lord Peter described in the beginning; she is able to go places and see and hear things that he and Parker could never hope to. Her role as a sidekick, in this case, is thus emphasized: she moves away from her investigative work at the beginning and comes to undertake inquiries for Wimsey in the case of *Unnatural Death*. She is called upon by Wimsey to assist him and while her detective work is insightful, she ultimately always refers back to Wimsey as the lead detective when working for him on his private cases.

Throughout the stories, Lord Peter and Miss Climpson continue to have a working and professional relationship, with Lord Peter coming to depend on Miss Climpson as his sidekick. Indeed, Miss Climpson recognizes her sidekick position when she tells Lord Peter in *Strong Poison*: 'Only let me know, at *any* minute of the night or day, and I will do my *very* best to help you' (original emphasis, Sayers [1930] 1960: 45). And when Lord Peter is depressed over lack of evidence and movement in the case, he openly relies on Miss Climpson to find it for him:

> 'I have a job', he said to her, more abruptly than was his wont, 'which I should like you to undertake yourself. I can't trust anybody else'.
> 'How *kind* of you to put it like that', said Miss Climpson. (original emphasis, Sayers [1930] 1960: 125)

Upon her introduction in *Unnatural Death*, Miss Climpson remains the sole official professional female sidekick to Lord Peter Wimsey who reappears throughout the series: she actively searches for clues and solutions to the problems he presents to her. Indeed, Miss Climpson's detecting abilities are key to solving the overall case in *Strong Poison*, which also introduces the series' other particularly noteworthy female character who occupies a temporary sidekick position, Harriet Vane. Climpson's intervention on the original jury directly saves Harriet from the gallows, and she thus opens up the potential for Harriet's relationship with Wimsey to develop as the series goes on.

After the introduction of Harriet, Miss Climpson rather fades from the stories, though is mentioned briefly to show she is still engaged in work with the Cattery. In *Gaudy Night* Harriet even contemplates asking for Miss Climpson's help. For the purposes of the story, and for Harriet and Peter to work out their own personal relationship in addition to Harriet's status as potential sidekick, detective or equal partner to Peter however, Harriet learns Miss Climpson is not available:

> [S]he hung up the receiver with a sinking heart. Why she should be surprised to learn that Miss Climpson was absent from Town "engaged on a case" she could not have said. It seemed vaguely monstrous that this should be so; but it was so. (Sayers [1935] 1949: 198)

Harriet Vane

While Miss Climpson's spinster status ensures that her relationship with Lord Peter remains strictly professional, Harriet Vane's role as a potential love interest for Wimsey complicates the construction of both her role as a sidekick and the detective/sidekick relationship more broadly. Sexually available and attractive female detectives were rare in the Golden Age of detective fiction, and as Julian Symons argues, after they had solved their case, these 'lady' detectives 'presumably settle down again to domesticity' (Symons 1972: 87). Indeed, the concept of 'attractive' female characters in detective fiction was so controversial that a rule was invoked by the Detection Club stating that the unity of the detective story was 'damaged' by an insertion of a love interest (1972: 108).[3] Symons also quotes Sayers, who herself said that characters in detective novels lived '"more or less on the *Punch* level of emotion" and, if they were to be considered more seriously, their emotions would "make hay of the detective interest"' (1972: 108). So why, therefore, was Harriet Vane introduced as a love interest for Lord Peter Wimsey when it seemed that Sayers both disagreed with the concept of providing a love interest or storyline in detective fiction, and had already inserted sufficient commentary on the role of women in her society through the character of Miss Climpson?

The answer comes through looking at the progression of the characters of both Harriet Vane and Lord Peter Wimsey as they move through the four main novels that they are in together: how they navigate their relationships with each other and with the mysteries that they are involved in. Specifically, in what role do they see themselves, place themselves or place each other, within the mystery: detective, sidekick or partners? Additionally, the inclusion of Harriet Vane as love interest gives Sayers the opportunity to further broaden her discussions of the role of women in society and the detective genre than she could with Miss Climpson's professional oscillation between detective and sidekick. With the added love interest between Harriet Vane and Peter Wimsey, Sayers allows herself to write characters who do not have 'every vestige of humanity [...] ruthlessly expunged' (Sayers 1937b: 76) which she also decried.

Rather, characters in the detective novel can become, as she states in 'Aristotle on Detective Fiction', [...] *good* [...] endowed with some sort of human dignity [...] *appropriate* [...] and like the reality [...] with some moderate approximation in speech and behaviour to such men and women as we see about us' (original emphasis, Sayers [1936] 2012: 177–178). Thus, over the course of the four novels with Peter and Harriet, Sayers directs the focus of her stories more towards creating characters who are good, appropriate, and realistic while moving away from the more recognizable and classic detective story. Indeed, she subtitles her final novel, *Busman's Honeymoon*, as 'A Love Story with Detective Interruptions' ([1937a] 2012).

While the relationship between Harriet and Peter moves towards an emphasis on character development, it additionally should be stated that Sayers was also interested in the idea of women detectives and women characters in the detective genre. In her introduction to *Great Short Stories of Detection, Mystery and Horror* (also published as *The Omnibus of Crime*), Sayers commented directly on women detectives:

> In order to justify their choice of sex, they are obliged to be so irritatingly intuitive as to destroy that quiet enjoyment of the logical which we look for in our detective reading. Or else they are active and courageous, and insist on walking in physical danger and hampering the men engaged on the job. Marriage, also, looms too large in the view of life; which is not surprising, for they are all young and beautiful. Why these charming creatures should be able to tackle abstruse problems at the age of twenty-one or thereabouts, [...] it is hard to say. Where do they pick up their worldly knowledge? Not from personal experience, for they are always immaculate as the driven snow. Presumably it is all intuition. (1929: 15–16)

Miss Climpson, as a spinster and therefore in no danger of being this young and 'charming creature', is an effective argument against this specific type of female detective whom Sayers despairs of. However, as effective as Miss Climpson is for the discussion of women's place in society, as Laurel Young argues in 'Dorothy L. Sayers and the New Woman Detective Novel', her role is not the main point of the story; this commentary is not the main focus of the story, it is the mystery that comes first (2005: 43). Thus, though Miss Climpson is an effective sidekick and detective who highlights how women are both necessary in the workplace and that they have a right to do the job which they are best suited and which they want to do, her narrative consistently remains submerged in the wider detective plot.

Therefore, it is with Harriet Vane that Sayers ultimately concentrates her conversation on women in society most firmly. Harriet's character can be broken down into four basic categories, corresponding with each of her four stories—love interest, sidekick, detective and then equal partner—although it must be clarified that these definitions are fluid and transition into each different story. Thus, while the treatment of Miss Climpson and the social conventions she breaks are only secondary to the plot of the novels in which she appears, in Harriet Vane, Sayers creates a more complex conversation that dominates and finally *supersedes* the mystery.

Love Interest: Strong Poison *(1930)*

When introduced to Harriet Vane in *Strong Poison*, she is on trial for the murder of her lover. She is no 'immaculate' heroine; Harriet obviously possesses some worldly knowledge. It is also made clear from the beginning of the story that Peter is invested in this case in a personal and emotional way: the love interest of the whole case comes at the very beginning. The meeting between Harriet and Peter is written so that the reader understands the depth of Peter's feelings for Harriet. While waiting to meet Harriet in the prison, 'Wimsey sat down and waited, a prey to curious sensations' ([1930] 1960: 34). During their interview together, Harriet smiles at Peter and 'his heart turned to water' ([1930] 1960: 35). After Peter leaves the prison, where he has already proposed to Harriet he ruminates on how 'jolly' their life will be together:

> poor kid, I would damn well work to make it up to her – she's got a sense of humour too – brains – one wouldn't be dull – one would wake up and there'd be a whole day for jolly things to happen in – and then one would come home and go to bed – that would be jolly, too – and while she was writing, I could go and mess round, so we shouldn't either of us be dull – . (Sayers [1930] 1960: 39)

Peter works to solve the murder of Harriet's dead lover, with the increased pressure that if he fails, the woman he loves will most likely be hanged for a crime he feels certain she did not commit.

Though much of the female detection in *Strong Poison* is completed by Miss Climpson and the other members of her 'Cattery', Harriet offers insight into the death of her lover, but more poignantly, it is her imprisonment that reveals how society condemns professional women who deviate from socially constructed gender norms. The assumption that Harriet is guilty of the murder of her lover is based upon her nonconformity to her gendered role: she first refuses an absurd offer of marriage and then refuses to perform 'as woman' for the court. In *Strong Poison*, Harriet as a detective or Harriet as a sidekick is not the focus; rather she is shown to be a successful and professional woman, whose very success caused her lover to be jealous of her. Additionally, the research she was doing for her next book—she is a detective fiction author—creates much of the evidence for the initial case against her: her lover had been poisoned by arsenic and she had bought arsenic under several assumed names to see how it could be done for the plot of her next novel (Sayers [1930] 1960: 10–12).

While Harriet's first appearance in *Strong Poison* deliberately positions her as a potential love interest for Peter, she also offers Sayers the opportunity to discuss women and how they are perceived in society, as well as set up her character to continue to be an influence and connection with Lord Peter. Her character undergoes significant changes and roles in *Have His Carcase, Gaudy Night*, and *Busman's Honeymoon*. It is in these stories, in her relationship with Peter, that Harriet becomes first sidekick, then acts as detective but ultimately is an equal partner to Peter. In this movement and changing of roles, Sayers experiments with detective fiction in having a character inhabit many of the genre's roles while at the same time using the characters to discuss the necessity for equality between the sexes. Harriet is professionally an author of detective fiction, but in the various experiences of the stories, she once again blurs the distinction between sidekick and detective. While Miss Climpson is called upon (and paid) by Lord Peter to help him solve his cases, how Harriet enters into the mysteries, and how she sees herself in relation to the mystery itself, helps to codify her first as sidekick and then detective. In *Have His Carcase* Harriet fulfils a sidekick role before she can move into the role of detective in *Gaudy Night* and *Busman's Honeymoon*.

Sidekick: Have His Carcase *(1932)*

Have His Carcase opens humorously, referencing Harriet's recent escape from the gallows and Peter's offer of marriage: 'The best remedy for a bruised heart is not, as so many people seem to think, repose upon a manly bosom. Much more efficacious are honest work, physical activity, and the sudden acquisition of wealth' (Sayers [1932] 1976: 7). Divided into thirty-four chapters, each chapter of *Have His Carcase* discusses a point of evidence of the case. The opening chapters initially display Harriet's ability to be a detective, when she conscientiously examines a corpse she finds on a beach and takes notes on it for the police before the body is taken away by the tide. How she sees herself in gathering this information, however, is always in relationship to how the two detectives she knows would assemble evidence. After an initial moment of understandable weakness is quickly overcome, she contemplates how best to react to the situation:

> 'The great thing,' Harriet found herself saying, after a pause, 'the great thing is to keep cool. Keep your head, my girl. What would Lord Peter Wimsey do in such a case? Or, of course, Robert Templeton?' (Sayers [1932] 1976: 14)

Robert Templeton is the hero of Harriet's detective stories and she follows guidance from him as she examines the body. Of course Harriet has written the Robert Templeton stories and therefore seemingly is following advice from herself, yet the nuance of the situation comes from how Harriet positions herself to a detective, even if she is seeking advice from her own fictional detective:

> [Robert Templeton] was a gentleman of extraordinary scientific skill, combined with almost fabulous muscular development. He had arms like an orang-outang and an ugly but attractive face. She conjured up this phantom before her in the suit of rather loud plus-fours with which she was accustomed to invest him, and took counsel with him in spirit. (Sayers [1932] 1976: 14)

Pushing the image of Peter Wimsey (almost the exact physical opposite of her own creation) firmly from her mind, she constructs how Templeton would examine the body and then proceeds to follow in a likewise manner. She takes on a sidekick role to her own detective: she separates the research and the professionalism which she has accomplished as a writer, and uses that information to guide her when she could be overwhelmed in a stressful situation which allows her to examine the dead body in an organized manner.

Then, when Harriet gives her statement to the police, the Inspector is surprised that a 'young lady' is so composed about murder and comments on her poise:

> 'It's a miracle to me, the way you handled it. Why, most young ladies would have run away'.
> 'Well you see', explained Harriet, 'I know what ought to be done. I write detective stories, you know'. (Sayers [1932] 1976: 37)

Thus it is clear that Harriet's ability to examine the body is influenced by her occupation as an author. In *Strong Poison*, Harriet and Lord Peter make up detective stories to amuse themselves while Harriet is locked in prison (Sayers [1930] 1960: 56–57), but it is in *Have His Carcase* that Sayers specifically shows how Harriet's professional work as an author—not just her life experiences—assists her in detection: she starts her detective work by positioning herself as a sidekick to her own fictional detective.

How Harriet positions herself as a sidekick to her own fictional detective is perhaps a much-nuanced point and one which could be argued against: after all, she does accomplish her task and steady herself while doing all of the detecting work and notes while examining the body in the first place. Where her true sidekick role comes into clear focus is once Lord Peter enters to essentially take over the case himself. Initially, it may appear as if Harriet and Peter are equal detectives in *Have His Carcase*, yet Sayers positions Harriet in a subordinate, even a sidekick role, to Lord Peter. She does this in several ways, and in doing so, uses the opportunity to once more bend the definition of sidekick while also discussing the balance of equality in the relationship between Peter and Harriet.

Harriet's respected position with the police in *Have His Carcase* is dependent upon Lord Peter's name; they base her innocence in this case on the evidence of her innocence established by Peter in *Strong Poison* ([1932] 1976: 38) and additionally ask him for information on her personally ([1932] 1976: 174, 333–334). Thus Harriet becomes 'protected' by Lord Peter and her feeling of forced gratitude is one which haunts her through the stories and makes it difficult to recognize her own worth to Peter. *Have His Carcase* discusses the difficulty of being forced into the 'protected' role, and how hard it is to come out of it. Harriet is not fully under suspicion of the police because of her connection with Lord Peter, yet in his protection of her, he undermines any chance of romantically being with her:

> Then why did you come?
> So that you might not have to send for me.
> *Oh!*
> There was a strained pause, while Wimsey painfully recalled the terms of the message that had originally reached him …
> And finally, the certainty that the best way out of a bad situation was to brazen it out – Harriet's word – even if it meant making a public exhibition of his feelings, and the annihilation of all the delicate structure of confidence which he had been so cautiously toiling to build up between this scathed and embittered woman and himself. (Sayers [1932] 1976: 173, 174)

This forced protection, while keeping Harriet from being harassed by the police, also forces her into a sidekick role, and ultimately, delays the satisfying romantic conclusion to their relationship. As the detective who comes to solve the case and to ensure Harriet is not once again arrested for murder, Peter takes on the detective role and puts Harriet into his sidekick role. Sayers ensures that this is clear and uses the famous detective sidekick pair, Holmes and Watson, to make her case.

When Peter first comes to Wilvercombe, the scene of the murder, Harriet is seen as the main detective (though she sees herself as under the guidance of Robert Templeton) and Peter acknowledges this when he first greets her with 'Good morning, Sherlock' ([1932] 1976: 47). He asks Harriet to give him the details of the murder and even wonders why she did not call him to come solve the case: 'bearing in mind that I'm a corpse-fan, don't you think you might, as man to man, have let me in on the ground-floor?' ([1932] 1976: 48–49). At the police station, examining the photos of the body Harriet had taken, Peter once again calls her 'Sherlock' ([1932] 1976: 55). The movement of Harriet into a full sidekick role to Peter comes immediately once Peter has received all the facts of the case, and has examined what there is of the physical evidence. Discussing the evidence and bantering with Harriet, Peter laughingly places her as his sidekick, 'These are deep waters, Watson' ([1932] 1976: 59). Harriet's reaction to this name is not presented, the sergeant interjects, and Wimsey declares his next step in searching for evidence. However, when Wimsey announces his intention of going to town, Sayers writes that 'Harriet, who had been preparing to say that she had work to do and could not waste time rubber-necking round Wilvercombe with Lord Peter, experienced an unreasonable feeling of having been cheated' ([1932] 1976: 59). It is unclear, however, if she feels cheated out of his company, or cheated out of helping to gather evidence in the case. Perhaps it is both.

Throughout the rest of the story, Harriet is mostly referred to as Watson by Peter and she even takes on this role in a playful encounter as Peter examines the evidence of a horseshoe. After Peter has given a list of information, deduced from the horseshoe, Harriet exclaims: 'Holmes, this is wonderful! How do you do it?' to which Peter replies: 'Perfectly simple, my dear Watson' (Sayers [1932] 1976: 210). Harriet's role becomes clearly that of sidekick, as she works on the cipher or other tasks that Wimsey has given to her. Though there are a few instances where Harriet goes out to do detecting work on her own, such as when she 'vamps' the main suspect, Henry Wheldon, in 'The Evidence of the Snake', she relies on Peter to take the information she gives him and make use of it towards the ultimate solving of the case.

Harriet, though put into the sidekick role in *Have His Carcase*, is also given a position of authority as an author. At the inquest the detached narrator writes: 'The next witness was Harriet Vane, who gave a detailed account of the finding of the body.[…] Harriet was a good witness on these points, her training as a mystery-writer having taught her to assemble details of this kind coherently' (Sayers [1932] 1976: 272). Harriet's status as an author is commented on several times, and her knowledge and insights into the case often are drawn from her experience as a writer. Peter acknowledges her worth in solving the case as a writer as well: 'Harriet! It's your business to work out problems of this sort—how do you propose to tackle this one?' (Sayers [1932] 1976: 431). Her insights into the case stem from her professional ability as an author and this is always made clear; ultimately, however, she does not connect all the evidence of the case to find a final solution—'"Of course!" she said.

[…] "I never thought about it in connection with the murder"' ([1932] 1976: 443, 444). She is placed into the sidekick role in *Have His Carcase* through having to be protected by Peter, and in addition to how Peter sees his role in the case and his wish to be the main detective who solves it. Her sidekick position ultimately means that Harriet feels subordinate to Peter and cannot become romantically involved with him. Yet is it her experience as sidekick, coupled with her professional life as an author, which enables her to take on the case in *Gaudy Night*. And it is Peter's response to her dealings with this case, which ultimately allows them to acknowledge each other as equals.

'Admission of Equality' (Sayers [1935] 166): **Gaudy Night** *(1935) and* **Busman's Honeymoon** *(1937)*

Sayers uses *Gaudy Night* to move Harriet from love interest, to sidekick, to detective, to finally equal partner with Peter, and highlights Harriet's academic and personal worth from all of her experiences and professional work. She declares in her article of the same name, that *Gaudy Night* is new and exciting, as she 'bring[s] the love-problem into line with the detective-problem, so that the same key should unlock both at once' (1937b: 85). This bringing together of these problems then constructs a book, she claims, where 'the plot and the theme [are] actually one thing, namely, that the same intellectual honesty that is essential to scholarship is essential also to the conduct of life' (1937b: 87).

Returning to Oxford for the first time since she has graduated, Harriet attends a Gaudy with her old friends and colleagues. Receiving a poison letter, but thinking that it is simply one of the myriads that has plagued her since her trial, Harriet dismisses the incident from her mind. Then, she is asked by the Dean of her old Oxford College, Miss Martin, to investigate cases of vandalism and poison-pen letters, which have been happening with alarming frequency at the women's college:

> We should be very glad to have your advice […] Not that one expects a detective novelist to be a practical policeman; but I know that you have taken part in one real investigation, and I feel sure you know a lot more than we do about tracking down malefactors. (Sayers [1935] 1949: 58)

Harriet 'smiles wryly' over the Dean's letter, which innocently references Harriet detecting abilities from 'the benefit of [her] experience' and gives little thought as to whether this is an insensitive thing to say. The 'worldly knowledge' that Sayers lamented as lacking in the 'young and inexperienced woman detective', is ascribed to Harriet; she possesses knowledge and experience, not only from being a successful author with a degree from Oxford, but also from having a lover, from being acquitted from the gallows, and from participating—albeit as sidekick to Lord Peter—in solving a case of her own. Though the Dean's letter lacked tact, the Dean was able to see that Harriet possessed the abilities and experience—notwithstanding her reputation—that made her the most fitting candidate to do the required detective work.

After Harriet learns that Miss Climpson is engaged elsewhere on a case, Harriet then becomes a fully-fledged detective in *Gaudy Night*. She is able to successfully take care of herself, and she thus moves away from the protected sidekick figure that she manifested in *Have His Carcase*. She is also the direct contrast to typical female detectives lamented by Sayers (1929: 15). Indeed, Harriet saves herself from possible harm, recalling Peter's disgust at distressed heroines in thrillers:

> She remembered Peter's saying to her one day: 'The heroines of thrillers deserve all they get. When a mysterious voice rings them up and says it is Scotland Yard, they never think of ringing back to verify the call. Hence the prevalence of kidnapping.' (Sayers [1935] 1949: 277)

Additionally, Harriet also learns to defend herself, sparring with Peter to withstand potential attacks (Sayers [1935] 1949: 286). This ends up saving her life after she is attacked by the poison-pen author, who, at the end of the novel, becomes almost driven to a frenzy in her quest for revenge.

What seems to be most important for Harriet's progression to 'detective', however, is the confidence Peter places in her abilities and his refusal to behave as an over-protective male. This is growth in the character of Peter, as well as Harriet, as Peter learns to give Harriet space and not fly to her side once he learns she is in potential danger. Harriet herself acknowledges this new aspect of Peter's character as she contemplates how to solve the vandalism in *Gaudy Night*:

> More generously still, he had not only refrained from offers of help and advice which she might have resented; he had deliberately acknowledged that she had the right to run her own risks. 'Do be careful of yourself';

> 'I hate to think of your being exposed to unpleasantness'; 'If only I could be there to protect you'; any such phrase would express the normal male reaction. Not one man in ten thousand would say to the woman he loved, or to any woman: 'Disagreeableness and danger will not turn you back, and God forbid they should.' That was an *admission of equality*, and she had not expected it of him. (my emphasis, Sayers [1935] 1949: 166)

While Harriet's full detective abilities in part seem to stem from her treatment by Peter, and his refraining from coming to protect her as he did in *Have His Carcase* (where she was then placed in the sidekick role), this is further evidence on how Sayers worked into her fiction a discussion of equality, as well as playing with the sidekick role of the detective genre. Harriet became a sidekick in *Have His Carcase* partly from her lack of confidence, but mostly because she was placed in that role by Lord Peter. In *Gaudy Night*, she briefly becomes a detective, sees herself as equal to Peter, and successfully navigates her personal life, because she is finally and fully offered dignity and equality by Peter.

Though Harriet ultimately asks Peter for help in solving the vandalism at Oxford, this does not diminish her equality with him. Her intelligence and skills are highlighted through her own unique talents of being a detective fiction author and scholar. Harriet presents Peter with her notes and he admires her organization: 'I'll say one thing for the writing of detective fiction: you know how to put your story together; how to arrange the evidence' (Sayers [1935] 1949: 222). Thus, Harriet's variously competing roles of detective, sidekick, writer and love interest to Peter finally come to terms with one another at the end of *Gaudy Night*. Her status as equal partner, scholar and accomplished writer allows Sayers to address women's roles in the professional world, and the necessity of bringing women into the professional sphere.

Harriet and Peter's progression towards mutual recognition of equality transcends the pairs' abilities as detectives; it is also tied to their romantic relationship. The equality in their love partnership thus further blurs the line between Harriet's portrayal as both detective and sidekick as the novels work through their multifaceted relationships. Though Peter had always acknowledged Harriet as an equal and as the woman he hoped to marry, it is only once Harriet recognizes that he *also* acknowledges her as an equal *detective*, he no longer forces her into the sidekick role, that she is finally able to actually marry him. Once married, they become true equals, and ultimately fully solve a case together, as a married couple, in *Busman's Honeymoon* ([1937a] 1976).

Busman's Honeymoon, or 'A Love Story with Detective Interruptions', fully highlights the importance of equality and the importance of mutual respect that Peter and Harriet have for one another. Spending their honeymoon in their new home, they find the corpse of the previous owner in the cellar the day after their wedding night there. Grappling with learning to live together, while simultaneously solving a case for the first time as true partners, there are many scenes and discussions of what this means for Harriet and Peter in their married life. A culminating scene comes towards the close of the case, as Harriet realizes that in finding the murder, her husband becomes a hangman. Finding the truth is what matters to them both, but she does not know if she can be so intimately connected with the man who ultimately sends murderers to the gallows. Peter declares that 'Well, Harriet, we are married now. We are bound, I'm afraid the moment has come when something will have to give way—you, or I—or the bond' (Sayers [1937a] 1976: 343). Their argument continues, until Peter offers to give up detecting:

> His voice was the voice of a beaten man. She was appalled, seeing what she had done.
> Peter, you're mad. Never dare to suggest such a thing. Whatever marriage is, it isn't that.
> Isn't what, Harriet?
> Letting your affection corrupt your judgement. What kind of life could we have if I knew that you had becomes less than yourself by marrying me? […]You *must* do what you think right. Promise me that. What I think doesn't matter. I swear it shall never make any difference.
> He took her hand and kissed it gravely.
> Thank you, Harriet. That is love with honour.
> They stood so for a moment; both conscious that something had been achieved that was of enormous – of overmastering importance. (Sayers [1937a] 1976: 343–344)

The thing of overmastering importance is their acknowledgement of the judgement and worth of the other and the other's opinion. Their equal partnership, coming at the end of their growth of character through their four novels together, highlights Sayers's emphasis on equality between the sexes, and the importance of recognizing the qualities and worth of another person, as well as their specific individual talents both in their private and professional spheres.

Conclusion

Across the Lord Peter Wimsey novels, Sayers thus manages to effectively play with the detective genre's conventions of roles—having fluctuating sidekicks and detectives—while at the same time inserting her own commentary for equality between the sexes: the importance of recognizing the potential and abilities of even those who are unconsidered by society, such as the superfluous spinsters or the women who do not preform to their gender. Peter hires Miss Climpson for her 'magnificent abilities' and is able to fully respect her without the complication of personal feelings. And the respect that Peter offers Miss Climpson—acknowledging her intelligence and her ability to do her job—is the same respect that Harriet realizes he fully offers to her in *Gaudy Night*.

While Miss Climpson's roles as detective and sidekick remain strictly professional, they thus open the space for Harriet Vane's character and the social conversation she embodies, to become aligned with and eventually come to supersede the detective plot. Sayers includes discussion of Harriet's professional and personal life. Therefore, though Harriet's marriage to Peter has been criticized as undermining the strong woman that she was originally portrayed to be, through her marriage Harriet is actually able to finally bring herself to an equal level with Peter, not as needing to be rescued and not needing to remain as love interest (as she is in *Strong Poison*), not as a sidekick (as she is in *Have His Carcase*), not as a detective (as she is in *Gaudy Night*), but rather, as Harriet realizes at the end of *Gaudy Night*, as a true partner (as she finally becomes in *Busman's Honeymoon*). Thus, while Kathleen Gregory Klein argues that the parameters of Golden Age detective fiction helped to keep the position of women in society unchanged and that it 'reaffirmed the old rules for women's behaviour' and therefore controlled 'the reading public's perceptions of women' (1995: 121), I contend that Sayers' writing directly contradicts Klein's argument. Sayers created female characters whose fluctuating roles as sidekicks and detectives expand the conventions of the detective genre.

Her additional portrayal of the dignity and respect offered to these characters in their professional and private spheres successfully challenges both the detective fiction characters' conventions as well as the prevailing social constructions and perceptions of women in her society.

Notes

1. Miss Climpson is introduced as Miss Alexandra Katherine Climpson in *Unnatural Death* ([1927] 1947: 31). In *Strong Poison*, however, her name is written as Miss Katharine Climpson ([1930] 1960: 40).
2. See 'Are Women Human?' and 'The Human-Not-Quite-Human' for further evidence of Sayers's views on the relationship between women and men and women's place in the workplace.
3. Sayers explains that the Detection Club was 'a private association of writers of detective fiction in Great Britain, existing chiefly for the purpose of eating dinners together at suitable intervals and of talking illimitable shop [...] If there is any serious aim behind [it], it is to keep the detective story up to the highest standard that its nature permits, and to free it from the bad legacy of sensationalism, clap-trap and jargon with which it was unhappily burdened in the past' ([1931] 2011: 1–2).

Reference Lists

Berglund, Birgitta. 2000. Desires and Devices: On Women Detectives in Fiction. In *The Art of Detective Fiction*, ed. Warren Chernaik, Martin Swales, and Robert Vilain, 138–152. New York, NY: St. Martin's Press.

Bredesen, Dagni. 2010. Introduction. In *The First Female Detectives: The Female Detective (1864) and Revelations of a Lady Detective (1864)*, ed. Dagni Bredesen, i–xxix. Ann Arbor, MI: Scholars' Facsimiles & Reprints.

Campbell, SueEllen. 1995. The Detective Heroine and the Death of Her Hero: Dorothy Sayers to P.D. James. In *Feminism in Women's Detective Fiction*, ed. Glenwood Irons, 12–28. Toronto, ON: University of Toronto Press.

Christie, Agatha. (1930) 1976. *The Murder at the Vicarage*. In *Sleeping Murder & The Murder at the Vicarage*, 172–379. New York, NY: Dodd, Mead & Company.

Doyle, Arthur Conan. (1887) 1987. *A Study in Scarlet*. In *The Complete Illustrated Sherlock Holmes*, 13-53. United Kingdom: Omega Books.

Forrester Jr., Andrew. (1864) 2010. *The Female Detective*. In *The First Female Detectives: The Female Detective (1864) and Revelations of a Lady Detective (1864)*, ed. Dagni Bredesen, 1–164. Ann Arbor, MI: Scholars' Facsimiles & Reprints.

Joannou, Maroula. 1995. *'Ladies, Please Don't Smash These Windows': Women's Writing, Feminist Consciousness and Social Change 1918–38*. Oxford: Berg Publishers.

———. 1999. The Woman Writer in the 1930s—On Not Being Mrs. Giles of Durham City. In *Women Writers of the 1930s: Gender, Politics, and History*, ed. Maroula Joannoa, 1–15. Great Britain: Edinburgh University Press.

Kestner, Joseph. 2003. *Sherlock's Sisters: The British Female Detective, 1864–1913*. England: Ashgate Publishing Ltd.

Klein, Kathleen Gregory. 1995. *The Woman Detective: Gender and Genre*, 2nd ed. Urbana, IL: University of Illinois Press.

Lewis, Jane. 1984. *Women in England 1870–1950: Sexual Divisions and Social Change*. Sussex: Wheatsheaf Books.

Sayers, Dorothy L. (1926) 1972. *Clouds of Witness*. London: New English Library.

———. (1927) 1947. *Unnatural Death*. London: Victor Gollancz Inc.

———. 1929. Introduction. In *The Omnibus of Crime*, ed. Dorothy L. Sayers, 9–46. New York, NY: Harcourt, Brace and Company.

———. (1930) 1960. *Strong Poison*. London: Landsborough Publications Limited.

———. (1931) 2011. Introduction. In *The Floating Admiral, Certain Members of the Detection Club*, 1–3. London: HarperCollins *Publishers* Ltd.

———. (1932) 1976. *Have His Carcase*. London: Victor Gollancz Ltd.

———. (1935) 1949. *Gaudy Night*. London: Victor Gollancz Ltd.

———. (1936) 2012. Aristotle on Detective Fiction. In *The Philosophy of Sherlock Holmes*, ed. Philip Tallon and David Baggett, 167–180. Lexington, KY: University Press of Kentucky.

———. (1937a) 1976. *Busman's Honeymoon*. London: Victor Gollancz LTD.

———. 1937b. Gaudy Night. In *Titles to Frame*, ed. Denys Kilham Roberts, 73–95. London: Thomas Nelson & Sons Ltd.

———. (1938) 1946. Are Women Human? In *Unpopular Opinions*. Dorothy L. Sayers, 106–115, London: Victor Gollancz Ltd.

———. (1942) 1982. Talboys. In *Striding Folly*. Dorothy L. Sayers, 91–124, Canada: New English Library.

———. 1946. The Human-Not-Quite-Human. In *Unpopular Opinions*. Dorothy L. Sayers, 116–122, London: Victor Gollancz Ltd.

Symons, Julian. 1972. *Bloody Murder*. Great Britain: Penguin Books.

Trembley, Elizabeth A. 1995. Collaring the Other Fellow's Property: Feminism Reads Dorothy L. Sayers. In *Women Times Three: Writers, Detectives, Readers*, ed. Kathleen Gregory Klein, 81–100. Bowling Green, OH: Bowling Green State University Popular Press.

Wallace, Diana. 1999. Revising the Marriage Plot in Women's Fiction of the 1930s. In *Women Writers of the 1930s: Gender, Politics, and History*, ed. Maroula Joannoa, 63–75. Edinburgh: Edinburgh University Press.
Wodehouse, P.G. 1977. Forward. In *Rex Stout: A Biography*, John McAleer, xv–xvi. Toronto, OH: Little, Brown and Company.
Young, Laurel. 2005. Dorothy L. Sayers and the New Woman Detective Novel. *Clues* 23: 39–53. http://search.proquest.com.proxy.lib.uwaterloo.ca/docview/2152713506?accountid=14906. Accessed 7 Mar 2018.

CHAPTER 8

'Pretty, but Not so Pretty…': Marlowe's Female Sidekicks and the Domestication of Hard-Boiled Detective Fiction

Alexander N. Howe

Introduction

> There were sounds of strangled fury as I hung up on him. Almost immediately the telephone started to ring again. I hardly heard it. The air was full of music. (Chandler [1958] 2002b: 971)

American detective fiction is typified by the hardboiled school that often features a lone investigator or solitary private eye. It is far from accidental that one of the first actions in Dashiell Hammett's *The Maltese Falcon* (1930), not the first but arguably one of the most widely recognized early hardboiled novels, is to kill off Sam Spade's partner, Miles Archer. Certainly, a 'partner' is not exactly a 'sidekick', but the point to be taken is that the very idea of collaboration and investigative partnership in American detective fiction is problematic. In this chapter, I argue that Raymond

A. N. Howe (✉)
University of the District of Columbia, Washington, DC, USA

L. Andrew and S. Saunders (eds.), *The Detective's Companion in Crime Fiction*, Crime Files, https://doi.org/10.1007/978-3-030-74989-7_8

Chandler counted this limitation among the many problems presented by the hardboiled genre, which was already well-established when he began writing in 1933. Interestingly, he chooses to re-examine the sidekick, a common feature of the classic detective story, in the form of two women: Anne Riordan from *Farewell, My Lovely* (1940) and Linda Loring from *The Long Goodbye* (1953), *Playback* (1958), and *Poodle Springs* (1962, 1989). Riordan is a fascinating and able investigator herself, while Loring becomes Philip Marlowe's wife, a narrative arc unheard of in hardboiled fiction of the time. These female sidekicks, while untraditional, allow Chandler to reach beyond the limits of the hardboiled genre and illuminate the often insular masculine perspective of Marlowe's ongoing critique of American experience, thus setting a significant precedent for subsequent hardboiled fiction.

It almost goes without saying that Arthur Conan Doyle's John H. Watson, Sherlock Holmes's unswerving attendant and chronicler, is the stereotypical sidekick. He is a relatively competent assistant who serves as the reader's surrogate in the story and documents the brilliance of the great detective. While we try (and fail) to keep up with the masterful detective, we simultaneously identify with the sidekick and know that we are just a bit smarter—a point made as early as by Ronald Knox in his seminal work, 'Studies in the Literature of Sherlock Holmes'. Holmes's gruff dismissal of Watson's confusion, and other character traits, is a fixture of the narratives; however, the two friends clearly have a deep affection and respect for one another. Amusingly, Rex Stout went so far as to claim that 'Watson Was a Woman' in a lecture given in (1941) in New York City to the famous Holmesian group, The Baker Street Irregulars. His reasoning for this conclusion is all the more delightful: the Holmes-Watson relationship has all the hallmarks of a bad marriage. This is, argues Stout, found especially in Watson's ambition to 'understand' Holmes and his keen interest in domestic details. Though unmentioned by Stout, key aspects that support this (literal) feminization of Watson undoubtedly include his emotion and 'romanticism'—a complaint Holmes repeats regarding Watson's writing (Doyle [1891] 1992: 90). This argument is pushed further when Stout claims that 'A Scandal in Bohemia' actually depicts Holmes meeting his future wife, Irene Watson, significantly undercutting one of the most interesting women in all of detective fiction.

Stout's playful theory is obviously meant as a lark, but it reveals a commonplace reduction of the Watsonian counterpart, or sidekick, to a doddering old man, in the vein of Nigel Bruce from the Sherlock

Holmes films of the 1930s and 1940s. Looking at the source texts with more care, Watson is actually a far more able partner, skilled in analysis and diagnosis—a basic requirement of his profession as a doctor. The back and forth between the sidekick and detective, in which the sidekick voices questions shared by the reader, has become a ubiquitous tool of exposition in a majority of texts using this narrative device. More recent television adaptations of the Holmes stories, particularly *Elementary* on CBS (2012–2019) and the BBC's *Sherlock* (2010–2017), have done a far better job of reaffirming Watson's skill and merit. For example, in *Elementary*, Lucy Liu plays Joan Watson, Holmes's physician and accomplice, and develops a more equitable and largely platonic partnership with the detective, something that has remained a difficult feat in the masculine space of detective fiction.

The greater power of the sidekick that adopts this standard Watsonian pattern is often missed: the sidekick is an author. Though constantly bested by the detective, and often by the reader, the sidekick is a proficient and often-artful writer. Watson's personality has become the gold standard for this character, but of course, Doyle borrowed the structure from Edgar Allan Poe's stories featuring the detective C. Auguste Dupin, published between 1841 and 1844. The narrator of the Dupin tales is nameless and figures less prominently than Watson; however, many critics have correctly argued that Dupin's counterpart is his equal (Lewis 1990: 100), as the sidekick's art (writing) is ingeniously silent, much like Dupin's own ratiocination. Indeed, Jacques Derrida suggested that discounting the narrator was a key misstep in Jacques Lacan's own allegorical reading of 'The Purloined Letter' (Johnson 1988: 221–222). Poe draws close attention to his narrator's doubling (or sharing) of the detective's literary skills. The two meet at 'an obscure library in the Rue Montmartre' and are in fact 'in search of the same very rare and very remarkable volume', and later they share a residence and spend their days in a 'book-closet' both 'reading, writing, or conversing' ([1841] 1975: 144, 208). Poe's narrator is more literary than Doyle's Watson, reminding us of the power of authorship; however, the more middle-class appeal of the doctor and the clearer systematization of mystery surely account for the greater success of the Holmes-Watson template.

These characteristics of the sidekick are developed throughout the Golden Age of detective fiction by authors such as Agatha Christie, Dorothy L. Sayers, and Rex Stout; however, they are significantly displaced with the emergence of hardboiled detective fiction in the 1920 and 1930s, which is fundamentally a chronicle of the crisis in white masculinity in America at the beginning of the twentieth century in the face of rapid social changes. In the essay 'The Simple Art of Murder' (1944), Chandler declares that this new fiction is about language and 'rude wit', but it is wise to remember that the hardboiled hero who 'down these mean streets must go [...] neither tarnished, nor afraid' is at the same time solitary and 'lonely' ([1944] 1972: 20, 21). John G. Cawelti suggests that an emphasis upon 'personal choice and action' distinguishes the hardboiled from the law and order of classic detective story (1976: 142), a turn to individualism in response to the chaos and injustices of the new American city. It is unsurprising, then, that the sidekick is lost initially in this format, as this character inevitably speaks to community and connection. This shift might be typified by Chandler's choice to use first-person narration in the Marlowe stories, which make the efficacies of a sidekick narrator structurally impossible: the reader no longer has an intermediary (or rival), and the detective's authority is no longer supported by the faith of the sidekick. Narratives are now told ostensibly in real time, without the protective post hoc ordering that was the Watsonian art, leaving the detective all the more isolated and vulnerable.

Chandler's Marlowe is perhaps the loneliest of the 'lone wolf' detectives ([1942] 2002a: 548). Nearly all of the novels open with Marlowe sitting alone in his office reflecting upon his work and, often, the degraded state of his contemporary California. He has neither secretary nor sidekick, and moments when he reflects upon cases with other characters are few and far between. Unlike the fair play found in the classic story, a bulk of Marlowe's reasoning occurs offstage—still alone and out of the reader's view. The great threat to Marlowe's relative safety is women, a danger true of most hardboiled fiction. Much has been written about Marlowe's infamously strict knightly code and its concomitant misogyny, and as critics identified early on, for Marlowe, women fall into a familiar strict juxtaposition of the Madonna and whore. As Megan Abbott summarizes, '[Marlowe's] masculinity obtains in his refusal to contaminate himself, refusal to involve himself sexually with a woman. Masculine means a hermetically separated space constituted in opposition to the feminine' (2002: 54). Not all Marlowe's women are, as Abbott concedes, plundering vamps, but all women must remain 'untouchable' in some way (2002: 54). Obviously lacking a Watsonian sidekick or partner—that is, genuine male camaraderie—the hardboiled detective's solitary existence is threatened all the more by female contagion.

Chandler himself was well aware of the failings of this position, and much scholarship has been written about Marlowe's own critical self-reflection through humour, wit and what Scott Christianson has called 'hardboiled conceit'—pointed, often-jarring metaphors and similes used in an effort to organize the chaos of modern experience through a 'direct assertion of power through language' (1989: 158). However, equally as important to Chandler's criticism of mid-century masculinity is his return to the device of the sidekick through two women in the series: Anne Riordan, who serves as a more traditional collaborator, and Linda Loring, who ultimately becomes Marlowe's wife. Admittedly, regarding this latter development, Dashiell Hammett established some precedent with his husband and wife crime-solving team, Nick and Nora Charles in *The Thin Man* (1934). Hammett was a great experimenter with genre, and the largely comic story of *The Thin Man* is no exception. Marlowe's characterization actually owes a good deal to Nick Charles. The latter is world-weary, yet sharp and self-effacing, particularly about his profession, typified in his famous comment at the end of the novel: 'Murder doesn't round out anybody's life except the murdered's and sometimes the murderer's' (Hammett [1934] 1992: 201). Nora Charles, though limited by her role as wife to the detective, is an able sidekick and is penetratingly insightful. Indeed, Hammett gives Nora the final line of his career as a novelist: '[I]t's all pretty unsatisfactory' ([1934] 1992: 201), a comment on her husband's summation of the case and the detective genre itself. While Marlowe is inevitably more critical about his own authority (and story), Chandler similarly places final judgment in the hands of his female sidekicks.

Anne Riordan

Anne Riordan first appears in *Farewell, My Lovely*—only the second Marlowe novel—and she accomplishes the unprecedented task in hardboiled fiction of becoming the detective's collaborator and undesired sidekick. Like many critics, Abbott reads Riordan as a 'Gal Friday' character and another of Marlowe's untouchable women (2002: 54). She is the daughter of the former (honest) police chief of Bay City, which immediately provides her entrée into Marlowe's world. She possesses a sharp flirtatious wit, but is quick to blush when sexualized comments cross a line. Riordan is appropriately introduced after Marlowe is knocked unconscious early in the novel, a signature Chandlerian trope that emphasizes that rationality, or 'using one's head', is not necessarily the key to success. We do not see Riordan initially, rather we hear her laugh at the unconscious Marlowe whom she finds lying next to a dead man. Though she initially quavers, her voice becomes strong: 'It meant what it said', as Marlowe observes ([1940] 2002a: 256). Importantly, Riordan repeatedly asks Marlowe for his 'story' ([1940] 2002a: 256). As with all good sidekicks, she herself will help develop this story, which is clear in her own hard-bitten bravado. In this first meeting, Riordan's forceful questions repeatedly best the detective, who replies, 'I get it. You ask the answers. He-man stuff' ([1940] 2002a: 256).

Riordan begins the larger investigation of the novel herself through some unrequested sleuthing, which effectively results in her becoming Marlowe's unsolicited sidekick. Her inquiries lead her, with Marlowe in tow, from the murdered man, petty criminal Lindsay Marriott, to Helen Grayle and her husband Lewin Lockridge Grayle. Marriott had hired Marlowe to help ransom a jade necklace that had been stolen from Mrs. Grayle. Grayle, at Riordan's insistence, ultimately hires Marlowe to find the still-missing necklace. Riordan is thus responsible for beginning the initial case of the novel, which then allows Marlowe to investigate the connections between the theft and Moose Malloy's search for his lost girlfriend, Velma Valento. At the conclusion of the novel, Velma confesses to everything: turning Malloy over to the police and sending him to prison; using Marriott to keep the Florians from exposing her, now a woman of means, as a former low-class singer; and conspiring to have Marriott (and Marlowe) killed. When Malloy comes forward to embrace her despite her treachery, she shoots him twice in the heart and escapes only to take her own life several months later in Baltimore when cornered by the police. In the concluding lines of the novel, in a conversation with Lieutenant Randall, Marlowe recalls *Othello* and suggests that Velma/Helen killed herself to save Mr. Grayle from the embarrassment of a trial. She knew that Grayle 'loved not wisely, but too well' and wished to spare him, which Randall dismisses as 'just sentimental' ([1940] 2002a: 442). Marlowe concedes the point and calls his theory 'Probably all a mistake anyway', and the more logical Riordan would undoubtedly agree ([1940] 2002a: 442).

As Gill Plain has pointed out, Marlowe's sentimental reading, which reduces the hardboiled novel to a tragic love story, figures the greater tension of the novel between mythologized masculine ideals set against the forbidden feminine (2001: 62). The hulking Moose Malloy represents this ideal—and he is 'worth looking at', as Marlowe notes ([1940] 2002a: 201)—and naturally Grayle/Valento signifies its greatest threat. Plain further argues that sensuality appears in Chandler's work 'predominantly in the depiction of men,' a defence mechanism in support of Marlowe's stilted erotics, with which 'the impossibility of the consummation of desire is redoubled' (2001: 62). The reasoning here is obviously sound; however, Anne Riordan also has an odd place in this mythology. Her hardboiled quips and firm questions of Marlowe already code her as somewhat masculine, which curiously destabilizes Marlowe's typical prohibitions. Reflecting at the office the next day, Marlowe comments on less attractive aspects of Riordan's appearance, such as her 'narrow forehead', 'small and inquisitive' nose, an upper lip 'a shade too long', and a mouth 'a shade too wide'; however, he admits, 'She had a nice smile. She looked as if she had slept well. It was a nice face, a face you get to like. Pretty, but not so pretty that you would have to wear brass knuckles every time you took it out' ([1940] 2002a: 270–271). Her 'small' and 'inquisitive' nose recalls Holmes's 'hawklike' nose, a comparison confirmed when Riordan claims to have 'a strain of bloodhound' ([1940] 2002a: 273) in her, which likewise recalls the description of Holmes as a 'sleuth-hound' ([1891] 1992: 185). She is openly aware that this is unladylike, and tempers her claim: 'Oh I know I'm just a damned inquisitive wench' ([1940] 2002a: 273). Her masculine coding appears again as Marlowe reviews her apartment. We are told that: 'There was nothing womanish in the room except a full length mirror with a clear sweep of floor in front of it' ([1940] 2002a: 351). But Riordan at the same time is ever-playful with Marlowe, suggesting that she is likewise interested in him in a way that is unique to his experiences with women.

Riordan's great affinity with Watson is the fact that she is a writer, one of the first details revealed to Marlowe as she holds him at gunpoint during their first meeting. As she states, 'Strange how curious people can be, isn't it? I write a little. Feature articles' ([1940] 2002a: 260). The self-effacement here needs to be taken with a grain of salt, as she utters this just after putting her gun back in her pocket—this after Marlowe returns it to her. Just as the hardboiled speech of men, her words likewise promise a violent, yet productive force. Riordan's power of authorship is most visible in her snide criticism of Marlowe and his role as a detective—a task that typically falls upon Marlowe himself in his narration. In a heated moment early on, Riordan scolds Marlowe, saying, 'Probably you'd like me to mind my own business, is that it? And not have ideas you don't have first. I thought I was helping a little' ([1940] 2002a: 313). Marlowe claims that he needs no help, but in a later scene at Riordan's apartment—which becomes his '[s]anctuary' ([1940] 2002a: 350)—the sidekick's value is resoundingly apparent. Importantly, Riordan has a pencil behind her ear as Marlowe arrives staggering and drugged after escaping Dr. Sonderberg's liquor-cure facility. Presumably, she was hard at work on a project before Marlowe arrived; however, so too is she now effectively prepared to get the latest version of Marlowe's story. Marlowe is hurt and weakened, but Riordan does not demure to a simple motherly role. She offers prodding questions and conclusions about the case, along with wise-cracks at Marlowe's stubbornness and the apparent 'indecency' of a 'simple case' for the detective ([1940] 2002a: 353).

In the midst of this dazed back-and-forth, Marlowe and Riordan have a productive moment of collaboration thinking through the psychic Jules Amthor's connection with Lindsay Marriott. Her impatience with Marlowe in this exchange cements her role as author: 'Why the thing stands out so far you could break off a yard of it and still have enough left for a baseball bat' ([1940] 2002a: 352). Marlowe is impressed: 'I ought to have said that one', I said. 'Just my style. Crude. What sticks out?' ([1940] 2002a: 352). Even Marlowe must recognize the sharpness of Riordan's Chandlerian metaphor, and here and elsewhere, Riordan's linguistic talents do in fact order the chaos of the narrative. Riordan's playful impatience has marked their collaboration from the beginning. For example, at the start of the case when Riordan arranges a meeting for her and Marlowe with Helen Grayle, Riordan overstays her welcome—Grayle clearly wishes to be alone with Marlowe—asking questions about the stolen necklace. Finally leaving the house, she waits for Marlowe in the driveway to debrief with him. He initially offers only suggestive comments about the interview, forcing Riordan to steer the investigation and direct his attention back to important details and additional leads. Here again, she keeps pace with Marlowe, in both insight and insolence: 'Sometimes I hate men. Old men, young men, football players, opera tenors, smart millionaires, beautiful men who are gigolos and almost-heels who are – private detectives' ([1940] 2002a: 313).

All of these characteristics undeniably cast Riordan as masculine and thus unthreatening. However, she is not completely untouchable in the manner that critics have claimed. In the conversation at her apartment, Riordan suggests, with eyes 'a little sly' ([1940] 2002a: 354), that

Marlowe spend the night at her house to recuperate. While seduction is likely not on her mind, she is infuriated when Marlowe accuses her of this and refuses to stay. She drives him home 'like a fury', a description more in keeping with Marlowe's other women ([1940] 2002a: 356). Riordan's ambiguity is further apparent when read against the numerous jibes about marriage which appear in *Farewell, My Lovely*—more than any of the other novels and most in response to Riordan. At her house, Marlowe jokes, 'A fellow could settle down here... Move right in. Everything set for him', to which Riordan responds: 'If he was that kind of fellow. And anybody wanted him to' ([1940] 2002a: 352). This is already common sparring for the two; however, as he leaves the apartment, he again reviews the living room: 'I looked back a moment before I closed the door. It was a nice room. It would be a nice room to wear slippers in' ([1940] 2002a: 355).

Riordan thus offers the temptation of domesticity, something that is far more appealing to Marlowe than he himself is ready to admit. Near the conclusion of the novel, in this same intimate space, the two share a summation of the case over drinks, in the manner of Holmes and Watson. She curses at Marlowe, asking to be kissed (the detective refuses), and chides him for not explaining the Moose Malloy dimension of the case, as she would have that known Grayle was Valento 'right away' ([1940] 2002a: 436, 439). Riordan's complaint has been shared by countless Chandler readers throughout the years, as Marlowe's greatest deductions all too often occur off-stage, as it were, and make use of unshared details. Through this shared irritation, the reader identifies all the more with Riordan. Dennis Porter argues that Riordan 'posed a problem for Chandler that he was unable to solve satisfactorily within the terms of the hard-boiled formula and its myths' (1981: 187). From this perspective, Marlowe must forsake Riordan, lest a more intimate relationship topple her from the detective's idealizations (Madden 1998: 8). However, Chandler's greatest talent as an author was pushing beyond the limits of the genre through Marlowe's irony, and this is certainly on display throughout the detective's acquaintance with Riordan—frequently, via Riordan's own comments on the absurdity of Marlowe's romantic reservations. It is little wonder, then, that Chandler said that Riordan was 'the kind of girl Marlowe would have married, had he been the marrying kind' (qtd. Durham 1963: 39).

Linda Loring

Linda Loring, from *The Long Goodbye*, Chandler's final completed Marlowe novel, is the woman that Marlowe ultimately does marry. Indeed, while Porter may well be correct that Riordan was a 'problem' that Chandler could not unravel, Loring is a daring solution to this dilemma attempted by the author—one that deserves far more attention in criticism than it has hitherto received. Loring is the daughter of the exorbitantly wealthy Harlan Potter, who made his fortune in newspapers, among other things ([1953] 2002b: 515). Like Riordan, Loring is blunt, diligent and inquisitive, although she does not have the investigative abilities or aspirations of her predecessor. Also like Riordan, Loring is a departure from Marlowe's other women, as she is neither an idealized 'glossy' version of love, nor a monstrous siren. Importantly, Loring is also the sister-in-law of Terry Lennox, the man with whom Marlowe develops a deep, sentimental and infamous friendship that is ultimately betrayed. She and Lennox, then, offer a reversal of the man–woman pairing more common to the series: here the woman is ultimately chosen as an object of desire—and Marlowe does indeed consummate a relationship with Loring—while the man, Lennox, is rejected. Though Marlowe's reaction to Lennox's betrayal is in many ways childish and melodramatic, the connection, understanding and sympathy that Marlowe imagines he finds in him are ultimately found in Loring.

While she is not the gumshoe character that Riordan is, Loring sees through Marlowe and matches his wit with ease. Whereas Riordan—with a good deal of frustration and wit—attempted to understand Marlowe, Loring actually succeeds. This fact is already on display during Loring's first conversation with Marlowe when she astutely accuses him of being a 'bit of a sentimentalist' for coming to the bar he used to frequent with Terry for a gimlet in his honor ([1953] 2002b: 614). This meeting was in fact the result of Loring's own detective work, as she wished to track down the man who helped Terry escape to Mexico after the murder of her sister, Sylvia Lennox. She and Marlowe discuss the details of Terry's apparent suicide, and Loring's deductive powers are increasingly evident as she and Marlowe reconstruct probable events from that night, and she persuasively corrects Marlowe's theory regarding Terry's motive ([1953] 2002b: 616). Naturally, their conversation contains plenty of sparring, and at evening's end Marlowe suggests that they had 'quite a fight', to which Loring offers an incisive retort worthy of the detective: 'You mean you had – and mostly with yourself' ([1953] 2002b: 621).

The next day Loring visits Marlowe at his office and offers all the familiar quips regarding his profession and workplace. She arranges a meeting for Marlowe with her father which takes place shortly after their first conversation—Marlowe actually meets the parents, as it were—and she correctly identifies that the $5000 dollar bill that Marlowe has in his office belonged to Lennox and further deduces that it was Marlowe who drove him to Tijuana to escape from the suspicion that he murdered his wife ([1953] 2002b: 671). Sean McCann suggests that the $5000 bill represents many of the novel's preoccupations, particularly the 'decadent wealth and dangerous abundance of the postwar world', which threatens to reduce Lennox's generosity and friendship to a cheap bribe and a disposable commodity rather than a unique human connection (2000: 180). McCann argues that Marlowe defeats this danger by refusing to spend the note; rather, he keeps it as a token of his friendship with Lennox, calling it his 'portrait of Madison', a phrase and meaning that only he understands, according to McCann (2000: 181). The reading of this gesture is undeniably accurate; however, Linda Loring understands immediately its significance for Marlowe, quite apart from simple bribe. What is interesting about this particular scene is that Loring correctly reads, and preemptively solves, the larger case. She asks Marlowe if Terry gave him a list of Silvia's (his murdered wife's) lovers, and more pointedly asks if the drunken author Roger Wade was on that list, as only a 'lunatic or savage drunk' could have so brutally murdered Silvia ([1953] 2002b: 671). Further, Linda sees through Marlowe's suggestion that he has taken the case only because Wade's publisher has asked that Wade be kept sober long enough to finish a book. Loring understands and respects that Marlowe does it out of a sense of obligation to Terry. Importantly, in the midst of this sparring, Marlowe accuses Linda of 'getting pretty corny' ([1953] 2002b: 673) in her overly dramatic ridicule of Marlowe's talent and his debt to Terry, which is likewise keenly perceptive given Marlowe's pained sentiment at the end of the novel.

Loring is not the writer that Riordan is; however there is a moment near the end of the novel that links her more directly with Riordan as a sidekick. She warns Marlowe about his safety and Eileen Wade's accusations that he effectively killed her husband Roger through negligence. She asks if he knows how they shoot tigers:

> 'They tie a goat to a stake and then hide out in a blind. It's apt to be rough on the goat. I like you. I'm sure I don't know why, but I do. I hate the idea of you being the goat. You tried so hard to do the right thing – as you saw it'. ([1953] 2002b: 783)

As Riordan before her, Loring uses an overwrought Chandlerian metaphor, importantly during a conversation in which she asks Marlowe to run away with her to Paris—thus inviting a drastic revision to Marlowe's own narrative. He refuses, but the two meet again at the end of the novel and famously go to bed together after some playful flirting and champagne. When Marlowe and Loring at long last embrace, Linda is 'without a trace of acting or affectation' and 'starry-eyed' ([1953] 2002b: 800). The celestial hyperbole notwithstanding, Marlowe has opened his hermetically separated masculinity to another, and the consequences for the genre will prove to be vast.

The chapter after their tryst is, incredibly, entirely about marriage, and it begins with Loring proposing to Marlowe, who responds by saying that 'it wouldn't last six months' ([1953] 2002b: 801). Marlowe's observations about American marriage are typically comical and interestingly focus on domestic space: 'twenty years all the [husband] has left is a work bench in the garage. American girls are terrific. American wives take in too damn much territory' ([1953] 2002b: 802). Loring matches Marlowe's sarcasm, but she does finally break down in tears and retorts, 'Suppose it lasted six months or a year or two years. What would you have lost except the dust on your office desk and the dirt on your venetian blinds and the loneliness of a pretty empty kind of life?' ([1953] 2002b: 803). Loring's choice of metaphors is again unerring, as she cuts to the heart of Marlowe's odd merger of the professional with the personal (as well as the hardboiled aesthetic), which results in both a spatial and emotional emptiness. The ambition of this chapter cannot be understated, and Loring's proposal and the frankness of their conversation on marriage is a remarkable development in Marlowe's characterization.

In *Playback*, the final novel-length Marlowe installment based on an older, abandoned film script, Loring appears in the final chapter, and the two conclude this conversation of marriage. Loring again proposes and Marlowe offers his reservations, but he turns again to domestic space as metaphor to express his change of heart:

> I reached for my drink. I looked around the empty room – which was no longer empty. There was a voice in it, and tall slim lovely woman. There was a dark hair on the pillow in the bedroom. There was that soft gentle perfume of a woman who presses herself tight against you, whose lips are soft and yielding, whose eyes are half blind. ([1953] 2002b: 970)

The room is suddenly full if not with meaning, then at the very least a connection. The concluding line of the novel reads: 'The air was full of music' ([1953] 2002b: 971). Philip Marlowe is in love, not with an idealization or prohibition, but rather with a woman in the here and now. Linda Loring is neither a Gal Friday nor a sleuth-hound character, but she possesses many of Anne Riordan's qualities—including her powers of deduction and linguistic play. Loring is thus a continuation of Chandler's reflections on the possibilities of collaboration, and as sidekicks, she and Riordan help to crack the case, as it were, along with Marlowe's fear of contagion and strategies of insularity. Linda Loring's diminished role in *Playback* is curious, but it is important to remember that the original film script drafts from which the novella is created did not contain Philip Marlowe as the protagonist. Still, Chandler remained committed to including this progression in Marlowe's characterization. In correspondence, he writes that his hope that Loring is the 'right woman' for Marlowe, and he supports his choice by arguing that there is nothing to be gained with Marlowe marrying just a 'nice girl'; rather, if he married a woman whose 'ideas about how to live were completely antagonistic to his [...] there would be a struggle of personalities and ideas of life' ([1962] 1997: 247). The development of this struggle is certainly exciting and innovative for the genre, but there was no place for this in *Playback*; rather, it was to be developed in his next Marlowe story.

One of the final projects that Chandler takes on and ultimately abandons is 'The Poodle Springs Story', which documents the early days of Marlowe's marriage and his first case as a married man. Linda is the first word of the story, and the five chapters actually finished by Chandler contain numerous disappointing marriage jokes and newly wed innuendos. Chandler's class commentary falls flat, and the dialogue is without prior refinements; however, the author's search, even in draft form, for the mode of the detective's marriage is fascinating. Marlowe himself is often lusty, but giddily and devotedly so, and while his playful jests at Linda's affluence become pointed at times, they are said with sympathy and affection in Chandler's chapters. In the 1980s, the Chandler estate commissioned Robert B. Parker to 'complete' the draft novel to celebrate what would have been Chandler's 100th birthday. Parker had the unenviable task of finishing a novel that was off to a shaky start in the style of the one of the great American literary stylists. His Chandler-inspired metaphors are often clunky and the plot is unnecessarily complicated, but both these things could also be said of Chandler. However, the greatest failing of the completed version of the story is Parker's treatment of Linda Loring. After Chandler's opening pages, she is limited to stock socialite wife appearances, emerging for most part by the pool, at a dinner parties, or over drinks in the kitchen.

Halfway through the novel, Parker begins including strife in the marriage, as Marlowe fails to find a place for himself within it. The breaking point comes when Marlowe is arrested and goes missing for a night. Linda suggests that 'This isn't working' (1989: 209), and shortly after this fight, the two have another frank conversation and arrive at the conclusion that they have separate lives and 'can't seem to [live] together', after which Linda suggests that she will have her attorney draw up divorce papers (1989: 237). Marlowe moves back to L.A. the next day, but the two have a sentimental reunion at the end of the novel. Loring appears in Marlowe's apartment after the case concludes, demanding that Marlowe make love to her. Interestingly, Marlowe asks for clarification about what it means, and Linda offers: 'It means […] that we love each too much to give each other up. We can end the marriage but we cannot end the love. Probably we can't live together. But why must that mean we can't be lovers?' (1989: 289). And the final word of the novel is 'forever', a word uttered by the two as their 'voices merged', as Marlowe says, and they fall into embrace (1989: 290). Parker is a gifted reader and writer of detective fiction, and preserving Marlowe's knightly code of renouncement—via the alibi of unending love—and abandoning the second path that Chandler offered is obviously in keeping with the protagonist's original characterization. However, scripting the ongoing negotiations and collaborations (both personal and professional) of the Marlowe-Loring marriage offered a far greater reward. That this path seemed impossible even for the likes of Parker suggests just how innovative Chandler's final plans for Marlowe ultimately were.

At the risk of degenerating into a sort of biographical criticism, I will conclude with a brief discussion of the short story, 'The Pencil', published originally as 'Marlowe Takes on the Syndicate' (1959), which was written in (1958) shortly before Chandler's death, making it the final Marlowe story. Old and quite ill by this time, Chandler chooses to return to the character Anne Riordan as Marlowe's spirited accomplice, interestingly foregoing a return for Loring. In this brief story, we see Marlowe stripped of his more graceful wit, and Chandler's more incisive characterizations are largely gone. The story begins when Marlowe is approached by a gangster, Ikky Rosenstein, who is supposedly leaving the mob and needs help to escape. As it turns out, this individual is not who he claims to be, and he is actually trying to arrange the killing of the real Rosenstein with Marlowe's unwitting assistance. To complicate matters further, Marlowe himself apparently once put away a connected mafia lieutenant, and he is likewise being set-up for either death or prison in his complicity.

In the story, Riordan's character remains largely unchanged, which Marlowe once more establishes using domestic space as a sort of mirror. Looking around Riordan's apartment, he notes: 'There were few changes, not many' ([1959] 2002c: 1238). However, the familiarity of Marlowe's relationship with Riordan now seems amplified by the years of their acquaintance. He immediately thinks of her to monitor the airport looking for hit men flying in from Las Vegas, given both her skill and secrecy ([1959] 2002c: 1236). As was true of *Farewell, My Lovely*, her appearances are brief; however, here she is an able (and presumably paid) collaborator working as an actual field operative. Her day job remains writing about 'young love' for 'shiny magazines' ([1959] 2002c: 1238), here a more explicit doubling of Marlowe's (and Chandler's) own dramatic productions of love and sentiment. Marlowe and Riordan are more flirtatious than before, and the latter more sexualized. In fact, Marlowe kisses her 'long and hard' after the pair joke about why they never married, and Riordan laments being a virgin at the age of twenty-eight ([1959] 2002c: 1241). However, there is also now a sadness and loneliness to Riordan. Marlowe comments that her work as a writer 'wasn't her life', but further, '[s]he didn't really have a life' ([1959] 2002c: 1238)—a detail that makes the detective and his sidekick two of kind. Marlowe brushes off Riordan's declarations of love with the tired claim that he is too 'shop-soiled' for her ([1959] 2002c: 1241), and this more intimate conversation is not developed. Marriage is mentioned in one other prominent place when Marlowe is reunited with police investigator Bernie Ohls on the phone to discuss the Rosenstein case. The detective complains, 'I haven't had a fight in years. I'm getting lonely', and Ohls immediately responds, 'well, get married' ([1959] 2002c: 1248).

As James Tate has suggested, the weaknesses of the story and dialogue are themselves Chandlerian and common in the author's work, as is Marlowe's self-mockery that 'anticipates the reader's rejection by voicing it first' (1998: 28). Beyond this, both Marlowe and Riordan are self-conscious of themselves as ideas. Riordan's question regarding her virginity suggests exactly this, and Chandler himself is undoubtedly reflecting—with appropriate humour and a bit of self-reproach—upon the limits of female characterization in hardboiled narratives. This in turn is also Chandlerian, as Marlowe's more monstrous women bristle (and often bite) against their hardboiled flatness. Riordan and Loring offer something like another way for Chandler, but tired and sick at the end of his life, he saw plainly that he had not seized the opportunities that such characters present, and he could only mark the absence of such realized potential. The women's snide preemption of readers' criticism suggests exactly this, and the very choice of returning to Riordan at the end of his life seems proof enough of this notion. To these ends, Riordan effectively has the final word in the story, and thus the series, when she teases Marlowe: 'What I like about you, apart from your enormous personal charm, is that when you don't know an answer you make one up' ([1959] 2002c: 1270), which recalls Nora Charles' conclusion in *The Thin Man* that 'it's all pretty unsatisfactory' (1992: 201). On this note, Chandler's career as a writer of hardboiled stories ends with Marlowe and Riordan drinking champagne at Romanoff's, a repetition of Marlowe's prior celebration with Linda Loring at the end of *The Long Goodbye*.

Conclusion

With Anne Riordan and Linda Loring, the only women to appear in multiple Marlowe stories—including the final four works—Chandler created two of the most remarkable hardboiled women of the time. It seems evident that the primary way in which Chandler thought of writing a strong female hardboiled character was to cast her, to a greater or lesser extent, as a sidekick. Riordan comes closer to the mark here, although Loring shows great acumen and incredible, yet unrealized, potential in her own right. At the level of structure, each is a solution to the problem that the notion of a sidekick, or even collaboration, has in the hardboiled genre. Admittedly, these solutions are enmeshed with Chandler's deep irony and are thus somewhat idiosyncratic. While the Watsonian sidekick documents the detective's mastery, Chandler's female sidekicks reveal the detective's limitations. In this, the violently misogynist heterosexual narrative of the noir and hardboiled worlds is both marked and (in part) revised.

Interestingly, Chandler's version of the female sidekick is not replicated or significantly developed elsewhere in the genre. Among the early hardboiled writers, only Mickey Spillane's secretary and sometimes collaborator Velda comes nearest to Chandler's sidekicks; however, her alternately sexualized and idealized position for the detective, Mike Hammer, makes her quite a problematic example of this figure. A much later possibility from the early 1970s is Susan Silverman, the girlfriend of Robert B. Parker's Spenser, who is herself a practicing psychologist and often offers insight into ongoing cases. However, there remains a significant distance in her relationship with the detective, even as it develops, and Spenser's violent partnership with Hawk inevitably mediates this connection. There is undoubtedly a structural component to the lack of influence of Chandler's female sidekick. George Grella writes of hardboiled detective's inability to produce long-lasting relationships, suggesting that 'his condemnation or rejection of other human beings unites him with the alienated and lost of American fiction' (85). The loneliness of this new frontier hero remained one of the defining features of the character, as did the threat posed by women. That no one took up Chandler's specific challenge is thus perhaps not so surprising, although there can be little doubt that the more general movement towards collaboration and intimacy beginning during what Lewis Moore has termed the Transitional Period of hardboiled fiction (1964–1977) owes a tremendous debt to Chandler's work (73).

Speaking of Chandler's legacy, McCann argues that the author's greatest achievement—in addition to his meticulous stylization and romantic vision of the city—was granting emotional complexity and reflection to the detective. Prior sleuths were detached professionals, but in Chandler 'heroes are men who feel things intensely' (2010: 52). The inner-dialogue of Marlowe's first-person narration amplifies this emotion and documents the detective's distaste for the fallen state of the city. McCann suggests that 'The detective who is brash in Daly, and icy in Hammett, is a sorrowful man in Chandler', and it is this disappointment that makes the lone detective attune to the social injustices of his world (2010: 55–56). This very model becomes predominant as the hardboiled genre develops from the 1970s forward to include previously marginalized voices and unseen populations within the city. That this characterization has been so influential, and has remained the predominant focus of criticism, speaks to the insight of Chandler's revision of the original hardboiled format. But loneliness is nothing if not a longing for connection, and this aspect of Chandler's Marlowe is at times lost in favour of his more dramatic wistfulness. This is a telling reminder of the audacity and innovation of Chandler's intimate construction of the female sidekick.

Prior to Chandler's work, sidekicks and collaborators are virtually non-existent in the hardboiled sub-genre. Equally as important, is Chandler's prescience of the need for hardboiled realism to venture into domestic spaces and relationships, including marriage. The turn in focus to developed romantic relationships and the mundane details of domestic life in hardboiled fiction beginning in the late 1970s, much of which was written by women featuring female detectives, is similarly indebted to the author. The hardboiled detectives, along with their partners and spouses, of Sue Grafton, Sara Paretsky, Marcia Muller and Bill Pronzini share this inheritance. Chandler's female sidekicks and his explorations of marriage and domestic space are ultimately nothing other than the demand for the revision and renewal of hardboiled characterization itself—a task that was subsequently achieved by authors such as these. As with so many aspects of the genre, Chandler was here an original practitioner.

References

Abbott, Megan. 2002. *The Street Was Mine: White Masculinity in Hardboiled Fiction and Film Noir*. New York: Palgrave Publishing.

Cawelti, John G. 1976. *Adventure, Mystery, and Romance: Formula Stories as Art and Popular Culture*. Chicago and London: University of Chicago Press.

Chandler, Raymond. (1940) 2002a. *Farewell, My Lovely*. In *Raymond Chandler: The Big Sleep, Farewell, My Lovely, The High Window*, 201–442. Everyman's Library Edition. New York: Alfred A. Knopf.

———. (1942) 2002a. *The High Window*. In *Farewell, My Lovely*. In *Raymond Chandler: The Big Sleep, Farewell, My Lovely, The High Window*, 445–656. Everyman's Library Edition. New York: Alfred A. Knopf.

———. (1944) 1972. The Simple Art of Murder. In *The Simple Art of Murder*, 1–22. New York: Ballantine Books.

———. (1953) 2002b. *The Long Goodbye*. In *Raymond Chandler: The Lady in the Lake, The Little Sister, The Long Goodbye, Playback*, 465–817. Everyman's Library Edition. New York: Alfred A. Knopf.

———. (1958) 2002b. *Playback*. In *Raymond Chandler: The Lady in the Lake, The Little Sister, The Long Goodbye, Playback*, 821–971. Everyman's Library Edition. New York: Alfred A. Knopf.

———. (1959) 2002c. The Pencil. In *Raymond Chandler: Collected Stories*, 1233–1270. Everyman's Library Edition. New York: Alfred A. Knopf.

———. (1962) 1997. *Raymond Chandler Speaking*, ed. Dorothy Gardiner and Kathrine Sorley Walker. Berkeley, CA: California UP.

Chandler, Raymond, and Robert B. Parker. 1989. *Poodle Springs*. New York: Berkley Books.

Christianson, Scott R. 1989. Tough Talk and Wisecracks: Language as Power in American Detective Fiction. *Journal of Popular Culture* 23 (2): 152–162.

Doyle, Arthur Conan. (1890) 1992. The Sign of the Four. In *The Complete Sherlock Holmes*, 89–158. New York: Barnes and Noble Books.

———. (1891) 1992. The Red-Headed League. In *The Complete Sherlock Holmes*, 176–190. New York: Barnes and Noble Books.

Durham, Philip. 1963. *Down These Mean Streets, A Man Must Go: Raymond Chandler's Knight*. Chapel Hill, NC: University of North Carolina Press.

Grella, George. 1988. The Formal Detective Novel. In *Detective Fiction: A Collection of Critical Essays*, ed. Robin W. Winks, 84–102. Woodstock, VT: Countryman Press.

Hammett, Dashiell. (1930) 1992. *The Maltese Falcon*. New York: Vintage Books.

———. (1934) 1992. *The Thin Man*. New York: Vintage Books.

Johnson, Barbara. 1988. The Frame of Reference: Poe, Lacan, Derrida. In *The Purloined Poe: Lacan, Derrida, and Psychoanalytic Reading*, ed. John P. Muller and William J. Richardson, 213–251. Baltimore: Johns Hopkins University Press.

Knox, Ronald A. 1911. Studies in the Literature of Sherlock Holmes. http://www.diogenes-club.com. Accessed 19 July 2018.

Lewis, Ffrangcon C. 1990. Unraveling a Web: Writer Versus Reader in Edgar Allan Poe's Tales of Detection. In *Watching the Detectives*, ed. Ian A. Bell and Graham Daldry, 97–116. London: Macmillan.

Madden, David. 1998. Anne Riordan: Raymond Chandler's Forgotten Heroine. In *The Detective in American Fiction, Film, and Television*, ed. Jerome H. Delamater and Ruth Prigozy, 3–11. Westport, CT: Greenwood Press.

McCann, Sean. 2000. *Gumshoe America: Hard-Boiled Crime Fiction and the Rise and Fall of New Deal Liberalism*. Durham, NC and London: Duke University Press.

———. 2010. The Hard-Boiled Novel. In *American Crime Fiction*, ed. Catherine Ross Nickerson, 42–57. Cambridge: Cambridge University Press.

Moore, Lewis D. 2006. *Cracking the Hard-Boiled Detective: A Critical History from 1920s to the Present*. Jefferson, NC: McFarland Press.

Plain, Gill. 2001. *Twentieth-Century Crime Fiction: Gender, Sexuality and the Body*. Chicago and London: Fitzroy Dearborn Publishing.

Poe, Edgar Allan. (1841) 1975. The Murders in the Rue Morgue. *The Complete Tales and Poems of Edgar Allan Poe*, 141–168. New York: Vintage Books.

Porter, Dennis. 1981. *The Pursuit of Crime*. New Haven, CT: Yale University Press.

Stout, Rex. 1941. Watson Was a Woman. http://www.nerowolfe.org. Accessed 19 July 2018.

Tate, James O. 1998. Raymond Chandler's Pencil. In *The Detective in American Fiction, Film, and Television*, ed. Jerome H. Delamater and Ruth Prigozy, 27–35. Westport, CT: Greenwood Press.

CHAPTER 9

The Anti-Sidekick: Raymond 'Mouse' Alexander, Double Consciousness and the Subversion of the Sidekick in Walter Mosley's *Easy Rawlins* Mysteries

Nathan Ashman

Introduction: Double Trouble

Author of fourteen novels featuring African American war-veteran-turned-private-detective Ezekiel 'Easy' Rawlins, Walter Mosley is renowned for his work's unyielding exposure of the racial subjugation and violence underlying not only American history and culture, but the very traditions of the hardboiled crime novel itself. In a genre where non-white races are frequently marginalised, victimised and delimited by the overwhelming force and discriminatory practices of white social power, Mosley's protagonist, Easy Rawlins, allows vital access to previously demarcated identities, cultures and spaces. Equally central to Mosley's work is Easy's long-serving, psychopathic sidekick and best friend, Raymond 'Mouse' Alexander. First appearing in *Devil in a Blue*

N. Ashman (✉)
University of East Anglia, Norwich, England, UK

L. Andrew and S. Saunders (eds.), *The Detective's Companion in Crime Fiction*, Crime Files, https://doi.org/10.1007/978-3-030-74989-7_9

Dress (1990), the small-statured yet unflinchingly violent 'Mouse' is an enduring presence throughout the Rawlins mysteries, operating as Easy's conduit to the brutal and racially schematised topography of post-war Los Angeles. Yet Mouse's role is rather different to that of the traditional sidekick. As Fredric Svoboda suggests, the detective's sidekick frequently operates as a 'surrogate for the reader', a point of identification who is typically 'inferior' to the detective and often comic (2001: 230). Mouse, on the other hand, is a menacing, volatile presence in the Rawlins mysteries, offering not comfort and familiarity, but unpredictability and threat. Although ostensibly Easy's best friend, Mouse's volatility and brutality continually compromise the detective's efforts to move beyond a life of injustice, violence and corruption. Mouse's role as sidekick is far more complex than a simple inversion of traditional genre paradigms, as his often-fraught relationship with Rawlins becomes inexorably intertwined with the broader racial politics of the city. The doubling between Easy and Mouse is illustrative of Mosley's intricate examination of the African American experience and the 'complex double consciousness' that Bernard W. Bell identifies as 'the special burden and blessing of Afro-American identity' (1989: 35).

This concept of double consciousness is most frequently aligned with W. E. B. Du Bois's seminal text *The Souls of Black Folk* (1903), particularly its articulation of an inescapable double bind that characterises black identity in America. Du Bois characterises this idea of 'double consciousness' as a profound sense of 'looking at one's self through the eyes of others, of measuring one's self by the tape of the world that looks on in amused contempt and pity'. This becomes most forcefully articulated through a splitting of subjectivity, the forging of an irreconcilable 'twoness,—an American, a negro; two souls, two thoughts, two unreconciled strivings; two warring ideals in one dark body, whose dogged strength alone keeps it from being torn asunder' (2017: 5). Du Bois outlines the complex development of black identity when positioned outside of a dominant culture, a marginality that not only prompts a cyclical interchange between conflicting desires and expectations, but that simultaneously triggers a violent splitting of the self. Chester J. Fontenot sees this notion of double identity as expressive of the inherent 'otherness' that lies at the core of Du Bois's discourse on black American identity (2001: 8). Not only does such splitting prevent the development of a fully integrated subjectivity, it also severely damages the potential for cultural cohesion.

Such instances of doubling punctuate Mosley's work and are most potently spotlighted via the relationship between Easy and Mouse as detective and sidekick respectively. Indeed, Scott McCracken reads Mouse as both 'childhood friend and alter ego', arguing that he signifies Easy's own hidden, criminal potentialities (1998: 169). This is supported by Richard Gray, who suggests that Mouse's violence and 'casual conscience-less approach to things' contrast dramatically and add 'depth' to Mosley's representation of Rawlins, whilst also operating as a reminder of the 'dark currents running within the protagonist' (2012: 734). Mouse's function as counterpart to Easy has been similarly confirmed by Mosley himself, who in a 1993 interview with Charles Silet, reveals that Easy's character was in fact borne out of 'his relationship, his feeling for this guy Mouse' (Silet 2011: 19). This chapter explores the connection between detective and sidekick in Mosley's work, examining how the bond between these two characters potently illustrates Easy's attempts to reconcile the conflicting facets of his racial identity in a culture dominated by white social power. Whilst in some respect Easy strives for a reputable and legitimate suburban life as characterised by the myth of the American Dream, Mouse's presence is a perpetual reminder that this dream is demarcated and energised by underlying racial prejudices. As such, this splitting between detective and sidekick becomes representative of a haunting double consciousness that Easy repeatedly combats throughout Mosley's works.

This connection between these discourses of double consciousness and the fraught relationship between Mouse and Easy has been touched on before by several critics. Roger A. Berger, for instance, identifies such moments of doubling between detective and sidekick as symptomatic of Mosley's 'strategic and pragmatic' explorations of race, deliberately 'reflecting or almost parodying Du Bois's notion of an African American double consciousness' (1997: 291). The parodic strategies of Mosley's work—as chiefly manifested via the relationship between Mouse and Easy—have been similarly recognised by Laura Quinn, who argues that instances of parody can be traced beyond Mosley's uses of the 'double consciousness' trope to include his comparably ironic imitation of both the 'doppelganger, and the popular convention of the sidekick' (2010: 124). Although this chapter similarly attempts to elucidate the ways in which Mouse is employed as a 'rhetorical device', one that heightens 'the political edge' of Mosley's work, it will provide a more sustained analysis of how double consciousness operates within the texts than previous critical examinations (Quinn 2010: 124).

Subverting the Sidekick: The Spectre of Mouse

The sidekick has been an enduring archetype since the birth of detective fiction and generally operates as a foil for the brilliant yet inscrutable sleuth. Often this relationship is characterised by a sense of intellectual or physical hierarchy, as the sidekick functions to accentuate or decipher the investigator's brilliance. Typified most obviously via the Holmes/Watson dynamic, Heather O'Donoghue argues that, 'plainly, the sidekick shows the hero in a flattering light' (2012: 42). Although this is perhaps a slight oversimplification, O'Donoghue underscores the typical 'narratological' purpose of the sidekick as a conduit between the reader and 'the lone (and often loftily taciturn) investigator' (42). Whereas the sidekick is characteristically intelligible and identifiable, the investigator remains more peripheral and furtive, often literally operating on the margins of the text. Holmes's liminality in *The Hound of the Baskervilles* (1902) (as well as other narratives such as 'The Man with the Twisted Lip' [1891]) is indicative of this form of narratological framework that deliberately propagates the mystery and unpredictability of the investigator.

In Mosley's work, this dynamic is complicated to the point of inversion. Unlike the typical sidekick, Mouse is often conspicuous by his absence in the Rawlins's mysteries. In this sense, Mouse transgresses what Charles Rzepka identifies as the traditional 'modal' function of the sidekick or companion, which is to essentially mediate or control the reader's 'access to information' (2005: 20). In contrast, Mouse is typically 'off screen' for the majority of Easy's cases and only scantily contributes to the actual process of investigation, usually through 'strong-arm' work. Nor does he act as a biographer or chronicler of the detective's adventures. Instead, like Holmes, Mouse frequently exists on the margins, a 'supernatural' presence who 'always arrives just when he is needed' (Wilson 2003: 41).

Although many critics have similarly aligned Mouse's narrative function with that of the traditional sidekick, his continual infringement of the supposed, generally accepted 'sidekick rules'—as active antagonist rather than passive ally—might bring one to question the extent to which he can be persuasively aligned with the conventions and expectations of this particular archetype (Gray 2012: 734). Yet, I would argue that it *is* this very transgressiveness that marks Mouse as a significant and unique iteration of the sidekick tradition. In the same way that Easy Rawlins decentralises the traditionally white subjectivity of the hard-boiled private eye, Mouse dismantles the conservative strictures of the detective's sidekick through his oscillating representation as saviour and threat. In this sense, Mouse's role is more that of an 'anti-sidekick' than anything else, a somewhat paradoxical position necessitated by the corrupt, violent and racially schematised urban milieu of post-war Los Angeles. As Quinn suggests, Mouse 'exceeds conventional sidekick containment' and in doing so critiques 'the power relations inherent in that convention' (2010: 125). Whilst the relationship between Easy and Mouse is fraught with an underlying sense of ambivalence, the detective's success and survival is still reliant on the capriciousness and ruthlessness of his oldest companion. As Easy himself recognises: 'in the hard life of the streets, you need somebody like Mouse at your back' (Mosley 1996: 63). This is most frequently evidenced when Easy finds himself in situations of impending peril, occasions that almost authenticate Mouse's uses of ruthless violence. It is here that the flexibility and diversity of the sidekick model becomes most apparent, as Mouse is able to fulfil his function as companion and redeemer whilst skirting the traditional expectations of the form.

This sense of paradox is equally evident in the effect Mouse has on Easy's subjectivity. Whilst the sidekick frequently operates to reveal the detective or to render his identity more distinct, Mouse's antithetical attributes of merciless brutality and unyielding loyalty often prompt the inverse. Not only does Easy become the conduit through which the reader gains access to the enigmatic Mouse, but Mouse's ferocity also leads Easy to question his own sense of self, as well as his position in a society structured around various institutions of white power. This sense of ambivalence that characterises Mouse and his relationship with Easy—being at once a 'caring and loyal man' whilst simultaneously cold, brutal and 'desensitised to death and violence'—is symptomatic of Mosley's work more broadly, particularly regarding questions of identity (Wilson: 41). Yet, if there is contradiction rooted in this detective/sidekick dynamic, it is also, as mentioned, one devoid of hierarchy. The detective and the sidekick are two sides of the same coin: to analyse Mouse is to analyse Easy, and vice versa.

Mouse's enigmatic marginality is no more evident than in the first of the Rawlins mysteries, *Devil in a Blue Dress* (1990). Set in 1948 Los

Angeles, the opening pages of the text not only immediately foreground Mosley's complex appraisal of racial identity, but also his self-conscious and systematic deconstruction of the hardboiled and sidekick traditions. Having recently been fired from his job at Champion Aircraft, the narrative commences with Easy drowning his sorrows at his friend Joppy's bar, uncertain and fearful of how he will be able to afford future mortgage payments on his modest house. Unbeknownst to Easy, his troubles amplify when the debonair yet menacing Alright DeWitt incongruously enters the bar, a man whose whiteness becomes absurdly exaggerated by his choice of attire. As Easy observes:

> It's not just that he was white, but he wore an off-white linen suit and shirt with a panama straw hat and bone shoes over flashing white silk socks. His skin was smooth and pale with just a few freckles [...] He stopped in the doorway, filling it with his huge frame, and surveyed the room with pale eyes; not a colour I'd seen in a man's eyes. (1990: 9)

Whilst immediately prefiguring the stark racial tensions that will saturate the text, here Mosley simultaneously reclaims the previously liminal locales of white hardboiled fiction, particularly the 'alien space' of the 'black bar' (Messent 2013: 98). Indeed, it is no coincidence that this opening scene of *Devil in Blue Dress* is strikingly reminiscent of Raymond Chandler's *Farewell, My Lovely* (1940), where Philip Marlowe follows the large and, like DeWitt, similarly incongruous Moose Malloy into a neon-lit 'dine and dice emporium' where the patrons are 'all negroes' (Chandler 2010: 5). In Chandler's work, the space of the black bar is codified exclusively as one of otherness and threat, one that ultimately occasions violence:

> The chanting at the crap table stopped dead and the light over it jerked out. There was a sudden silence as heavy as a waterlogged boat. Eyes look at us, chestnut coloured eyes, set in faces that ranged from grey to deep black. He turned slowly and the eyes in them glistened and stared in the dead alien silence of another race. (5)

Through a clear inversion of perspective that positions Easy at the centre of the narrative, Mosley's opening deliberately destabilises the rigid racial tropes, perspectives and topographies that typify the traditional hardboiled crime novel. Whereas Chandler unambiguously depicts blackness as unfamiliar and threatening, Mosley instead ensures that it is 'whiteness, not blackness' that is shown as 'other and alien' (Messent: 98). The cataloguing of De Witt's whiteness is extended to his bleached 'pale' eyes, a clear replication and ironic subversion of Chandler's comparable focus on eyes as a signifier of blackness in *Farewell, My Lovely*. De Witt's presence is unfamiliar and unwanted in Joppy's bar, the inflated almost grotesque description of his twisted 'pink lips' and 'slithery' serpentine handshake indicating an underlying sense of deceit and danger (Mosley 1990: 10–11).

It is during this exchange that the spectre of Mouse first appears. After being introduced, Albright offers Easy a chance to accrue some quick cash doing covert investigative work. Albright is searching for the missing Daphne Monet, a mysterious young blonde woman known to frequent black bars and jazz clubs: establishments that Albright 'can't go in' because he is not the 'right persuasion' (Mosley 1990: 26). Although Easy accepts the proposition, he is unsure of De Witt's ultimate motives and unsettled by the man's likeness to his childhood friend Raymond 'Mouse' Alexander, particularly his disconcerting sneer which reminds Easy of the way 'Mouse was always smiling, especially when misfortune happened to someone else' (28). Immediately Mouse's role as anti-sidekick begins to materialise, as he emerges more as a source of threat and anxiety for Easy than reassurance and companionship. Almost a direct manifestation of Freud's 'ghastly harbinger of death', the menacing apparition of Mouse subtly anticipates Easy's continual struggle to negotiate the conflicting facets of both his past and his identity in the series as whole (2003: 142).

Easy's trepidation transpires to be well founded, as De Witt's promise of quick cash steadily escalates into a complex and multifaceted narrative of murder and violence that starkly illuminates the entrenched corruption and racial hostility at the centre of the city and its institutions. Easy's primary motivation for accepting De Witt's proposal is deeply grounded in his desire for an honest and legitimate suburban life. Indeed, Carlyle Van Thompson argues that 'keeping and maintaining the American Dream' is central to the tension between Mouse and Easy Rawlins throughout Mosley's series (2010: 93). Van Thompson draws parallels between Rawlins and Jay Gatsby, arguing that both are 'desperately desiring' individuals 'willing to take enormous personal risks' in the pursuit of prosperity and upward social mobility. Rawlins 'love affair' with his modest and 'diminutive house' becomes a central aspect of the narrative, as well as the driving force behind his attempts to remain distant from his violent childhood friend Mouse (Van Thompson: 93). Atypically of the sidekick, Mouse is a menacing and peripheral presence in the early sections of *Devil in Blue Dress*, a phantom who is circuitously mentioned by Easy in association with a tumultuous past of poverty and crime he is eager to forget. This is one of the many ways Mouse operates against the sidekick tradition, destabilising Easy's identity rather than cementing it.

Thus, when Mouse sends a letter to Easy informing the latter of his impending arrival in Los Angeles, Easy's immediate reaction is to run, to 'pack [his] bags and leave town' (Mosley 1990: 53). Mouse's arrival and position as anti-sidekick lucidly expounds the ambivalence and duality of Easy's fraught subjectivity in Mosley's texts, an irrepressible tension induced by his location on the borderland between the promise of the future and the burden of the past:

> The only time in my life that I had ever been completely free from fear was when I ran with Mouse. He was so confident there was no room for fear. Mouse was barely five-foot-six, but he'd go up against a man Dupree's size and you know I'd bet on the Mouse to walk away from it. He could put a knife in a man's stomach and ten minutes later sit down to a plate of spaghetti.
>
> I didn't want to write Mouse and I didn't want to let it lie. In my mind he had such power that I felt I had to do whatever he wanted. But I had dreams that didn't have me running in the streets anymore; I was a man of property and I wanted to leave my wild days behind me. (Mosley 1990: 47)

Easy's ambivalence towards Mouse and, by extension, his own history is rendered palpably clear via this paradoxical response. Whilst Easy's memories of Mouse are aligned with notions of freedom and fearlessness, the attendant recklessness and violence of this 'wild' past are no longer compatible with Easy's position as a 'man of property'. As such, Mouse illustrates a key conflict in the Rawlins mysteries, one that is engendered by Easy's conflicting desires and allegiances. Whereas Easy exists on the liminal borderland between conservative white power structures and delimited black spaces, Mouse is the embodiment of a form of uncompromising black masculinity that refuses to comply with a society and system of justice that has systematically failed to protect and serve his welfare. The relationship between these two characters becomes symptomatic of the irreconcilable division that defines Easy's double consciousness. As 'home owner, businessman and family man', on the one hand, Easy has 'a respectable, proto-bourgeois identity'. Yet, on the other, he 'has a quasi-criminal identity, formed by his childhood experiences and connection to the underworld', or, more specifically, to Mouse (McCracken: 169).

'Why'd You Kill Him?': Violence, Duality and the Anti-Sidekick

Mouse's liminal yet dynamic presence in the Rawlins's mysteries is most starkly manifested in the form of 'the voice', a symbolic embodiment not only of Easy's assembly with the sidekick, but of the detective's broader identification with the impoverished and subjugated black communities of his youth. The 'voice' is a particularly strong presence in both *Devil in a Blue Dress* and *A Red Death* (1991) and unambiguously actualises the fraught 'dualism' of Easy's existence throughout the series (Lock 2001: 80). The 'voice' operates as both an internal alter ego and a survival mechanism, one that first emerges during Easy's service in the Second World War. Recalling an occasion when he and 'two buddies' are pinned down by sniper fire in Normandy, Easy is directed by this voice to 'get off yo' butt when the sun comes down n' kill that motherfucker. Kill him an' rip off his fuckin' face with yo' bayonet, man' (Mosley 1990: 105–106). The diction of 'the voice' is starkly antithetical to Easy's typical narration, hinting at a connection not only to Easy's more turbulent and hostile Texas upbringing, but to the more brutal and racially demarcated patois of Mouse. Described as 'hard' and 'only emerging at the worst times', the rage of 'the voice' not only becomes a figurative extension of both Mouse's ruthlessness (and opportune interventions) in the Rawlins mysteries, but simultaneously spotlights the fluxing frontiers of identity that Mouse and Easy continually negotiate throughout Mosley's work. In this sense, the internal voice operates as a further indicator of Easy's double consciousness, one that replicates his complex and oscillating association with Mouse. Manifested symbolically through the rage of 'the voice'—and literally via his timely intrusions in Easy's cases—Mouse's role as sidekick becomes intimately bound up with ideas of lawlessness and survival. Whilst these violent interventions are welcomed by Easy in moments of impending death, Mouse frequently emerges as a barrier to Easy attaining the life of respectability and stability that he craves.

The connection between double consciousness and narrative voice in Mosley's work has been similarly identified by Helen Lock, who points to the disjunction between the 'standard' English of Easy's narration and the more colloquial street talk we see in the dialogue he holds with other characters, particularly Mouse. For Lock, this 'double voice' is emblematic of the inherent 'ambivalence' of Easy's 'self-perception' (80). Although an educated man striving for respectability and success, Lock argues that Easy deliberately 'downplays his education in much the same way that he hides his wealth, for related reasons of community solidarity' (80).

Easy's intricate negotiation of identity is underlined in *A Red Death*, when he deliberately camouflages his ownership of several rental properties, pretending instead to be the handyman. In the process, he perpetuates the myth that the buildings are owned by 'some white lady Downtown' (Mosley 1991: 14). The motive for this subterfuge is linked to his role as private investigator, specifically his reputation amongst the poverty-stricken and marginalised local community that he serves. As Easy states: 'I had a reputation for fairness and the strength of my convictions among the poor. Ninety-nine percent out of a hundred-black folk were poor back then, so my reputation went quite a way' (15). The implication here is clear; Easy fears that his success will compromise his reputation and authenticity in the black neighbourhoods in which he operates. Here, ownership and affluence become parasitically connected to white power and, by extension, black subjugation. The anxieties over authenticity, ownership and power are exacerbated, once again, by the uncertainty and danger of Mouse, who emerges more as a source of threat than protection in *A Red Death*. Having disappeared after the events of the previous novel, Mouse is once again back in LA, this time pursuing his ex-wife, Etta Mae, who has fled with their son, LaMarque. Both are hidden and protected by Easy, a deceit that is energised by the detective's own feelings for Etta Mae. Despite Easy's desire to flee to Mexico with mother and son, the end of the text sees Mouse and Etta Mae reconciled, a union that destroys Easy's fantasy of forging his own pseudo 'nuclear family' (McCracken 1998: 173). Once again, the duality that underlies the relationship between detective and sidekick in Mosley's work frequently culminates in an obstruction to Easy's desires and identity. Mouse operates in a unique space between fortification and annihilation, placing Easy in a perpetual state of deferral.

Mouse and Easy are certainly not the only characters to be profoundly affected by these complex negotiations of identity and race. The finale of *Devil in a Blue Dress* explicitly actualises these undercurrents of identity splitting that mark the text throughout. Yet perhaps more significantly, the denouement of the novel also brutally exposes the duality that punctuates Mouse's role as anti-sidekick, as he shifts from saviour to cold-blooded murderer in the space of a few pages. After a complex investigation, Easy eventually discovers that De Witt Albright represents Todd Carter, a wealthy businessman who had recently been in a relationship with Daphne Monet until she vanished with thirty thousand dollars of his money. After driving to confront Albright at his Malibu ranch house, Easy soon finds himself caught in a shootout. Outnumbered and outgunned, it is only the dramatic arrival of Mouse with 'smoking pistol in hand' that saves Easy—and Albright's hostage Daphne Monet—from certain death. Taking 'the little man in [his] arms' and hugging him 'like [he] would hug a woman', Easy's gratitude towards Mouse is short-lived, as he is soon faced with the violent consequences of Mouse's intervention (1990: 207). After binding and interrogating barman and Albright conspirator Joppy, Mouse's seeming heroism is almost immediately juxtaposed with an act of callous and unflinching brutality, one that vividly emphasises the ambivalence that defines his role as sidekick:

> [Mouse] turned casually to his right and shot Joppy in the groin. Joppy's eyes opened wide and he started honking like a seal. He rocked back and forth trying to grab his wound, but the wire held him to the chair. After a few seconds, Mouse levelled his pistol and shot Joppy in the head. One moment Joppy had two bulging eyes, then his left was just a bloody, ragged hole.
> Mouse stood up and said, 'So let's get that money, honey'. He picked up [Daphne's] clothes from behind the couch and dropped the heap in her lap. Then he went out of the front door. (Mosley 1990: 206)

The savagery and coldness of Joppy's execution is rendered all the more potent by the unsparingly clinical tone via which Easy details the scene. The description is starkly devoid of emotion, relating the execution with a detachment that only enhances its visceral brutality. It is here that the sidekick's true motives become clear, as Mosley is quick to dampen any sense of heroism that may have been associated with Mouse following his rescuing of Rawlins. As much as Mouse is driven by a desire to protect Easy—like one might expect from a traditional sidekick—it also becomes demonstrably apparent that his involvement in the case is equally directed by personal and financial gain. The complexity of Mouse's position as sidekick is starkly illuminated here, as his ostensible function as protector and companion is perpetually bound up with a ruthlessness and unpredictability that often threatens to derail Easy's investigations and ultimate search for justice. Mouse's interventions always come at a price and this relates as much to the stability of Easy's subjectivity as to money or violence.

In the aftermath, Daphne Monet is revealed to be gangster Frank Green's half-sister Ruby Hanks, an African American woman passing as white. Ruby's passing becomes inextricably bound up with text's broader engagements with identity splitting, particularly the dualism between Mouse and Easy. As the dust settles following Joppy's execution, Easy angrily confronts Mouse for committing what he perceives as a senseless and avoidable murder, desperately asking: 'Why'd you kill him?'. Whilst carelessly 'whistling and wrapping his money in a package fashioned from brown paper bags', Mouse justifies executing Joppy because he was the 'cause of all [Easy's] pain' (209). He then admits to the additional murder of Frank Green, which elicits more disapproval and guilt from Easy. Unable to reconcile their perspectives, Mouse accuses Easy of 'aspiring to whiteness' in the same way as Ruby (Demirtürk 2012: 17).

Here the schematisation between Mouse and Easy once again becomes reflective of the text's broader engagement with double consciousness, as the brutality and remorselessness of Mouse emerges as a 'carnivalesque' manifestation of 'everything that Easy is trying to leave behind' (McCracken: 170). Through his role as anti-sidekick, Mouse becomes allegorically illustrative of what Fernandes defines as the 'wilful outsider who operates at counter-purposes to the ethics responsible for his oppression' (2008: 121). This certainly accounts for the deep complexity and uncertainty that defines Mouse's position, as operating at 'counter-purposes' to a hegemonic culture accountable for his subjugation often means operating in opposition to Easy and his investigations. As McCracken suggests, Easy 'operates on the edge, between the conformist structures of white society and the closed space of the black ghetto', on the very seam 'between what a racist society defines as culture and non-culture' (1998: 169). Mouse on the other hand refuses to co-operate with a system of power that persistently fails to safeguard or promote the lives and values of him and others like him. As Easy says of Mouse: 'Raymond was proof that a black man could live by his own rules in America when everybody else denied it' (Mosley 2003: 201).

In the Rawlins series, the irreconcilable tension between detective/sidekick is certainly atypical of these kinds of partnerships. Whilst on the one hand Mosley positions Mouse as a protective companion (and an assurance against death), he simultaneously embodies a violence and brutality that threatens to destroy Easy's attempts to forge a new form of black male subjectivity. Whereas Easy sees such acts of violence as an expression of his best friend's savage and unhinged nature, for Mouse such ruthlessness is intimately bound up with an acceptance of his own 'essential' black masculinity. As Fernandes suggests, what is 'at stake' in Mouse's violence 'is the construction of the self beyond the dominant narrative's grasp' (2008: 121). In other words, such acts become intrinsically connected to Mouse's self-definition and to his resistance to a hegemonic culture of white power. In a racially fractured culture where 'black bodies are symbolic sites of crime' and in which the criminal justice system fails 'to provide justice and safety for the black urban poor', Mouse takes these concepts of law and justice into his own hands (Demirtürk 2012: 17). Whilst sidekick to Easy, he is simultaneously—and often antithetically—accepting of his position as outsider, and subsequently criticises the detective not only for condemning his acts of violence, but for attempting to inhabit a position in-between these violently demarcated racial topographies:

> 'You just like Ruby,' Mouse said.
> 'What you say?'
> 'She wanna be white. All the years people tellin' her how she light skinned and beautiful but all the time she knows that she can't have what white people have. So, she pretend and then she lose it all. She can love a white man but all he can love is the white girl he think she is.'
> 'What's that got to do with me?'
> 'That's just like you, Easy. You learn stuff and you be thinkin' like white men be thinkin'. You be thinkin' that what's right fo' them is right fo' you. She look like she white and you think like you white. But brother you don't know that you both poor niggers. And a nigger ain't never gonna be happy 'less he accept what he is.' (Mosley 1990: 209)

Here, Mouse draws a direct correlation between Ruby and Easy, particularly for what he perceives as their comparable disavowal of an 'authentic' black subjectivity. Whereas Ruby appropriates the visual, physical signifiers of whiteness in the process of passing, Easy's 'whiteness' is the result of a schizophrenic subjectivity catalysed by the inescapable burden of his own double consciousness. Mouse's diction once again illuminates the varying and intermingled sites of racial contestation—such as language and space—that Easy must negotiate, whilst concurrently underlying the double bind of the detective's identity. Crucially, Mouse as anti-sidekick is a symbol of the perennial and inescapable marginality of African American identity in a society structured around monolithic structures of white social power. As McCracken suggests, in 'this context, Mouse's advice can be understood not so much as a definition of Easy's essential nature, but as the necessity of performing a black identity within and against the constraints of racism' (1998: 171). Mouse encourages Easy to embrace a similarly liminal position in this unbalanced paradigm of racial power, inferring that any potential for resistance stems from rejecting the unachievable and hollow aspirations of whiteness and the consequent negation it exacts.

Mouse's unorthodox positioning as anti-sidekick is perhaps at its most apparent in *Black Betty* (1994). Set in 1961—five years after the previous instalment *White Butterfly* (1992)—the novel opens with a dream sequence in which Easy recounts the cold-blooded murder of Bruno Ingram at the hands of Mouse in an alley behind 'John's Bar'. What begins as a verbal altercation over an unpaid wager ends with Mouse pulling out his 'long .41 calibre pistol' and emptying the cylinder into Bruno's chest, with each bullet throwing the victim's body 'up against the pork butcher's back door again and again' (1994: 4). As Easy wakes from the murderous nightmare memory, we learn that Mouse was subsequently incarcerated for manslaughter and has been in the state prison in Chino for the ensuing half decade. Easy describes himself as experiencing a similar kind of incarceration, what he terms 'a prison of guilt, a prison of [the] mind' (1994: 6). Short of cash, Easy is hired by a white private investigator to find Elizabeth Eady (a.k.a. 'Black Betty'), a domestic servant who has been missing since the recent death of her wealthy white employer. Yet what begins as a seemingly straightforward case soon degenerates into a maelstrom of violence, corruption and scandal.

Easy's search for 'Black Betty' is problematised further by the release of the rage-fuelled Mouse, who is hell-bent on finding and murdering the man who ratted on him to the police. Although Mouse has narrowed it down to three possible snitches, he is still ultimately unsure of who is responsible. When Easy questions: 'But if you don't know now how you gonna know?' Mouse replies: 'Either I find out or I'ma kill all three of'em. But one way or another, I'ma get the man who did it' (1994: 72). *Black Betty* signals a clear shift in Mouse's role as sidekick, as the dynamic between the two men becomes more adversarial than in any of the previous texts. As Leroy Panek suggests, unlike *White Butterfly* where Easy uses Mouse and the 'threat of violence to intimidate white businessmen who seek to buy his properties', *Black Betty* sees Easy's relationship with violence undergo 'significant changes' (2000: 201). Indeed, Charles Wilson notes that *Black Betty* is the first time that Easy does not use Mouse 'in any way to assist in the solving of cases'. Instead, he serves to remind Easy to 'avoid all unnecessary violence in his life, especially given his role as father' (2003: 62). Although Easy can prove that none of the men on Mouse's hit list turned him in, the detective recognises that Mouse's rage will not be abated until he enacts some form of revenge: 'He couldn't help himself, I knew that. He needed to kill somebody, and even though it would hurt him he'd kill me if there was nobody else to blame' (1994: 316). Easy decides to direct Mouse's rage into what Wilson describes as a 'constructive effort' and subsequently leads him to Martin Smith (2003: 62). Smith, a pseudo-father figure to Easy who helped raise him as a boy, is in the throes of terminal cancer and had previously asked Easy to euthanise him, which Easy had refused to do. Although the death of Martin is therefore arguably an act of mercy, *Black Betty* is nonetheless bookended by two ruthless, cold-blooded murders, both committed at the hands of Mouse:

> Mouse had come in and asked him who had turned him in and Martin said that he'd done it. He said the Lord wouldn't let him keep quiet on that. And Mouse shot him. A sixty-year-old man dressed in a small boy's clothes, but all Mouse saw was the man who'd turned him over. So, he shot him and walked out of the empty house. (1994: 320)

The almost traumatised tone Easy adopts to recount the scene is distinctly reminiscent of the language he uses to describe the equally ruthless murder of Joppy in *Devil in a Blue Dress*. In both cases, the conflict and ambivalence that defines the relationship between Easy and Mouse as detective and sidekick is certainly palpable. Crucially, the 'paradox of

Mouse' represents a hostile and conflicted iteration of the sidekick tradition. Whilst Easy often relies on Mouse to support and facilitate his investigations, *Black Betty* simultaneously exposes the literal and symbolic threat that the sidekick poses to the detective in Mosley's work.

It is in the next volume in the series, *A Little Yellow Dog* (1996), that Mouse's violence reaches a crescendo, one that causes him to reflect on a transgressive lifestyle that he had previously considered 'part of a big ole puzzle, a piece' (1996: 7). After murdering his friend Sweet William Dokes, a distraught Mouse breaks down in front of Easy, 'blubbering' and 'shaking' uncontrollably in remorse (66). From this moment, Mouse 'renounces his violent past' and becomes converted to a pseudo form of 'religious fundamentalism' (Bryant 2003: 223). Uncertain of what triggered Mouse's uncharacteristic display of guilt, Easy reflects: 'I didn't know what to say. Maybe just sitting there is what changed him. Maybe being in my company, coming from my house, he got the idea to go straight' (1996: 66). After two years of doing custodial work at Easy's rental properties and staying clear of the streets, Mouse's new diplomatic approach to conflict resolution is comically displayed in a meeting with gangsters Puddin' and Tony near the climax of the text:

> 'See that Easy?' Mouse was jubilant.
> 'What?'
> 'Aint no need to get all mad an' surly. All you got to do is talk. People will listen. You know Etta been tellin' me that for years an' I jus' ain't never paid her no mind'. (Mosley 1996: 324)

Ironically, it is Mouse's decision to retreat from a life of violence that leads to his seeming demise. When he later agrees to accompany Easy to broker a deal for Jackson Blue's life, he does so with the express intent of avoiding bloodshed. As he tells Easy: 'I don't have a gun on me but that's just because I don't wanna kill nobody right now. I mean, if I had to I could get me a firearm. But right now I just wanna see what it's like to live wit' your family an' work at a job' (320). Indeed, after the exchange turns sour, Mouse sacrifices himself for Easy, pushing the detective out of the line of fire before being shot twice by gangster Sallie Munroe. Seemingly mortally wounded, this act of sacrifice is one of redemption for Mouse that reaffirms the partnership between the two men. Despite Mouse's rogue status and often uncontrollable violence in Mosley's works, his role as loyal sidekick and saviour to Easy is ultimately reaffirmed through death.

'The Ghastly Harbinger of Death': Return of the Mouse

In his reading of *A Little Yellow Dog* (1996), William R. Nash sees Mouse's 'apparent death' at the hands of gangster Sallie Munroe as a bifurcating moment in the Rawlins mysteries. Signifying more than just a 'striking plot twist', he argues that the death of Mouse provides the opportunity 'for a resolution, as Easy finds a way out of his street mentality and embraces a new world' (1999: 304). In doing so, Nash suggests that Mosley provides a final solution to the impasse that pervades the Rawlins mysteries; the incompatible conflict between domestic life and the violent pull of the streets. For Nash, Easy's escape from the magnetic underworld of the streets is symbolically intimated at the end of the text via the detective's description of himself 'an astronaut who had completed his orbit of earth and now [...] was pulled by some new gravity into a cold clean darkness' (1999: 308). Nash sees this imagery as a symbol of Easy's 'transcendence of the double consciousness that has plagued him'. In other words, the death of Mouse—and of the dualism that their relationship represents—allows Easy to 'pull out of the orbit of the double conscious life', thus signifying 'new possibilities for him in the process of identity formation' (1999: 304). Nash's assessment forcefully recognises Mouse's somewhat usual, if not antithetical, position in the sidekick paradigm. Rather than cementing or reinforcing the detective's subjectivity, Mouse often destabilises Easy's sense of self by frustrating this process of identity construction. His role as sidekick is thus permeated with challenging contradictions, as he embodies the role of both guardian and killer.

For Nash, Easy's ultimate transcendence beyond the 'orbit' of double consciousness is further compounded by the coincidence of Mouse's death with the assassination of John F. Kennedy, a convergence that not only signifies the shift of momentum in the Civil Rights struggle during the mid-sixties, but the emergence of a new 'black consciousness' produced by a 'growing resistance to the double-consciousness-producing marginalization of the social order' (1999: 304–305). Although in part convincing, overall Nash's reading is severely problematised by the ultimate return of Mouse in the later Rawlins novels. Although Mouse is initially resurrected in Mosley's collection of short stories *Six Easy Pieces* (2003), it is his most recent Rawlins mystery *Charcoal Joe* (2016) that reasserts this unbreakable doubling between Mouse and Easy as detective and sidekick. By extension, the persistence of Easy's double consciousnesses is similarly and simultaneously reaffirmed. After almost dying himself in *Blonde Faith* (2007), we find Easy in a much less tumultuous position at the beginning of *Charcoal Joe*. Set in the late spring of 1968, the beginning of the text sees Easy in a rare state of financial and personal security. With a loving partner he is due to marry, two well-provided-for children and a legitimate detective agency formed with partners Saul Lynx and 'Whisper' Natly, the opening pages see Easy reflecting on the fortunate trajectory of his life. Yet, the equilibrium of this moment is soon disrupted by the impromptu return of Mouse, a return that draws Easy back into the violence and injustice of the mean streets:

> In the last year and a half, I had been as close to death as a living being can get and climbed my way back up into a world that seemed new and hopeful. I had two great kids, a perfect island woman that I would soon propose to, a profession I was good at, friends that I liked and access to powers that most people in Los Angeles (white or black) didn't even know existed.
>
> I had built the kind of life that I wanted, and once Bonnie said yes, everything would be perfect.
>
> The buzzer on my desk sounded
>
> 'Yes?' I said, pressing the button on the console.
>
> 'Raymond Alexander for you, Mr Rawlins,' Niska said.
>
> 'On the phone?' I asked, maybe a little hopefully.
>
> 'No, dude,' Mouse called from the background. I could hear him on the phone and through my open door. 'I'm right here.'
>
> 'Send him on in,' I said, thinking there was a reason that optimism didn't come naturally to people like me. (Mosley 2017: 6–7)

Here Mosley offers a parodic subversion of the Holmes/Watson paradigm, one that typifies Mouse's role as anti-sidekick. In the same way that Holmes frequently 'pulls Watson away from the marital home', here it is Mouse's return that causes a disruption to Easy's (for once) settled domestic life (McCrea 2011: 92). Mouse asks Easy to investigate a case on behalf of 'Charcoal Joe', a violent mob boss currently serving time in prison. The LAPD is currently holding young physicist Dr. Seymour Braithwaite on suspicion of murder, a charge that Joe wants dropped. What begins as simple case soon escalates into a complex narrative of double-crossing and death, one that shatters Easy's new-found domesticity.

Mouse's resurrection in *Six Easy Pieces*—where he reveals that he was saved by the voodoo magic of a witch doctor called Mama Joe—and subsequent appearance here in *Charcoal Joe*, re-establishes the inextricable bond and subversive power that defines his and Easy's relationship as anti-sidekick and detective, one that extends beyond mere friendship to encompass a deeper facet of African American identity. Indeed, Jennifer Larsen argues that Mouse's 'nonchalant' return from the dead causes the two men to establish a new kind of partnership grounded on 'mutual accountability' (2016). For Larsen, this extends to Easy's acceptance of Mouse's violence as a necessary outcome of operating between the socially and racially schematised spaces of the city. Easy's ultimate embracement of Mouse's transgressive potentiality thus reaffirms the enduring connection between subjectivity and the detective/sidekick dualism in Mosley's work. Indeed, if Nash perceives the apparent death of Mouse in *A Little Yellow Dog* as the symbolic destruction of double consciousness, then the fact of Mouse's return is equally symptomatic of its very persistence.

The Freudian connotations of Mouse's repeated re-emergence are difficult to avoid. As Traci Carroll suggests, 'the disjunction between racial and national identity in Du Bois's concept of double consciousness bears a remarkable similarity to the binary opposition between consciousness and the unconscious in psychoanalytic thought, yet it also deconstructs Freud by drawing the imagined line of self-fracture' (1996: 189). In his paradigm, Carroll argues that the 'two poles of twoness, American and Negro, function as conscious and unconscious, black being the repository of a barely glimpsed truth about oneself whose complete access is prohibited or limited by racism' (1996: 189). Through his role as anti-sidekick, Mouse is a perpetual reminder of the very twoness that defines Easy's subjectivity, a conduit through which the 'barely glimpsed truth' of Easy's own darker capacities are realised. In the process, this relationship becomes central to Mosley's strategic subversion of the traditions of the hardboiled American crime novel and of the conventions of the sidekick mode. Whilst providing an 'other' perspective on the mechanisms of white masculinity that have traditionally energised the genre, the elaboration of the traditional role of helper into the exploration of black masculinity in Mouse and Easy is further testament to Mosley's more nuanced and complex examinations of race (McCracken 1998: 174). With more Rawlins mysteries likely in the future, it seems difficult to imagine a scenario where the fate of Easy is not inextricably bound up with that of his perennial double and anti-sidekick, Mouse.

References

Bell, Bernard W. 1989. *The Afro-American Novel and Its Tradition*. Amherst: The University of Massachusetts Press.

Berger, Roger A. 1997. "The Black Dick": Race, Sexuality and Discourse in the L.A. Novels of Walter Mosley. *African American Review* 31 (2): 281–294.

Bryant, Jerry H. 2003. *Born in a Mighty Bad Land: The Violent Man in African American Folklore and Fiction*. Bloomington: Indiana University Press.

Carroll, Traci. 1996. Invisible Sissy: The Politics of Masculinity in African American Bisexual Narrative. In *Representing Bisexualities: Subjects and Cultures of Fluid Desire*, ed. Donald E. Hall and Maria Pramaggiore, 180–206. New York: New York University Press.

Chandler, Raymond. (1940) 2010. *Farewell, My Lovely*. London: Penguin.

Demirtürk, E.Lâle. 2012. *The Contemporary African American Novel: Multititle Cities, Multiple Subjectivities and Discursive Practices of Whiteness in Everyday Urban Encounters*. Lanham: Farleigh Dickinson University Press.

Du Bois, W.E.B. 2017. *The Souls of Black Folk*. Seattle: AmazonClassics.

Fernandes, Jorge Luis Andrade. 2008. *Challenging Euro-America's Politics of Identity: The Return of the Native*. Abingdon: Routledge.

Fontenot, J. Chester. 2001. On Being a Problem in America. In *W.E.B. Du Bois and Race: Essays Celebrating the Centennial Publication of The Souls of Black Folk*, ed. Chester J. Fontenot, Mary Alice Morgan and Sarah Gardner, 1–10. Macon: Mercer University Press.

Gray, Richard. 2012. *A History of American Literature*. Chichester: Wiley Blackwell.

Larson, Jennifer. 2016. *Understanding Walter Mosley*. Columbia: University of South Carolina Press.

Lock, Helen. 2001. Invisible Detection: The Case of Walter Mosley. *MELUS* 26 (1): 77–89.

McCracken, Scott. 1998. *Pulp: Reading Popular Fiction*. Manchester: Manchester University Press.
McCrea, Barry. 2011. *In the Company of Strangers: Family and Narrative in Dickens, Conan Doyle, Joyce, and Proust*. New York: Columbia University Press.
Messent, Peter. 2013. *The Crime Fiction Handbook*. Oxford: Wiley.
Mosley, Walter. 1990. *Devil in a Blue Dress*. London: Serpent's Tail.
———. 1991. *A Red Death*. New York: Serpent's Tale.
———. 1994. *Black Betty*. New York: Simon & Schuster.
———. 1996. *A Little Yellow Dog*. New York: Simon & Schuster.
———. 2003. Gray-Eyed Death. In *Six Easy Pieces: Easy Rawlins Stories*, ed. Walter Mosley, 197–236. New York: Atria.
———. 2017. *Charcoal Joe*. London: Weidenfeld & Nicolson.
Nash, William R. 1999. Maybe I killed my own blood: Doppelgangers and Death of Double Consciousness in Walter Mosley's A Little Yellow Dog. In *Multicultural Detective Fiction: Murder from the "Other" Side*, ed. Gosselin J Adrienne, 303–324. New York: Garland.
O'Donoghue, Heather. 2012. Old Wine in New Bottles: Tradition and Innovation in Stieg Larsson's' Millennium Trilogy. In *Stieg Larsson's Millennium Trilogy: Interdisciplinary Approaches to Nordic Noir on Page and Screen*, ed. Steven Peacock, 35–57. Basingstoke: Palgrave.
Panek, LeRoy. 2000. *New Hard-boiled Writers, 1970s–1990s*. Bowling Green: Bowling Green Press.
Quinn, Laura. 2010. The Mouse Will Play: The Parodic in Walter Mosley's Fiction. In *Finding a Way Home: A Critical Assessment of Walter Mosley's Fiction*, ed. Owen E. Brady and Derek C. Maus, 121–132. Jackson: University Press of Mississippi.
Rzepka, Charles. 2005. *Detective Fiction*. Cambridge: Polity.
Silet, Charles. 2011. The Other Side of Those Means Streets. In *Conversations with Walter Mosley*, ed. Owen E. Brady, 16–28. Jackson: University Press of Mississippi.
Svoboda, Joseph. 2001. Detective Sidekicks. In *The Guide to United States Popular Culture*, ed. Browne B Ray and Pat Browne, 230. Madison: University of Wisconsin Press.
Van Thompson, Carlyle. 2010. *Black Outlaws: Race, Law and Male Subjectivity in African American Literature and Culture*. New York: Peter Lang.
Wilson, Charles E. 2003. *Walter Mosley: A Critical Companion*. London: Greenwood Press.

CHAPTER 10

72 Votes: Theorizing the Scapegoat Sidekick in *Batman: A Death in the Family*

Kwasu Tembo

Introduction: 1–900s and Crowbars

There has been surprisingly little scholarly attention paid towards the death of arguably the most famous sidekick in comic book history—Batman's companion, Robin. Although Dick Grayson is the most famous iteration of Robin, Jason Todd represents perhaps the most editorially and commercially problematic holder of the mantle. In Jim Starlin and Jim Aparo's 1988–1989 *Batman* story arc, *A Death in the Family* (hereafter *ADITF*), the then Robin (Jason Todd) is captured by the Joker and near-fatally bludgeoned with a crowbar. Left lying unconscious in a pool of his own blood, the Joker abandons Jason in a warehouse rigged to explode via delayed detonation. Perhaps the most unique aspect of this arc is that, unlike the death of Maxwell Lord at the hands of Wonder Woman, Superman's 'death' at the hands of Doomsday, or Supergirl's death at the hands of the Anti-Monitor, the death of Jason Todd was not purely an executive decision. Jason did not enjoy the widespread popularity of his predecessor in the Robin role, Dick Grayson, and DC Comics and

K. Tembo (✉)
Ashesi University, Accra, Ghana

L. Andrew and S. Saunders (eds.), *The Detective's Companion in Crime Fiction*, Crime Files, https://doi.org/10.1007/978-3-030-74989-7_10

then *Batman* editor Dennis O'Neil later observed that, since 'letters and conversations with fans indicated that few admired [Jason], many were indifferent to him, and a substantial number hated him', it was better to 'let the reader decide Jason's fate', instead of making a concerted editorial decision requiring redrafting the character (O'Neil 1993: 4). In order to do this, DC Comics set up two 1–900 number 50-cent hotlines which gave callers the ability to vote in favour of or against his death—thus generating publicity for the *Batman* title while also potentially ridding the comic of an unpopular character. Over 10,000 votes were cast. The final results of the vote were 5343 for and 5271 against, and Jason's fate was sealed. For all intents and purposes this arc, which received substantial mass media attention (and some criticism), appeared to be tantamount to a public execution. But, as I will argue, it can be more thoroughly understood as a complex form of scapegoating.

It should be acknowledged at this point that, although I will make the case for reading the event as being not dissimilar to a public execution, it is equally important to note that the vote was extremely close. There were almost as many people who wished to see Jason survive the ordeal as those who wished to see him killed. Jason may have been an unpopular character with some fans, but the Robin mantle had been a constant of the *Batman* mythos almost from the beginning of the character's publishing history. For many readers who voted to save Jason, their decision may have stemmed from a desire to preserve the status quo, or perhaps from a belief that, as the third Robin, Tim Drake, later declares, 'Batman *needs* Robin' (Wolfman 1989: 22). Moreover, while the violent death of key characters is commonplace in superhero comics, the wilful murder of a young sidekick at, potentially, his most emotionally vulnerable moment, as he attempts to find and reconnect with his birth mother, was perhaps a step too far for some readers. Based on the vote, then, it seems that Jason Todd was not universally despised by fans, but, crucially, the number of votes cast in favour of his death demonstrates a significant shift in attitude to Robin. It is a clear shift, an extreme response that so many votes were cast to kill of a *boy* sidekick; a boy who represents a mantle almost as old as that of Batman itself. What is key here is the shift in attitude that readers experience from Dick Grayson's Robin (who by comparison appears to be universally liked based on his longevity in comics) to Jason Todd's Robin. With Jason, just over half of those who cared enough to vote from the then readership wanted to see him killed off. Jason Todd, therefore, is one of the most interesting iterations of Robin not because of the convoluted publishing process that determined his diegetic fate, but because of the hatred he stirs in a dedicated group of comic book readers.

To theorize that Jason is arguably the most interesting incarnation of the Robin mantle simply because he is the first one to die outright would be, ironically, uninteresting. Superheroes and masked crime fighters die all the time in comic books, some more than once. Instead, I will illustrate that Jason's death makes him the most interesting Robin precisely because of *how* and *why* he dies in terms of literary anthropology. More explicitly, Jason's divisive effect on the DC Comics readership and the relationship between reader responses to both the character and DC's editorial decisions are also grounds to analyse not only this particular storyline and reader event, but also this particular iteration of Robin that both caused and facilitated them.

Before proceeding, I need to briefly explain a key term and its two modifications that perform a lot of work in my analysis. Jason Todd's death takes place on three diegetic levels: the *extradiegetic*, *diegetic* and *hyperdiegetic*, or in other words, 'our world', 'the narrative world' and worlds within worlds as 'a story within a story' respectively. The term *interdiegetic* refers to phenomena that move between these modalities of narrative (Genette 1980: 228; Hills 2002: 137). For Jason, life and/or death ultimately redounded to a margin of 72 votes. What are we to read in these 72 votes? Envy? Jealousy? Murder which transcends narrative boundaries between our world and the narrative one? Scapegoating of a child? Did readers choose death in the end because they were jealous of Robin's undeserved and unpopular proximity to Batman—a Robin many thought to be most unlike Batman in his impetuousness and lack of discipline? Did they just want to see what would happen and, in some way or other, satisfy a mordant curiosity? Or are we to see this as an extreme critique of Jason in his capacity as sidekick, or perhaps as a scapegoat punishment for his repeated insubordination against Batman and evident disrespect for the cowl and the mission behind it? The answer is, in fact, a combination of all the above. René Girard's fundamental interest in the relationship between desire, violence and scapegoating as the mediation and control of violence is particularly helpful here, as it provides a useful theoretical framework with which to conceptualize an event of complicit, publicly and interdiegetically determined death. I will attempt to provide a theoretical account for this controversial, if not pseudo-ritualistic, moment in the history of superhero comics by arguing that the justification of the violence committed towards Jason, as well as a scapegoat's death as a solution to the editorial problem of Jason Todd. In so doing, I will theorize the relationship between the role of sidekick in comic book crime fiction, and the function of scapegoating.

The 'Good' Robin: Dick Grayson and Setting the Standard for a Sidekick

The question this section will explore is deceptively simple: what makes a 'good' Robin? However, this question is actually in many ways a supplement of a more fundamental one, namely: what makes a good *sidekick*? Broadly speaking, a good sidekick performs a multitude of roles in their assistance of the principal superhero/costumed crime fighter that can generally be broken down into two categories I call 'hard' and 'soft' skills. Armed with weapons, vehicle, investigative and surveillance training, for example, a good sidekick can be viewed as a living weapon deployed by the hero to give them tactical superiority in their engagements. Whether known or unknown to the hero's target(s), a good sidekick can offer the hero the tactical advantage of additional force that will either surprise and overwhelm their foes, or dissuade them from engaging in the first place. Moreover, the good sidekick also diffuses the risk undertaken by the hero in their activities by becoming both a second target and additional threat to the hero's target(s), forcing the hero's target(s) to divide and weaken their force by fighting an enemy that can seemingly be in two places at once. In a less martial capacity, not all of the hero's manifold activities require the application of violence, in part or *in toto*, to achieve their objective(s). In instances in which persuasion is required, for example, a hero's enemies may, due to fear and a history of violence endured in past encounters with the hero, be more willing to negotiate with a good sidekick rather than suffer the damages, both emotional and physical, of the hero's hyper-aggression. Empathy, patience, emotional fortitude, maturity, discipline and adamant moral-ethical commitment are 'soft' skills that are just as, if not more, important as the 'hard' skills of stamina, pain tolerance, physical strength and athleticism in a good sidekick. There is one other, and perhaps slightly controversial, paradox underpinning the idea of a good sidekick: they must be simultaneously dispensable and indispensable, replaceable and irreplaceable, useless and useful. It is this paradox at the heart of the concept of the sidekick that I believe *ADITF* also ultimately exposes.

Perhaps one way to approach the question of what makes a good 'Robin' is to question exactly what 'Robin' means. If Robin as a sidekick can be thought of as an ancillary, albeit important, adjunct to Batman, then the value of the mantle is always-already determined by its relationship to Batman. According to Jake Black:

> [T]he boys [Batman] takes under his wing and into his household are more than symbols of his mission. With each new sidekick he brings in, he renews that solemn covenant he made [...] in Crime Alley. He needs a Robin. It gives him something tangible to fight for, when his true mission is cased in the emotional, the intangible. Without Robin, Batman's quest for justice and protection becomes hollow. It is vengeance for vengeance's sake. But with Robin, he can restore and preserve the parts of him that were destroyed long ago, giving his mission meaning and power in his own life and in the lives of those he helps. Robin's colourful costume reminds the Dark Knight that all is not as bleak as it may appear. There is still innocence out there, and that is above all other concerns, worth protecting. (Black 2009: 125–126)

Here, the paradoxes of the mantle become clear. According to Black, a 'good' Robin must remind Batman that there is innocence in the world that is worth protecting. Yet a good Robin must also be a disciplined and dedicated warrior who, alongside Batman, must continuously have that sense of innocence eroded by unending conflict with Gotham's broad and terrible array of evil. In this sense, a good Robin is not unlike a child soldier: an innocent combatant.[1] What Batman needs a good Robin to be (aside from level-headed, despite the psychological and physical tempestuousness of adolescence) is lethally efficient, but also to always obfuscate said lethality beneath a veneer of good cheer and the hopeful amiability of youth.

Let me acknowledge the fact that the Robin mantle, though seemingly perpetually in Batman's shadow, also casts its own umbra. The legacy established by Dick Grayson, the first Robin, is a weight of familial commitment, effective partnership and meaningful apprenticeship under which Jason Todd must toil. What makes Dick not only a 'good' Robin but *the best* Robin is precisely that he was not only able to endure the immense physical, psychological and emotional weights placed upon his youthful shoulders by Batman *as* Robin, but to subsequently move beyond the limits against his self-identity imposed by the Robin mantle itself. He is so successful in this regard that he develops an entire life independent of Batman. He leaves Gotham, attends university, co-founds and mentors numerous incarnations of the Teen Titans as Nightwing, a new mantle evolved out of both Robin and Batman. In a colloquial sense, Dick grows to become a sort of Batman 2.0.[2] As both Nightwing and a mature Dick Grayson, the character is shown to be just as capable, just as tenacious, dedicated, strong-willed and effective as both a man and a crime-fighter. Moreover, he is also shown to be deeply emotionally open (as evidenced by his intimate relationship with Starfire), mature, grounded, humorous and compassionate. While it is tempting to argue that what makes Dick a 'good' Robin is the fact that he is less psychologically and emotionally damaged than Batman, I feel it more accurate to say that Dick takes the time to balance the development of his abilities in pursuit of his duty as Robin with the development of his psychological and emotional well-being. This makes him better equipped to deal with his traumas in a way that his mentor and master, Bruce, is unable to do for himself, nor teach any subsequent Robin to do. While it seems tautological to suggest that Dick is able to do something Bruce is not, yet needs Bruce in order to be able to do it, one must keep in mind that not all Robins are the same. Beyond the undifferentiating scope of their training mission, and mentorship from Bruce, the way each individual boy beneath the mask expresses and represses his trauma is different. In this sense, what makes Dick Grayson the quintessential 'good' Robin is the fact that he is, by and large, able to do everything Batman is able to, yet also do more affective things that, though ephemeral, are crucial to the self-care and trauma processing necessary to the successful and healthy continuation of a crime-fighter's career, especially in a city as saturnine and psychotic as Gotham. In this way, by relinquishing his identity as Robin and re-creating it as Nightwing, Dick Grayson ultimately does what Bruce Wayne could not: move forward and move on. This process is not without its complexities; as Carsten Fogh Nielsen notes, Dick's decision to vacate the role of sidekick 'leads to a heated encounter with Batman [in at least some versions of the story], who refuses to accept that Dick Grayson/Robin will no longer act as his sidekick' (Nielsen 2008: 254). Based on Batman's reaction, the biggest question here is whether Dick is a good Robin for moving beyond the mantle, or a bad Robin for the same reason? This also raises another question: is a good Robin simply a more stable version of Batman?

There are, however, related ancillary questions that will prove important to the analysis to come. Does Dick Grayson's evolution make him a good or bad Robin to the *reader*? Is a good Robin one who survives, or one who dies for the mission? Is a good Robin one who is like Batman in character and crime-fighting, but one who ultimately remains resolutely attached to Batman? Is a good Robin like or unlike Batman? What matters most in determining whether a Robin is good or bad? Self-determination, moral rectitude, strength of will, independence and autonomy and/or discipline? Such considerations are even further troubled by the fact that, as Carsten Nielsen observes:

> Dick Grayson doesn't just free himself from Batman's influence and become a respected crime fighter in his own right, he does so using the very abilities and character traits he has acquired and learned from Batman. Most obviously, Nightwing uses the detective skills he has been taught by Batman and the physical and mental abilities he has developed through their mutual collaboration, in his own war against crime. Equally important but not nearly as obvious is the way Nightwing employs the courage, intelligence, and integrity that Batman has helped instil in him, to *liberate* himself from Batman's influence. (Nielsen 2008: 255; emphasis mine)

Nielsen's (presumably innocent) use of the word 'liberate' is particularly interesting here. Dick Grayson needed to literally escape, to free himself from the shadow of Batman, because he instinctively knew that being and remaining a sidekick was to risk being sacrificed for the mission. If viewed in this way, the question of whether or not Dick is a good Robin comes down to whether one believes his emancipation from Batman was, in any way, catalysed by self-preservation. Mary Borsellino observes that from Dick Grayson to Tim Drake, everyone who has taken on the role of Batman's sidekick has paid a severe price—the traumatic death of their parents—that, in view of its circuitousness throughout the history of the Robin mythos, is seemingly a prerequisite of the mantle (Borsellino 2009: 142). Is a 'good' Robin, then, one who has or is willing to pay what I call the mantle price? There are several disturbing implications to be drawn out from this: one: while not occurring to all Robins (Tim Drake for instance), the Robin mantle is typically predicated on the sustained trauma of the loss of their parents as the result of violent crime, which thematically acts as a type of prerequisite mirroring of the same trauma sustained by Batman himself. Two: all Robins must accept this. In this sense, a good Robin is not unlike a front-line soldier, a paradox of debilitating psychological, emotional and physical trauma, seemingly superhuman resolve, and perhaps most paradoxically of all, disenchanted yet unwavering faith in the mission. However, the question still remains as to how independent Dick Grayson is of Batman if he 'acquired and developed the capacities needed for him to become an autonomous human being, mainly by imitating and emulating a morally exemplary person, Batman'? (Nielsen 2008: 255). So, then, what makes a 'good' Robin? If a paradoxical mixture of loyalty and autonomy, subservience and independence, serfdom and enterprise form the psychologically, emotionally, and physically difficult core of the Robin mantle, then Dick Grayson arguably succeeds on all counts. In the last instance, his independence from Batman is not tantamount to an ultimate rejection of his mission's mandate or methods. It is an evolution of it.

On Jason Todd, a.k.a. the 'Bad' Robin

In view of the above discussion of Dick Grayson as the quintessential 'good' Robin, how is Jason a 'bad' Robin? Jason's status as a 'bad' Robin is largely based on the fact that the character does not fit neatly into the sidekick role established during Dick Grayson's tenure. While Dick is, both during and after his time, able to more or less successfully remain within the confines of the mantle, there is a tension, it seems, between the Robin identity and Jason Todd's identity. The idea of having a sidekick identity to slip into (or out of, in Jason's case) is an interesting one in terms of the development of the sidekick in crime fiction.

As Mathew Manning and Hanna Dolan note, Jason Todd, not unlike his predecessor, first appeared in a circus scene on the pages of *Batman* No. 357 (1983) (Dolan and Manning 2011: 201). Jason is the second character to assume the mantle of Robin, though while the initial reader response to him was generally favourable, Jim Starlin's run was not well received following the character's retconned origin in *Batman* No. 408–409 (1987). Part of the character's revamped origin casts Todd as a young destitute orphan living in an abandoned apartment tenement. Immediately, Jason's 'badness' is inherent in his initial encounter with his future foster father, teacher, mentor and patron: Batman. In a seemingly kismetic scene, Batman catches Jason attempting to strip and steal the tires off the Batmobile in Crime Alley, the same traumatic space in which Batman's parents were gunned down by the mugger Joe Chill (Finger and Kane 1939: 1–2; Starlin 1988: 2).

Bruce, on numerous occasions throughout the arc, describes his ward and partner as having a '*dangerously high* level of *aggressive energy* to work off', his demeanour as 'very *moody*. Resentful. Reckless', adding that his 'attitude is [likely] to get him *killed*' (Starlin 1988: 2–3). This assessment is further supported by numerous other allusions to Jason's psychological and emotional instability. In *Batman* No. 426 (1988), Bruce states, 'the boy's got a lot of *sorrow* to work out of his system' (Starlin 1988: 12). Jason's impetuousness, however, is immediately apparent even on the first page of the arc. On a raid of a child pornography racket, Bruce states: 'the bust was all set to go. *Robin* and I were in hiding, waiting for our police backups. Suddenly my partner runs out of *patience*. That's the way it goes sometimes with the best laid plans of *mice* and *man*' (Starlin 1988: 2). Robin shakes off Bruce's attempt to restrain him, yelling that his recklessness is simply an aspect of what he was trained to do, gleefully violating protocol to 'kick some tail' (Starlin 1988: 2). In the aftermath of their skirmish with the racketeers, Bruce takes Jason about the shoulders and remonstrates with him, asking 'don't you *understand*? These are *procedures* even *we* have to follow [...] What's worse, you nearly got yourself *killed* doing it [...] what do you *think* we're doing here!? *Playing some kind of game*?' Jason responds nonchalantly with a wry grin, saying over his shoulder 'of course. All life's a game' (Starlin 1988: 4).

Equally as apparent as Jason's burgeoning propensity for morally opprobrious behaviour are numerous sympathetic reasons that seemingly frame, contextualize, and, perhaps even justify this predisposition. It could be argued that Jason is the victim of circumstance; consider another instance of Jason's rebelliousness which emerges when he decides to pursue a lead concerning the true identity of his mother. He decides to disobey Bruce and proceed alone stating,

> I know what he'd say ... 'you're in *no shape* to be running an investigation!' Besides, Bruce *wouldn't care* about finding my real *mother*. All he gets off on is *catching crooks*. He probably couldn't even *understand why* I'd want to locate the woman. This *job's* all *mine*. *Can't depend* on *anyone* for help. (Starlin 1988b: 18–19)

However, the seemingly clear-cut delineation of Jason as a bad Robin in this and other moments throughout his career is complicated when Jason offers compelling support for his recklessness by asking the reader the rather profound question: 'How often, in life, do you get to *meet* your *own mother* for the *first time*?' (Starlin 1988b: 24).

It could be argued here that Jason feels unloved by Bruce. In the first quarter of the *ADITF*, Bruce has a choice: track down and stop the Joker from selling a nuclear warhead or find and retrieve Jason. He chooses the former, to which Jason retorts, 'sure, Bruce ... nothing *glamorous* about hunting down a *runaway*' (Starlin 1988b: 32). Later in *Batman* No. 428 (1988), Bruce admits the true reason for his neglect of Jason's psychological and emotional well-being stating in an inner monologue:

> It's just that I felt so adrift when I lost *Dick Grayson* as a partner. *The Batman* needed a *Robin* [...] I guess the truth is that I was lonely ... didn't want to go it alone. So what do I do? I bring a young *innocent* into this mad game. I must be insane. (Starlin 1988: 2)

Here, Bruce recognizes his mistake: 'I thought I had his *best interests* at heart when I rushed him into training to be the *new Robin*' (Starlin 1988c: 12). Despite these revelations, the question still remains, however: is Jason a bad Robin because of his innate characteristics, his trauma, or because he has been poorly trained, overseen, mentored and nurtured by Bruce?

Preceding the events of *ADITF*, Jason believes himself to be the son of Willis and Catherine Todd who raised him in Park Row, a rough district of East Gotham. The introductory issue of *ADITF*, reveals that his mother Catherine was a drug addict whose death by overdose resulted in Jason's orphanhood. His father, Willis, is revealed to have been a former medical student while simultaneously working as a hired thug for villain Two-Face (Starlin 1988: 12). Following an assignment gone awry, Willis suspiciously disappeared. After Bruce Wayne's attempts to institutionalize the boy, and Jason successfully assisting Batman to apprehend a gang of thieves, Jason eventually earns the mantle of Robin after six months of training. In *Batman* No. 428 (1988), Batman makes the observation that while Jason does not possess Dick Grayson's natural athleticism and acrobatic aptitude, Jason is most effective as Robin *if* and when he focusses his inexhaustible rage (Starlin 1988c: 3). Latent within this observation is also a premonition, namely, that left unsupervised, Jason's descent into the 'criminal element' is inevitable, thus ostensibly making Bruce Wayne's intercession in the boy's life seemingly exigent.

Max Allan Collins' reinterpretation of Jason and his origins in the *Batman* comic in 1986–1987 serves to portray him as rebellious or bad. Some of this registers as somewhat heavy-handed, namely in Jason's 'bad' habits which include smoking, swearing and acute unapologetic insubordination. The performance of his duties during his tenure as Robin is also portrayed as one fuelled by unbridled emotion, specifically anger and hostility, as well as instinct. Collins establishes this disequilibrium between emotional turmoil and duty as one that yields varying results. On the one hand, success can be measured in the form of Jason managing to single-handedly apprehend villains like Scarecrow. On the other, failure can be measured in the form of numerous instances where Jason's impatience impedes upon the success of the mission. This can be noted in *Batman* No. 426, where Jason's impatience foils the Dynamic Duo's chances of successfully executing raids against a terrorist training camp in Lebanon to interrogate the camp's training officer, Lady Shiva (Starlin 1988a: 12–22). Later in Chapter 2, even Jason acknowledges his own impetuousness in this regard. Staking out a hotel in Lebanon for a woman he suspects may be his mother, Jason says to himself: 'Guess I just wait here for her to show up. But what then? Do I just *walk up* and *ask* her if she's my *mother*? Guess I haven't really *thought* this all out yet' (Starlin 1988a: 30).

Jason's unpredictable and dangerous behaviour causes his patron and partner much psychological, emotional and even procedural/tactical unease. Seeking counsel from Alfred in *Batman* No. 426 (1988), Bruce remarks 'the kid's *losing* it. He *dived* into those *thugs* like someone looking to *die*' (Starlin 1988a: 3). Later in the same exchange, Bruce admits the possibility and fault that he 'may have started Jason as Robin *before* he had a *chance* to come to grips with his *parents' deaths*' (Starlin 1988a: 3). Alfred responds by pointing out the obvious in terms of the underlying complexity of Jason's life: 'Being your *partner* is not exactly the best *situation* for a teenager *adjusting* to such a loss' (Starlin 1988a: 5). Overhearing this exchange, Jason is subsequently suspended from active duty. This apparent demotion precipitates an interesting argument between the two. Bruce justifies his decision by stating 'a person's got to have his *head* screwed on *right* for this line of work' (Starlin 1988a: 6). Here, Starlin reveals an underlying ambivalence to Bruce and Jason's working and domestic relationship. On the one hand, Bruce is keenly aware of the danger of having an emotionally damaged child as a crime-fighting vigilante partner. Bruce declares openly that he is aware that

Jason is 'hurting' and that he has 'a lot of *anger* and pain inside [him which will] take *time* for [him] to get rid of' (Starlin 1988a: 6, 1988c). On the other hand, Bruce is also caught between the value of Jason's efficacy as a combatant, despite the youth's procedural and methodological divergences from Bruce's own. Bruce notes in a flashback sequence in *Batman* No. 428 (1988) that 'Jason took to the *training* like a fish to water. He was *quick* and *intelligent*. It was like training Dick again. But this kid had a *rebellious streak* in him' and later how 'right from the start [of the duo's career as such], there was trouble. This *new Robin* came with an overload of *emotional luggage*' (Starlin 1988c: 3). In this construction is also the underlying fact that Jason's efficacy as a combatant does not necessarily make him a good Robin.

This ambivalence simultaneously registers as pedagogical and parental malpractice. After all, how can it be that the greatest detective in the DC multiverse would fail to see the danger in the aforementioned behavioural markers in his younger, less experienced partner? This question arises in *Batman* No. 426 (1988) where Bruce is shown to be unable to discern the root causes of Jason's un-Robinly behaviour. Throughout the issue and arc more broadly, Bruce continually (and erroneously) assumes Jason's oscillating temperament is the result of him not having 'adjusted to the *death* of his *parents* [and that] he needs *time* to work out his *grief*, *time he wouldn't find* fighting crime by [Bruce's] side' (Starlin 1988a: 25). However, it is later revealed that Jason's temperament has been unbalanced by the fact that his mother, assumed dead, is in fact still alive. Are the most adverse effects of Jason's behaviour therefore compounded by either Bruce's negligence and/or ambivalence to the causes and treatments of Jason's psychological and emotional distress? Or is the answer here more tragic in that Bruce fails to recognize his ward and warrior's instability, or perhaps, *wilfully* chooses to be blind to it because it resembles all too closely (and therefore triggers) his own trauma? Bruce admits as much to himself in *Batman* No. 428 (1988) when searching the wreckage of the warehouse in which Jason and his mother are killed by the Joker. He says to himself, 'I warned you not to take on the Joker by yourself. I begged you to *wait*, Jason. But of course you *didn't*. You never listen. *Why*? *Why*?' (Starlin 1988c: 2). He is, however, remorseful over the situation. Bruce admonishes himself, stating 'why didn't I see that you were too young for this kind of work? How could I have been so *stupid*?' (Starlin 1988c: 2). All of this redounds to the same question: who or what is to blame for Jason's status as a bad Robin?

Prior to his death, the most ethically and morally problematic manifestation of Jason's emotional tumult appears in *Batman* No. 424 (1988). In the story 'The Diplomat's Son', serial rapist Felipe Garzonas evades prosecution on account of his father's diplomatic immunity. Jason finds one of Garzonas' victims, a girl named Gloria, dead after hanging herself due to fear of Garzonas' committing a third rape against her. Subsequently, Batman witnesses Garzonas fall 22 stories to his death, looking up to see Jason standing on the edge of a balcony. Jason alleges that Garzonas' death was due to fright, causing him to accidentally slip (Starlin 1988: 180–182). As a result, the circumstances of the character's tragic origin story come into direct conflict not only with the lethality of his crime-fighting outlook and its comparatively radical divergence from Batman's own code of conduct, but the ambiguity surrounding Jason's own sense of morality more generally.[3]

In view of this moral ambiguity and emotional instability, the resulting aspersions cast against Jason were potent enough to precipitate an editorial death sentence, one to be either confirmed or stayed by the reader. This decision was mediated by editorial feints and slips, all of which can be seen as tantamount to prosecutions and defences not only of Jason's actions, but his character as well. In 1988's *ADITF*, the demand for Jason's execution is somewhat troubled by the narrative basis informing the entire arc; namely, the sympathetic story of an orphan seeking his parents. This narrative portrays Jason as a confused, isolated, desperate, hopeful and ultimately tragic figure. In the story, Jason discovers Catherine Todd was not his biological mother. In an attempt to locate the latter, Jason uses his training to deduce three possible parental candidates including an Israeli Mossad agent and villainous Lady Shiva. The third, Sheila Haywood, an aid worker practising in Ethiopia, turns out to be his mother. After her suspiciously cool reception of him, Jason detects that Haywood is being blackmailed by the Joker, who intends to sell her medical supplies for profit following the U.S. government's seizure of most of his assets in the events leading up to *ADITF*. It is revealed that the Joker is exploiting Sheila's guilt and involvement in embezzlement from the aid agency as leverage. As part of their deal and her cover, she agrees to betray Jason, whom she has to also be Robin, to the Joker. After being briefly detained in an abandoned warehouse, the Joker severely beats Jason with a crowbar and subsequently leaves both him and his mother there under threat of a timed explosive set to detonate. At this point, the vote determining the fate of Jason took place.

The result of which was Jason and his mother failure to escape, the explosion of the device, the destruction of the warehouse, and both characters' deaths. Arriving too late, Batman finds their charred corpses in the debris (Starlin 1988: 2). Following these events, both Batman and the reader are left to contemplate the nature of Jason Todd as Batman's greatest failure, as an orphan betrayed, and/or as a careless and overzealous lost boy who reaped what he had so impulsively and thoughtlessly sown. These and other contemplations became more than subjective musings when O'Neil and DC made the decision to set up a dual 1–900 number voting system as the way to determine Jason's fate. The onus was placed squarely on the readers, who now had the ability to influence the story directly. Beginning on 15 September 1988, readers could call either of the two numbers and cast their vote for or against Jason's death within a 36-hour window. Over 10,000 votes were cast, those in favour of Jason's death winning by a margin of 72 votes.

As Mathew Manning (2011) suggests, Jason Todd's death is a far more personal death for Batman (perhaps barring only that of his biological son, Damian Wayne) and the Bat Family more generally than the circumstances surrounding the loss or moving on of other Robins. The Joker, who had hitherto been known for murdering anonymous victims (typically bystanders of his cat-and-mouse battles with the Dark Knight), made a victim of one of the Batman mythos' core characters.[4] *ADITF* has come to be regarded as one of the most important narrative events in the Batman universe. *ADITF* generated wide media coverage and deprecatory responses impugning the decision to kill Jason, a Robin, and whether consumers liked it or not, a pop-culture icon. Reactions came in from various news and print media including *USA Today* and *Reuters*, and collectively revealed that, on the one hand, the public and readership had contrasting understandings of Jason as an innocent victim versus a victim of his own making. On the other hand, the vote revealed the zeitgeist's fundamental misunderstanding and/or egregious oversimplification of the interdiegetic nature of Jason's death, its underlying structure based on the interaction between the reader, Batman and Robin. *Reuters* would reduce the complexities of Jason's death to the mere soundbite: 'a group of comic book artists and writers has succeeded in doing what the most fiendish minds of the century [...] have failed to accomplish' (*USA Today* qtd. in Weldon 2016: 149).

There is a little direct scholarship that seeks to theorize Jason Todd and his death. Of all Bruce Wayne's wards to wear the Robin mantle, Jason is the least commented upon in academic contexts. What little scholarship exists is often circuitous in that it uses Jason as either a case study within a broader discussion of Batman's ethics, or as a case study of DC's editorial decisions and socio-historical engagement with its readership. That said, Cara MacNeil-Donoghue investigates the nature of Robin in a helpful way. She uses various aspects of performance theory to first define what is meant by the term/mantle 'Robin' within the character's own mythosphere(s) and within the broader mythos of Batman, before subsequently comparing the first two holders of the mantle, namely Dick Grayson and Jason Todd. In so doing, she seeks to elaborate specific aspects of the character which she frames initially as the following questions: 'what makes a good Robin? How do we understand what a Robin is? Who makes a good Robin? Why do they make a good Robin?' (MacNeil-Donoghue 2015: 55). In this sense, she approaches Robin less as an individual, but more as 'a category, a type of performance' (MacNeil-Donoghue 2015: 55). Theoretically, this means that the mantle can be described to determine the value of the holder's state of being and their freedom of choice. In this sense, the value of Jason Todd, as *both* a Robin and as a victim, must be measured against his performance as Robin. In this, I follow the outline MacNeil-Donoghue sets down when she states that:

> [P]erformance is comprised of repeated action – one action doesn't 'make' you anything, but rather what you do repeatedly defines who you are. So what does Robin do repeatedly? First of all, Robin performs physical acts of bravery alongside the Dark Knight. Secondly, he maintains a sense of justice that (like Batman's) is devoid of personal involvement and permits the supremacy of an impartial system. Third, Robin maintains absolute loyalty to the Bat and is willing to take Batman's place for the sake of Batman, not for personal gain. (MacNeil-Donoghue 2015: 55)

Here, I would take MacNeil-Donoghue's insights slightly further. Ostensibly, Dick's smile and earnestly enthusiastic demeanour do not bespeak anything resembling pathological rage, nor do they reveal any vengeful malice. Quite the contrary, in fact, in the form of his ultimately grateful attitude despite the severity of his personal losses. While Dick is linked to all the other Robins, with the exception of Damian Wayne, in being an orphan, Dick does not possess the rage that comes from being an orphan that Batman and Jason do. As evidenced in his acrobatic artistry that turned pummelling criminals and reprobates into something of an art, Dick makes crime-fighting more beautiful by removing the envenomed motivation behind the action. This is in keeping with the manner in which the character is introduced into the *Batman* series in *Batman* No. 1 (1940). The issue features reader identification techniques including the Scout-like group the 'Robin's Regulars' and the ideological precepts disseminated in 'Robin's Code' that portray the character as not just a point of reader identification for the comic's young readers, but also explicitly as a role model. As I will later discuss, an important aspect of Robin as a point of reader identification is the space the character opens up in which readers could insert themselves, a space whose proximity to Batman is of primary significance here.

By contrast, Jason's unsublimated rage and anger make him most like the worst and, dare I say real or indissoluble, parts of Bruce, namely anger and the desire for vengeance. Even Damian, who is biologically most like Bruce in being his son, is like him only conceptually; that is despite their respective divergences, especially with regard to lethal force both are equally as committed, disciplined and dedicated to their missions. The conflict between Bruce and Damian arises in the differing methods of their respective missions. While Stephanie Brown most resembles her boyfriend Tim Drake as a Robin, in terms of being able, contentious, ambitious and highly skilled, Tim is most like Batman in terms of his natural deductive prowess and intelligence. Furthermore, in terms of the character's relationship to the mission and his own psychological makeup, Tim established a serviceable median between the dedication and discipline of Dick and a far more toned down (often occasional rather than ongoing) manifestation of Jason's impudence. In view of this contextualizing albeit cursory comparative glance at the performances of Robin, we can conclude as MacNeil-Donoghue does concerning Jason: he frequently 'diverges from the Bat Philosophy and this is part of the reason we do not read him as a good Robin' (MacNeil-Donoghue 2015: 59). In this sense, Jason is a 'bad' Robin for the exact reasons Dick Grayson is a good one. Jason is brash, insubordinate, proud and violent in ways that challenge as opposed to safeguard the mission. In this way, Jason's status as a 'bad' Robin must necessarily be a confluence of character traits, behaviours and reader opinion. It is this same confluence of circumstances, attributes and reception that underpinned the character's death. As suggested above, an inherent, and arguably most important, aspect of the Robin mantle is trust in Batman and obedience to him. In the pursuit of his own agendas of vengeance and self-discovery, as well as in the methods he brings to bear therein, Jason Todd is a 'bad' Robin precisely because, while the character's circumstances made it so that he had no choice but to rely on himself, he has no faith in Batman when given the choice. While he acknowledges the skills, abilities, resources and mission of his mentor, Jason does not respect Batman's approach to his mission (Starlin 1988a: 18–19). This is perhaps nowhere better expressed than in the scene after which, using not only the detective skills he was taught by Bruce but also his impressive resources in the form of the Batcave computer, Jason discovers three potential hits for the identity and location of his mother. When faced with the dilemma of how to proceed, he deliberates as follows, revealing his disregard for Batman's approach and his mission itself:

> So what do I do now? Take what I have to *Bruce*, ask for his *help*? *No way*! I know what he'd say ... 'you're in *no shape* to be running off on this type of investigation!' Besides, Bruce wouldn't care about finding my *real mother*. All he gets off on is *catching crooks*. He probably couldn't even *understand why* I'd want to locate the woman. (Starlin 1988b: 18)

The implication here is that despite Jason's insubordination, his attempt to save the woman who betrayed him, his own mother, should characterize him as a hero. But these narrative facts come into conflict with certain inextricable and contradictory external facts. Firstly, while DC has never repeated a 1–900 vote concerning a character's death since Jason's own, despite the backlash O'Neil and his staff garnered, the retrospectively short-sighted decision was ultimately theirs. Secondly, the voting system was, by any democratic standards of voting, crude in that there were no guarantees that the process would produce a fair or even accurate result. In his commentary for the *Under the Red Hood* (2010) documentary, O'Neil goes as far as to assign the outcome of the vote to a caller who allegedly repeatedly called the 1–900 for Jason's death in order to ensure it (Winick 2010).

This latent desire to avoid blame for and further theorization of Jason's death continues in O'Neil's foreword to *Robin: Tragedy and Triumph* (1993). In it, O'Neil offers a paradoxical description of Jason which, I contend, reveals the central aporia of Jason's status as being simultaneously both pure and impure victim of interdiegetic violence and editorial scapegoating. He describes Jason as 'an interesting, and somewhat spooky, case of a fictional character seizing control of his own destiny' on the one hand, and as 'a disturbed and sometimes disagreeable problem child' on the other (O'Neil 1993: 4). While O'Neil could simply have elected to kill Jason off outright, the melodrama, showmanship and sensationalism of the phone vote method was most certainly, at least in part, intended to engender interest, shock and an atmosphere of suspense and, with it, more sales. However, this editorial sidestepping does not absolve O'Neil and the DC editorial staff more broadly for the complicity in ensuring what increasingly appears to be a ritualized, albeit modern, interdiegetic murder through a faulty system, gauge and measure that ultimately encouraged the revelation and expression of the violence of readers' antithetical feelings towards Jason. While O'Neil claims, explicitly and implicitly, that Jason's death was his own fault and also unintended by the editorial staff, he claims precisely the opposite elsewhere (Langley 2012: 1; Pearson and Uricchio 1991). O'Neil states that DC's editorial team *consciously* portrayed Jason as increasingly 'bratty': 'when we were building up to the death of Robin', O'Neil confesses, 'we made him rebellious—he ran away, and in a way he got what he was asking for. He disobeyed Batman twice, and that's what led to his demise' (O'Neil qtd. from Benicio127 and Whitesycamore 2011). While O'Neil tends to speak about Jason at a remove, Starlin, who wrote the Batman issues leading up to and including *ADITF* has been far clearer in his resounding dislike not only of Jason as a character, but also of the mantle of Robin itself more broadly. Starlin has stated that he 'wanted to kill off Robin as soon as I started writing Batman. The idea of taking a kid along to fight crime is ludicrous' (Starlin qtd. in Benicio127 and Whitesycamore 2011). Here, the problem of Jason Todd is always already bifurcated between the boy himself and the mantle's capacities and duties as Batman's sidekick.

It is clear, therefore, that Jason Todd's death is a combination of editorial and reader decisions, the former requiring the latter and the latter only coming into existence due to the structures put in place by the former. As Benicio127 and Whitesycamore conclude in their widely quoted discussion of Jason Todd titled 'Who's to Blame? A Must-Read Essay on Jason Todd':

> Jason was doomed from the outset, written as he was by a creative and editorial team who were no longer sure what purpose the character of Robin was supposed to serve. It seems as though it was much easier for

> the editorial team of Starlin and O'Neil to blame an individual character for the 'failure' than to admit that who or what Robin in the modern era should be was in a state of uncertainty [...] And, really, who decides -- or should be the decision maker in a fictional character's life and death? Not the character, but the creators. (Benicio127 and Whitesycamore 2011)

In Jason's case, however, the decision to kill a fifteen-year-old boy was ultimately in the hands of the reader. In the events leading up to and including *ADITF*, O'Neil (1991) is further quoted stating that readers '*did* hate him [namely, Jason]', adding that he did not 'know if it was fan craziness – maybe they saw him as *usurping* Dick Grayson's position' (O'Neil qtd. in Weldon 1992 [2017]: 147, my emphasis). With both the diegetic and extradiegetic contexts surrounding Jason's death in place, I will now turn my attention to Girard's thought in order to theorize the diegetic violence and death Jason undergoes. In doing so, I will discuss why the character was the perfect scapegoat for the crisis of the Robin mantle and the role of comic-book sidekicks in the genre of crime fiction more broadly during 1980s Batman comics.

Violence, Mimetic Crisis, Death and Scapegoating in A Death in the Family

The purpose of this final section is to show that through *ADITF*, readers were given the ability to eliminate a character they both wanted to imitate and also of whom they subconsciously felt jealous. This jealously was, at least partially, based on viewing the character as undeserving of the Robin mantle due to his behaviour and his subsequent status as a 'bad' sidekick more broadly. To do so, I refer to the work of René Girard. The foundational concept of Girardian thought, outlined in his first text *Deceit, Desire and the Novel* (1961), is that all desire is mimetic, that is, desire is learned/borrowed/imitated from others and that this shared desire inevitably leads to conflict. When two individuals try to appropriate the same object, a mimetic crisis emerges, because both cannot have the same object at the same time. This results in violence emerging as a means of allowing both individuals a chance to remove one another as impediments to the acquisition of the desired object (Williams 1996: 8). The crisis of mimetic violence not only effects said individuals, but their mimetic rivalry extends beyond the confines of their dispute and threatens the integrity of their community as well. This crisis can only be quelled, for a time, by the scapegoat mechanism whereby the cause of the mimetic crisis is blamed on a sacrificial victim. The scapegoat's death is designed to defuse a mimetic crisis, sanctify the victim, and protect the cohesion of the community (Müller 1996).

When applied to the death of Jason Todd in relation to his role as sidekick and, I contend, scapegoat in *ADITF*, the immediate question is whether or not his death accomplishes *any* of these things. If we take the reader as the subject, Batman as the object, and Jason as the mediator, the primary desire at play here is the reader's desire to be either near and/or like Batman. The desire is ultimately for the reader to be the character who shares the most proximity with Batman, namely Robin. Jason, in being that character, becomes not only a mediator but also a rival of the reader's desire. This generates feelings of jealousy, envy and resentment, and the reader may, implicitly or explicitly, think that were they to occupy that same space of proximity, they themselves would be far better Robins than Jason. It is precisely Jason's status as a 'bad' Robin which engenders feelings of envy and dislike of the character in the reader. Conversely, Dick is not subjected to this antagonism, due to his status amongst readers as a 'good' Robin. This could very well be the result of Dick being the originator of the Robin role and the first claimant of the mantle and, as such, more likely to be generally accepted by readers. In this way, it should not come as a surprise that Jason would ultimately be judged against Dick and found wanting on account of not living up to the original and progenitor. Moreover, the fact of Dick's vacation of the Robin role and Jason's subsequent assumption of the Robin mantle suggests that the Robin role is a fluid, transferrable position. This means that, ultimately, a specific character does not own a monopoly on the mantle that that character adopts for a time. With the Robin mantle, there is no such thing as permanent tenure and thus the nature, value and efficacy of each and every occupant of the role may be challenged.

According to Girard, this type of mediation can be described as 'external' because Jason is a fictional character and, therefore, should be beyond the reach of the subject—the reader. However, due to O'Neil's editorial decision, the mediation at play between Jason and the reader became 'internal' because, for 36 hours, mediator (Jason) and subject (the reader) occupied the *same* diegetic space. Through a telephone call, readers could directly insert their intent, disapproval, jealousy and so forth into the story world. Regardless of how the vote unfolded in the end, this particular editorial method precipitated a mimetic crisis, because now Jason and the readers' relationship evolved beyond passive consumption of a fictional character beyond the readers' reach into something that they could actively affect. The reader could now not only influence Jason's existence in the story world, but in being given this power, compete against him. In voting against Jason, I speculate that numerous callers saw themselves as being better allies and partners to Batman than Jason, using their power to eliminate something they perceived to be a threat to his mission, namely Jason himself. O'Neil and DC's editorial decision not only highlighted the crisis of readers' resentment of Jason, as a bad mediator in being a 'bad' Robin, but, in opening up a type of wormhole between reader and character. In this way, the vote allowed the reader to act on their resentment, turning it, in effect, into violence that had visible, tangible consequences in the narrative. Therefore, the perennial violence of the Bat-verse which is typically contained in the DC Comics story worlds bursts out, spills and seeps through to other levels of reality through the simple device of a 1–900 number. Here, the telephone becomes a conduit into the story which carries violence, like gravity between dimensions, from one diegetic level to another. In this sense, O'Neil and his team allowed violence the temporary chance to move in all directions, in all realities, influencing, reacting against, and being influenced by the violence it encounters on each level. Put simply, the Joker did not kill Jason. The reader did. The reader's violent resentment travelled from heart, to mouth, through the receiver, into DC's switchboards, the writer's pen, the draftsman's pencil, and subsequently into the Joker's hand. In the last instance, the Joker's disdain and desire to punish Todd is undifferentiated from the same impulse in the reader. I argue that it is precisely Jason's role as sidekick that allows him to be such an effective scapegoat; one that allowed O'Neil and his DC editorial staff to exorcise their readership's discontent preceding and including the publication of *ADITF*.

In this sense, Jason's role as a sidekick is inextricably shaped by his function as a scapegoat. The relationship between the reader and Jason, set up in this antagonistic way as subject and mediator, means that 'the antagonists are caught in an escalation of frustration. In their dual role of obstacle and model, they both become more and more fascinated by each other. Beyond a certain level of intensity, they are totally absorbed and the disputed object becomes secondary, even irrelevant' (Girard qtd. in Williams 1996: 12). As a result, a transformation occurs in which readers move from being rivals against one another on the extradiegetic level, to being united, collective haters of the same object on the diegetic level, the same object that, previously, acted as an object of resentment and desire, namely Jason-as-Robin. The readers, who were once antagonists or mimetic rivals against one another, now mimic each other's hatred as opposed to desire for the same object, namely Jason. Here, the mantle of Robin becomes secondary to the wearer, one who is collectively viewed as unworthy of it, thereby becoming an effective scapegoat. In this sense, Jason Todd does not 'fit' the Robin role and so draws attention to himself as a person worthy of scapegoating in a way that Dick Grayson does not on account of his comparative obedience, focus, crime-fighting elegance and amiability. In the end, while Jason may not be considered as good a Robin as Dick Grayson, let alone a good Robin at all in the DC story worlds, he still is able to do something quite remarkable in the world of the reader as a scapegoat. While he may be seen as a disruptive force whose end is to break apart not only the mantle and sidekick role of Robin (and by extension the Bat-Family more broadly), I argue that he must also necessarily be seen as a binding force that helped keep the DC readership together and loyal to the brand. While O'Neil and his editorial team's decision to institute the vote seems innocuous on one hand, and deeply ethically problematic on the other, as a means of attempting to unify and protect the then disquieted community of readers, one cannot deny the simple genius of it. As a catalyst for fan backlash, the problem of Jason-as-bad-Robin/sidekick was, in fact, encouraged by the vote—it simultaneously moved copy and allowed for antagonistic reader-responses to be aired and repurposed.

Conclusion

My views on the tensions between Jason Todd, the mantle of Robin and the role of the sidekick in the *Batman* comics can be summarized as follows: Jason may indeed be regarded as a 'bad' Robin, but as a 'bad' Robin he makes a good scapegoat. Why has no other scholar or commentator read Jason's death in terms of a sinister, albeit seemingly oblique relationship between the roles of sidekick and scapegoat? Simply, because until now the ethical issues and debates surrounding the concept and the act of determining the life and/or death of a troubled fifteen-year-old boy have been sublimated in diegetic difference. This fact is obscured by certain persistent albeit outdated sentiments that regard comic book crime fiction as so-called low art. It is a critical sentiment given voice by polemic pundits such as Bill Maher that, despite the dexterity, longevity and complexities of the medium more broadly and the superhero genre more specifically, still exist (Maher 2018). I believe that the diegetic failure, but extradiegetic success, of Jason Todd as a bad sidekick but good scapegoat required readers to misunderstand what it was they participated in as well as their desire for it. In this way, *ADITF* relied upon readers' belief that the demand for a victim came solely from the editor, the character, or any other source save their own shared resentment against a character who did not fit the expected role of a 'good' Robin.

Notes

1. The concept of Robin being raised and deployed as a child soldier is famously taken up by Frank Miller's *All-Star Batman & Robin* (2005–2008). This theme is also analysed in Lucy Andrew's essay in this collection.
2. Dick does go on to eventually take up the mantle of Batman in Bruce Wayne's absence in Tony Daniel's *Batman: Battle for the Cowl* (2009).
3. There are numerous textual examples in which Batman pronounces, in some form or other, what can be described as a code of conduct, praxiological ethic, or oath which describes his mission. A good distillation of this comes from J.M. DeMatteis' *Batman: Absolution* (2002): 'we impose meaning on the chaos of our lives. We create form, morality, order. It's a choice we have to make every second of every day' (DeMatteis 2003: 46–47).
4. An arguable close second would be the Joker's paralysing of Barbara Gordon in Alan Moore's *The Killing Joke* (1988).

Reference List

Benicio127, and Whitesycamore. 2011. Who's to Blame? How Jason Todd Is Blamed for His Own Demise. *Fuckyeahjasontodd*. http://fuckyeahjasontodd.tumblr.com/post/1999047334/whos-to-blame-how-jason-todd-is-blamed-for-his. Accessed 12 June 2018.

Black, Jake. 2009. Robin: Innocent Bystander. In *Batman Unauthorized: Vigilantes, Jokers, and Heroes in Gotham City*, ed. Dennis O'Neil and Leah Wilson, 121–126. Dallas, TX: Benbella Books.

Borsellino, Mary. 2009. Gotham's First Family. In *Batman Unauthorized: Vigilantes, Jokers, and Heroes in Gotham City*, ed. Dennis O'Neil and Leah Wilson, 137–144. Dallas, TX: Benbella Books.

DeMatteis, J.M. 2003. *Batman: Absolution*. New York: DC Comics.

Derrida, Jacques. 1978. *Writing and Difference*, trans. Alan Bass. Chicago: University of Chicago Press.
Finger, Bill, and Bob Kane. 1939. *Detective Comics* 33, April. New York: DC Comics.
Genette, Gérard. 1980. *Narrative Discourse: An Essay In Method*, trans. Jane E. Lewin. New York: Cornell University Press.
Girard, René. 1977. *Violence and the Sacred*, trans. Patrick Gregory. Baltimore: Johns Hopkins University Press.
Hills, Matt. 2002. *Fan Cultures*. London: Routledge.
Langley, Travis. 2012. *Batman and Psychology: A Dark and Stormy Knight*. Hoboken: Wiley.
MacNeil-Donoghue, Cara. 2015. The Gray(son) Area: Performing Robin the Right Way. In *Dick Grayson, Boy Wonder: Scholars and Creators on 75 Years of Robin*, ed. Kristen L. Geaman, 54–66. Jefferson, NC: McFarland.
Manning, Mathew. 2011. *The Joker: A Visual History of the Clown Prince of Crime*. Connecticut: Universe Publishing.
Maher, Bill. 2018. Adulting. *Real Time with Bill Maher Blog*. https://www.real-time-with-bill-maher-blog.com/index/2018/11/16/adulting. Accessed 12 Dec 2018.
Müller, Markus. 1996. Interview with René Girard. *Anthropoetics* 2.1. https://anthropoetics.ucla.edu/ap0201/interv/. Accessed 11 Dec 2018.
Nielsen, Carsten Fogh. 2008. Leaving the Shadow of the Bat: Aristotle, Kant, and Dick Grayson on Moral Education. In *Batman and Philosophy: The Dark Knight of the Soul*, ed. Mark D. White, Robert Arp, and William Irwin, 254–268. Hoboken, NJ: Wiley.
O'Neil, Dennis. 1991. Notes from the Batcave: An Interview with Dennis O'Neil. Interview by Roberta E. Pearson and William Uricchio. In *The Many Lives of The Batman: Critical Approaches to a Superhero and His Media*, ed. Roberta E. Pearson and William Uricchio, 18–32. London: BFI Publishing.
———. 1993. Foreword. In *Robin: Tragedy and Triumph*, ed. Alan Grant and Chuck Dixon. New York: DC Comics.
Starlin, Jim. 1988a. *Batman* 426. New York: DC Comics.
———. 1988b.*Batman* 427. New York: DC Comics.
———. 1988c. *Batman* 428. New York: DC Comics.
———. 1989. *Batman* 429. New York: DC Comics.
———. 2015. *Batman* 424. In *Robin, the Boy Wonder. A Celebration of 75 Years*, ed. Dennis O'Neil, 160–183. New York: DC Comics.
Pearson, Roberta E. and William Uricchio. 1991. *The Many Lives of The Batman: Critical Approaches to a Superhero and His Media*. London: BFI Publishing.
Weldon, Glen. 1992 [2017]. *The Caped Crusade: Batman and the Rise of Nerd Culture*. New York: Simon and Schuster.

———. 2016. *The Caped Crusade: Batman and the Rise of Nerd Culture*. New York: Simon and Schuster.
Williams, James G., ed. 1996. *The Girard Reader*. New York: The Crossroad Publishing Company.
Winick, Judd. 2010. *Batman: Under the Red Hood*. Directed by Brandon Vietti. New York: DC Entertainment.
Wolfman, Marv. 1989. *Batman* 442, December. New York: DC Comics.

CHAPTER 11

'I'm Gonna Be the Best Friend You Could Ever *Hope* For—And the Worst Enemy You Could Ever *Imagine*': Frank Miller's *All Star Batman & Robin, the Boy Wonder* and the Problem of the Boy Sidekick in the Twenty-First-Century Superhero Narrative

Lucy Andrew

Introduction: Robin in Crisis

'Fuck Batman.' These are the first words uttered by the latest on-screen incarnation of the original Robin, Dick Grayson, in the first trailer for DC Comics' television series, *Titans* (2018–present).[1] This show offers a fresh take on the Teen Titans comic-book characters (1964–present), young superheroes (many of them sidekicks to more established heroes) who team up and take centre stage in the fight against crime. Robin,

L. Andrew (✉)
University Centre Shrewsbury, University of Chester, Chester, UK

L. Andrew and S. Saunders (eds.), *The Detective's Companion in Crime Fiction*, Crime Files, https://doi.org/10.1007/978-3-030-74989-7_11

sidekick extraordinaire, is often tasked with leading this motley crew. In the comics, Robin usually balances his duties as Titans' leader with his role as sidekick to the 'world's greatest detective', Batman. In *Titans*, however, this is evidently not the case. Something is rotten in the state of Gotham. Here, Robin (played by Brenton Thwaites, who was 28 when the series began) is Boy Wonder no more. Estranged from Batman, and preparing to head up his own team of young superheroes, this Robin—foul-mouthed, violent and blood spattered—in no way resembles the 'laughing, fighting young dare-devil' created by Bill Finger and Bob Kane in 1940 (Finger and Kane 1940a: 1). Instead, Thwaites's Robin seems to draw inspiration from a much more recent version of Dick Grayson's Robin origin story: Frank Miller's *All Star Batman & Robin, the Boy Wonder* (*ASBAR*), published between 2005 and 2008.[2]

As Alexandra Schulz fairly surmises, *ASBAR* is 'one hell of a mess', replete with 'lurid writing, relentless over-the-top grittiness, and equally over-the-top radical interpretations of beloved DC characters' (2015: 244). But *ASBAR*'s overwrought narrative style does serve a purpose. Set before Miller's *The Dark Knight Returns* (1986), in which an embittered Dick Grayson has been replaced by girl Robin Carrie Kelly, and *The Dark Knight Strikes Again* (2001–2002), where a now-deranged Dick is dropped into an active volcano by Batman, *ASBAR* represents a crisis point in Robin's career, offering an extreme and violent explication of the place of the boy sidekick in the twenty-first-century comic-book industry and superhero universe. Never one to shy away from profanity, violence and controversy, Miller draws upon, but explicitly rewrites, Finger and Kane's 1940 Robin origin story from *Detective Comics*, transforming Batman's first encounter with the Boy Wonder from a heroic rescue to a sinister kidnap. Miller problematises the earlier origin story, offering a disturbing new perspective on the adult detective/boy sidekick relationship in the process. This perspective, I suggest, is influenced not only by contemporary social and moral anxieties such as those stemming from recent child abuse scandals, but also by current narrative practices and preferences dictated by the comic-book industry. For a twenty-first-century audience, I contend, the boy sidekick, epitomised by Robin, is inevitably and necessarily a much more complex and troubling entity than his earlier incarnations.

In Pursuit of a Boy Sidekick: The Troubling Acquisition of Dick Grayson

In Finger and Kane's 1940 Robin origin story, Dick Grayson is a circus boy who is taken in by Bruce Wayne (a.k.a. Batman) after Dick's parents, the Flying Graysons, die in a trapeze accident—which turns out to be no accident. When Dick overhears local gangster Boss Zucco threatening circus owner Mr. Haly with more 'accidents' if he fails to pay his protection money, he is determined to go to the police but is intercepted by Batman, who warns him that 'this whole town is run by Boss Zucco. If you told what you knew you'd be dead within an hour' (Finger and Kane 1940a: 3). After establishing that his priority is to protect Dick, and proposing to hide him at Wayne Manor, Batman reveals that his own parents' murders prompted him to become a crime fighter. Dick expresses his wishes to join Batman on his crusade against Gotham's criminal element and, while Batman is initially reluctant and warns Dick about the 'perilous life' that he leads, he accepts Dick into the role of sidekick as 'the troubled face of the boy moves him deeply' (Finger and Kane 1940a: 3). After making Dick swear an oath 'never to swerve from the path of righteousness', Batman trains him in boxing and jiu jitsu and so Robin the Boy Wonder is born (Finger and Kane 1940a: 3).

Like Finger and Kane's Robin origin narrative, Miller's *ASBAR* begins with the death of Dick's parents although, in this version, there are some key differences. Rather than falling to their deaths during a trapeze routine, Dick's parents are shot in the head as they take their bow, making the scene both more violent and more strongly evocative of the deaths of Bruce Wayne's own parents. Perhaps more disturbing than the death of the Graysons, however, is Wayne's extended pursuit of their son. And there is no doubt that it *is* a pursuit. Unlike Wayne's apparently coincidental trip to the circus in Finger and Kane's narrative, in Miller's version Wayne admits to his date, journalist Vicki Vale, that 'I've had my eye on him for a while. He's *something* all right' (Miller 2005a: 10). As Batman, he continues to voice such predatory assertions in subsequent episodes, claiming 'I chose him with care. I did my homework' (Miller 2005c: 16) and 'I've had my eye on this Grayson for months' (Miller 2006: 4). As Schulz asserts:

> Right from the start, there's a creepy predatory element to a grown man stalking a young boy for his own purposes, an element that's consistently

> present in ASBAR [sic], such as when Batman later remarks that Dick 'just might *do*,' and that he needs him 'good and scared.' (2015: 252)

As Dick Grayson officially assumes the Robin mantle, Batman's assessment—'Fast hands, my little Robin. Fast hands, big mouth …' (Miller 2008b: 2)—only adds to the disturbingly predatory and sexualised representation of Batman's acquisition of his boy sidekick in *ASBAR*. Batman may be talking about Robin's skills with a paintbrush here, and his loud complaints about being used as 'child labor' (Miller 2008a: 2), but Miller's narrative lends itself to less innocent and more troubling readings.

In fact, *ASBAR* draws upon the much earlier and frequently referenced anxieties about the Batman/Robin relationship raised by psychiatrist Frederic Wertham in *Seduction of the Innocent* (1954). Here, Wertham argues that 'the Batman type of story helps to fixate homoerotic tendencies by suggesting the form of an adolescent-with-adult or Ganymede-Zeus type of love relationship' (1954: 190). The Comics Code, which was introduced late in 1954 in response to Wertham's study, declared that 'Illicit sex relations are neither to be hinted at nor portrayed' and 'The treatment of love-romance stories shall emphasize the value of the home and the sanctity of marriage' (qtd. in Brooker 2000: 144). As a result, the Bat-family expanded to include Batwoman as a potential love interest for Batman in 1956 and her niece, Bat-Girl, in 1961 as a possible girlfriend for Robin.[3] In *ASBAR*, by contrast, the presence of Bruce Wayne's female love interest, Vicki Vale, deliberately serves to underscore rather than diffuse the troubling sexual undertones and predatory nature of Bruce Wayne's pursuit of Dick Grayson. Throughout *ASBAR*, and particularly in the early episodes, Vicki Vale acts as a double of Dick Grayson in a way that draws interesting and worrying links between the roles of love interest and boy sidekick.

Jim Lee's illustrations accentuate the connections between Dick Grayson and Vicki Vale, particularly in the first episode of *ASBAR* where the visual narrative centres on these two figures. Both are introduced in full-page images that emphasise their physicality: Dick Grayson appears in a skin-tight, shiny leotard while performing a daring acrobatic routine to an admiring audience (Miller 2005a: 1); Vicki Vale is clad only in her underwear and a pair of heels as she dictates an article on superheroes while sipping a martini (Miller 2005a: 3). As different as their professions are, both Vicki and Dick have jobs that thrust them into the public eye. Both characters also become objects of *ASBAR*'s penetrative male gaze, as evidenced by the use of skin-tight costumes, full-page illustrations and a series of close-up images that fetishise their bodies. And both characters have caught the eye of one man in particular: Bruce Wayne/Batman. In fact, as Vicki Vale searches for the perfect 'costume' for her date with Bruce Wayne, she is pictured modelling three potential outfits—in red, yellow and green, the colours of the Robin costume in which Dick finally emerges in episode nine—before rejecting them in favour of a figure-hugging silver dress with a sheen to rival that of Dick's Flying Graysons costume (Miller 2005a: 6–7). In these early scenes, both Vicki and Dick are on display for the pleasure of Bruce Wayne.

The similarities do not end here. Vicki and Dick both begin proceedings as outsiders to Batman's violent world but soon become victims of it. As Dick's parents are murdered in front of him, the alternating close-up images of Vicki and Dick focus on their faces and their emotional reactions to the traumatic situation unfolding before their eyes. The shock etched across their faces (Miller 2005a: 12–13) soon turns to anger (Miller 2005a: 15) as the corrupt police arrive to silence them, bundling Dick Grayson into a police car and telling Vicki Vale to 'Go back to your *newspaper*, sexpot' (Miller 2005a: 14). It is notable that Vicki is the only character to intervene in the police's kidnap of Dick Grayson, telling them: 'I've seen what you cops do with your *hands*. What girl in Gotham *hasn't*? And who *knows* what you do to little *boys*?' (Miller 2005a: 15). Here, Vicki explicitly voices what has been implicit in the narrative so far—the possibility of adult male authority figures as sexual predators, preying not only on 'sexpot' female reporters, but also on vulnerable, twelve-year-old potential sidekicks. Vicki earns a punch in the mouth from a violent cop for her troubles and, in the episodes that follow, Vicki and Dick suffer parallel physical and emotional traumas at the hands of Batman: Vicki is left fighting for her life in the aftermath of the carnage caused by Batman as he steals Dick Grayson away from the police; meanwhile, Dick attempts to come to terms with the deaths of his parents and his double kidnap (by the police and Batman) while imprisoned by Batman in the dank, dark and rat-infested Batcave.

Both characters' victim status and passivity are, again, reinforced visually through their clothing as they attempt to recover from their parallel traumas. After requesting fresh clothes from Batman because 'I've still got mom and dad's blood and stuff all over me' (Miller 2006: 13), Dick awakens and notices that 'somebody's put me in silk pyjamas that are way too big for me' (Miller 2006: 17). On closer inspection, the pyjama top is adorned with a crest that is presumably that of the Wayne family, suggesting the imposition of an institutional identity upon the future boy sidekick (Miller 2007a: 20). The pyjama top also features three pom-poms, reminiscent of those attached to the shoes that Vicki Vale is wearing on her first appearance (Miller 2005a: 3), drawing yet another visual connection between these two figures. Similarly, Vicki herself suffers an enforced change of clothing as a result of her trauma at the hands of Batman. In episode six, she appears in a hospital gown and asks cub reporter Jimmy Olsen to aid her self-discharge from hospital by fetching 'my *clothes* from the *closet.* My *housekeeper* dropped off a fresh set—a nice enough *outfit*, and one with no *blood* on it' (Miller 2007b: 12). The fact that both Vicki and Dick are re-clothed in institutional attire while unconscious, without their consent, and to conceal or replace their own blood-soaked clothing, not only positions them as passive victims of violent trauma, but also as figures who are in danger of losing their own identities to Batman's violent Gotham.

In *ASBAR*, then, the potential sidekick and the potential girlfriend occupy the same ground: both catch Bruce Wayne's eye through their physical attributes and impressive visual performances; both become objects of the narrative's male gaze and fall prey to the macho violence of Gotham City and its law enforcers (official and vigilante alike); both suffer physical and mental trauma as a result. It is true that they both resist the victim status that accompanies this trauma and attempt to reshape their identities. We never see the outfit that Vicki changes into—she disappears from Miller's unfinished narrative at this point with the suggestion that she intends to find out the truth about Batman and Dick Grayson—but there is again a parallel here with Dick's narrative. Just as Vicki casts off the institutional garb that identifies her as trauma victim in favour of an outfit provided by her housekeeper, so Dick sheds the Wayne pyjamas and fashions his own costume with materials brought to him by Bruce Wayne's butler, Alfred (Miller 2008a: 15, 21). But neither character's attempt to reassert their agency is wholly successful, as Vicki disappears from the narrative after episode six and Batman later rejects Dick's 'Hood' costume and, by extension, his attempt to craft his own sidekick identity (Miller 2008a: 21). Most importantly, perhaps, the connection between Vicki and Dick emphasises just how precarious the role of the boy side-kick truly is. By Miller's reckoning, the boy sidekick, like the female love interest, is an abused, marginalised, disempowered, decorative, potentially sacrificial figure—in danger of being discarded or replaced at a moment's notice so long as he performs a purely practical rather than emotional function for Batman. Just as Vicki serves as 'arm candy' for Bruce Wayne, so Dick is in danger of becoming merely another weapon in Batman's extensive arsenal. In the aftermath of the death of Jason Todd, the second Robin, in the 1988 *A Lonely Place of Dying* story arc, future Robin Tim Drake tells past Robin Dick Grayson that 'Batman *needs* Robin' (Wolfman 1989: 22). Tim may be right. But, regardless of whether he *needs* Robin, in *ASBAR*, Miller suggests that Batman should never have acquired his boy sidekick to begin with.

The Boy-Sidekick-in-Training: The Batman/Robin Power Imbalance

When Robin was first introduced to the Batman comics in 1940, one of his key functions was to lighten the tone of this initially dark series with its violent, brooding hero. Bob Kane, co-creator of the Dynamic Duo, observes that 'Robin lightened up the mood of the strip and he and Batman would engage in punning and badinage as they defeated their adversaries' (Kane qtd in Brooker 2000: 56). 'Sorry, boy, but I'm going up!' Robin declares as he wrestles a member of Boss Zucco's gang to the ground and jumps up onto a girder in his first outing as Boy Wonder (Finger and Kane 1940a: 8). Batman is similarly playful as he joins the fray, tackling Boss Zucco from above: 'Mind if I join the party, Zucco? So sorry to drop in unexpectedly this way ...' (Finger and Kane 1940a: 9). Despite being considerably darker in tone, in *ASBAR*, Dick Grayson does, like his earlier incarnation, lighten the mood—this time not through 'punning and badinage', but through his apparent disdain for Batman's world. Miller here pokes fun at the larger-than-life trappings of the original comics as Dick demands, 'What the Hell's a "ward"?' (Miller 2005b: 8), brands the Bat-Mobile 'totally queer' (Miller 2005c: 19), declares that '*tights* really *blow chunks*' (Miller 2006: 17) and that 'a *costume* is queer *enough*, but why a *mask*?' (Miller 2008a: 7). Moreover, when Batman introduces Dick to the Batcave, asking, 'Is this cool or *what*?', Dick replies with studied indifference: 'Yeah. I guess it's okay. I mean, I've seen better, but I guess this is okay' (Miller 2006: 12). In typical adolescent style, Dick is equally apathetic when confronted Batman's now-famous, much-parodied proclamation, 'I'm the Goddamn *Batman*. [...] I'm gonna be the best friend you could ever *hope* for—and the worst enemy you could ever *imagine*', responding with a witheringly dismissive, 'Sure, man. Whatever' (Miller 2005b: 9). In this respect, the boy-sidekick-in-training provides some of the light relief that the original Dick Grayson brought to the role, although here the humour is at the expense of Batman and the original comics rather than the Dynamic Duo's criminal opponents.

As well as lightening the tone of the Batman comics, Kane observes that '[m]ore significantly, the addition of Robin gave Batman a permanent relationship, someone to care for, and made him into a fatherly big brother rather than a lone avenger' (Kane qtd in Brooker 2000: 56). As a result, Mark Napolitano argues, 'Batman instantly became a less violent vigilante' (2013: 147). Dick Grayson's introduction performs similar functions in *ASBAR*. After his kidnap in episode two, Dick recognises that Batman is 'that lonely. He's all alone' (Miller 2005b: 21). In episode seven, Black Canary suggests to Batman that he should attempt to combat this loneliness: 'All I'm trying to *say* is that your *perspective* on things might find itself a tad bit readjusted by the occasional *conversation* with somebody ... somebody you're not *punching* in the *face*, that is' (Miller 2007c: 12). While Batman and Robin's relationship certainly cannot be characterised as a friendship at this point—to Batman, Dick is a 'brat' (Miller 2005a: 12) and 'little snot' (Miller 2005b: 19), while Dick brands Batman 'The bastard. Damn monster', 'crazy', 'lunatic', 'such a tool', 'a creep' (Miller 2005b: 14, 15, 16)—as boy-sidekick-in-training, Dick does offer a form of companionship to Batman. He is someone with whom Batman can converse and share his superhero existence, despite Dick's feigned disinterest in Batman's world.

Dick's presence humanises Batman to the point where the Dark Knight expresses fondness for his would-be sidekick, reluctantly admitting that 'I'm starting to like this little snot' (Miller 2008a: 6). More than this, as his emotional connection to Dick strengthens, Batman grows a conscience. After Dick proves his detective prowess by choosing to interrogate rather than kill his parents' murderer, Batman gives Dick his seal of approval, telling him to 'get yourself a costume and a mask' but then almost immediately asking himself, 'What am I doing, playing the father ...? This is the dumbest move I've made in my whole life' (Miller 2008a: 7). Later, in the midst of an encounter with Green Lantern in which Batman and Robin begin to bond as they team up to mock their fellow superhero, Batman begins to question his impact upon his would-be sidekick: 'From out of nowhere I start to think about the kid. About whether I've saved his life—or wrecked it' (Miller 2008a: 16). In episode nine, after the newly christened Robin nearly kills Green Lantern, it seems that Batman has his answer:

> What have I done? What have I accomplished? I've done plenty. I've taken an adept and taught him to fight. I've taught him how to kill. And that's all I've taught him. I rushed things. I dragged him into my world. I was reckless. I rushed it. I had years—years to learn my path. I had wise gurus and the gentle hand of dear old Alfred. I had years to learn every side of lethal power. I had years to learn the great thoughts of great men. All he's had is weeks in the hands of a joy-riding, cackling lunatic. I had years—to grieve. To grieve. That's where it started ... (Miller 2008b: 19)

Again, *ASBAR* speaks back to the 1940 Robin origin story, drawing attention to the lack of both physical and emotional training that Dick undergoes in preparation for the Robin role. In Finger and Kane's version, Batman's training of Robin is perfunctory. Robin's physical training plays out over three panels before he emerges as the fully-fledged Boy Wonder and though his first assignment apparently takes place '[m]any months later ... after strenuous work and study ...' (Finger and Kane 1940a: 4), none of this 'work and study' is recorded in the narrative itself. Moreover, any form of emotional adjustment to the Robin role is omitted altogether from Robin's origin story. Within the panels of the comic, Dick is not given time to mourn his parents' deaths, just as Miller's Batman concludes that '[t]here's no time for grief. There's no room for grief' (Miller 2005b: 19). Thus, *ASBAR* points to some key omissions in the original story, where Robin's training—his arduous transformation from civilian to sidekick—takes place out of sight and, thus, out of mind of the comic's readers.

Through his crisis of conscience, Miller's Batman recognises the mistakes that he has made in his training of Robin and attempts to put them right as he prays for 'a second chance. A fresh start' (Miller 2008b: 21). The final, full-page illustration of episode nine of *ASBAR* offers a potential opportunity for this 'fresh start' as Batman is pictured embracing Robin at the burial site of Dick's parents. Here, Batman finally allows his boy sidekick to grieve the death of his parents and finally allows himself to show human emotion, holding Robin in a fatherly embrace (Miller 2008b: 22). This image offers a stark contrast to the closing illustration of the first episode of *ASBAR*, where Batman violently hoists Dick high into the air and tells him, 'You've just been ***drafted***. Into a ***war***' (Miller

2005a: 22). Throughout the narrative, there has been a power imbalance between the violent Batman (never Bruce Wayne—he is always in costume when he engages with Dick) and the traumatised Dick Grayson, who does not truly shed his civilian identity until episode nine. As Schulz suggests, 'Bruce holds all the power and Dick none' (2015: 254). At first glance, the touching emotional moment at the end of episode nine appears to act as an equalising scene, suggesting a progression in Batman's relationship with his protégé who, in the guise of Robin, is now seemingly deserving of Batman's affection.

However, in actuality, the Batman/Robin relationship is no less unbalanced than the Batman/Dick Grayson relationship: it is parasitic rather than symbiotic. For while Dick humanises Batman, Batman himself is a parasite, draining Dick's humanity by inducting him into the sidekick role. Initially, Batman seemingly allows Dick to craft his own sidekick identity, telling him to 'get to work on your *costume*. And get yourself a damn mask' (Miller 2008a: 9). Yet when Dick appears in a costume inspired by 'some old *movie* about Robin Hood' that his father made him watch and declares 'I'm Hood' (Miller 2008a: 21), Batman is quick to demonstrate the impracticality of his costume design, pulling the hood over his eyes and demanding, 'Lose the hood. You're Robin' (Miller 2008a: 22). This may, in part, be Miller's way of rejecting the Robin Hood inspiration behind Finger and Kane's creation, but Batman's rejection of Hood also denies Dick a connection to his civilian Grayson identity. In fact, when Dick makes his debut as Robin in episode nine, it is not just the hood that he has lost. His makeshift costume has been replaced in its entirety by one which closely resembles the 1940 Robin costume (Miller 2008b: 2). In Finger and Kane's narrative, the costumed Robin appears fully formed and, beyond his brief training with Batman, there is no indication of exactly how his sidekick identity has been crafted—and *who* has crafted it. *ASBAR* suggests that Dick is a passive recipient of the Robin identity—an identity constructed entirely by Batman. In light of this, the emotional scene at the Graysons' burial site takes on a new significance. The embrace which humanises Batman dehumanises Dick Grayson. The words '[w]e mourn lives lost. Including our own', coupled with the simple 'Grayson' rather than the full names of Dick's parents on the headstone beside him, is suggestive of the death of Dick Grayson in the birth of Robin. There is a sense that, by embracing Batman and, by extension, his sidekick identity, Dick is coming to terms with the loss of his boy self and civilian identity. Becoming a boy sidekick, *ASBAR* suggests, is a serious business involving great sacrifice: of innocence; of humanity; of selfhood.

The Boy Sidekick Emerges: The Corruption of Robin

Dick Grayson's loss of innocence and dehumanisation is further exacerbated in his role as Robin, where he is thrust into a world of violent criminals. Dick's first expression of enthusiasm for Batman's world occurs at the end of episode five as he surveys Batman's weapon collection in the Batcave: 'It's full of stuff. And all the stuff is clean and sharpened and polished and ready to use' (Miller 2007a: 21). On the following page, Dick brandishes a gleaming axe, the hint of a smile on his face for the first time since his parents' deaths as he proclaims, 'Cool' (Miller 2007a: 22). Dick's appreciation of Batman's weapons continues in episode eight as he reports that the Batcave is full of 'Cool stuff. Cool weapons. Lots of cool weapons' (Miller 2008a: 14) while selecting a bow and arrow as his own weapon of choice. When he finally appears as Robin in episode nine, Dick does not brandish any weapons, but manages to do considerable damage to Green Lantern with his bare fists, forcing Batman to perform an emergency tracheotomy on the fallen hero before pronouncing, 'Congratulations, kid. You're not a *murderer*' (Miller 2008b: 17). Perhaps more worrying than Robin's violence is his admission that 'I almost killed a man tonight. A man who never did me any harm. And I enjoyed every second of it. More than I ever enjoyed anything. I wanted to kill him' (Miller 2008b: 18). In the final episode of *ASBAR*, Robin's brief reappearance confirms his violent nature:

> a twelve-year-old dynamo dances like a pixie across a filthy room and makes a bullet of his fist and crushes a good man's trachea—like it's a stalk of celery, he crushes it, crushes it, crushes it ... almost killing that good man at my bidding, at my bidding. (Miller 2008c: 7)

Miller's boy sidekick is a violent, monstrous creation—a deadly weapon for Batman to wield against his foes. On the surface, such a sidekick could not be further from his 1940 equivalent, who was introduced not only to lighten the tone of the comics and to provide companionship for Batman, but also as a point of reader identification and, thus, a role model for the comics' younger readers (Bell 2015: 9). Robin's moral function is emphasised in the first issue of the *Batman* comic with the creation of the 'Robin Regulars', who were encouraged to abide by 'Robin's Code: Readiness; Obedience; Brotherhood; Industriousness; Nationalism'

(Finger and Kane 1940b: 53). Yet even this early Robin is a product of Batman's violent world. In an interview for *Dick Grayson, Boy Wonder*, comic-book author Marv Wolfman admits that '[o]nce I was a teenager I never much liked Robin as the kid partner. I never understood why Batman would put this pun-spouting 10 year old in constant danger' (Geaman 2015: 272). In Finger and Kane's origin story, Robin's first outing sees him landing 'among the murderous gunmen' of Boss Zucco's gang, armed only with a sling shot, 'like David fighting Goliath' (Finger and Kane 1940a: 9). 'Goliath' almost wins as Robin slips and clings to a girder as a gunman steps on his fingers, but the Boy Wonder survives as he 'twists his body up and around the girder. Kicking the gunman off the girder into space!' (Finger and Kane 1940a: 10). Although the result of this clash is not depicted, there is little doubt that the gunman has fallen to his death. While Robin's elimination of the gunman could here be excused as self-defence, two pages later he again shows a decided lack of concern for the welfare of his criminal foes as, on Batman's instructions, he calmly snaps a photo of Boss Zucco pushing a fellow gangster to his death in order to capture the evidence that will send Zucco to the electric chair. At the end of the story, when Bruce tells Dick, 'I ought to whale on you for jumping those men alone', Dick replies, 'Aw! I didn't want to miss any of the fun! Say, I can hardly wait till we go on our next adventure!' (Finger and Kane 1940a: 12). From his earliest outing, it seems, Robin has a taste for violence. In *ASBAR*, Miller makes this implicit violence *explicit*, drawing attention to the morally problematic nature of introducing a boy sidekick into the dangerous criminal environment of the adult crime fighter.

Miller's text, however, does not just respond to Finger and Kane's Robin origin story, but is also in dialogue with more recent narratives that deal with the Boy Wonder's beginnings. During the period in which *ASBAR* was being published, DC Comics introduced a new future Robin—the fourth character to assume the Robin mantle long term—in the form of Bruce Wayne's biological son, Damian.[4] Damian Wayne is a laboratory baby, produced by his mother, Talia al Ghul, without Batman's knowledge or consent. Talia is a deadly assassin and daughter of the infamous R'as al Ghul and Damian is brought up within his grandfather's League of Assassins. As I have argued elsewhere, 'Damian is not only a spoilt brat who thinks that he is entitled to the Robin role but is also an emotionally damaged, murderous child from a broken home' (Andrew 2017: 195). On his first outing as a crime fighter in Gotham (and not yet in the role of Robin) Damian kills a criminal called the Spook, proudly brandishing his severed head and telling a horrified Tim Drake that 'In the League of Assassins, we showed our enemies no mercy. [...] We killed anyone who got in our way' (Morrison et al. 2006: 23). When Tim challenges Damian's behaviour, Damian attacks him and leaves him for dead, cobbles together his own Robin costume and tells Batman 'He quit, father. There's a new Robin now' (Morrison et al. 2006: 30). Damian turns to the Robin costumes on display in the Batcave to complete his look although, tellingly, he opts for part of Jason Todd's costume over that of Dick Grayson—an indication of the type of Robin that he will become: criminal, reckless, destined to die.[5]

There is an interesting visual connection between Damian's makeshift Robin costume in the *Batman* comic and Dick's homemade Hood costume in *ASBAR*. Both Damian and Dick appear in black tights and sporting a dark cape with a hood—neither of which are features of the iconic Robin costume. Both of these costumes are short-lived as Grant Morrison's Batman denies Damian the mantle of Robin, while Miller's Batman rejects Dick's Hood identity. Published in January 2008, just over a year after Damian's premature attempt to become Robin in November 2006, Miller's 'Hood' scene clearly nods to Morrison's Damian episode. By drawing this link, *ASBAR* perhaps foreshadows Dick's own premature entrance into, and violence within, the Robin role. Reckless, bloodthirsty, desperate to prove themselves, these Robins are disasters waiting to happen. In the twenty-first century, it seems, Batman's boy sidekick is no longer a suitable role model for his young audience. More crucially, perhaps, the position of sidekick appears to be a wholly unsuitable job for a boy—wondrous or otherwise.

Why So Serious? New Century: New Sidekick

Why, though, do these problematised Robin figures become prominent in the twenty-first century? What has prompted the transformation of the boy sidekick from 'a laughing, fighting young dare-devil' (Finger and Kane 1940a: 1) to a mentally disturbed, violent vigilante? Certainly, Miller and Morrison's dark Robins fit tonally with the landscape of post-9/11 America, and the focus on the potential abuse of these figures at the hands of adult guardians responds to a contemporary culture in which child abuse scandals are rife. Moreover, these 'bad' boy sidekicks emerge at a time when anxieties about boyhood violence and criminality have been exacerbated by atrocities such as the Columbine High School massacre in Jefferson County, Colorado, in 1999, perpetrated by two adolescent male attackers.[6]

Yet the representation of the boy sidekick is not only affected by real-life events and anxieties, but also by developments within the comic-book industry. Many twenty-first-century superhero narratives are imbued with a gritty realism and dark tone not often seen in the Golden Age of American comics.[7] As Angela Ndalianis asserts, 'The comic book superheroes have multiplied and, in the process, become more complicated. Clear demarcations of a moral order have blurred and become confused' (2009: 8). The darker superhero narrative became a mainstream phenomenon early in the twenty-first century through a proliferation of superhero films, beginning with Marvel's *X-Men* (2000) and reaching its zenith with Christopher Nolan's *Dark Knight* trilogy (2005–2012), launching what Jeffrey A. Brown suggests is 'a new golden age for superheroes' (2017: 2). Yet the trope of gritty realism that became dominant in DC's superhero films for a time through Nolan's *Dark Knight* trilogy and Zach Snyder's *Man of Steel* (2013) and *Batman v. Superman: Dawn of Justice* (2016) has much earlier roots in the comic-book industry.[8] Will Brooker notes that:

> [T]he underlying discourse of opposition between a 'dark' serious Batman and a 'camp', light Batman has a long-established history. The same distinctions were used to distinguish Tim Burton's 1989 *Batman*, Frank Miller's 1986 *Dark Knight Returns* and Denny O'Neil's early 70s 'darknight detective' stories from the previous bad Bat-object, the 1960s TV show. (2012: 104)

In fact, Nolan's *Dark Knight* trilogy credits the work of O'Neil and Miller as key inspirations (Brooker 2012: 57–62). Another key change to the superhero comics that can be traced back to the 1970s is a shift in narrative structure. Henry Jenkins observes that:

> As the comic book franchises take shape, across the Golden and Silver Ages, their production is dominated by relatively self-contained issues; readers turn over on a regular basis as they grow older. [...] Somewhere in the early 1970s, this focus on self-contained stories shifts towards more and more serialization as the distribution of comics becomes more reliable. Readers have, by this point, grown somewhat older and continue to read comics over a longer span of their lives; these readers place a high value on

> consistency and continuity, appraising both themselves and the authors on their mastery of past events and the web of character relationships within any given franchise. (2009: 20)

Here, we see the rise of the graphic novel—the publication of complex and extended narrative arcs, often aimed at a more mature audience and sometimes appearing across several different comic-book titles. This format allows not only for plot development, but also for a depth of characterisation and relationship development that was missing from earlier comics. It grounds superheroes in reality and fills in some of the gaps—temporal, logical, emotional and moral—that existed in the Golden Age comic-book narratives.

These tonal and structural shifts posed several problems for the representation of the boy sidekick. For example, for Robin, the focus on character development would inevitably mean growing up, rebelling against his father figure and, eventually, maturing out of the boy sidekick role. Furthermore, the darker tone of the comics jars with the light and bright representation of Dick Grayson and, as Schulz observes, 'as comics became grittier and Gotham City's violence more realistic, it now potentially invites the unfortunate implication of a grown man building a traumatized orphan into a child soldier' (2015: 252). Miller makes this implication explicit in *ASBAR* through Batman's first words to Dick Grayson: '[o]n your *feet*, soldier. You've just been *drafted*. Into a *war*' (Miller 2005a: 21–22). From the 1970s onwards, Dick Grayson does begin to mature in response to this new comic-book environment. As Fernando Gabriel Pagnoni Berns and César Alfonso Marino suggest, '[i]n this new scenario, Robin, became "more of a liability than an asset," so he was sent to attend the fictional Hudson University in New Carthage (New York)' (2015: 28). Dick becomes the 'Teen Wonder' in 1970 and in 1984 he finally vacates the role of boy sidekick as he progresses to an adult superhero identity: Nightwing.[9]

The shift from series to serial format also had implications for the Boy Wonder. Catherine M. Vale asserts that 'In almost every Batman story from Robin's inclusion to 1943, Robin is captured by criminals and thought to be dead' (2015: 102). In the 'self-contained issues' (Jenkins 2009: 20) of the early comics, this constant danger was relatively unproblematic. The repeated formula of these narratives reassured readers that Robin would remain safe: the villain would be thwarted by the end of each issue and Robin would inevitably be saved. However, the shift towards continuing story arcs from the 1970s onwards removes this safety net and the boy sidekick's peril becomes all too real—thus inviting constant accusations of child endangerment and posing a significant threat to the long-term survival of the boy sidekick. The second Robin, Jason Todd, succumbs to this threat as he is blown up by the Joker in Jim Starlin's *A Death in the Family* story arc (1988) after the infamous telephone vote in which readers decided that Jason should die from his wounds.[10]

While Jason is a criminalised figure (and, as Kwasu Tembo argues in this volume, potentially a 'bad' Robin) who proves unpopular with readers because of his differences to Dick Grayson, the third Robin, Tim Drake, is a much more grounded figure. He is reluctant to take on the Robin role and yet feels a responsibility to do so, and the comics follow his struggle to balance his sidekick identity with his civilian identity. Additionally, Rob Lendrum notes that 'some changes have occurred to avoid any implications of a man/boy love relationship. The new Robin still lives with his own father and he wears a more modest costume with full-length green pants' (2004: 70). Tim's training is also a lot more protracted and he has to pass a series of tests in order to enter the sidekick role officially. This Robin has his own comic, aimed at a younger audience than the *Batman* title.[11] In issue ten of the *Robin* comic, a time-slip storyline allows Tim to meet a young Dick Grayson as Robin and gain a direct seal of approval from the earlier Robin who, impressed with Tim's detective skills, responds, 'I can see how you got your job. *Robin*' (Dixon et al. 1994: 22). While Tim is both a 'good' and fairly realistic Robin, whose skillset is more cerebral than physical, he still clashes tonally with the aesthetic of the darker, 'adult' Batman narratives. Here, Robin is removed altogether. Brooker asserts that seminal story arcs such as '*Year One* and *The Long Halloween* avoided any mention of Robin simply by setting their stories before his arrival in Batman's life', a tactic followed in Nolan's *Batman's Begins* (2005) where, Brooker argues, 'the selective tradition of key texts which *Batman Begins* constructs as its source material marginalised Robin to the point of disappearance' (Brooker 2012: 124).[12]

With the mainstreaming of the dark, grittily realistic superhero narrative in the twenty-first century—particularly through the success and influence of Nolan's *Dark Knight* trilogy—it becomes considerably more challenging to find a suitable place for the boy sidekick. He does not fit neatly into this dark aesthetic and, consequently, the most successful representations of the contemporary boy sidekick are those that, like

ASBAR, explicitly address this tension and problematise the sidekick role, constructing an image of the boy-sidekick-in-crisis. A further structural change within the comic-book metanarrative also offers new possibilities for the Robin role. Jenkins asserts that:

> Today, comics have entered a period where principles of multiplicity are felt at least as powerfully as those of continuity. Under this new system, readers may consume multiple versions of the same franchise, each with different conceptions of the character, different understandings of their relationships with secondary figures, different moral perspectives, exploring different moments in their lives, and so forth. (2009: 3)

Such multiplicity allows for a much broader exploration and interrogation of the boy sidekick identity. Here a plethora of Robins can co-exist: Miller's abused and abusive Dick Grayson (2005–2008); Morrison's biological Bat brat assassin, Damian Wayne (2006–present); Chris Yost and Fabian Nicieza's Red Robin (2009–present)—the new superhero identity adopted by an angst-ridden Tim Drake after he is ousted from the Robin role by Damian; Lee Bermejo's teenage vigilante Robin wannabees in *We Are Robin* (2015–2016). Despite their differences, these figures have something in common: a sense of turmoil and a thirst for violence. In the twenty-first century, the boy sidekick has become the ultimate problem child.

The twenty-first-century explosion of superhero narratives has a further repercussion for the boy sidekick. As the superhero market continues to expand into the mainstream—as film franchises spill out into television series—it is not just the big hitters who are handed starring roles. In the past few years, Marvel in particular have created (albeit rather short-lived) television series revolving around some of their more obscure comic-book characters, such as *Jessica Jones* (2015–2019), *Luke Cage* (2016–2018) and *Iron Fist* (2017–2018). With *Titans* (2018–present), DC have taken this practice a step further by extending the focus from minor superheroes to young sidekicks. Here, sidekicks are no longer sidelined, but take centre stage. Admittedly, Dick Grayson is hardly a 'boy' sidekick here.[13] But there is little doubt that *Titans* offers a fresh and in-depth perspective on the problematic Robin role. As Thwaites's Robin so eloquently puts it, 'Fuck Batman.' It is time for the sidekick to have his say.

Notes

1. The words are spoken by Dick in the first episode of *Titans* in the first scene in which we see him in action as Robin. 'Where's Batman?', a criminal asks him, to which Dick replies, 'Fuck Batman', before proceeding to violently attack and incapacitate the entire criminal gang. This scene sets the tone for how Robin is portrayed in the series: violent; relentless; out of control. Jason Todd is depicted as a similarly violent and troubled figure when he makes his debut in 'Jason Todd' (1.6).
2. In the first season of *Titans*, Dick Grayson struggles with his superhero identity after leaving behind Bruce Wayne/Batman, a crisis which comes to a head when he meets the new Robin, Jason Todd ('Jason Todd', 1.6). In 'The Asylum' (1.7), Dick burns his Robin costume and, in the next episode, he admits that 'Being Robin doesn't work anymore. But not being Robin doesn't either. Not without some help' ('Donna Troy', 1.8). He finally reconciles with Bruce Wayne at the beginning of season two, telling Bruce that 'I know you only did what you knew. What you thought was best for me' ('Trigon', 2.1) and he takes on his new superhero identity of Nightwing in the final episode of season two ('Nightwing', 2.13).
3. Ironically, when Batwoman reappeared in DC Comics in 2006 after a long absence, she was now represented as an openly lesbian character.
4. Carrie Kelly, who took on the Robin role in Miller's *The Dark Knight Returns* (1986), is excluded from the official Robin chronology. Stephanie Brown, girlfriend to the third Robin, Tim Drake, briefly occupied the Robin role in 2004 before returning to her former superhero role of Spoiler
5. As Kwasu Tembo discusses in this volume, the second Robin, Jason Todd, was killed off as a result of a reader phone-in vote in 1988. Damian Wayne, who officially takes over the Robin role from Tim Drake in the 2009 *Battle for the Cowl* storyline, is killed by Heretic, an adult clone of himself, in *Batman Incorporated* in 2013. However, in true comic-book style, he is resurrected and returns to the Robin role at the end of 2014. Notably, when the third Robin, Tim Drake, reluctantly assumes the Robin mantle after Dick Grayson refuses to return to the role, he wears Dick Grayson's old costume on his first outing as Robin, suggesting that he is a legitimate candidate for the Robin role (Wolfman 1989: 7).
6. For further information on the Columbine High School massacre, see Ralph W. Larkin, *Comprehending Columbine* (2007).
7. The exact date range of the Golden Age of American comics is disputed, but *DC Comics: Year by Year* identifies the Golden Age period as 1938–1955 (Cowsill et al. 2014: 8).
8. Marvel, meanwhile, have begun to react against this gritty realism prominent in Nolan and Snyder's DC superhero films, embracing the comic

potential of its stable of superheroes in the Marvel Cinematic Universe (MCU), which was established with *Iron Man* in 2008. Particularly zany additions to the MCU include *Guardians of the Galaxy* (2014), *Ant-Man* (2015), *Guardians of the Galaxy Vol. 2* (2017), *Thor: Ragnarok* (2017) and *Ant-Man and the Wasp* (2018), whilst *Spider-Man: Homecoming* (2017) offers a superhero take on the traditional teen romantic comedy. Film franchises such as Marvel's *Kick-Ass* (2010–2013) and *Deadpool* (2016–present) and the comics from which they are adapted demonstrate Marvel's increasingly tongue-in-cheek and metafictional representation of superheroes. While the gritty realism of the Nolan era has now dissipated to a degree in DC adaptations, the darkness of tone persists in many newer DC outputs such as *Suicide Squad* (2016), *Joker* (2019) and the aforementioned *Titans* television series (2018–present).

9. Dick Grayson first appears as Nightwing in issue 44 of *Tales of the Teen Titans* in July 1984.
10. For a detailed discussion of this telephone vote and Jason Todd's death, see Kwasu Tembo's chapter in this volume.
11. Tim Drake appeared as Robin in three miniseries between 1991 and 1993, before starring in the long-running *Robin* comic from 1993 to 2009.
12. There is a nod to the Robin identity in *The Dark Knight Rises* (2012) in the figure of police detective John Blake who reveals at the end of the film that his first name is Robin. This 'Robin', however, is an adult figure who has more in common with Dick Grayson's Nightwing than the Boy Wonder.
13. In his appearance in Marvel's *Captain America* film (2011), boy sidekick Bucky Barnes is similarly recast as an adult companion to Steve Rodgers (a.k.a. Captain America). In *Titans*, it is Dick's successor in the Robin role, troubled teen Jason Todd, who more clearly fits the young sidekick position. Jason only plays a minor role in the first season of *Titans*, but is promoted to regular cast member in season two.

References

Andrew, Lucy. 2017. *The Boy Detective in Early British Children's Literature: Patrolling the Borders Between Boyhood and Manhood*. Basingstoke: Palgrave Macmillan.

Bell, J.L. 2015. Success in Stasis: Dick Grayson's Thirty Years as Boy Wonder. In *Dick Grayson, Boy Wonder: Scholars and Creators on 75 Years of Robin, Nightwing and Batman*, ed. Kristen L. Geaman, 8–27. Jefferson, NC: McFarland & Company, Inc., Publishers.

Berns, Fernando Gabriel Pagnoni, and César Alfonso Marino. 2015. Outlining the Future Robin: The Seventies in the Batman Family. In *Dick Grayson, Boy Wonder: Scholars and Creators on 75 Years of Robin, Nightwing and Batman*, ed. Kristen L. Geaman, 28–39. Jefferson, NC: McFarland & Company, Inc., Publishers.

Brooker, Will. 2000. *Batman Unmasked: Analyzing a Cultural Icon*. London and New York: Continuum.

———. 2012. *Hunting the Dark Knight: Twenty-First Century Batman*. London and New York: I. B. Taurus.

Brown, Jeffrey A. 2017. *The Modern Superhero in Film and Television: Popular Genre and American Culture*. New York and London: Routledge.

Cowsill, Alan, Alex Irvine, Matthew K. Manning, Michael McAvennie, and Daniel Wallace. 2014. *DC Comics Year by Year: Updated Edition*. London: Dorling Kindersley.

Dixon, Chuck, Tom Grummett, and Ray Kryssing. 1994. *Robin* 10, September. New York: DC Comics.

Finger, Bill, and Bob Kane. 1940a. *Detective Comics* 38, April. New York: DC Comics.

———. 1940b. *Batman* 1, Spring. New York: DC Comics.

Geaman, Kristen L. 2015. Interview with Marv Wolfman. In *Dick Grayson, Boy Wonder: Scholars and Creators on 75 Years of Robin, Nightwing and Batman*, ed. Kristen L. Geaman, 271–273. Jefferson, NC: McFarland & Company, Inc., Publishers.

Jenkins, Henry. 2009. 'Just Men in Tights': Rewriting Silver Age Comics in an Era of Multiplicity. In *The Contemporary Comic Book Superhero*, ed. Angela Ndalianis, 16–43. New York and Abingdon: Routledge.

Larkin, Ralph W. 2007. *Comprehending Columbine*. Philadelphia: Temple University Press.

Lendrum, Rob. 2004. Queering Super-Manhood: The Gay Superhero in Contemporary Mainstream Comic Books. *Journal of Arts, Sciences and Technology* 2 (2): 69–73.

Miller, Frank, and Jim Lee. 2005a. *All Star Batman & Robin, the Boy Wonder* 1, September. New York: DC Comics.

———. 2005b. *All Star Batman & Robin, the Boy Wonder* 2, November. New York: DC Comics.

———. 2005c. *All Star Batman & Robin, the Boy Wonder* 3, December. New York: DC Comics.

———. 2006. *All Star Batman & Robin, the Boy Wonder* 4, March. New York: DC Comics.

———. 2007a. *All Star Batman & Robin, the Boy Wonder* 5, July. New York: DC Comics.

———. 2007b. *All Star Batman & Robin, the Boy Wonder* 6, September. New York: DC Comics.
———. 2007c. *All Star Batman & Robin, the Boy Wonder* 7, November. New York: DC Comics.
———. 2008a. *All Star Batman & Robin, the Boy Wonder* 8, January. New York: DC Comics.
———. 2008b. *All Star Batman & Robin, the Boy Wonder* 9, April. New York: DC Comics.
———. 2008c. *All Star Batman & Robin, the Boy Wonder* 10, August. New York: DC Comics.
Morrison, Grant, Andy Kubert and Jesse Delperdang. 2006. *Batman* 657, November. New York: DC Comics.
Napolitano, Mark. 2013. 'Elementary, My Dear Robin!' Batman, Sherlock Holmes, and Detective Fiction Fandom. In *Fan Phenomena: Batman*, ed. Liam Burke, 142–152. Bristol: Intellect Books.
Ndalianis, Angela. 2009. Comic Book Superheroes: An Introduction. In *The Contemporary Comic Book Superhero*, ed. Angela Ndalianis, 3–15. New York and Abingdon: Routledge.
Schulz, Alexandra. 2015. Darkly Deconstructing the Dynamic Duo: Dick Grayson in Frank Miller. In *Dick Grayson, Boy Wonder: Scholars and Creators on 75 Years of Robin, Nightwing and Batman*, ed. Kristen L. Geaman, 244–261. Jefferson, NC: McFarland & Company, Inc., Publishers.
Vale, Catherine M. 2015. 'The Loyal Heart': Homosocial Bonding and Homoerotic Subtext Between Batman and Robin, 1939–1943. In *Dick Grayson, Boy Wonder: Scholars and Creators on 75 Years of Robin, Nightwing and Batman*, ed. Kristen L. Geaman, 94–111. Jefferson, NC: McFarland & Company, Inc., Publishers.
Wertham, Frederic. 1954. *Seduction of the Innocent*. New York: Rinehart & Company, Inc; Toronto: Clarke, Irwin & Company, Ltd.
Wolfman, Marv. 1989. *Batman* 442, December. New York: DC Comics.

Televised Material

Berlanti, Greg, Akiva Goldsman and Geoff Johns, creators. *Titans*. DC Universe, 2018–present.
1.1, Titans. 12 October 2018.
1.6, Jason Todd. 16 November 2018.
1.7, Asylum. 23 November 2018.
1.8, Donna Troy. 30 November 2018.
2.1, Trigon. 6 September 2019.
2.13, Nightwing. 29 November 2019.

CHAPTER 12

'World's Long on Academics, Morse, but Woeful Short of Good Detectives': Lewis, Hathaway, and Endeavour; the Changing Roles of Colin Dexter's Sidekicks

David Bishop

Introduction

This chapter explores the many variations of sidekick found in Colin Dexter's *Inspector Morse* novels, and in the three extant television series based on his characters, *Inspector Morse* (1987–2000), *Lewis* (2006–2015) and *Endeavour* (2012–). It argues that the role of sidekick within the Morse narrative universe is not fixed and that characters can (and do) transition across different roles and functions across different series. Few narrative universes in crime fiction have evolved from a single author's novels into two related television series scripted by numerous dramatists, before once more returning to the exclusive work of a single writer, and the range of approaches taken to representing Dexter's characters in various forms thus offers an opportunity to examine how depictions of sidekick characters respond to their means of creation, and the medium

D. Bishop (✉)
Edinburgh Napier University, Edinburgh, UK

L. Andrew and S. Saunders (eds.), *The Detective's Companion in Crime Fiction*, Crime Files, https://doi.org/10.1007/978-3-030-74989-7_12

for which they are created. In addition, the considerable length of time during which these series have been produced—from the late 1970s to the present—provides the chance to see how Morse and Lewis function in different roles, as sidekick and detective.

It is firstly necessary to define what is actually meant by the term, 'sidekick'. Sarah Dimick proposes examining the roles of detective and sidekick 'through the lens of differentiated responsibility', where the sidekick essentially 'perform[s] the brutal physical work necessary to protect the cerebral detective' (2018: 22). Elsewhere, Fedwa Malti-Douglas argues for a different function, suggesting that the sidekick

> provides [the reader] with someone either to identify with or to feel superior to, as the case may be. Furthermore, if the reader is at a loss and is unable to untangle the story […] the presence of this companion, who is usually also at a loss, gives the reader confidence. (1988: 67)

While Dimick defines the sidekick as mere muscle and Malti-Douglas highlights the character's potential for generating reader empathy, Stephen M. Zimmerly goes further by listing four different roles that a sidekick can fulfil:

> [a] 'narrative gateway' through which the reader can better understand an enigmatic protagonist; as a 'devil's advocate' to provide conflicting views; as 'comic relief' to an otherwise serious hero; or as a 'foil' to contrast with the protagonist. The roles […] not only overlap and combine […] they can shift, especially for sidekicks who appear in extended storylines. (2019: 2)

It is worth noting that Zimmerly also expresses reservations about using the term 'sidekick', acknowledging that there is a 'dismissal inherent in the term' with the relevant character being positioned as 'an afterthought […] there is a connotation of usefulness, but not necessity' (2019: 4).

Let us apply these definitions to Dexter's characters. Dimick and Malti-Douglas present the role of sidekick as fixed, even static, but this is simply not true of the sidekicks found in the Morse narrative universe, and particularly not in the adapted television series. However, Zimmerly's last statement—that the roles of a sidekick can shift across long series—is far more accurate for Dexter's characters, which feature in 13 novels and numerous television episodes. The role occupied by a sidekick in the Morse narrative universe changes, depending on which novel one is reading or which series one is watching.

Ultimately, I would contend that the many variations proposed above demonstrate there is no one-size-fits-all definition for the term 'sidekick', aside from the common factor of the character fulfilling a supportive role. The nature of that role and how the sidekick interacts with their detective can vary considerably, as will become apparent in this chapter's analysis of the different approaches taken with Dexter's characters since they first appeared in 1975.

Morse and Lewis in Print

Oxford police detectives Inspector (later Chief Inspector) Morse and Sergeant Lewis first appeared in Colin Dexter's debut novel *Last Bus to Woodstock* (1975), with the characters going on to feature in twelve subsequent novels and eleven short stories. The early novels found a considerable readership, and by 1981 had won two Silver Dagger awards from the Crime Writers' Association of Great Britain. But it was the *Inspector Morse* television series that propelled Dexter's novels up the best-seller lists. A hit with both critics and audiences, the screen version of Dexter's characters won BAFTA awards in 1992 and 1993 for best drama (Bishop 2011: 10). The series attracted up to 18 million viewers in the UK (Bishop 2011: 239), and was sold to more than 200 countries world-wide (Hayward 2009). It is therefore understandable that, as Neil McCaw notes, 'for the most part it is the TV incarnation of the detective [Morse] that has been discussed rather than the Dexter novels' (2011: 63). This chapter redresses that imbalance a little, by first examining the relationship between Morse and Lewis on the page, and the shift in Dexter's approach to them after the television incarnation, *Inspector Morse*, became a success.

Morse and Lewis are introduced in chapter two of *Last Bus to Woodstock*. Morse 'knew Sergeant Lewis only slightly, but soon found himself pleasurably impressed by the man's level-headed competence' (Dexter 1975: 10). The inspector expresses dismay that Lewis never studied Latin at school, but decides the sergeant is 'nobody's fool [...] a man of some honesty and integrity' (Dexter 1975: 12). During their initial encounters, Dexter establishes Lewis as a valuable foil for Morse, largely through their contrasting investigatory approaches. Morse lacks capacity for the mundane yet necessary aspects of police work, feeling 'impatient and bored with the trained and thorough pedanticism with which his sergeant probed and queried' (Dexter 1975: 25). Lewis, meanwhile, fulfils the role of policing competence, as Morse acknowledges: 'he knew it had to be done and he knew that Lewis was doing it well' (Dexter 1975: 25). In fact, the sergeant acts as the guardian of procedural responsibility; when Morse suggests illegally searching a suspect's property, Lewis is appalled and stomps off to the police canteen in protest (Dexter 1975: 91). This fulfils the 'devil's advocate' role proposed by Zimmerly, with the sergeant on the side of upholding the law. As the pair's first case together concludes, Morse cheerfully patronises the sergeant: '[w]e'll make a detective of you yet' (Dexter 1975: 174). Of course, Lewis is *already* a police detective in name and rank, but that does not matter to Morse; to him, a true detective solves murders not with painstaking procedure, but with imagination, instinct and intellect. This ideology informs most of Morse's existence; while Lewis struggles with the simple coffee-time crossword in the *Daily Mirror* tabloid, Morse takes pride in solving the fiendish cryptic crossword in *The Times* broadsheet newspaper, and in *The Dead of Jericho* (1981) he boasts: 'I happen to be blessed with the most brilliant brain in Oxford' (9). But these leaps of intuitive reasoning can, and do, send investigations awry, requiring the procedurally driven Lewis to intervene. In *The Dead of Jericho*, for example, Morse theorises that a woman hanged herself to fulfil the myth of Oedipus, after discovering she was unwittingly sleeping with the son she gave up for adoption long before (159). Lewis disproves this elegant hypothesis via routine enquiries, that reveal the woman's son, in fact, died of meningitis at the age of three (164).

Dexter never turns Lewis into a comic relief sidekick, despite Morse's frequent attempts to belittle him. For example, in *The Riddle of the Third Mile* (1983), Morse teases: '[d]on't underestimate yourself, Lewis – let me do it for you!' (Dexter 1983: 335), while in *The Secret of Annexe 3* he quips: '[l]ife *is* complex, Lewis. Not for *you*, perhaps' (Dexter 1986: 121). Morse finally pushes Lewis's forbearance to the limit as the body count mounts in *Service of all the Dead*. When the sergeant tries to raise a legitimate point, Morse—frustrated at losing control of the case—shouts at Lewis at length before accusing him of 'farting around with piddling nonsense' (Dexter 1979: 321):

> Lewis walked out, making sure to slam the door hard behind him. He'd had just about enough, and for two pins, he'd resign from the force on

the spot if it meant getting away from this sort of mindless ingratitude. (Dexter 1979: 321)

Nonetheless, despite the occasionally-terse relationship he has with Morse, Lewis appears content to remain a sidekick. In *Last Seen Wearing* (1976), the sergeant recognises that 'he would never make an inspector' (Dexter 1976: 502), and by *The Dead of Jericho* Lewis is happy to be associated with

> the phenomenon of Morse [...] [f]or all his superior's irascibility, crudity, and self-indulgence, Lewis has taken enormous pride – yes, *pride* – in his friendship with the man whom almost all the other members of the Thames Valley Constabulary had now come to regard as a towering, if somewhat eccentric, genius. (Dexter 1981: 105)

The sergeant thus represents everything Morse is not, as Morse himself notes in *The Riddle of the Third Mile*: 'Lewis was placid, good-natured, methodical, honest, unassuming, faithful, and (yes, he might as well come clear about it!) a bit *stolid*, too' (Dexter 1983: 235). Morse's errant genius and Lewis's stolid honesty can, and do, provoke comparisons to Sherlock Holmes and Doctor John Watson. In fact, Dexter directly invites these comparisons, such as when Lewis helps Morse solve a tricky crossword clue in *Last Seen Wearing*: 'Sherlock Holmes picked up *The Times*, wrote in the answer and beamed at his own Doctor Watson' (Dexter 1976: 428). John Scaggs, for example, contends that Dexter 'structures his fiction around a Holmes/Watson relationship, the grumpy, intellectual, opera-loving Chief Inspector Morse and his sidekick Detective Sergeant Lewis, who is unimaginative, but reliable and diligent' (Scaggs 2005: 50). Martin Priestman agrees that Morse and Lewis are 'a lopsided duo' with 'the traditional appeal of the Holmes-Watson format', but also suggests that Dexter presents 'police work as collective, grim and often untidy, rather than as merely an elegant intellectual exercise' (2003: 178–179). However, I would argue that the prose relationship of Morse and Lewis is significantly different from that of Holmes and Watson. Indeed, Doyle deployed Watson as a first-person narrator in a manner that fulfils Zimmerly's definition of sidekick as narrative gateway that enables the reader to observe and to better understand Holmes. Conversely, Dexter uses third-person narrative positions throughout his texts, giving readers access to the thoughts and feelings of both Morse and Lewis, along with other characters' perceptions of them. Lewis is also an effective policeman in his own right and is more than willing to challenge Morse when necessary. While Holmes's deductions are based on observation and scientific methodology, Morse regularly employs leaps of imaginative reasoning and guesswork, and while Watson marvels at Holmes' feats of deductive reasoning, Lewis finds plenty to fault with the intuitive leaps of logic that Morse favours. In *Last Bus to Woodstock*, for example, Lewis openly despairs of Morse's approach:

> The real trouble was that he always had to find a complex solution to everything, and Lewis had enough experience of police work to know that most criminal activity owed its origins to simple, cheap, and sordid motives. What the great man couldn't do, for all his gifts, was put a couple of simple facts together and come up with something obvious. (Dexter 1975: 433)

Another significant difference is that while Holmes and Watson are private sleuths who occasionally work alongside the police, Morse and Lewis solve crimes from within the hierarchical world of policing. Their relationship is thus informed by rank, a system that codifies the role of senior and junior officers—detective and sidekick—through the chain of command. Whereas Holmes and Watson are equals in their social position if not in their investigative roles and abilities, Morse always holds the power of rank over his sidekick Lewis.

Dexter had published seven Morse novels when the television rights to his characters were optioned, with the first episode of *Inspector Morse* broadcast in January 1987 (Bishop 2011: 119). The author wrote six further novels over the next twelve years, in which Morse's character stayed largely the same even after the televised series began airing. Interestingly however, Dexter admitted to altering how he wrote Lewis in response to the show's casting of a visibly young actor, Kevin Whately, as the sergeant: '[m]y view of Lewis has changed [...] I've solved the problem by ignoring it and not giving him too much physical description' (Sanderson 1991: 20). From *The Wench Is Dead* (1989)—the first novel published after the television debut of *Inspector Morse*—through to the final instalment, *The Remorseful Day* (1999), the author avoids mentioning Lewis's age. He keeps his Welsh wife, but their children are absent until that final novel where Lewis helps a previously-unmentioned son with his homework (33)—reflecting the fact that the television version of Lewis has a teenage son.

Dexter also makes a number of sly nods to Lewis's on-screen portrayal in the later novels. In *The Way Through the Woods* (1992), for example, the sergeant recalls two past trips overseas—three weeks in Australia, and two weeks in Italy (141). These match television stories that took Morse and Lewis to Australia ('Promised Land', broadcast in 1991), and Italy ('The Death of the Self', broadcast in 1992). As *The Way Through the Woods* concludes, Morse asks if Lewis would like a bottle of Newcastle Brown ale—a reference to the northern city that the sergeant calls home on television (Dexter 1992: 261). But, overall, the characterisation of Lewis as *sidekick* remains the same in Dexter's later novels, despite the changes made to his character.

In print, then, Lewis is portrayed as Morse's competent and honest sidekick, yet he also does far more than simply perform brutal physical work, provide a source of reader empathy, or even provide a narrative voice or window for the reader to observe Morse in action. Lewis is the series' guardian of police-procedural responsibility, making him a valuable and utterly necessary foil for Morse's idiosyncratic and instinctual approach to detection. Dexter thus employs Lewis as a devil's advocate, yet at the same time he also shows how the sidekick can be an effective policeman and/or detective in their own right.

Morse and Lewis on Screen

The television series *Inspector Morse* keeps its title character much as he is on the page, but his sidekick, Lewis, undergoes a far more comprehensive reinvention. Gone is the grandfather several years older than Morse, replaced by a man perhaps a decade younger (their relative ages are not stated, but Kevin Whately, the actor playing Lewis, was nine years younger than his counterpart John Thaw). Lewis becomes Morse's junior in both years and experience, while the inspector becomes an occasional father figure for Lewis. This is most explicit in the cricket-themed episode 'Deceived By Flight' (1989), where Lewis goes undercover with an amateur team, playing a match while Morse watches idly. The sergeant makes a catch, but when he turns proudly to see if Morse witnessed it, the inspector is asleep.

On television, Lewis still lacks university qualifications or any knowledge of literature. He also remains a family-oriented character, but his wife is now from Oxford rather than Wales, and his children are teenagers. However, Lewis's own background undergoes an even more substantial change. In print, he is a character with no fixed place of origin, while on screen he is from the North East, with a strong accompanying accent. As Stijn Reijnders states, 'the cultured, historic and academic environment of Oxford fits seamlessly with the intellectual, somewhat snobbish character of [...] Morse' (2009: 172). The reinvention of Lewis's background thus creates a North/South divide, signalling him more overtly as an outsider in the university town, and also rather callously signifies a class distinction between detective and sidekick.

In its first two series, *Inspector Morse* stayed close to Dexter's source material, with each script adapting either one of his novels or a story supplied by the author. The first episode to be aired was 'The Dead of Jericho' (1987), where Lewis initially works with another inspector but already knows Morse by reputation: 'I've heard he's meant to be a very clever man' ('The Dead of Jericho': 1.1). Morse acquires both the case and Lewis during this episode, but the new pairing is not an immediate fit, evident when Morse sneers at Lewis's early morning enthusiasm: '[y]ou're one of those people who has breakfast, aren't you?' ('The Dead of Jericho': 1.1). However, by the second episode ('The Silent World of Nicholas Quinn', 1987), the two detectives display a more easy familiarity, as if they have been together for years: 'I do hope this is not going to be one of our sordid cases, Lewis,' Morse laments ('The Silent World of Nicholas Quinn': 1.2). Lewis is very much a sidekick here, although his unwitting comments often prompt a vital connection, such as in 'The Sins of the Fathers' (1990) where the sergeant's uncultured use of English makes Morse realise who killed the final victim. This happens so often on screen that such moments have their own catchphrase: 'You've done it again, Lewis!' Variations of this can be found in 'The Silent World of Nicholas Quinn' (1987), 'Ghost in the Machine' (1989), and 'Twilight of the Gods' (1993), amongst others.

Inspector Morse increasingly portrays Lewis as a devil's advocate, the sidekick ready to challenge Morse's attitudes and easy disregard for procedure. In 'Last Seen Wearing' (1988), for example, the sergeant berates Morse for having little interest in a missing person case until someone dies: '[w]ell, you've got your body, sir. You were so keen to have a murder. You should be happy' ('Last Seen Wearing': 2.2). The detectives have a blazing row in 'Driven to Distraction' (1990) when Morse proposes illegally searching a suspect's business premises—echoing their clash in *Last Bus to Woodstock*. Lewis categorically refuses to have any part in such an act: '[t]here's no procedure. It's crime solved like a crossword puzzle and I'm sick of it' ('Driven to Distraction': 4.3).

The arrival of new producer Chris Burt for the third series of *Inspector Morse* (broadcast in 1989) brought a shift away from adaptation to commissioning original scripts based on Dexter's characters. It is no coincidence that this sees Lewis 'taking a more active role in solving cases [...] [and acting] as a comic foil, pricking his superior's lapses into pomposity' (Bishop 2011: 151). In later series, Lewis becomes more willing to confront Morse's often-warped notion of what constitutes being a detective, signalling that he does not remain static as a sidekick and actually progresses towards a more equal partnership with Morse. I would argue this is a consequence of the shift from page to screen, moving to a narrative form where stories must be externalised and the dramatic need for conflict encourages writers to have their lead characters clash. As Helen Davis argues: 'Lewis matures as the program continues through the eighties into the nineties, and he is increasingly seen as a partner in this duo rather than a fledgling' (Davis 2001: 138). She describes Lewis as Morse's essential counterweight:

> Morse's commitment is more truly a reflection of his fascination for a puzzle [...] it demonstrates how inappropriate and non-productive it would be for Morse to have an acolyte as his assistant. Lewis's vision of the job is totally vindicated [...] Intuitive theorizing will only get you so far. It requires painstaking legwork to break the case. (140)

While the relationship between Morse and Lewis grows closer on screen, they remain separated by rank. Where the sergeant is content with his position in print, the on-screen Lewis shows greater interest in career progression. During 'Who Killed Harry Field?' (1991), Morse finds a copy of the *Police and Criminal Evidence Act* on Lewis's desk. To Morse, it means one of two things: either '[Lewis] hasn't got enough work, or his wife wants him to be an inspector' ('Who Killed Harry Field?': 5.3). Morse is thus a man of wild imagination, yet he is unable to conceive of his sergeant having any desire for promotion. Ultimately, Lewis chooses not to pursue higher rank—at least for now—because he is content where he is, signalling the development in his partnership with Morse. Indeed, the evolution of Lewis's relationship with his superior is made apparent when the detectives travel to the Australian outback in 'Promised Land' (1991). Lewis openly enjoys himself, but Morse finds it a hellish trip beset by heat, flies, country music—and the troubling revelation that he unwittingly had an innocent man jailed. Not long before the episode's bloody climax, Morse calls his sergeant 'Robbie' for the first time. The significance of this moment is set up earlier, when Lewis tells another character that 'Robbie' is a name used only by his friends ('Promised Land': 5.5).

Additionally, Julie D. O'Reilly suggests that 'sidekicks normalize their otherwise atypical protagonists' (2009: 61), and this is certainly the case with Lewis and Morse on screen. The sergeant does 'normalize' Morse's atypical talents, and provides a bridge between him and others who may be unaware of Morse's acerbic nature—be they other police officers or civilians. For example, in 'The Secret of Bay 5B' (1989) the sergeant explains to the unmarried Morse how the Lewis family marks appointments and important events like birthdays on a shared calendar, which leads to a breakthrough in the case that Morse would not have otherwise made ('The Secret of Bay 5B': 3.4). Secondly, in 'Greeks Bearing Gifts' (1991) it is Lewis who smooths things over after Morse is typically abrasive with the interpreter Jocasta Georgiadis ('Greeks Bearing Gifts': 5.4). Furthermore, when Morse is being door-stepped and pilloried by the tabloids in 'Happy Families' (1992) for reading books and liking classical music, it is Lewis who openly speaks up in Morse's support, rather than the ambitious Superintendent Holdsby ('Happy Families': 6.2).

Inspector Morse ended as a regular television series in 1993, but Dexter continued writing new novels, which continued to provide fresh material for a handful of one-off specials broadcast from 1995 to 2000. These took the show back to its source material, with each new episode adapting one of Dexter's original texts. In 'The Way Through the Woods' (1995) Morse is busy writing a report for the chief superintendent, so Lewis works with another inspector called Johnson, who is soon to take charge of a regional crime squad. Johnson offers Lewis a chance to become an inspector, but Morse interferes in matters. Finally, Lewis snaps: 'I've proved myself a decent detective, but you're such a bloody arrogant, self-centred bastard you'd rather die than ever admit it!' ('The Way Through the Woods': 8.1). Morse congratulates Lewis on the potential promotion but warns it will come with a price. He is proven right when Johnson assaults a suspect. Afterwards, Morse defends Lewis to his rival: 'Detective Sergeant Lewis is nobody's fool, Johnson – least of all yours' ('The Way Through the Woods': 8.1). The door to promotion finally opens for Lewis in the final episode of *Inspector Morse*, 'The Remorseful Day' (2000). The bitter irony for Lewis is that it takes Morse's death to finally elevate the sergeant from sidekick status to protagonist-detective in his own right. Nonetheless, the characterisation of Lewis as a sidekick displays clear evidence of evolution in the 33 episodes of *Inspector Morse*, broadcast across 13 years. He progresses from a sergeant whose unwitting comments prompt moments of inspiration for his detective to a far more active participant in solving their cases. Furthermore, Lewis becomes a true devil's advocate, while at the same time his behaviour and presence normalises the atypical Morse to create a touching friendship between the two characters on screen.

Lewis and Hathaway on Screen

Six years after the finale of *Inspector Morse*, one of Dexter's characters returns to the screen in a new series: *Lewis*. The sergeant, still played by Kevin Whately, is now a detective inspector. In the opening episode 'Lewis', he comes back to Oxford after a two-year secondment in the British Virgin Islands, but he is now a widower, and much changed by these tragic circumstances. Phil Wickham suggests that the new series

> fleshes out the role of Morse's previously upbeat sidekick to recreate its forebear's emphasis on world-weary experience. Lewis is now bereaved and, like Morse, is frequently at odds with his superior and modernity [...] *Lewis* may appeal to the older viewer in its distaste for the ways in which individuals are subsumed into an institutional machine. (2010: 77)

Assisting Lewis is Detective Sergeant James Hathaway, a Cambridge theology graduate and former student priest. In an echo of the first episode of *Inspector Morse*, Hathaway is working for another detective when this story opens but is temporarily reassigned to work with Lewis. After they solve the case, Hathaway asks to continue as the inspector's sergeant. The two enjoy a more equal working relationship than Lewis experienced in his years with Morse. Like Morse, Hathaway's education far outstrips Lewis's, but the inspector's decades of police experience are a more than equal counterweight for Hathaway's academic prowess.

Lewis is thus repositioned from sidekick to title character, with Hathaway now positioned as sidekick. However, while Hathaway sometimes makes a few joking asides,[1] his function is not one of either comic relief or to act as the muscular sidekick, nor is he even a narrative pathway to help viewers better understand the detective. Instead, Hathaway operates chiefly as Lewis's foil, as the source of scholarly, cerebral or classical knowledge where it is required, and is thus designed to provide a Morse-esque contrast to Lewis himself, sometimes playing devil's advocate as the pair puzzle over a mystery. Indeed, Rosanne Welch suggests that Hathaway carries 'the Morse qualities of higher education and love of classic literature and music' (Welch 2016: 387).

However, while I agree that Hathaway can be seen as an attempt to create a neo-Morse character, manifesting the late inspector's intellectual side with Lewis recast in the role of older mentor, there is very little in how the sergeant operates as a *detective* that replicates Morse's approach. Hathaway's methods are actually far closer to those of Lewis, using police procedure and forensic evidence to solve cases, rather than wild, instinctive leaps of deductive reasoning. Indeed, when *Lewis* was unveiled, Whately admitted to concerns about being the heart of the series: 'Lewis was always set up as a sounding board, and the films were very much motivated by Morse himself' (Bishop 2011: 269). David Brown (2015) argues that:

> [T]o give this perennial sidekick his own show did – at first – seem a bit tenuous. It was akin to the doltish Captain Hastings or the baffled Dr Watson being handed their own spin-offs. [...] But thankfully, Lewis *did* have Hathaway. (2015: n.p.)

Phil Wickham, meanwhile, is more charitable in assessing the merits of *Lewis*:

> The show closely follows its predecessor's blueprint; a languorous pace, picturesque Oxford locations, and emphasis on performance and character [...] The complexity of human nature is the interest (rather than the whodunit) derived from experience, from an understanding that comes with age, in which morality can be an ambiguous and messy affair. (2010: 77)

Certainly, the most effective episodes focus on the two men's inner lives informed by their past experiences. A strong example is 'Life Born of Fire' (2008), in which Hathaway is forced to confront issues of sexuality and gender, and reveals the reason why he abandoned his studies toward joining the priesthood. Hathaway withholds the truth from Lewis, driving a wedge between them and putting lives (including his own) at risk as a consequence. However, *Lewis*'s procedural nature means each episode must stand alone, able to be viewed in any order—indeed, several series were originally screened in a different order to how they were filmed. This approach denies *Lewis* the chance to develop or revisit significant character arcs. Instead, both Hathaway and Lewis are required to return to their previous status at the end of each episode, being portrayed as individuals with slightly wounded souls who work together to solve crimes and indulge in occasional repartee.

It could be argued that Hathaway's intellect and Lewis's decades of experience combine to form perhaps a shadow version of Morse, but there is limited evidence to support this. Instead, I would propose an alternate theory: that Hathaway and Lewis are two sidekicks working together, functioning as mutual foils. Yes, Lewis holds a superior rank, but the younger man matches that with his superior education and grasp of modern technology. Crucially, Lewis treats Hathaway in many ways as an equal, despite their differences in experience and age. Together they are far more of a partnership than Morse and Lewis ever were in print or on screen.

The only significant change to the Lewis and Hathaway relationship occurs near the end of the show's ten years. Lewis retires at the end of series seven (2013), clearing a way for Hathaway to be promoted. Series eight (2014) opens with Hathaway as a detective inspector in Oxford, but incapable of delegation. Chief Superintendent Innocent implores Hathaway to hang on to his newest sergeant, DS Lizzie Maddox, in 'Entry Wounds' (2014). Short on personnel, Innocent persuades Lewis to come out of retirement as a consulting detective. She assigns him to help Hathaway and Maddox, putting Hathaway in the awkward position of giving orders to his former boss. But the two soon settle back into their comfortable twosome, with Maddox cast in the role of sidekick to both. Maddox quickly becomes severely underutilised; her arrival in series eight offers the chance to disrupt the male-centric focus of *Lewis*, but this potential goes unrealised. The character is never given much opportunity to show herself as anything more than a competent assistant to Hathaway and Lewis. Worse still, she gets downgraded to the role of 'damsel in distress' during 'Beyond Good and Evil' (2014), with Hathaway and Lewis racing to save Maddox after the killer leaves her for dead. She spends the rest of the episode in a coma, useful only to provide motivation for Hathaway, Lewis and Maddox's husband. This is a trope known as 'fridging', which J. Andrew Deman defines as 'sacrificing a female character in service of a male character's narrative' (2020: 12). It is disappointing to see Maddox—a rare example of a female detective in the Morse narrative universe—being used in such a retrograde manner. However, sidestepping the mishandling of Maddox in later episodes of *Lewis*, the series offers a new approach to the sidekick within the Morse narrative universe. Rather than the evolving sidekick and detective dynamic in Dexter's novels and *Inspector Morse*, this series presents two sidekick characters collaborating to solve crimes. The equality of their relationship becomes explicit in series eight and nine when both Lewis and Hathaway have the same rank: Detective Inspector. It is a pity that the purely procedural nature of *Lewis* and its means of production prevented it from fully exploiting the possibilities of this unusual dynamic.

Endeavour: A New Paradigm

To mark the twenty-fifth anniversary of *Inspector Morse*'s first appearance on television, a new one-off special—'Endeavour'—was broadcast in January 2012. Set in 1965, the story reinvents Dexter's Morse as an angry young detective constable struggling to find his way within a regimented police culture. One of many officers seconded to Oxford for a missing person's case, Morse becomes a sidekick to Inspector Fred Thursday, a no-nonsense copper with decades of experience and an eye for a good detective. Recognising the young Morse's ability, Thursday offers the chance to become his 'bagman' (a driver and aide-de-camp, an unofficial post usually held by a higher rank, usually detective sergeant): 'I'd see you right, make sure we get you through your sergeant's exam. With the proper encouragement, who knows?' ('Pilot').

The special episode was a success, achieving 'the highest audience for a new one-off drama on ITV1 in five years' (Bishop 2016). Seven series of *Endeavour* have followed, with an eighth in production at the time of writing. The two previous shows featuring Dexter's characters were scripted by numerous writers—15 across 33 cases in *Inspector Morse*, and 20 contributing to 33 *Lewis* stories. As noted above, that means each episode is effectively a standalone, with little (if any) narrative content linking them to past or future stories. However, writer Russell Lewis provides the script for every episode of *Endeavour*, as well as being one of the show's executive producers. In British television this is colloquially known as an 'authored drama', with a single writer responsible for all the scripts and the creative vision of a series or serial. Russell Lewis defines the role and destiny of each character—and he is the first writer to have sole charge of that in the Morse narrative universe since Dexter wrote the original novels. This means that *Endeavour* can, and does, have characters that undergo extended narrative arcs, and evolve in ways that are impossible for the show's television forebears due to the means of their creation. The authored drama approach confirms a contention by Torben Grodal that 'crime fiction is often produced within a frame of serialization. The detectors [...] are the constants, the agents with whom the viewers or readers resonate empathically in fiction after fiction' (2010: 71). In this final section, I will examine how Russell Lewis employs that frame of serialisation to present variations of the sidekick within *Endeavour*.

Rosanne Welch argues that pairing the young Morse with Thursday is 'continuing the balance of personalities set by the parent series' (2016: 387). However, I would suggest that *Endeavour* offers a more complex narrative approach, with Morse actually participating in a variety of relationships. While Dexter's novels and the previous television series focused largely on two-man teams, *Endeavour* presents a predominantly homosocial workplace ensemble. Hammarén and Johansson define homosociality as 'a mechanism and social dynamic that explains the maintenance of hegemonic masculinity', and 'one used to point at how men tend to bond, build closed teams, and defend their privileges and positions' (2014: 1). They propose that a distinction be made 'between vertical/hierarchical and horizontal homosociality', with the former 'as a means of strengthening power and of creating close homosocial bonds to maintain and defend hegemony', and the latter as 'relations that are based on emotional closeness, intimacy, and a nonprofitable form of friendship' (5). Hammarén and Johansson do concede that there are 'no absolute boundaries between these two approaches' (5). In *Endeavour*, most of the workplace relationships are examples of vertical homosociality, reflecting the rigid rank system of the police. But some of Morse's work relationships do match the horizontal approach. Thursday and Morse are the central pairing of *Endeavour* and the only characters to appear in every episode to date, aside from police surgeon Dr. Max DeBryn. The two detectives are a generation apart, but both are ex-army and come from a working-class background. They recognise each other's strengths and Thursday soon treats Morse as his equal in detection, if not in rank. Several episodes see them simultaneously yet separately identify the killer or a vital clue via different means. For example, in 'Girl' (2013) both deduce that there is undiscovered evidence at a remote public toilet—the scene of a recent murder—and travel there independently to find it.

There are significant differences in their policing approach, however. Thursday willingly resorts to violence, something that Morse does not countenance. In the first episode, Thursday sends Morse out of the room before bloodying the nose of a suspicious car dealer, while in 'Prey' (2016), Thursday beats a confession from a park keeper who targets vulnerable young women. In 'Coda' (2016), Thursday is ready to execute a gangster after a bank robbery goes wrong, but Morse convinces him to restrain himself. In 'Quartet' (2018), Thursday coaches a wife to help her avoid being accused of killing her abusive husband. Morse protests to the inspector that they are meant to uphold the law. 'Well, it's my way and I'm too set in my ways to change them now,' Thursday snaps ('Quartet': 5.5). From this perspective, then, the relationship between Morse and Thursday inverts Sarah Dimick's suggestion that the sidekick can be found 'performing the brutal physical work necessary to protect the cerebral detective' (2018: 22). Instead it is Thursday—the senior ranking officer—who does the more brutal work, while Morse takes the role of cerebral detective, unwilling to use violence. In series six of *Endeavour* (2019), a now-demoted Thursday works beneath a corrupt officer who favours rough justice, and he becomes what Maureen T. Reddy calls a 'violence machine', beating individuals to get information (2012: 164). It is Morse's intervention that eventually helps Thursday find his way back to the right side of the law.

O'Reilly's theory that 'sidekicks normalize their otherwise atypical protagonists' (2009: 61) is also inverted in the early series of *Endeavour*, as it is Thursday who helps to 'normalize' his sidekick, Morse, by inviting the young detective sergeant into the Thursday family home, and by coaching him to become a better policeman. In 'Girl' (2013) the inspector appoints Morse as his 'bagman', an action that attracts the attention of newly arrived Chief Superintendent Bright, and the ire of the displaced Detective Sergeant Jakes, who becomes intent on punishing his apparent usurper. Thursday urges Morse to 'learn his trade': 'I'm a good detective,' Morse protests. 'And a poor policeman,' the inspector replies—a deliberate echo by writer Russell Lewis of an exchange between Morse and the wife of a rival officer in the *Inspector Morse* episode 'Second Time Around' (1991) ('Girl': 1.1). But just as Thursday often struggles to contain his violent streak, so too is Morse unable—and often unwilling—to hide his intellectual talent. The young detective constable's arrogant belief in the correctness of his deductions is deft writing by Russell Lewis, planting seeds of the character that is Dexter's Morse. In 'Girl', for example, Morse openly contradicts Chief Superintendent Bright in front of other officers by identifying the owner of an abandoned bicycle as an older, left-handed cleric of limited means—a feat of deductive reasoning worthy of Sherlock Holmes ('Girl': 1.1). Yet Morse also makes basic blunders, such as wrongly arresting a gas meter collection man, and failing to properly investigate a young female suspect to whom he is obviously attracted simply because he does not believe she is guilty. These errors give Jakes a chance to highlight Morse's weaknesses as a policeman. Stubborn single-mindedness helps Morse solve the case—but also nearly ends his career.

The first four series of *Endeavour* see Morse stuck as a detective constable, with a sergeant—Jakes—between him and Thursday. The inspector recognises Morse's potential, and slowly cajoles him towards higher rank. In 'Prey', Morse laments that he is not sergeant material, and Thursday replies 'you're inspector material, but there's no short cut' ('Prey': 3.3). When Morse finally becomes a sergeant, he believes it more than justified: 'I've earned these stripes many times over' ('Muse': 5.1). By 'Quartet' (2018), Thursday believes Morse is ready to succeed him. 'You've always been ready. You just needed someone to tell you, that's all' ('Quartet': 5.5). Despite Thursday's support, the other officers dismiss Morse due to the expectations of rank, or simply due to personality clashes. The antagonistic DS Jakes openly perceives Morse as a threat, and uses his superior rank to undermine or belittle him. In 'Fugue' (2013), for example, Jakes rejects a clue left in a hidden space simply because Morse found it: '[n]ot as if anybody normal would think to look there' ('Fugue': 1.2). When investigating a murder at a factory ('Rocket': 2013), Jakes delights in making Morse take statements from dozens of workers. In 'Home' (2013), Morse sees the sergeant out on a date with Thursday's grown-up daughter Joan, but tells nobody. Jakes offers an illicit look at the sergeant's exam paper in return, but Morse refuses: 'I'm trying to do you a favour,' Jakes insists. 'You're trying to buy me off,' Morse replies ('Home': 1.4). Jakes continues mistreating Morse until the series two finale (2014s 'Neverland'), when a historic abuse scandal at a boys' home is uncovered. Morse deduces Jakes was one of the victims but keeps the sergeant's secret. They work more easily together after this, until Jakes ultimately leaves in 'Arcadia' (2016).

Morse famously never finished his Oxford degree, but that university background—alongside his knowledge of literature, opera and other classical music—marks him out as different in a station of policemen who do not share these interests. 'Most of the lads have got you down as a bit of a queer fish,' the uniformed Constable Strange tells Morse in 'Girl', 'Standoffish. Rude. You've got to rub along with people in this job if you want to get on' ('Girl': 1.1). Indeed, Morse's relationship with Strange charts an intriguing trajectory, particularly as some viewers of *Endeavour* will be aware of Strange's position as Morse's superior in the original *Inspector Morse* series. The two characters first meet in *Endeavour* as constables during 'Girl'—Morse a detective, Strange in uniform. They quickly become friends, with Strange helping Morse study for the sergeant's exam later in the episode. Morse seeks Strange's help to interview the factory workers in 'Rocket', giving him a chance to do more than stand guard. Morse thus treats Strange as an equal colleague, despite his limitations as a detective. When Morse visits his dying father in 'Home', he suggests that Strange be seconded to help with enquiries as an acting detective constable. Strange is grateful, seeing it as another rung on the career ladder: 'Little acorns, matey' ('Home': 1.4). Like Lewis in Dexter's novels, Strange is aware he lacks Morse's imagination: in 'Trove' (2014), Strange asks Morse's advice about joining the Freemasons, and suggests that he could not advance his career on his own merit alone: '[w]e haven't all got your brain, matey,' he explains. 'Some of us need a leg up' ('Trove': 2.1). Strange is soon promoted to sergeant, while Morse remains a constable. 'It's nothing you couldn't do,' Strange tells Morse in 'Prey', 'rank's not about brains, it's about playing the game. Or not, in your case. You rub people up the wrong way' ('Prey': 3.3). Strange is destined to become a chief superintendent, while Morse will never rise higher than chief inspector. Strange's comment in 'Trove' echoes an observation his older self makes in the television adaptation of 'The Dead of Jericho' (1987): 'You're a clever sod, but you don't say the right things to the right people' ('The Dead of Jericho': *Inspector Morse* 1.1). Strange becomes a detective sergeant after Jakes' departure, and finds himself giving Morse orders. It is awkward at first, yet the pair remain friends until Morse objects to using force on a suspect. 'Let's get one thing straight, matey,' Strange warns. 'You don't tell me, I tell you. Job calls for brains, you'll be the first in the queue. Something like this, leave it to those who've got the sand' ('Coda': 3.4). Their previous friendship is restored only after Morse himself is promoted to sergeant.

The Morse and Strange relationship is therefore a useful example of what Hammarén and Johansson define as horizontal homosociality (2014: 5), and disrupts the typical detective/sidekick dichotomy. But the homosocial workplace ensemble is disrupted in 'Arcadia' when uniformed WPC Shirley Trewlove begins assisting the detectives. She proves herself an intelligent young officer with a gift for solving puzzles, and impresses Morse by deducing the solution to a mysterious explosion that defeats his reasoning. Thereafter, he encourages Trewlove to make contributions to cases. 'She's a very capable officer,' Morse says when asked about her. 'Doesn't suffer fools' ('Arcadia': 3.3).

Elsewhere, Russell Lewis uses the way Morse treats lower-ranked colleagues in *Endeavour* to foreshadow how he will behave as an older man in *Inspector Morse*. The young Morse's attitude to those cast as his sidekick relies not on their rank, but on how much potential they show. Strange is limited but dependable, with little malice to his nature. Trewlove is a bright, intelligent constable, and thus earns Morse's respect. But Morse finds Detective Constable George Fancy far less impressive when he arrives in 'Muse'. Thursday asks Morse to train the new detective constable: 'You've got rank now. That brings responsibilities' ('Muse': 5.1). As ever with Dexter's characters, their choice of newspaper puzzle is shorthand for their level of intelligence. When Fancy first appears, he is pondering where to draw the circle on a 'Spot the Ball' photo—not exactly a promising start. Fancy asks if he will make decent mates at the police station; 'If you go in for that sort of thing,' Morse replies ('Muse': 5.1). The new man happily admits he only joined the job for the social life—and the chance to impress young women. 'Let's just keep it to work and we'll get along fine,' Morse warns ('Muse': 5.1). Later, he catches the constable listening to loud rock music in an unmarked police car while on duty. 'Is this your idea of discreet observation?' Fancy admits forgetting to book in evidence. 'You're not paid to forget,' Morse snaps, 'you're paid to remember.' However, he later takes the blame for Fancy's mistake, accepting an unjustified rebuke from Thursday: 'You're a sergeant now, you want to look sharp' ('Muse': 5.1).

In 'Cartouche' (2018), Thursday chides Morse for his dismissive treatment of Fancy. 'You shouldn't be so hard on the boy. It's encouragement he wants. A bit of praise goes a long way' ('Cartouche': 5.2). Fancy volunteers to visit pubs and cafes that a murdered man may have visited. 'If he comes back with anything more than a skinful, I'll eat my hat', Morse says ('Cartouche': 5.2). Fancy somewhat inevitably proves Morse right, returning half-cut, and it seems that their relationship can never progress due to Fancy's lack of maturity. Fancy dies in the series five finale, 'Icarus' (2018), gunned down during a shoot-out while trying to prove himself after an earlier dressing down from Morse. Morse does not say so out loud, but he is clearly all too aware of his role in events that led to Fancy's death, and helps explain Morse's reluctance to re-engage with his colleagues in the first episode of series six, 'Pylon' (2019). It is also an example of Russell Lewis proposing a possible explanation for the eventual misanthropic nature of John Thaw's Morse. The means of creation employed by the two previous series adapting Dexter's characters makes such nuances unlikely, but the authored approach available to Russell Lewis with *Endeavour* enables him to craft a much longer, more subtle narrative.

Overall, among all the different incarnations of the Morse narrative universe, it is *Endeavour* that presents the most intriguing and certainly the most multi-faceted approach to the sidekick. The young Morse functions both as sidekick and detective in *Endeavour*. He is sidekick to Detective Inspector Thursday, while simultaneously having officers younger than himself and/or lower in rank operate as his sidekick—a relationship with which he is clearly uncomfortable. Furthermore, the central relationship between Morse and Thursday inverts several definitions of sidekick noted earlier in this chapter. Here, the detective performs the brutal physical work to protect the cerebral sidekick. Morse is thus both sidekick and atypical protagonist, normalised by his relationship with a more 'typical' detective.

Conclusion

In summary, the characters created by Dexter and developed by other writers in subsequent television adaptations make apparent the considerable range of variations possible for depicting a sidekick. The different approaches to the characters of Lewis, Hathaway and the young Morse demonstrate that the function of the sidekick is neither fixed, nor static; that a sidekick can become a detective in their own right, while a detective can fill many of the roles and functions associated with a sidekick. The four strands of the Morse narrative universe underline how significant the means of creation can be for the depiction of a sidekick. Finally, I would argue that *Endeavour* surpasses Dexter's novels in the depth and complexity of its characterisation of the sidekick, reinventing Morse as someone simultaneously able to occupy the roles of both sidekick and detective in a predominantly homosocial workplace environment. There is certainly a wealth of material in the Morse narrative universe worthy of further exploration and interpretation by adaptation studies scholars.

Note

1. In 'Expiation' (2007), for example, Hathaway (rather snidely) tells Chief Superintendent Innocent, 'I'm not smug, ma'am, […] it's just the unfortunate shape of my face' ('Expiation': 1.4).

Reference List

Bishop, David. 2011. *The Complete Inspector Morse*. London: Titan.

———. 2016. *Endeavour: The Complete Inspector Morse*. Edinburgh: Vicious Imagery.

Brown, David. 2015. Lewis Airs Its Final Episode—But Have We Really Seen the Last of Hathaway? *RadioTimes.com*. https://www.radiotimes.com/news/2015-11-10/lewis-airs-its-final-episode-but-have-we-really-seen-the-last-of-hathaway/. Accessed 13 Aug 2018.

Davis, Helen. 2001. Inspector Morse and the Business of Crime. *Television & New Media* 2 (2): 133–148.

Deman, J. Andrew. 2020. Busting Loose: Ms. Marvel and Post-Rape Trauma in X-Men Comics. *Journal of Graphic Novels and Comics*. Published online 3 May 2020: 1–14. https://doi.org/10.1080/21504857.2020.1757477. Accessed 17 July 2020.

Dexter, Colin. 1975. *Last Bus to Woodstock*. In *The Third Inspector Morse Omnibus*. London: Pan.

———. 1976. *Last Seen Wearing*. In *The Second Inspector Morse Omnibus*. London: Pan.

———. 1979. *Service of All the Dead*. In *The First Inspector Morse Omnibus*. London: Pan.

———. 1981. *The Dead of Jericho*. In *The First Inspector Morse Omnibus*. London: Pan.

———. 1983. *The Riddle of the Third Mile*. In *The Second Inspector Morse Omnibus*. London: Pan.

———. 1986. *The Secret of Annexe 3*. In *The Second Inspector Morse Omnibus*. London: Pan.

———. 1989. *The Wench is Dead*. In *The Third Inspector Morse Omnibus*. London: Pan.

———. 1992. *The Way Through the Woods*. In *The Fourth Inspector Morse Omnibus*. London: Pan.

———. 1999. *The Remorseful Day*. London: Macmillan.

Dimick, Sarah. 2018. From Suspect to Species: Climate Change in Antti Tuomainen's The Healer. *Mosaic: An Interdisciplinary Critical Journal* 51 (3): 19–35.

Grodal, Torben. 2010. High on Crime Fiction and Detection. *Projections* 4 (2): 64–85.

Hammarén, Nils, and Johansson, Thomas. 2014. Homosociality: In Between Power and Intimacy. *SAGE Open* 4 (1): 1–11. https://doi.org/10.1177/2158244013518057. Accessed 13 Aug 2018.

Hayward, Anthony. 2009. Philip Jones: Television Executive Who Sold 'Inspector Morse' to the World. *The Independent*, July 10.

Malti-Douglas, Fedwa. 1988. The Classical Arabic Detective. *Arabica* 35: 59–91.

McCaw, Neil. 2011. *Adapting Detective Fiction: Crime, Englishness and the TV Detectives*. London: Continuum.

O'Reilly, Julie D. 2009. The Legacy of George and Bess: Sidekicks as Normalizing Agents for the Girl Sleuth. *Clues: A Journal of Detection* 27 (1): 61–73.

Priestman, Martin. 2003. Post-war British Crime Fiction. In *The Cambridge Companion to Crime Fiction*, ed. Martin Priestman, 173–190. Cambridge: Cambridge University Press.

Reddy, Maureen T. 2012. Race and American Crime Fiction. In *The Cambridge Companion to American Crime Fiction*, ed. Catherine Ross Nickerson, 135–147. Cambridge: Cambridge University Press.

Reijnders, Stijn. 2009. Watching the Detectives: Inside the Guilty Landscapes of Inspector Morse, Baantjer and Wallander. *European Journal of Communication* 24 (2): 165–181.

Sanderson, Mark. 1991. *The Making of Inspector Morse*. London: Macmillan.

Scaggs, John. 2005. *Crime Fiction: A New Critical Idiom*. Abingdon: Routledge.

Welch, Rosanne. 2016. Transmitting Culture Transnationally: The Characterisation of Parents in the Police Procedural. *New Review of Film and Television Studies* 14 (3): 386–401.

Wickham, Phil. 2010. *New Tricks* and the Invisible Audience. *Critical Studies in Television* 5 (1): 69–81.

Zimmerly, Stephen M. 2019. *The Sidekick Comes of Age: How Young Adult Literature is Shifting the Sidekick Paradigm*. Lanham: Lexington.

Televised Material

Dexter, Colin, creator. *Inspector Morse*. Zenith Productions. 1987–2000.

———. 1.1. The Dead of Jericho. 6 January 1987.

———. 1.2, The Silent World of Nicholas Quinn. 13 January 1987.

———. 2.2, Last Seen Wearing. 8 March 1988.

———. 3.1, Ghost in the Machine. 4 January 1989.

———. 3.3, Deceived By Flight. 18 January 1989.
———. 3.4, The Secret of Bay 5B. 25 January 1989.
———. 4.2, The Sins of the Fathers. 10 January 1990.
———. 4.3, Driven to Distraction. 17 January 1990.
———. 5.1, Second Time Around. 20 February 1991.
———. 5.3, Who Killed Harry Field?. 13 March 1991.
———. 5.4, Greeks Bearing Gifts. 20 March 1991.
———. 5.5, Promised Land. 27 March 1991.
———. 6.2, Happy Families. 11 March 1992.
———. 6.3, The Death of the Self. 25 March 1992.
———. 7.3, Twilight of the Gods. 20 January 1993.
———. 8.1, The Way Through the Woods. 29 November 1995.
———. 8.5, The Remorseful Day. 15 November 2000.
Dexter, Colin, creator. *Lewis*. ITV Studios. 2006–2015.
———. Pilot. Lewis. 29 January 2006.
———. 1.4, Expiation. 4 March 2007.
———. 2.3, Life Born of Fire. 9 March 2008.
———. 8.1, Entry Wounds. 10/17 October 2014.
———. 8.3, Beyond Good and Evil. 7/14 November 2014.
Lewis, Russell, deviser. *Endeavour*. Mammoth Screen/Masterpiece. 2012–.
———. Pilot. Endeavour. 2 January 2012.
———. 1.1, Girl. 14 April 2013.
———. 1.2, Fugue. 21 April 2013.
———. 1.3, Rocket. 28 April 2013.
———. 1.4, Home. 5 May 2013.
———. 2.1, Trove. 30 March 2014.
———. 2.4, Neverland. 20 April 2014.
———. 3.2, Arcadia. 10 January 2016.
———. 3.3, Prey. 17 January 2016.
———. 3.4, Coda. 24 January 2016.
———. 5.1, Muse. 4 February 2018.
———. 5.2, Cartouche. 11 February 2018.
———. 5.5, Quartet. 4 March 2018.
———. 5.6, Icarus. 11 March 2018.
———. 6.1, Pylon. 10 February 2019.

CHAPTER 13

Mooncakes and Squashed Fly Biscuits: Otherness in the *Wells and Wong* Series

Alice Nuttall

Introduction

Since its debut in 2014 with *Murder Most Unladylike*, Robin Stevens' *Wells and Wong* series has become a successful part of the middle-grade detective canon, a genre of mystery stories aimed primarily at readers aged 8–12. Following the adventures of Daisy Wells and Hazel Wong, two students at an exclusive English boarding school in the 1930s, the books contain loving homages to works from the Golden Age of detective fiction, particularly the works of Agatha Christie and Dorothy L. Sayers. However, the series also offers an original take on the 'child detective' premise. Some of the most prominent aspects of the *Wells and Wong* stories that have led them to stand out are the characterisations and interactions of the two titular heroines.

Hazel Wong is the daughter of a rich Hong Kong banker. She and her father share a particular love of all things English, and so he sends her to Deepdean, an English boarding school. There, the serious, kind and thoughtful Hazel meets her new best friend, the Honourable Daisy Wells.

A. Nuttall (✉)
Oxford, UK

L. Andrew and S. Saunders (eds.), *The Detective's Companion in Crime Fiction*, Crime Files, https://doi.org/10.1007/978-3-030-74989-7_13

Daisy initially seems to Hazel to be a 'perfect English Miss', but is in fact a much more complex and unexpected person than the Blytonesque stereotype Hazel had anticipated (Stevens 2014: 64). Hazel narrates the series, and is often cast in the sidekick role, particularly in the earlier novels. These dual, linked roles are emphasised by the nickname 'Watson', given to her by Daisy, who casts herself as Holmes.

Much of the internal conflict and the humour of the series is driven by the contrast between Hazel and Daisy, which is emphasised in almost every aspect of their characterisation, including their physical appearances:

> Look at Daisy and you think you know exactly the sort of person she is – one of those dainty, absolutely English girls with blue eyes and golden hair [...] I, on the other hand, bulge all over like Bibendum the Michelin Man; my cheeks are moony-round and my hair and eyes are stubbornly dark brown. (Stevens 2014: 4)

The only traits that the two heroines initially seem to have in common are their intelligence and their flair for solving mysteries. In fact, this is how they become friends in the first place. Hazel is the only person to understand that '[t]he Daisy Wells we all pashed on was, in short, not real at all, but a very clever part' (Stevens 2014: 117). By discovering that Daisy is 'not jolly-good-show at all' (Stevens 2014: 4), but instead a highly intelligent, somewhat unnerving person who 'always has to *know* things' (Stevens 2014: 117, original emphasis), Hazel wins her respect, and they form their detecting duo; Daisy taking the role of President and lead detective, and Hazel first as Secretary, then Vice-President, but almost always in the role of sidekick.

Hazel's sidekick role is, in part, a result of Daisy's dominating personality, which is established both through their friendship dynamics and by Daisy's position as a popular figure at school. While Hazel is Watson, the sidekick, narrator and recorder, Daisy is Holmes, the coldly logical detective who frequently drives the action. The Detective Society itself is constructed to correspond with these roles, something set out at the very beginning of the first book:

> Daisy Wells is the President of the Detective Society, and I, Hazel Wong, am its Secretary. Daisy says that this makes her Sherlock Holmes, and me Watson. This is probably fair. After all, I am much too short to be the heroine of this story, and whoever heard of a Chinese Sherlock Holmes? (Stevens 2014: 3)

At least at this early stage, then, Hazel has accepted her sidekick role, and this is again partly a result of the personality contrast between herself and Daisy. However, it is also a result of her role as Other, an outsider in the otherwise overwhelmingly white world of Deepdean and in the wider English and European settings explored in later novels. Hazel's racial Otherness plays an important role in her experiences and development throughout the series, as narrator, sidekick, and heroine.

Hazel as Other

As the *Wells and Wong* stories, with a few exceptions,[1] are told from Hazel's perspective, we are frequently shown Hazel's first-hand experiences of being Othered in the Western social settings in which she is immersed. She is treated as an oddity so often that she is surprised by the few occasions that her differences are ignored:

> Mr Perkins looked at me, and I braced myself for the usual stare, or gasp, or angry look – the way English people usually behave when they see me for the first time. But for once I was surprised. Mr Perkins took in my brown hair and dark eyes and round face and nodded in greeting, just as though I was not remarkable at all. (Stevens 2016: 43)

More often, Hazel is on the receiving end of shocked and curious reactions, or occasionally outright aggression. When she and her father board the Orient Express in *First Class Murder* (2015b), a passenger tells Hazel's father's secretary 'You, sir! Move your servants!' (Stevens 2015b: 19), while Mr. Young, an English tutor that the group encounter on their Nile cruise boat in *Death Sets Sail* (2020), speaks 'loudly and slowly' to Hazel and her father and sisters, prompting Hazel to think 'I could tell that he expected us not to be able to understand English' (Stevens 2020: 53). Daisy's Aunt Saskia is similarly hostile:

> 'Daisy – Daisy, dear,' – she pulled Daisy towards her again and muttered like a foghorn – 'there seems to be AN ORIENTAL in your hall.' She said it as though I were a bear, or a snake. (Stevens 2015b: 21)

The secondary characters' placement of Hazel in an inferior role—as a servant, a depersonalised 'Oriental', or an animal—contribute to Hazel's sidekick status. To the social circles encountered throughout the books, with the exception of *A Spoonful of Murder* (2018a), it seems natural that Daisy, the white British aristocrat, should be the leader, while the Chinese Hazel should be the follower and sidekick. While Hazel's social status in Hong Kong is equivalent to Daisy's in England, and her economic status is certainly higher, British and European society cannot perceive this, and so Hazel is assumed to be secondary to Daisy. This pushes her further into the stereotypical view of the role of sidekick, a role that has often been viewed as ancillary to that of the hero—although, as Hazel and her literary forebear Watson have shown, this is an overly simplistic reading of the sidekick role.

The constant Othering that Hazel faces shapes her perspective on the societies and spaces in which she moves. Her treatment affects her view of the English and other European settings and groups of people that she encounters throughout the series:

> I can sometimes forget that I'm different. But as soon as I leave school I remember all over again. The first time people see me they stare at me and sometimes say things under their breath. Usually they say them out loud. I know it is the way things are, but I wish I was not the only one of me – and I wish that the *me* I am did not seem like the wrong sort of *me* to be. (Stevens 2015a: 8, original emphasis)

Hazel's feeling of being 'the wrong sort of me' leads her to develop a dual sense of self; the English persona she adopts in order to fit in, and which, as an Anglophile, she enjoys exploring, and her Chinese self, which remains hidden throughout much of the series. The tension between these two selves informs much of Hazel's character. While she may wish that she was not 'the only one of [her]', this wish has only very recently been granted—until a later instalment in the series, *Top Marks for Murder* (2019), Hazel is the only young woman of colour in the series' Western settings.[2] When the glamorous Amina El Maghrabi joins Deepdean in *Top Marks for Murder*, it is evident that she is very different from Hazel:

> the sight of Amina had startled me. I am used to bring the one girl at Deepdean who does not look like all the rest – and used to being gently looked down on for it. But here was darker-skinned Amina making all the pale English misses fawn around her. Was it simply because she looked as though she expected nothing less? (Stevens 2019: 13)

The 'gently looked down on', secondary role that Hazel occupies for much of the series partly influences her position as sidekick; however, Hazel's own negotiation and management of her identities is also a factor in her own creation of both her detective and her sidekick role.

Many of Hazel's actions throughout the series are based on her attempts to fit in with English society. To counteract her Otherness at school, she emulates the other girls, a process of 'camouflaging' that she describes in detail in *Murder Most Unladylike*:

> In Maths, I added up a sum wrong three times in a row, and in my French composition I told Mamzelle that I had brown eyes and a long black horse. When I read this out, I got my first ever giggle from the second form, and after lessons, Lavinia walked all the way back up to House with me – silently, but without leaving me behind at all. (Stevens 2014: 207)

Hazel's actions here echo Clare Bradford's description of schools in children's literature as 'a liminal space where differences of class, gender, sexuality, ethnicity, and race are played out' (Bradford 2007: 159). The space of the school allows Hazel to experiment with her 'English self', refining and perfecting her camouflage (and indeed, enjoying playing this role) in an environment that provides its inhabitants with room for this kind of experimentation. However, despite hiding her Otherness behind the scruffiness and 'don't-care' attitude that she has observed in her English classmates, Hazel is determined to remain herself on the inside. Her pride in her Hong Kong background, and her complex feelings over her need to hide it, is particularly apparent through the metaphor of the moon cakes that Hazel's mother sends her in the first book:

> The brown paper parcel was full of lotus-paste moon cakes from our kitchen. They are my favourite food, sweet and heavy on my tongue, like nothing here in England; but all the same I wish my mother would not send them. Lavinia saw one once, and for weeks after told everyone that I ate heathen pies. (Stevens 2014: 120–121)

During a key scene in *Murder Most Unladylike*, when the girls are planning a midnight feast, Hazel puts aside the mooncakes in favour of bringing a walnut cake from Fortnum and Mason's—a more socially acceptable, English choice that is far less likely to raise comment from her classmates.

As the series continues, and Hazel grows in confidence, the balance between her dual 'selves' shifts. This is particularly evident during the heroines' trip to Hong Kong. However, even in her earliest adventures, Hazel learns to use her Otherness to her advantage, by exploiting the assumptions others make about her. This is true for mundane activities, such as her Art lessons. In *Murder Most Unladylike*, Hazel notes:

> I always enjoy Art. This is less to do with the Art itself, and more to do with the fact that to The One [her art teacher], Hong Kong is part of a magical, made-up place called The Orient; because I am from there, he thinks I must be a natural artist [...] So I copy Chinese dragons out of books that I find in the library, and The One is delighted. (Stevens 2014: 251)

Hazel takes the notion of 'Orientalism as a Western style for dominating, restructuring, and having authority over the Orient' (Said [1978] 2003: 3), and turns it back on the Orientalist, in this case The One, by using his biases to win herself high marks in Art and coast through the lessons, giving herself more time and energy for activities that interest her, such as her detective work. Hazel is used to regulating and moderating her behaviour and the way she is perceived in order to fit in, rather than acting impulsively as Daisy does. This allows her to adopt roles that appear non-threatening and make her easy to overlook, thus making it possible for her to manoeuvre herself into positions where she can covertly gather information. This mobility is an important aspect of Hazel's sidekick role, as she is less likely to be observed than Daisy. In addition to this, the actively thoughtful way in which Hazel engages with and processes English society places her in the position to process situations set up by the more impulsive and proactive Daisy.

As well as being a key part of her character, and the internal conflicts that she overcomes during the course of the series, Hazel's Otherness is central to her role as sidekick. Being an outsider gives her a more detached position than the other characters (with the exception, to some extent, of Daisy). Hazel has been placed in a position where she must keenly observe the behaviour of those around her in order to fit in, and so she notices out-of-character behaviour more easily than someone who has been immersed in English society since birth and who therefore has no need to be as hyper-observant. Hazel's position thus allows her to consider her adopted community and the crimes that occur within it from a more distanced perspective, and so places her in an ideal position to solve these crimes. In order to camouflage herself, Hazel has had to observe and emulate many of the social traditions and customs of English society, despite many of them making little sense to her.[3] This has the added bonus of making it particularly clear to her when things are out of the ordinary, such as when she visits Daisy's home of Fallingford:

> I know all about parents not speaking – at home there are weeks when my mother and father talk to each other through me, as though I'm a living telephone – but this [the coolness between Daisy's parents] seems to be something else entirely. (Stevens 2015a: 11)

While Daisy is also operating from a position of relative detachment, she has personal connections to English society, and the associated biases, that Hazel does not. This is true not only when the crime involves her own family, as in *Arsenic for Tea* (2015a), but in her school environment and in wider society. This is not only because, as Hazel notes, 'The English have a habit of being related to nearly anyone you can mention', but also because Daisy, despite her differences to those around her, is viewed by her peers as an insider within English society, unlike the consistently Othered Hazel (Stevens 2014: 45). As a cultural insider, Daisy has the freedom to act more directly and provoke reactions from potential suspects without being considered anything more than a little eccentric, as we see in *Murder Most Unladylike* when she crawls across a classroom floor to gather evidence. Hazel, however, is already hypervisible, and would face greater social consequences were she to overtly deviate from English cultural norms; for example, she is unable to talk publicly about her father's second wife Jie Jie at school, despite the fact that she feels closer to Jie Jie than she does to her own mother. Because of her visible Otherness, Hazel must develop a quieter, more covert detective role, which corresponds more closely to the position of the sidekick.

Hazel's detached position allows her to consider the guilt or innocence of various murder suspects more objectively. For example, in *Murder Most Unladylike*, she objects to Daisy's immediate ruling-out of Miss Hopkins, and in *Mistletoe and Murder* (2016), her Otherness also makes her an advocate for objectivity in the case of the law itself:

> I imagined what would happen to Alfred [another citizen of Hong Kong studying in England] if we accused him of murdering two Englishmen. Would he be given the opportunity to explain himself? Or would PC Cross and the rest of the police, and a jury and judge, simply look at the colour of his skin and make up their minds on the spot? (Stevens 2016: 286)

While Daisy focuses on solving the immediate puzzle of the murder, Hazel concentrates on the long-term implications of the detection process, in keeping with her position as narrator. As sidekick, she is the foil to Daisy, concerned with the consequences of their actions rather than the direct results. Hazel's racial Otherness is not the only aspect of her identity that influences her role as detective and sidekick, however. Her gender, and the relationship between her gender and her race, are also important considerations when analysing Hazel's role in the series.

Hazel's Parallel Identities

Intersectionality, a term coined by black feminist academic and writer Kimberlé Crenshaw, describes the way that the multiple privileged or marginalised identities belonging to one person interact and the impact of this interaction on the person's experiences in society. Crenshaw refers specifically to the experiences of black women, who simultaneously experience sexism and racism.[4] We might expect Hazel's status as a young woman of colour to intersectionally influence the way she is treated; however, this is not necessarily the case. Hazel is often categorised alongside the men of colour whom she occasionally meets. This is particularly clear in *Mistletoe and Murder*, when the racist Chummy comments 'What's this? […] Another Chinese? Isn't it a bit much? Why, we English will begin to feel outnumbered soon!' when he sees Hazel and Alfred standing together (Stevens 2016: 60). However, the axes of racism and sexism in the Western social settings explored in the *Wells and Wong* series seem to run parallel, rather than intersect. The stories explore the ways that racism inhibits the male privilege that the young men of colour may have otherwise experienced; as bell hooks notes, 'race and class status determine the degree to which one can assert male domination and privilege' (hooks 1990: 59), and *Mistletoe and Murder* focuses closely on the ways that George and Alfred are unable to command the situations around them in similar ways to their white male counterparts. However, while the stories focus on both the racism and the sexism which Hazel experiences, they do not generally look at the ways that these two aspects of discrimination intersect for her. Hazel is often overlooked for being a girl as well as for being from Hong Kong, but rarely discriminated against specifically for being a girl from Hong Kong. Similarly, while Amina is racially Othered at many points throughout *Top Marks for Murder*, this does not overtly intersect with her gender; on this axis, she is placed in the same category as other popular girls at Deepdean. Indeed, before meeting her, Hazel reflects that Amina 'had captured every imagination, in much the same way as the Honourable Daisy Wells had done when I first arrived at Deepdean' (Stevens 2019: 12).

The sexism that Hazel faces is something she can frequently use to her advantage when detecting. Unlike the men of colour around her (her father in *First Class Murder*, and Alfred, George and Harold in *Mistletoe and Murder*), Hazel is not considered to be suspicious by the officials attempting to solve the crime in question. It is assumed that, as a girl, she would be incapable of planning or committing a murder, despite the fact that many of the murderers in the series have been women. Meanwhile, men of colour are immediately coded as a threat, as Alfred is in *Mistletoe and Murder*. This is useful for Hazel's detective work, but perhaps unrealistic, as 'neither race nor [...] gender operate alone ... They do so within a system of simultaneous interrelated social relationships' (Andersen and Collins 2007: 62). It is surprising that, within the context of the series, Hazel is viewed as suspicious only when she has a personal connection to the victim, and when she inhabits a social setting—Hong Kong—where she is a (relatively) dominant figure, rather than an Other. If she is compared to 'a snake or a bear' by the racist society she inhabits, it seems likely that she would be viewed as the potential perpetrator of the crimes that she investigates.

The lack of scrutiny placed on Hazel outside of Hong Kong gives her freedom to investigate crimes that George, a young Anglo-Indian man, does not have. This is made particularly clear by the differing methods that Hazel and George use in order to carry out their detective work. Hazel is able to sneak around Deepdean after dark, pose as ill in the sanatorium and then gather evidence, or hover on the edges of the crowded carriages in the Orient Express in order to observe the other characters. Meanwhile, George must make himself overly obvious in order to gather information:

> It's strange how good George is at tailing people [...] He knows that, because of the colour of his skin and his Indian surname, no-one could ever not notice him, and so he uses that. He leans against a wall adjusting his cuffs or staring into a mirror at a fleck of dust in his shoulder, in the middle of the room but apparently completely uninterested in what anyone else is saying. (Stevens 2017: 114)

If Hazel experienced intersectional oppression during the series as a result of her race and gender, then we might expect her to perhaps be suspected of the crimes that she investigates during her time in England and on the Orient Express. Instead, the only time Hazel is a potential suspect is, again, when she is at home in Hong Kong. Hazel seems to experience racism and sexism as discrete categories, rather than as part of an intersectional oppressive structure. While Hazel is often overlooked in favour of Daisy, it is strongly implied that this is less because of Daisy's white privilege than it is because of Daisy's beauty, and her forthright personality. It could be argued that Daisy's beauty is linked to her white privilege, as Western beauty standards centre whiteness; Imelda Whelehan notes that women of colour are 'rarely [...] associated with ideal-type femininity' in white-centric social contexts' (Whelehan 2000: 156). However, within the context of the *Wells and Wong* series, I believe that the physical contrast between Daisy and Hazel is constructed in such a way that the difference between the ethnic backgrounds of the two girls is not a factor in this aspect of their relationship. When Hazel compares her own appearance with Daisy's, she focuses on factors such as the differences between their heights and weights, aspects of physical appearance that are not racialised; if Hazel were white and English, she would still make the same comparisons. Hazel's occupation of the sidekick role is partly a result of her lack of conformity to beauty standards—she is not a dashing, glamorous figure like Daisy—but the same structure would be enacted if Daisy had chosen to investigate mysteries with one of the other white girls at her school, such as Lavinia or Beanie. Similarly, when she first appears in *Top Marks for Murder*, Amina's appearance is described in glowing terms, with Kitty commenting "she's terribly glamorous. I wish my hair looked like hers!" (Stevens 2019: 9). Amina's physical appearance puts her in the same social category as Daisy, while Hazel's places her in the same category as Beanie and Lavinia, suggesting that Stevens has created a deracialised beauty standard at least within her school setting.

It is not until Hazel is reunited with her family in *A Spoonful of Murder* that the series delves into specifically East Asian beauty standards. Here, her thoughts on beauty are similar to those explored by Suwen Tan in her personal essay about being a plus-size East Asian woman: 'We're meant to be skinny. We're meant to have bony wrists and fit XS. We're the reason that if you order clothing from China on Ebay you should order XXL' (Tan 2018). Hazel compares herself (and is compared by Daisy) unfavourably with her mother, who is described from her first appearance in terms that fulfil the beauty standards which would be applied to a rich Chinese woman in 1930s Hong Kong:

> My mother stepped forwards, taking the little dancing steps that she has to with her bound feet, and bowed to Daisy. Her hair was cut in a new style, a fashionable, wavy bob, her face was carefully painted and her curved lips were red. In her white *cheongsam* she looked very lovely – and very forbidding. (Stevens 2018a: 33)
> [...]
> Ooooh, *Hazel!* It's so chic! Just like your mother. Now I see why you're so odd about clothes and so on. You don't think you could ever match up to her. (Stevens 2018a: 193–194)

Meanwhile, in England, Hazel's feelings of inferiority next to Daisy with regards to her appearance put her in the same category as her white classmates, rather than in a separate, racialised category. At Deepdean, Hazel's weight is described in similar terms to Beanie's smallness, or Lavinia's larger and more muscular build; all three girls exist outside of the beauty standard that Daisy embodies, without race being a major factor in their difference. Interestingly, the other girls in Daisy and Hazel's house also play a role as temporary members of the Detective Society and assisting in solving various mysteries; however, when Lavinia, Beanie and Kitty, who is described as the most conventionally attractive of the three, work together, Kitty often takes the lead. The ease with which the girls fall into these clearly delineated roles suggests that conforming to social beauty standards is a trait associated with a leader (something that also becomes apparent when it is revealed that Hazel's mother has taken a lead role in the plot to kidnap Teddy), whereas sidekicks can fall outside this standard, potentially drawing less attention and keeping the unobtrusive mobility described earlier.

Similarly, Daisy's dominance over Hazel in terms of her personality is not racialised throughout the story. The only time when Hazel's race plays a role in their interactions is during a flashback in *Murder Most Unladylike*, when Hazel is newly arrived at the school and Daisy repeatedly refers to her as 'foreign girl'. This is no longer a factor in their relationship, as Daisy has overcome her racism and now values Hazel as her closest friend, although she is still a domineering figure. We can assume that Hazel and Daisy's relationship dynamic would be the same even if Hazel were white and English, as Daisy is established as holding sway over many other girls in school:

> At lunch time Daisy held a royal audience with her shrimps. As well as Betsy North, she has a trio of identical second formers who are loyal to her [...] They have a sort of collective pash on Daisy, and think everything she does is marvellous [...] When she told them she wanted their help, they nearly went into a collective faint. (Stevens 2014: 190–191)

Both of the girls are dismissed by society at large because of their gender; they are even categorised according to gender by people who are aware of their abilities, as we see in Inspector Priestley's description of their work as their 'Young Miss Marple routine' (Stevens 2014: 281). On the axis of gender, Daisy is Othered in a similar way to Hazel. However, it is also clear from a close analysis of her character that sexist Othering is not the only kind of Othering that Daisy experiences.

Daisy as Other

Daisy, as Holmes to Hazel's Watson, occupies a complex position in the series. As Hazel herself notes, Daisy is a far more typically heroic character; she 'always has to go rushing head over heels into things like a dog after a rabbit' and 'is whippet-thin and tall, with glorious golden hair', while Hazel is 'short and round' and far more reticent and thoughtful (Stevens 2015a: 4). Daisy assigns herself the role of President, and makes the major decisions regarding the investigations, ordering Hazel around. She initially assigns Hazel the role of Secretary of the society, a much more auxiliary position than her own. As 'The Honourable Daisy Wells', she occupies a central and privileged position within society from birth, and has built on this by making herself into the kind of 'jolly-good-show' upper-class English girl that society expects her to be (Stevens 2014: 4).

Her show of conformity is underlined by her repeated refrain to the adults around her that 'I shall marry a Lord'. She is, on the surface, the 'privileging norm' that casts Hazel as 'peripheral', both in terms of their personal dynamic and the with regards to the impact of their privileged and marginalised racial identities (Ashton et al. 1989: 3). However, while Daisy's façade mirrors society's expectations, her real personality makes her far more Other than she might initially appear.

While I am mindful of the fact that it is often problematic to apply specific identities to fictional characters when these identities are not explicitly stated, I argue that Daisy Wells is deliberately coded from the beginning of the series as having two other marginalisations, parallel to her gender-based marginalisation. It is often implied that Daisy is neuroatypical. She processes information and social cues differently to Hazel and the other girls at school. This is apparent in factors such as her sense of humour. When buying a Christmas card for the boys in *Mistletoe and Murder*, Hazel reports Daisy's reaction to a card featuring two cats pulling a Christmas cracker: 'Daisy had laughed until she cried when she saw it. "Funny!" she had finally gasped. "Because cats don't have opposable thumbs, you see!" (Stevens 2016: 160). It also comes across in her interactions with the people around whom she feels comfortable enough to let down her guard. In *Mistletoe and Murder*, Daisy is inadvertently insensitive about Alexander's romantic interest in her, and Hazel's unrequited love for him:

> 'You're quite mad about him. You gape at him like a fish. It's exactly the way *he* looks at *me*.' Then she blinked. 'Oh,' she said. 'I'm sorry. I shouldn't have said that, should I?' [...] I shook my head, ears ringing. (Stevens 2016: 251)

Regarding her frequent misunderstanding of social cues, Daisy herself laments 'Sometimes I do think that I shall never understand people' (Stevens 2016: 331). Daisy is able to observe and analyse social situations accurately, but treats them as part of a puzzle or problem, rather than engaging with them on the neurotypical social level that Hazel does. Daisy's potential neuroatypical status makes her Other to the people around her, creating a further link between her and Sherlock Holmes, who has also been read as neuroatypical.[5]

Daisy's social Otherness is not only a clue that she may possibly be neuroatypical; it also links to the fact that she is queer-coded throughout the series. In *Murder Most Unladylike*, she has a 'pash' on Miss Hopkins, her games mistress, and when Alexander joins the cast, Daisy is baffled by Hazel's attraction to him. Although Daisy often talks about 'marrying a Lord', it is clear from context that this is a private joke that she is making about society's expectations for a girl in her social position, not a genuine aspiration. When speaking candidly about relationships, Daisy tells Hazel 'I'm not marrying anyone. I keep trying to explain to you – men do not interest me. I'm not like you' (Stevens 2016: 250). George, who has Daisy-like powers of observation, concurs, telling Hazel 'I don't think she's the sort of person who falls in love' (Stevens 2016: 219). In *Death in the Spotlight* (2018b), Daisy is explicitly shown to be a lesbian, falling in love with young actress Martita, in a truly Holmesian manner: 'Love is idiotic, and I despise it, but Martita is simply so *pretty*' (Stevens 2018b: 176). In an interview with Penguin Books, Stevens states 'I have known since […] *Arsenic for Tea* that if Daisy was ever to fall in love, she'd fall for a girl, not a boy […] It matters desperately to me that Daisy, like many of my favourite people and some of my most loyal readers, is queer' (Stevens and Morris 2018). In the final book in the series, *Death Sets Sail*, when the girls travel to Egypt with Amina, Hazel realises 'Daisy was not in Egypt for adventure at all, no matter what she had said to me. She was here for Amina' (Stevens 2020: 48), a relationship that is realised towards the end of the novel:

> I saw Amina shake back her long dark hair, lean upwards and touch her lips to Daisy's. The look on Daisy's face – bewilderment and utter delight – made me turn away at last, cheeks burning. This was something I ought not to have intruded on. (Stevens 2020: 261)

In the same way as Hazel's markers of social status and power are, as explored earlier, invisible and therefore do not mitigate the Othering treatment that she receives from English society, Daisy's Otherness is invisible—in the case of her sexuality, by necessity, as while she would not be at risk of legal repercussions (as discussed between Hazel and Martita in *Death in the Spotlight*), she would still face severe social consequences for being an out lesbian in the late 1930s. The other lesbian couples we encounter during the series, such as Miss Parker and Miss Bell, or Frances Crompton and Theresa Johnson, must pose as housemates in order to avoid ostracism. Having to remain in the closet is the clearest example of how Othering impacts Daisy's life; however, it also means that she is covertly rather than overtly Othered, unlike Hazel, whose Otherness is permanently visible. The Othering explicitly inflicted on Hazel shifts her into the role of sidekick, whereas Daisy will not be overtly Othered by society unless she chooses to come out (she does, of course, experience the effects of prejudice and Othering by being forced to stay in the closet). Daisy is not automatically perceived as Other by a prejudiced society in the way that Hazel is; as a result, society still supports and upholds her role as leader.

Daisy's Otherness impacts Hazel's role as sidekick. Their social interactions with the other girls at Deepdean, and with people in other social settings, often involve Hazel dealing closely with the people they encounter, while Daisy makes the plans and analyses the facts. Daisy's logic makes her an excellent detective but can cause her to miss or misinterpret some of the more random, emotionally driven behaviour around her. This is particularly apparent when she and Hazel discover the affair between Daisy's mother and Mr. Curtis in *Arsenic for Tea*; Daisy's surprise and shock show both the reader and Hazel that she had missed the rather obvious clues of their attraction towards each other. Daisy's method of coping with the discovery is in keeping with her usual way of viewing society; '[s]he had taken all the real things that had happened yesterday, and in her head she had turned them into the wooden parts of a puzzle' (Stevens 2015a: 62). Daisy's neuroatypical Otherness allows her to consider the actions of those around her more logically, even when they are personally close to her. This can give her the advantage of a greater sense of objectivity when solving crimes, and it also acts as a foil for Hazel's ability to understand people on a more instinctive, less analytical level. Daisy analyses suspects' behaviour and applies cool logic, while Hazel is ready to step in and point out any potentially messy and illogical alternative possibilities, making them a perfect detective team.

Otherness in Hong Kong

A Spoonful of Murder differs from the rest of the series in a fundamental way—it is set outside of Europe, in Hazel's home, Hong Kong. Here, we see Hazel for the first time without her role of racial Other, something which has an enormous impact not only on her sidekick role in the story, but on her demeanour and personal feelings. As Bradford notes, 'tropes of travel and movement across space are endemic in children's literature generally, [but] in postcolonial texts they take on particular inflection, rehearsing colonial journeys involving the dislocation of colonised people from their ancestral homes' (Bradford 2007: 14). While the *Wells and Wong* series is set in a colonial era, it can potentially be viewed as a post-colonial text, as one of Stevens' motivations in writing was to challenge Orientalist portrayals of Chinese characters in detective literature. When writing about Ronald Knox's rules of detective literature[6] in *Cream Buns and Crime* (2017), Stevens comments on Rule 5, 'No Chinese person must figure in the story', stating 'This is the rule that cause me sleepless nights as a child, and still upsets me today. I went to school with plenty of Chinese girls, and I could not understand why they weren't allowed to be in books [...] I wrote a detective novel with a Chinese heroine just to upset Ronald Knox' (Stevens 2017: 73). While, as Stevens emphasises in her afterword to *A Spoonful of Murder*, 'a British-American upbringing is not a Hong Kong Chinese one', and she has no personal experience that corresponds to Hazel's, she also mentions the extensive research that she undertook in order to write Hazel, and the sensitivity reading that has been carried out for her novels by people who do share Hazel's background. Because of these considerations, I argue that the *Wells and Wong* series can be viewed as a postcolonial text, as it is written specifically to challenge and counter colonialist stereotypes and to centre Othered figures.

Hazel's journey in *A Spoonful of Murder* does the inverse of Bradford's analysis; while still corresponding with her emphasis on the colonial journey, the girls reverse it when Hazel returns to her ancestral home, counteracting the sense of dislocation that she has experienced during her time in England. Upon arriving in Hong Kong, Hazel reflects 'No one looks at me oddly. I'm not strange, and that is a wonderful feeling, like opening up your hand and realising that you have been clenching the muscles of it for far too long' (Stevens 2018a: 50). Not only is Hazel a cultural insider; she occupies a position of privilege in Hong Kong that is comparable to, and which perhaps even surpasses, Daisy's back in England. Hazel comments to herself that 'In England I was always in Daisy's shadow. But here *I* was the famous one. Sai Yat had heard of me. Not simply us, the Detective Society, but *me*' (Stevens 2018a: 228). Hazel's 'opening up' is a key part of this instalment in the series; she comes into her own during the investigation in Hong Kong, which is, in large part, a result of her insider knowledge. Even Daisy acknowledges that, in this environment, Hazel must 'take the lead' (Stevens

2018a: 117), although she refuses to consider giving up her Presidential authority.

In Hong Kong, then, it is Daisy who occupies the position of racial Other. However, she does not experience it in the same way that Hazel does in England and Europe. Rather than '[adapting] to wherever she is, like a brightly-coloured lizard' (Stevens 2018a: 8), as Hazel expects, Daisy finds Hong Kong somewhat difficult to navigate. She is thrown off-balance by the local customs, such as the mourning ceremony where she and Hazel must crawl up the front steps of Hazel's house to honour her dead grandfather, and by the food:

> Daisy had tried *congee* for the first time and was not enjoying it. She stared at her bowl, muttering 'This is absolutely not like rice pudding at *all*,' with a betrayed expression on her face. (Stevens 2018a: 68)

However, while Daisy's whiteness does elicit some attention from the people around her ('People on the street turned to look at Daisy, at the flash of her gold hair, and she looked back at them haughtily – but, I saw, with a little twitch of nerves' [Stevens 2018a: 161]), she does not experience the racial discrimination or stereotyping that Hazel does in England. Hazel is frequently referred to as 'an Oriental', and has to deal with stereotypical assumptions, such as the idea that '[her] father ran the opium trade' (Stevens 2014: 44). In Hong Kong, by contrast, Daisy is merely overlooked: 'In England we are Miss Wells and Miss Wong, but here we were both realising that I was the daughter of Vincent Wong, and Daisy was simply my friend' (Stevens 2018a: 81). Her white privilege means that she still fits in with the formal social occasions in Hong Kong, where 'everyone Chinese is pretending to be Western', and she quickly establishes a friendly rapport with Mrs. Svenssen. As noted by Bridget Byrne, 'whiteness is more than a conscious identity, it is also a position within racialised discourses as well as a set of practices and imaginaries [...] As such, it plays a part in constructing the identities that white people *do* expect' (Byrne 2006: 3, original emphasis). This is particularly true of the Empire-centric 1930s; Daisy expects to occupy a central position in whatever social setting she inhabits, an expectation which is, to some degree, self-fulfilling, and is distressed and thrown off-balance on the few occasions when she does not.

However, while Hazel is not a racial Other in Hong Kong, her gendered Otherness remains, and is indeed heightened. The conflict of the earlier parts of the narrative revolve around the presence of Teddy, Hazel's new baby brother, who, she feels, has usurped her position as her father's favourite child:

> 'Having a boy matters. Boys are … boys are more important than girls. I mean, of course they're not *really*, but that's what people think.'
> 'That's just the same as in England!' Daisy said dismissively.
> […]
> I sighed. Daisy was quite sure that she understood, but I knew that she didn't. A boy was everything in Hong Kong. A brother would *change* things. (Stevens 2018a: 42)

Teddy's presence means that Hazel is pushed away from her father, quite literally—her new brother takes her old room, next to the ones belonging to her parents, and Hazel is moved to a different part of the house. However, Hazel's privileged position in upper-class Hong Kong means that, unlike in England, she is not able to use her gender marginalisation to fly under the radar and gather information to help her investigation. Instead, they are 'closely watched', to guard against potential kidnaps that are a risk for all rich children in Hong Kong:

> I had grown up hearing horrid stories about children who were kidnapped. It's quite common in Hong Kong, among families who are as rich as mine. That is why we always have maids and chauffeurs with us, why we are kept in the house so much. If we go out alone, we might be taken. (Stevens 2018a: 94)

Shifting into a leadership role is accompanied by losing the mobility that Hazel had as an overlooked, sidekick character in England and Europe. Partly as a result of this, and partly because of the social structure of Hong Kong, Daisy and Hazel have to resort to a far greater level of subterfuge in order to investigate during their stay. Back at Deepdean, they could get around the school at night by feigning illness or climbing out of a window; in Hazel's compound, they must befriend a garden servant and be smuggled out of the gates under a pile of garden waste, in order to avoid being detected by the guard dogs. However, Hazel's social and financial privilege means that she is able to deal with important figures in Hong Kong, including the Triad leader, Sai Yat, who speaks 'directly to her' when assuring her that the Triad did not kidnap Teddy (Stevens 2018a: 208).

In Hong Kong, Hazel lacks some of the inadvertent benefits of the marginalisation that she experiences in England; she is focused upon far more intently, and so finds it more difficult to carry out the covert work that is an important part of her detection process. However, Hong Kong is also where it becomes clear that Hazel is moving from sidekick to joint leader with Daisy—even Daisy acknowledges that she is 'quite a different Hazel ... *far* more difficult to order about' (Stevens 2018a: 340). *A Spoonful of Murder* makes it clear that Hazel's Otherness is circumstantial, and something that she has learned to work with, rather than it being an integral part of her character. The same is true of her role as sidekick. In *A Spoonful of Murder*, Hazel comes into her own, drawing on both her English and Chinese selves to create her own self-actualised character, something cemented by the fact that she enrols her new Hong Kong comrades into the Detective Society by having them repeat her and Daisy's official oath—in Chinese. By the end of the novel, Hazel has shed much of her sidekick role; although she is not President, it is clear that she will no longer be relegated to Secretary. In *Death in the Spotlight*, Hazel refuses to return to her sidekick role, despite being back in an environment far more suited to Daisy than to her—they are in England, among Daisy's family, and acting in a stage play, something that appeals far more to the confident and dramatic Daisy than the quiet, shy Hazel. While Daisy takes charge through much of the investigation, Hazel is no longer occupying the straightforward sidekick role that she has in previous novels. Instead, she overrules Daisy on several points, particularly when insisting that they must consider Martita a suspect despite Daisy's feelings for her. She takes the lead on several occasions, escaping her guardians to travel across London and investigate a lead in a chase scene, and stands up to Daisy far more easily than she has done in previous novels:

> 'We're solving a murder, not going to a tea party!' I said – and then I saw from Daisy's rather shocked face that what had come out of my mouth was one of the things that, a few months ago, I might have kept inside my head. (Stevens 2018b: 213)

Hazel's confidence continues upon the girls' return to Deepdean in *Top Marks for Murder*, where, following Hazel overruling Daisy's complaints about changes in the dorm, Lavinia comments 'You've changed, Hazel ... Look at you, telling Daisy what to do!' (Stevens 2019: 7). By the end of the series, in *Death Sets Sail*, Hazel realises the extent to which she has changed, gaining a level of confidence and self-belief that, at the beginning of the series, would have seemed out of her reach:

> I got a strange, vertiginous, flashing moment where I saw myself from the outside, a girl who was standing up straight, her shoulders set, determination on her face. That girl looked important, like a person who mattered, like a detective. (Stevens 2020: 264)

While Hazel is not the same kind of hero and leader as Daisy, her recognition that both her Otherness and sidekick status are circumstantial, and can be used by her to achieve her goals and solve the mysteries that she encounters, allow her to create a more powerful position for herself than the one she has been socially assigned—and also, increasingly frequently, to challenge both the Othering that she encounters and her sidekick role. By *Top Marks for Murder*, Hazel feels comfortable asserting her role as joint heroine with Daisy:

> 'I will always stay alive,' said Daisy. 'I am the heroine.'
> 'So am I!' I said.
> 'An interesting thought,' said Daisy. 'What if you were the heroine all along? No, that wouldn't be anywhere near as good a story.' (Stevens 2019: 282)

As well as ironically pushing against the fourth wall, this exchange shows that the 1930s society of the series is wrong for 'gently [looking] down on' Hazel because of her position as a young woman of colour and as a sidekick. Hazel's journey throughout the *Wells and Wong* books shows the reader that the boundaries between roles are fluid and that sidekicks can be heroes too.

Notes

1. Some of the short stories, such as *The Case of the Blue Violet*, are narrated by Daisy instead of Hazel.
2. In *Mistletoe and Murder*, three young men of colour join the cast, including a key secondary character, George.
3. This is apparent in Hazel's observations on the English attitude to money: 'One of the most important things I have learned is that, in England, the more money you have, the less you mention it … Even my father, who loves all things English, finds this odd' (Stevens 2015a: 36).

4. Kimberle Crenshaw, 'Demarginalizing the Intersection of Race and Sex: A Black Feminist Critique of Antidiscrimination Doctrine, Feminist Theory and Antiracist Politics,' *University of Chicago Legal Forum: Vol. 1989: Iss. 1, Article 8*. Available at: http://chicagounbound.uchicago.edu/uclf/vol1989/iss1/8. Crenshaw's original text on intersectionality focused on a group of black women who had experienced both sexism and racism in the workplace, but who were told that they could only claim discrimination on the grounds of sexism *or* racism, not both. Crenshaw argues that black women's gender and race shape the ways in which they experience both sexism and racism.
5. Discussion of Sherlock Holmes as potentially autistic can be found in publications such as *Psychology Today* (Karl Albrecht. 2011. 'Did Sherlock Holmes Have Asperger Syndrome?' *Psychology Today*. https://www.psychologytoday.com/gb/blog/brainsnacks/201110/did-sherlock-holmes-have-asperger-syndrome. Accessed 27 May 2020) and *The Telegraph* (Hayley Dixon. 2013. 'Sherlock Holmes Is Autistic, Leading Charity Claims'. *The Telegraph*. https://www.telegraph.co.uk/culture/10521128/Sherlock-Holmes-is-autistic-leading-charity-claims.html. Accessed 27 May 2020).
6. Ronald Knox's 10 Commandments of Detective Fiction can be accessed at Gotham Writers. https://www.writingclasses.com/toolbox/tips-masters/ronald-knox-10-commandments-of-detective-fiction.

References

Albrecht, Karl. 2011. Did Sherlock Holmes Have Asperger Syndrome? *Psychology Today*. https://www.psychologytoday.com/gb/blog/brainsnacks/201110/did-sherlock-holmes-have-asperger-syndrome. Accessed 27 May 2020.

Andersen, Margaret L., and Patricia Hill Collins. 2007. *Race, Class and Gender: An Anthology*. Belmont: Thomson Higher Education.

Ashton, Bill, Gareth Griffiths, and Helen Tiffin. 1989. *The Empire Writes Back: Theory and Practice in Post-Colonial Literatures*. London: Routledge.

Bradford, Clare. 2007. *Unsettling Narratives: Postcolonial Readings of Children's Literature*. Waterloo, Canada: Wilfrid Laurier University Press.

Byrne, Bridget. 2006. *White Lives: The Interplay of "Race", Class and Gender in Everyday Life*. Abingdon: Routledge.

Crenshaw, Kimberle. 1989. Demarginalizing the Intersection of Race and Sex: A Black Feminist Critique of Antidiscrimination Doctrine, Feminist Theory and Antiracist Politics. *University of Chicago Legal Forum: Vol. 1989: Iss. 1, Article 8*. Available at: http://chicagounbound.uchicago.edu/uclf/vol1989/iss1/8. Accessed 25 May 2020.

Dixon, Hayley. 2013. Sherlock Holmes Is Autistic, Leading Charity Claims. *The Telegraph*. https://www.telegraph.co.uk/culture/10521128/Sherlock-Holmes-is-autistic-leading-charity-claims.html. Accessed 27 May 2020.

hooks, bell. 1990. *Yearning: Race, Gender, and Cultural Politics*. Boston: South End Press.

Knox, Ronald. *Ronald Knox's 10 Commandments of Detective Fiction*. Gotham Writers. https://www.writingclasses.com/toolbox/tips-masters/ronald-knox-10-commandments-of-detective-fiction. Accessed 25 May 2020.

Said, Edward. (1978) 2003. *Orientalism*. London: Penguin Books.

Stevens, Robin. 2014. *Murder Most Unladylike*. London: Puffin Books.

———. 2015a. *Arsenic for Tea*. London: Penguin Books.

———. 2015b. *First Class Murder*. London: Penguin Random House.

———. 2016. *Mistletoe and Murder*. London: Puffin Books.

———. 2017. *Cream Buns and Crime*. London: Puffin Books.

———. 2018a. *A Spoonful of Murder*. London: Penguin Books.

———. 2018b. *Death in the Spotlight*. London: Puffin Books.

———. 2019. *Top Marks for Murder*. London: Puffin Books.

———. 2020. *Death Sets Sail*. London: Puffin Books.

Stevens, Robin, and Charlie Morris. 2018. Robin Stevens: 'It Matters Desperately to Me That Daisy Is Queer'. Penguin. https://www.penguin.co.uk/articles/children/2018/nov/robin-stevens-on-daisy-coming-out-murder-most-unladylike.html. Accessed 24 Nov 2018.

Tan, Suwen. 2018. I Was 12 Years Old the First Time a Relative Said I Was Fat. That Was Just the Beginning. Mamamia. https://www.mamamia.com.au/asian-women-body-image/. Accessed 15 July 2018.

Whelehan, Imelda. 2000. *Overloaded: Popular Culture and the Future of Feminism*. London: The Women's Press Ltd.

CHAPTER 14

Sherlock's Legacy: The Case of the Extraordinary Sidekick

Dominique Gracia

Introduction

Arthur Conan Doyle's Sherlock Holmes seems, in one way or other, to inform almost all detective stories now told. As readers and viewers, we can spot a Holmesian trait in an official or unofficial detective—perhaps especially in the latter—with ease. In this chapter, I want to investigate the relationship between Doyle's Holmes stories and a particular sub-genre of television detective series that is becoming increasingly common, which I dub the 'extraordinary-sidekick' series. I intend to look not only at the resemblance between Holmes and the extraordinary-sidekick figure, but also how these series respond to a particular underexplored legacy of Doyle's Holmes stories: societal mistrust of professional law enforcement. Extraordinary sidekicks, I suggest, are an attempt to resolve some of the problems with professional policing that the Holmes stories highlight. Typically, in stories involving an unofficial detective, the police need have only one attribute: 'they must never be right about whodunnit' (Green and Finch 1997: 26). One 'leitmotif of Holmes criticism' is to identify

D. Gracia (✉)
University of Oxford, Oxford, UK

L. Andrew and S. Saunders (eds.), *The Detective's Companion in Crime Fiction*, Crime Files, https://doi.org/10.1007/978-3-030-74989-7_14

times when 'he shows up officialdom' (the 'official police'[1]), and this is often mimicked in comedic television detective series through absurd or caricatured professionals who are 'an obstacle to truth' (Reitz 2004: 75).[2] However, latent mistrust of *competent* professionals is, I suggest, a legacy of Doyle's work that also still affects the detective stories that we tell today, and the extraordinary-sidekick figure can help us to better understand that legacy.[3]

To help delineate our extraordinary-sidekick sub-genre from the broad range of detective series, I propose the following working definition of the extraordinary sidekick: someone with either an innate or acquired ability or specialist knowledge base, who stands outside the usual law-enforcement structure, who routinely works alongside a single detective or small team of detectives, and who is used by them as a resource to improve the quality of law enforcement. Building on this definition, I here begin to develop a taxonomy of the extraordinary sidekick. I demonstrate how they both mimic and differ from Holmes, but also look behind the characterological influence of Doyle's unofficial detective to examine the purpose and function of these characters and what they tell us about how we think about policing.[4] Victorian detective stories like Doyle's Holmes stories co-occurred with 'the development of the modern police force' (Thomas 1999: 4), and like today's television detective series, they rendered crime, which was 'an increasingly serious moral and social problem', 'an entertaining pastime' (Cawelti 1976: 105). That detective stories entertain does not, however, render benign the law-enforcement profession that they illustrate. Professional policing and its methods remain contentious, as evidenced by Alex Vitale's 2017 polemic, *The End of Policing*, which traces the historical roots of the police force and its contemporary problems. While I focus in this chapter on the inner frames of extraordinary-sidekick series and the relationship of their narrative content to Doyle's stories, my argument thus also relates to our real-world relationship with policing itself.

I argue that extraordinary sidekicks support professional detectives in ways that plug a trust gap, while their very existence perpetuates and requires that gap. My analysis eschews more traditional detective series that feature what Mareike Jenner has called 'genius detectives', such as *Inspector Morse* (1987–2000) or *Endeavour* (2012–), as well as police procedurals like *Silent Witness* (1996–) that focus on 'specialists', such as forensics experts and pathologists, as defined by Sue Turnbull. Such series also address mistrust of professional law enforcement, but in distinct ways.

The extraordinary-sidekick sub-genre reflects circumstances in which the capability of the professionals is simultaneously low and high, like Doyle's Detectives Gregson and Lestrade, who are 'the pick of a bad lot', 'quick and energetic, but conventional' (1901: 37). This is starkly illustrated in the early series of *The Mentalist* (2008–2015), in which former supposed psychic, Patrick Jane, joins the fictional California Bureau of Investigation (CBI) in order to pursue and capture the serial killer, Red John, who has murdered his family. When Jane appears to quit the CBI midway through the first series, Detective Teresa Lisbon, described by her boss as having a 'very promising career', reassures her team of their inherent professional capability: 'We closed cases before he came. We'll close cases now that he's gone' ('Red John's Friends': 1.11). However, when Jane appears to quit again at the beginning of series 2, Lisbon suggests that following Jane's unconventional 'shortcuts' had made the team 'slack and unprofessional' ('Redemption': 2.1). Success and professional competence are an unstable combination.

What Makes for an Extraordinary Sidekick?

As my definition suggests, in contrast to the 'conventional' official professional, the extraordinary sidekick is usually a sort of consultant, engaged in law enforcement almost accidentally. The extraordinary sidekicks that I discuss in this chapter come from a range of professions and backgrounds, but they are *not* private detectives, setting them apart from Holmes himself. As noted above, my definition excludes medical examiners, forensic pathologists and profilers. While such characters feature heavily in the literature regarding crime and detective television series, they are so closely embedded within the police structure that they cannot be said to stand outside the usual law enforcement system.[5] Although in some respects my definition resembles Turnbull's definition of 'specialists'—people with 'a particular gift or knowledge set' and appearing either as 'a consultant' or in a way that is 'central to the investigation in ways that would be unlikely in "real" life' (2014: 125, 127)—and she includes some of the characters that I identify as extraordinary sidekicks as 'specialists', there are critical distinctions between 'specialist' and extraordinary sidekick. The extraordinary sidekick's skills are of a particularly extreme nature and are much less obviously connected to the formal criminal justice structure. In essence, the extraordinary sidekick is one to whom Lucifer Morningstar's ludicrous ditty of 'Crime-solving Devil.

It makes sense. Don't overthink it!' might be readily adapted (the series implausibly features the Devil in the employ of the LAPD) ('Candy Morningstar': *Lucifer* 2.14). Crime-solving pathologists simply *do* make sense, even where television depicts them unrealistically. Thus, they cannot be extraordinary sidekicks.

Before making the case for considering extraordinary characters such as Patrick Jane and Lucifer Morningstar as *sidekicks*—which may initially seem counterintuitive—I want to explore exactly what makes them extraordinary, as it is the Holmesian extraordinariness of these characters that allows the legacy of latent mistrust in professional detectives to often go unnoticed. What makes extraordinary sidekicks obviously extraordinary—an innate or acquired ability, or specialist knowledge base—derives largely from Holmes: 'I have a lot of special knowledge which I apply to the problem, and which facilitates matters wonderfully' (Doyle 1901: 30). Although Detective Gregson describes himself and Holmes as 'both brain-workers', the extraordinary sidekick's 'brain-work' is, like Holmes', always of a different type to the professional's (89). A good example of this comes in *White Collar* (2009–2014), where brilliant forger and con man, Neal Caffrey, partners with the head of the New York White Collar division of the FBI, Agent Peter Burke, to solve a range of fraud and theft cases similar to Caffrey's own crimes. Here, academic achievement, embodied in the FBI trainees who Burke disparages as 'Ivy League co-eds', contrasts with Caffrey's illicit knowledge gained through his extensive criminal career. In the pilot episode, the FBI is caught out when a rigged vault explodes, destroying evidence against a forger. Caffrey's ability to identify the Canadian banknote security strip, which mystifies Burke's agents, in the debris of that explosion prompts Burke to accept Caffrey's proposal of a partnership ('Pilot': 1.1).

Some other extraordinary sidekicks share Caffrey's criminal knowledge and his art of deception, such as government-agent-turned-criminal Raymond Reddington (*The Blacklist*, 2013–) and illusionist Cameron Black (*Deception*, 2018), but extraordinary sidekicks more commonly bring to bear either unusual scientific knowledge or unusual insight into the human condition.[6] Occasionally, a physical trait distinguishes the extraordinary sidekick, rather than a body of knowledge, as with *The Sniffer* (2013–), whose extraordinary sense of smell allows him to detect criminals and criminal activity in a remarkable way, and Brian Finch, who in *Limitless* (2015–2016) is one of the few people able to take the cognition-enhancing drug NZT without lethal side effects. More commonly, however, it is how the extraordinary sidekick thinks—how they 'apply' their 'special knowledge'—that allows them to supplement the official force with the 'imagination' that Holmes criticises professionals for lacking, which could allow an 'extremely competent officer' to 'rise to great heights in his profession' (Doyle 1894a: 9).[7] For example, Will Graham's 'empathy disorder' ('Amuse Bouche', *Hannibal* 1.2), which is described as the power of 'imagination', allows him to intuit the motives and emotions of serial killers and help the FBI identify them ('Apéritif': 1.1). In many episodes, crimes are shown being rewound in Graham's mind so that he can occupy the position of the killer as the acts are committed. For example, when confronted with a family annihilation scene around a laid dinner table, Graham mentally rewinds the scene and sniffs cooking food before declaring, *a propos* of no evidence: 'Family dinner. I wasn't invited. I take my seat at the empty plate', and then 'I brought my new family to this home invasion'. These insights, and Will's subsequent declaration that the mother's 'body position' shows 'acceptance ... Forgiveness, even', lead the team to look into the family's missing child as the key suspect ('Oeuf': 1.4).

Holmes describes his own work as the 'scientific use of the imagination' (Doyle 1902: 67), and crime-novelist-cum-extraordinary-sidekick Richard Castle offers a meta-textual example of this in *Castle* (2009–2016), using his authorial imagination to solve crimes. This is the premise of the pilot episode, where crimes are based on his own novels and his obvious knowledge of these is useful to the police ('Flowers For Your Grave': 1.1), but subsequent episodes establish that his ability to think through different and unusual scenarios will be the primary resource he can offer the police. In the second episode, he declares that 'the neighbour [being the murderer] would make a better story', giving an imagined description of the circumstances that might have led to him carrying out the murder that is so convincing that it prompts the police to begin investigating everyone living in the victim's building ('Nanny McDead': 1.2).[8] More broadly, several extraordinary sidekicks share Holmes' musical abilities almost as a form of shorthand for an unusual working of the mind. CIA-agent-turned-psychologist, Dr. Dylan Reinhart tells Detective Lizzie Needham in the first episode of *Instinct* (2018–2019) that he has a 'phonographic memory', and he turns out to be an excellent musician ('Pilot': 1.1). Similarly, Lucifer's musical skill is often used as a recognisably human marker of extraordinary ability that helps to make the character less of a caricature, with his self-accompanied renditions often indicating his developing emotional capability, as with his version of 'All Along the Watchtower' ('Everything's Coming Up Lucifer': *Lucifer* 2.1).

That these characters are extraordinary according to the model provided by Holmes is thus fairly easy to establish. However, *prima facie*, few of them hold up against most people's heuristic for the category of sidekick. Ron Buchanan suggests that the sidekick is 'a lesser figure', 'present to assist the central character and to act as a surrogate for the audience', or a 'confidant', 'sounding board', or 'buffer' to the hero(ine) (2003: 15, 18, 24). By this analysis, the professional detectives might be the sidekicks, which would appear to be supported by the fact that these series are routinely named after the extraordinary individual. This question of primacy sometimes surfaces narratively. In *Lucifer*, new Lieutenant Marcus Pierce identifies Detective Chloe Decker as 'Lucifer's partner', offending her, as she thinks Lucifer is *her* partner ('They're Back, Aren't They?': 3.1).[9] Similarly, towards the end of *White Collar*, Caffrey and Agent Burke bicker about which of them is the 'student' in their crime-solving partnership and which the 'master', with this awkward exchange forming a sort of capstone to Burke's regular chaffing of Caffrey about how many times Burke has captured and imprisoned him ('Return to Sender': 6.2).

I want to argue in support of Burke and Decker, and Decker's ex-husband's, who dubs Lucifer her 'sidekick' ('Lucifer, Stay. Good Devil': *Lucifer* 1.2), by recommending the counterintuitive position that the extraordinary individuals are sidekicks within the parameters of the shows themselves, in contrast with Holmes. There are three reasons for this, which relate closely to my definition of extraordinary sidekick. First, these characters are defined by a tenuous, marginal relationship to law enforcement, which is itself the central character. Second, they have an unusually stable interpersonal and narrative relationship with their professional counterpart, distinct from the more erratic Doyleian official/unofficial detective relationship. And third, they are deployed by law-enforcement agencies, often explicitly, as a usable/consumable resource. These characters are thus secondary structurally, if not narratively.

The tenuous nature of their relationship with law enforcement means that those characters who have their own investigative agenda, or their own 'Moriartys' (such as Red John in *The Mentalist*), must work within the law-enforcement structure to which the professionals grant access. They do not, and cannot, pursue detective work alone. For example, while suspended and inserting himself into an apparent Red John case,

Jane asserts ownership: 'This is my case' ('Pilot': *The Mentalist* 1.1). The tension between Jane's claim to all information about Red John and the locus of the official detectives is a key plot point for the entire series, with Jane regularly stepping out of bounds as a consultant to pursue Red John, but always being contained within or supported by the official law-enforcement structure in one way or another. For example, he quits the CBI to prove a murderer's innocence in exchange for his offer of information on Red John, but his official colleagues also take time off to pursue the same case ('Red John's Friends': 1.11), and when Jane plants bugs in Agent Bosco's office because the latter refuses to share information with him ('The Scarlet Letter': 2.2), he is caught and temporarily imprisoned, and he has to rely on Agent Lisbon's leverage over Bosco to evade charges ('Black Gold and Red Blood': 2.6). In contrast, Holmes positions himself as an aide to both 'Government detectives' and 'private ones', who call on him when they are stumped, but he works independently of both forms of institutionalised law enforcement, and is entirely free to do so (Doyle 1901: 29).

Extraordinary sidekicks are thus also fundamentally distinct from extraordinary law-enforcement officials who also ape Holmes, such as the titular character in *River* (2015), or Detective Saga Noren in *The Bridge* (2011–2018). The latter form part of Jenner's group of 'genius detectives', as do some of my extraordinary sidekicks, but we can distinguish genius *professional* detectives and the extraordinary sidekick. Authority and its symbols, such as firearms and handcuffs, form a dividing line. In *Instinct*, this is broached head-on when Dr. Reinhart tells Detective Needham, 'If we're going to work together, I would like to have a gun' ('Wild Game': 1.2). She refuses, and Reinhart has to supply himself with one. Other extraordinary sidekicks are less cavalier. Jane, for example, regularly ducks aside for the professionals to make an arrest with firearms drawn, especially early in the series. He flees an armed killer in the pilot, racing past just-arrived Agent Wayne Rigsby while shouting, 'You're late! Draw your weapon!' ('Pilot': *The Mentalist* 1.1), and in the following episode, a machete-armed gang member races towards Jane in the road and is deflected only by a violent tackle from Lisbon ('Red Hair and Silver Tape': 1.2). Jane's vulnerability in the face of armed criminals distinguishes him from the professionals. Holmes' instruction, 'You will need your handcuffs, Inspector. You can leave the talking to me', might be the watchword of the extraordinary sidekick, while a professional 'genius detective' would need to supply both (Doyle 1905b: 87).

In addition, the extraordinary sidekick's complementary function to professional law enforcement is often manifested through the sidekick's sidekicks. Crime-solving teams assembled from the extraordinary sidekick's own professional background, such as former spy Julian Cousins (*Instinct*), Charlie Eppes' fellow academics Amita Ramanujan and Larry Fleinhardt (*Numb3rs*, 2005–2010), and con man Mozzie (*White Collar*), structurally reinforce the extraordinary sidekick's contingent status in a law-enforcement context because they are shown leading others outside the formal structure but do not—and cannot—lead the team within it. For example, although Mozzie participates in several operations with the FBI team, he is also involved in illicit schemes with Caffrey outside that structure and encourages Caffrey not to abandon their criminal lifestyle.[10] Mozzie treats Agent Burke with suspicion, referring to him dismissively as 'Suit', and Burke's wife (with whom Mozzie develops a friendship) as 'Mrs. Suit'. Caffrey's contingent status working with the FBI, during which he is regularly threatened with return to prison and treated with (not undue) mistrust, is thus reinforced by this external partnership.

With the narrative demand for the extraordinary sidekick to be an accidental detective, somehow ill-suited for professional law enforcement, comes the requirement to explain their continued deployment. Holmes is regularly described as giving the police his 'co-operation' (Doyle 1894a: 2) or being 'associate[d] … in [their] investigation[s]' (Doyle 1905b: 75), an 'amateur companion' of the police (Doyle 1901: 52), but not a fully integrated part of their process. Although Lestrade is the most frequently mentioned professional in the Holmes stories, a range of other professionals engage with Holmes in identical ways, including Inspectors Gregson, Hopkins and Barnes, who appear several times, while a significant proportion of cases do not involve any of these professional figures at all. By contrast, the extraordinary sidekick's implausible career in law enforcement is usually justified through the interpersonal relationship between them and the professionals.

While most extraordinary-sidekick series feature a department ensemble, there is always a single professional who serves as their access point into the law-enforcement structure. Some series explain this through pre-existing relationships, including fraternal (*Numb3rs*), student–teacher (*Perception* 2012–2015; *Professor T* 2015–2018), or of childhood friends (*The Sniffer*). However, largely, the law-enforcement official begins as a sceptical professional 'partner' who becomes emotionally—and sometimes romantically—attached to their sidekick. While

Holmes is 'only answerable to [him]self' (Doyle 1905b: 87) and works regularly on his own account or across police forces, the extraordinary sidekick becomes, to a greater or lesser extent, answerable to higher-ups in a particular professional force. The antagonistic relationship between Holmes and the 'official police'—who he often causes to be 'angry' (Doyle 1893d: 249) or speak in an 'injured' tone (Doyle 1901: 108)—is necessarily mellowed by the quality and persistence of the personal relationship between the two primary figures in extraordinary-sidekick series. It is rare for extraordinary sidekicks to work wholly with another professional detective besides their usual partner, or alone. For example, Castle works with detectives other than Kate Beckett only a handful of times (such as in 'Headhunters': *Castle* 4.21 and 'Need to Know': 6.3), and for a short period in series 7 becomes a licensed private investigator. Yet the usual equilibrium always reasserts itself in a way that is alien to the Holmes stories. The Castle-Beckett partnership always swiftly re-establishes itself (as in 'Undead Again': 4.22 and 'Number One Fan': 6.4), and the brief ban on Castle working with the police while a licensed PI is lifted so that he can be reinstated as Beckett's consultant ('Reckoning': 7.15).

Thus, while Holmes takes offence at being mistaken for a professional officer—'Fancy his having the insolence to confound me with the official detective force!' (Doyle 1893c: 194)—the extraordinary sidekick's outsider status is more tempered. The recent adaptation *Sherlock* (2010–2017) provides a noticeable contrast with extraordinary-sidekick series. In the pilot, Detective Inspector Lestrade begs Holmes to help with a difficult case: 'Will you come?', he repeats twice. Holmes emphasises his independence by refusing to go with Lestrade to the crime scene in a police car and complaining that others on the force 'won't work with [him]' ('A Study in Pink': 1.1). Extraordinary sidekicks are far more embedded within professional workplace structures. They would usually have a desk or designated space within the professionals' office environment, albeit sometimes a space that sets them apart as somehow other, as in *Limitless*, when Finch works in a storage area. They work on cases when instructed to, barring moments of disobedience that are narratively driven, often travel with their professional 'partner' to crime scenes and interviews, and receive the cooperation of others on the professional team, often building friendships with them, such as the friendship that arises between Lucifer and forensics specialist Ella Lopez.

The extraordinary sidekick thus could be interpreted as an unusual merging of the characteristics of Holmes and Watson into a single figure, set in a stable relation with a single professional detective. The term 'sidekick' helps us to keep in mind the subtle distinctions between these extraordinary characters and Holmes, including the contingent nature of their detective work and the close personal link between them and the professionals who allow them to undertake that work. The final criterion that 'sidekick' helps us to keep in mind is that the extraordinary sidekick is a finite resource at the disposal of the professional, who brings the unconventional into the 'conventional' with a view to concluding the case. It is here that there is perhaps the greatest contrast with Holmes.

Lestrade describes Holmes as having 'been of use to the force once or twice in the past' so that 'we owe you a good turn at Scotland Yard' (Doyle 1905a: 37), but Holmes sums up the truth of his relationship with the professionals when he remarks drily: 'I am not retained by the police to supply their deficiencies' (Doyle 1893c: 179). Holmes is his own resource, then, as when he describes how he has 'been using [him]self up rather too freely' in pursuit of Moriarty (Doyle 1894d: 257). By contrast, the extraordinary sidekick is often in danger of being used up by their professional counterpart *precisely* to 'supply their deficiencies', a fate that they seem unable to avoid. Graham in *Hannibal* is an exemplar of this use of the extraordinary sidekick as a consumable resource. His friend, psychiatrist Dr. Alana Bloom, criticises Special Agent Jack Crawford for involving Graham in law-enforcement work, saying that '[she] wouldn't put him out there' and warning Crawford: 'you really don't want me commenting on this in any official capacity' because 'it wouldn't reflect well on you' ('Apéritif': 1.1). Bloom sees Crawford as misusing Graham in a damaging way, while she 'just want[s] everybody to leave [Graham] alone' ('Sorbet': 1.7). Bloom is vindicated when Graham comes to doubt his own sanity and fear that working with the FBI has turned him into a cannibalistic murderer.

Less dramatically, the language of resourcing is often part of the initial justification for bringing the extraordinary sidekick into the law-enforcement structure. Detective Decker describes Lucifer as a 'valuable resource' when arguing for him to be allowed to continue working for the LAPD ('Sweet Kicks': *Lucifer* 1.5). Finch, at least while he is taking the neuro-enhancer NZT, is framed by Agent Rebecca Harris as a 'resource' to be exploited when she encourages her boss to allow her to work with him ('Pilot': *Limitless* 1.1). And in *Deception*, illusionist Black makes a 'pitch' to the FBI emphasising his possible utility to them ('Forced Perspective': 1.2). This language of resourcing also emerges through the possessive nature of the professional–sidekick relationship. For example, when Caffrey gets a new handler, Agent Burke struggles to accept this change, even though it is essential because of his own promotion. He worries that someone other than himself will be fooled by Caffrey, allowing him to escape or return to crime. That Caffrey does both several times while working with Burke only feeds this anxiety, and while in part this reflects the quasi-paternal friendship Burke feels for Caffrey, it is also true that the latter is a 'prized possession', as his fellow crook Keller tells him ('Au Revoir': *White Collar* 6.6).

That the extraordinary sidekick is in some way owned by their professional partner is evident when their usefulness becomes a double-edged sword. Caffrey's success rate leads to his being denied his freedom several times in order to force him to continue to work with the FBI. At the end of series 3, an agent who wishes to force Caffrey to join his own team in Washington D.C. destroys Caffrey's chance of a commutation ('Judgment Day': *White Collar* 3.16), while at the end of series 5, the Director of the FBI refuses to sign Caffrey's release because of his utility to the Bureau ('Diamond Exchange': 5.13). Jane, similarly, is enticed back into law enforcement under false pretences, having been told that all charges against him for killing Red John would be dropped, only for this to be reneged on once he has returned to the US ('My Blue Heaven': *The Mentalist* 6.9). The almost forcible retention of the extraordinary sidekick demonstrates their value as a resource.

All three of these characteristics—contingency, stability of relationship with a partner, and being used as a resource—are encapsulated in the term 'sidekick'. By positioning these characters as sidekicks, they become supplementary to a larger system, which they in turn underpin. And it is only from this vantage point that we can understand how they can plug the trust gap that plagues professional law enforcement.

Put to Good Use: Plugging the Trust Gap

In a historical example with echoes of *Castle*, Kate Thomas notes that 'the Holmes stories were, at one time, required reading in the Metropolitan Police force training', in what can only be described as internalised mistrust of the force's own capabilities (2009: 388). As Green and Finch note, Doyle's Lestrade is 'the plodding Scotland Yard man', 'nominally in charge' but 'sometimes inept and always baffled'. They suggest that when he brings cases to Holmes it is 'in desperation' or, crucially, because he is 'conscious of his own lowly social standing in an era in which the police detective was still looked down on' (1997: 343). Extraordinary sidekicks' existence reflects, and tries to ameliorate, this fact of Holmes' world: the police cannot be trusted to get to the right answer on their own, and they need the assistance of someone extraordinary to bolster their appearance of competence with the public.

While 'detective fiction' is 'invest[ed] in the notion that the common and the trivial can be mastered—or be made to make sense—if only the proper methods are used', the extraordinary sidekick highlights that the 'proper methods' may not be those of institutionalised police forces (Thomas 2009: 378). Perhaps because of incompetence, a lack of 'imagination', being too 'conventional', or because 'the mere sight of an official-looking person seals men's lips' (Doyle 1901: 37, 88), there is always a risk that justice might not be done. This problem is structural, rather than an individual complaint about Lestrade or Gregson, and the extraordinary-sidekick sub-genre reflects this by showing how the problem affects even the most impressive and competent professionals.

Scholars such as Caroline Reitz and Jonathan Nichols-Pethick have looked beyond the detective genre's reputation as 'essentially conservative' to focus on 'the detective narrative's relation to a *liberal* critique of imperialism's "things as they are"'. Reitz is describing the detective fiction literary genre and its relationship with *fin-de-siècle* imperialism, but the twist she offers to this relationship between state power and policing is valuable for us too:

> [D]etective fiction works toward public acceptance of authority and even solidifies imperial position not because of a wholesale endorsement of power but because it reimagines authority as consistent with, rather than an alternative to, milder liberal principles. (2004: 67)

Or, as Nichols-Pethick puts it, detective stories are 'an important site of cultural production', 'where our deepest commitments to the meaning of citizenship and to the maintenance of our communities are put to the test' (2012: 22). Detective stories, then, are still a way of imagining a world with better policing, which the extraordinary-sidekick sub-genre does with outré stories that nevertheless reflect a real-world core of mistrust in the methods and capabilities of the police, even when they appear to be competent and fighting for justice.

Sherlock vividly illustrates this mistrust 'at source', as it were, ostentatiously establishing the antagonistic relationships between Holmes, the police and the press through Holmes' remote-control interjections into a police press conference. Three times, journalists receive text messages reading 'Wrong!', immediately contradicting statements by Lestrade. Detective Constable Donovan protests (privately) at Lestrade's inability to 'stop [Sherlock] doing that', to which Lestrade replies: 'If you can tell me how he does it, I'll stop him' ('A Study in Pink': 1.1). Lestrade here expresses both wry acknowledgement of the professionals' inadequacy and an acceptance of the mistrust with which the journalists (and so the public) view the police, which Holmes feeds. The professionals continue to have a 'lowly social standing'.

Kate Thomas argues that Doyle's Holmes and the Baker Street Irregulars 'better the official organ of social control', that is to say, the police, because the latter cannot recognise 'the significatory power of details' and so 'replace them with generic, inherited, and inadequate master narratives' (2009: 378). Indeed, in Holmes stories past and present, the police are largely characterised as generating much heat but little light. In Doyle's stories, a reference to 'energy' usually codes for ineffectual work that might, nevertheless, be praised in the press. Thus, Detective Athelney Jones gives 'an immense display of energy' in erroneously arresting four people (Doyle 1890: 118), while Mr. Forbes 't[akes] up the case with a great deal of energy' but little effect (Doyle 1894c: 226). Such 'energy' might be effective in other circumstances. As Agent Lisbon tells Jane: 'Sometimes, the obvious guy did it. *Most* of the time, the obvious guy did it' ('Pilot': *The Mentalist* 1.1). But extraordinary cases that diverge from such 'generic narratives' require extraordinary sidekicks to help the professionals succeed in mastering the 'significatory power of details' and become a 'better… organ of social control'.

Aside from cases that are too unconventional for the 'obvious guy' to be the culprit, there are several other reasons why law-enforcement professionals might be met with mistrust, which the extraordinary sidekicks also help ameliorate. Holmes, in the Doyle stories, criticises Gregson and Lestrade because 'they have their knives into one another', suggesting a self-interestedness that is antithetical to good police work (1901: 37). In the extraordinary-sidekick sub-genre, working with an extraordinary sidekick is often damaging to a professional's career prospects at the same time that it ensures justice is done. Thus, for example, at one stage Burke advises a junior agent, Jones, not to 'take [Caffrey] on' because '[he]'ll regret it' ('Live Feed': *White Collar* 5.10). The negative consequences for the professional are sometimes so extreme that they find themselves on the wrong side of the law. For example, Burke is arrested for a murder committed by Caffrey's father ('In the Wind': 4.16), and it takes Caffrey's forgery of a confession from his father to free Burke, highlighting the contrast between justice and the outcomes that standard professional methods provide ('At What Price': 5.1). The prospective taint that can come from working with the extraordinary sidekick derives from the fact that they themselves can pose a risk to law and order. In this regard, the sub-genre bolsters trust in the professionals because of how they manage the risky, potentially hostile "other" in their midst.

The common accusation by the professional force that Holmes is 'not very practical' (Doyle 1893d: 250), or has too many 'theories' (Doyle 1890: 105) continues to plague the extraordinary sidekick, who often relies on probabilities rather than proof, as when Jane's shrewd guesses about the murderer of a young teenage girl result in the killing of a man by his wife and are vindicated only by the unexpected discovery of the girl's diary ('Pilot': *The Mentalist* 1.1). However, mistrust of the extraordinary sidekick is qualitatively different to mistrust of the professionals. While the competence of the latter is doubted, mistrust of the extraordinary sidekick is by and large mistrust of their motivations, not their abilities.

What motivates the extraordinary sidekick to participate in detective work varies. Jane's motivation in *The Mentalist* is explicitly 'personal revenge', and he refuses to concede that he finds it 'worthwhile' to work on cases that do not pertain to his personal mission to catch Red John ('Redemption': 2.1). *Hannibal* provides a further interesting example of uncertain motives. Crawford is routinely unable to determine whether Graham is on his side. In part, this instability is driven by Crawford's unwillingness to trust his own extraordinary sidekick and accept that Dr. Hannibal Lecter might be a cannibalistic murderer, but Graham *does* waver between a commitment to law enforcement and his friendship with Lecter. This has tragic consequences at the end of series 2, when he betrays Crawford by calling Lecter to warn him that the police are on their way to arrest him ('Mizumono': 2.13).

As in the case of Graham, whose extraordinary empathic abilities allow Lecter's psychopathy to influence him, the threat posed by the extraordinary sidekick arises from their extraordinary ability, which must be in some way contained by working with the professionals. This is a powerful extension of how Holmes's capacity to 'ma[k]e a highly efficient criminal' (Doyle 1905d: 197) is curtailed by him being 'on the side of the force, and not against it' (Doyle 1894b: 210). Even setting aside those who are known criminals, such as forger and con man Caffrey and criminal mastermind Reddington, extraordinary sidekicks are often arrested. Castle is arrested repeatedly (including in 'Flowers For Your Grave': *Castle* 1.1; 'A Deadly Affair': 3.1; 'Probable Cause': 5.5; and 'Driven': 7.1), while mathematician Charlie Eppes is arrested and has his FBI security clearance revoked for passing information to scientists in Pakistan in the spirit of academic collaboration ('When Worlds Collide': *Numb3rs* 4.18).

What enables the extraordinary sidekick to continue working with the professionals irrespective of these uncertainties is their reciprocal relationship of trust or faith with their primary professional partner. Tom Ue and Benjamin Poore have explored in detail the function of faith in Holmes stories, including *Sherlock*, with Ue concluding that 'Watson's faith in Holmes is [...] developed through having witnessed repeated demonstrations of Holmes's abilities' (2017: 91). However, Poore suggests that 'the belief in Holmes's powers is largely a faith-based practice', with there being a gap between his '(misleadingly) proclaimed methods and the frequently successful results he achieves' (2013: 159, 161). In the extraordinary-sidekick sub-genre, this trust or faith has to be reciprocal in order for the trust gap to be plugged. The willingness of the professional partner to trust, or have faith in, their extraordinary sidekick can vary as the latter's motivations are called into question, but trust in their extraordinary abilities is quickly established through 'repeated demonstrations' and is rarely undermined in any serious way. This is true even when confidence in these abilities is undermined for the purpose of narrative tension, as is routinely the case in *Perception*, in which psychologist Dr. Daniel Pierce's schizophrenia often results in him and those around him questioning his insights. It is only Agent Kate Moretti's trust in Pierce, and his reciprocal trust in her, that allows him to continue to act as an extraordinary sidekick who can plug the trust gap.

Conclusion

In beginning this chapter, I identified a paradox in how law-enforcement professionals of series in the extraordinary-sidekick sub-genre are treated: as both competent and incapable, striving for justice but unable to achieve it 'by the book'. In many of the cases featured in extraordinary-sidekick series, the extraordinary sidekick is uniquely essential, calling into question whether traditional law-enforcement methods could have solved the crime. Detective series have often been linked historically to crises in policing, and in particular crises of confidence in the police, because 'viewers always view in contexts, both social and discursive', which 'set definite limits on the range and possibilities of interpretation' (Storey 2010: 23). For example, Mark Duguid notes that *Cracker* (1993–1995, 1996, 2006), one of the earliest examples of a series featuring a profiler working with the police, aired during a period when the British police's actions were under intense scrutiny (2009: 49). However, I have not offered here a detailed analysis of the early twenty-first century in the hope of identifying a historical or sociological cause for the extraordinary-sidekick sub-genre because it is clear that there can be no one-to-one correspondence between current events and the varied extraordinary sidekicks who appear on our screens. Instead, I have suggested that the basic premise of the extraordinary-sidekick sub-genre—the very existence of the character type—represents a way of thinking through the possibility that 'the problem is policing itself', as the front cover of Vitale's *End of Policing* declares. By examining these series, I have sought to shift the angle from which we view them to tell us more about the persistence of mistrustful attitudes towards professional law enforcement.

Having spent this chapter comparing contemporary figures with the larger-than-life Holmes, I want to end with an informative comparison with another *fin-de-siècle* detective, Martin Hewitt, an early Holmes 'clone'. John Greenfield suggests that Hewitt represented the late-Victorian middle class more accurately than Holmes through a 'quiet professionalism' that mirrored their positions as 'experts' in the new fields of 'science, engineering, teaching, journalism, government service, public health and welfare, sociology, and business administration' (2002: 20–21). Unlike Holmes, Hewitt is cheerful, polite and formerly a professional lawyer, who has turned to private detective work after discovering his peculiar powers of deduction. Reflecting now with a historical perspective, we might include the police in the group of new 'experts' also. But while the professional middle class has continued to grow in the twentieth and twenty-first centuries, it is Holmes who has held our interest, not Hewitt. This illustrates the mistrust in which law-enforcement professionals continue to be held, more than a century and a half after the professionalisation of detective police work.

Reitz identifies in detective fiction 'not a renunciation of authority, but an argument for the necessity of better authority', a 'power' that involves 'a union or, in the words of Doyle, a "cross-indexing" of domestic and foreign knowledge' (2004: 69, 76). While Doyle's story and Reitz have in mind the 'cross-indexing' of domestic and foreign intelligence (Doyle 1919: 122),[11] in the extraordinary-sidekick sub-genre, we see the 'cross-indexing' of professional and extraordinary abilities. The genre plays with the possibilities of uniting these two to ameliorate the deficiencies of both and obtain a 'better authority'. That a 'better authority' is required, even when professional officers are wholly competent, is an untold legacy of Doyle's own time, which the continued influence of his iconic detective has helped perpetuate.

Notes

1. The phrase 'official police' is used repeatedly in the Holmes stories, as when Holmes says he 'will represent the official police until their arrival' (Doyle 1905c: 112) or Detective Peter Jones is described as an 'official police agent' (Doyle 1893a: 48).
2. A recent example of this might include local detectives Sherlock Hobbs and Tina Teventino in the comic paranormal detective series *Dirk Gently's Holistic Detective Agency* (2016–2017), whose professional competence is humorously limited. For example, Teventino is, when we first meet her, high and drunk and sleeping in her car, and she remains thus for the whole working day ('Space Rabbit': 2.1). After keeping some of the series' main characters—who are at that point on the FBI Most Wanted list—imprisoned for a few days, Teventino begins to allow them to roam the police station freely, letting them dress up in old uniforms and other clothes from evidence ('Two Broken Fingers': 2.3).
3. 'Professional' is another qualifier used to distinguish between Holmes and police officers, as when Detective Lestrade is referred to as 'the professional' (Doyle 1919: 162) and Inspector Martin is referred to as Holmes' 'professional colleague' (Doyle 1905b: 78).
4. The extraordinary sidekick is typically male and overwhelmingly white. Examining this lack of diversity is beyond the scope of this chapter, but an interesting analysis could be undertaken regarding the depiction of 'extraordinary' and its roots in the Holmes stories.
5. Examples from these groups include Dr. Quincy (*Quincy M.E.*, 1976–1983), Frank Black (*Millennium*, 1996–1999), Dr. Sam Waters and Dr. Rachel Burke (*Profiler*, 1996–2000), Dr. Sam Ryan and Dr. Nikki Alexander (*Silent Witness*, 1996–), Dr. Spencer Reid (*Criminal Minds*,

2005–2020), Dr. Moira Isles (*Rizzoli and Isles*, 2010–2016), Dr. Henry Morgan (*Forever*, 2014–2015), Agent Holden Ford (*Mindhunter*, 2017–2019), Dr. Daniel Harrow (*Harrow*, 2018–), Dr. Laszlo Kreizler (*The Alienist*, 2018–), and Dr. Max Liebermann (*Vienna Blood*, 2019).

6. Those who bring to bear unusual scientific knowledge include Dr. Charlie Eppes (*Numb3rs*, 2005–2010); Dr. Temperance Brennan (*Bones*, 2005–2017); and Dr. Beaumont Rosewood (*Rosewood*, 2015–2017). Those who bring to bear unusual insight into the human condition include Patrick Jane, Allison DuBois (*Medium*, 2005–2009, 2009–2011); Shawn Spencer (*Psych*, 2006–2014); Richard Castle (*Castle*, 2009–2016); Dr. Daniel Pierce (*Perception*, 2012–2015); Will Graham (*Hannibal*, 2013–2015); Lucifer Morningstar; Professor Jasper Teerlinck (*Professor T*, 2015–2018; and its German remake, *Professor T*, 2017–); Dr. Dylan Reinhart (*Instinct*, 2018–2019); and Dr. Martin Whitly (*Prodigal Son*, 2019–2021).
7. Holmes also criticises Lestrade for his lack of 'imagination' in 'Norwood Builder' (Doyle 1905a: 42).
8. The killer eventually turns out to be a neighbour, although not the one Castle had picked out in his story-telling.
9. This tension also arises in series from related genres, such as in superhero series *Luke Cage* (2016–2018). At one point, bulletproof Cage calls Detective Misty Knight his 'sidekick'. Knight retorts, 'Who says you're not my sidekick?', and Cage replies, with an expression of confusion, 'Me. It's my show' ('On and On': 2.7). Although he means this in the sense of 'running the show', the nod to the series' own mediality illustrates the narrative tension that can arise between professionals and extraordinary individuals.
10. Series 3 ends with them escaping to an island with no extradition treaty.
11. Doyle describes Holmes' activity at the beginning of 'Bruce-Partington Plans' as 'cross-indexing his huge book of references' (1919: 122), and as Reitz explains, the story reflects the need to bring domestic and international policing together in the national interest. The act of 'cross-indexing' is one that Doyle obviously associates with Holmes' approach, appearing also at the start of the much earlier 'Five Orange Pips', when Holmes is found 'cross-indexing his records of crime' (Doyle 1893b: 108).

References

Buchanan, Ron. 2003. "Side by Side": The Role of the Sidekick. *Studies in Popular Culture* 26 (1): 15–26.

Cawelti, John G. 1976. *Adventure, Mystery, and Romance: Formula Stories as Art and Popular Culture*. Chicago: Chicago University Press.

Doyle, Arthur Conan. 1890. *The Sign of Four*. London: Spencer Blackett.

———. 1893a. The Adventure of the Red-Headed League. In *The Adventures of Sherlock Holmes*, 29–56. London: George Newnes.
———. 1893b. The Adventure of the Five Orange Pips. In *The Adventures of Sherlock Holmes*, 107–127. London: George Newnes.
———. 1893c. The Adventure of the Blue Carbuncle. In *The Adventures of Sherlock Holmes*, 156–180. London: George Newnes.
———. 1893d. The Adventure of the Noble Bachelor. In *The Adventures of Sherlock Holmes*, 235–260. London: George Newnes.
———. 1894a. The Adventure of Silver Blaze. In *The Memoirs of Sherlock Holmes*, 1–31. London: George Newnes.
———. 1894b. The Adventure of the Greek Interpreter. In *The Memoirs of Sherlock Holmes*, 191–213. London: George Newnes.
———. 1894c. The Adventure of the Naval Treaty. In *The Memoirs of Sherlock Holmes*, 214–255. London: George Newnes.
———. 1894d. The Final Problem. In *The Memoirs of Sherlock Holmes*, 256–279. London: George Newnes.
———. 1901. *A Study in Scarlet*. London: Ward, Lock & Co.
———. 1902. *The Hound of the Baskervilles: Another Adventure of Sherlock Holmes*. London: George Newnes.
———. 1905a. The Adventure of the Norwood Builder. In *The Return of Sherlock Holmes*, 31–60. New York: P.F. Collier & Son.
———. 1905b. The Adventure of the Dancing Men. In *The Return of Sherlock Holmes*, 61–92. New York: P.F. Collier & Son.
———. 1905c. The Adventure of the Solitary Cyclist. In *The Return of Sherlock Holmes*, 93–118. New York: P.F. Collier & Son.
———. 1905d. The Adventure of Charles August Milverton. In *The Return of Sherlock Holmes*, 187–208. New York: P.F. Collier & Son.
———. 1919. The Adventure of the Bruce-Partington Plans. In *His Last Bow: Some Reminiscences of Sherlock Holmes*, 122–171. London: John Murray.
Duguid, Mark. 2009. *Cracker*. London: British Film Institute.
Green, Joseph, and Jim Finch. 1997. *Sleuths, Sidekicks and Stooges: An Annotated Bibliography of Detectives, Their Assistants and Their Rivals in Crime, Mystery and Adventure Fiction, 1795–1995*. Cambridge: Scolar Press.
Greenfield, John. 2002. Arthur Morrison's Sherlock Clone: Martin Hewitt, Victorian Values, and London Magazine Culture, 1894–1903. *Victorian Periodicals Review* 35 (1): 18–36.
Jenner, Mareike. 2016. *American TV Detective Dramas: Serial Investigations*. Basingstoke and New York: Palgrave Macmillan.
Nichols-Pethick, Jonathan. 2012. *TV Cops: The Contemporary American Television Police Drama*. London and New York: Routledge.

Poore, Benjamin. 2013. Sherlock Holmes and the Leap of Faith: The Forces of Fandom and Convergence in Adaptations of the Holmes and Watson Stories. *Adaptation* 6 (2): 158–171.
Reitz, Caroline. 2004. *Detecting the Nation: Fictions of Detections and the Imperial Venture*. Athens, OH: Ohio State University Press.
Storey, John. 2010. *Cultural Studies and the Study of Popular Culture*. Edinburgh: Edinburgh University Press.
Thomas, Kate. 2009. Arthur Conan Doyle and Isabella Beeton. *Victorian Literature and Culture* 36 (2): 375–390.
Thomas, Ronald R. 1999. *Detective Fiction and the Rise of Forensic Science*. Cambridge: Cambridge University Press.
Turnbull, Sue. 2014. *The TV Crime Drama*. Edinburgh: Edinburgh University Press.
Ue, Tom. 2017. The Truth Will Set You Free: Implicit Faith in Sherlock and London Spy. *Journal of Popular Film and Television* 45 (2): 90–100.
Vitale, Alex S. 2017. *The End of Policing*. London: Verso.

Televised Material

Biller, Kenneth, and Mike Sussman, creators. *Perception*. ABC Studios, 2012–2015.
Bokenkamp, Jon, creator. *The Blacklist*. Sony/Universal/Davis, 2013–.
Caron, Glenn Gordon, creator. *Medium*. Paramount Television/CBS Television Studios, 2005–2009; 2009–2011.
Carr, Caleb, creator. *The Alienist*. Paramount Television/Anonymous Content, 2018–.
Carter, Chris, creator. *Millennium*. Ten Thirteen/20th Century Fox Television, 1996–1999.
Coker, Cheo Hodari, creator. *Luke Cage*. Marvel Television/ABC Studios, 2016–2018.
———. 2.7, On and On. 22 June 2018.
Davis, Jeff, creator. *Criminal Minds*. ABC/Paramount/CBS, 2005–2020.
Dexter, Colin, creator. *Inspector Morse*. Zenith Productions, 1987–2000.
Eastin, Jeff, creator. *White Collar*. Fox Television Studios, 2009–2014.
———. 1.1, Pilot. 23 October 2009.
———. 3.16, Judgment Day. 28 February 2012.
———. 4.16, In the Wind. 5 March 2013.
———. 5.1, At What Price. 17 October 2013.
———. 5.10, Live Feed. 9 January 2014.
———. 5.13, Diamond Exchange. 30 January 2014.
———. 6.2, Return to Sender. 13 November 2014.
———. 6.6, Au Revoir. 18 December 2014.

Falacci, Nicolas, and Cheryl Heuton, creators. *Numb3rs*. CBS/Paramount, 2005–2010.
———. 4.18, When Worlds Collide. 16 May 2008.
Fedak, Chris, creator. *Deception*. Warner Bros. 2018.
———. 1.2, Forced Perspective. 18 March 2018.
Fedak, Chris, and Sam Sklaver, creators. *Prodigal Son*. Warner Bros./Fox, 2019–2021.
Franks, Steve, creator. *Psych*. NBC/Universal, 2006–2014.
Fuller, Bryan, deviser. *Hannibal*. NBC Studios, 2013–2015.
———. 1.1, Apéritif. 4 April 2013.
———. 1.2, Amuse-Bouche. 11 April 2013.
———. 1.4, Oeuf. 26 April 2013.
———. 1.7, Sorbet. 9 May 2013.
———. 2.13, Mizumono. 23 May 2014.
Gatiss, Mark, and Steven Moffatt, devisers. *Sherlock*. Hartswood Films/BBC Wales, 2010–2017.
———. 1.1, A Study in Pink. 25 July 2010.
Hanson, Hart, deviser. *Bones*. 20th Century Fox Television, 2005–2017.
Harthan, Todd, creator. *Rosewood*. Temple Hill/20th Century Fox, 2015–2017.
Heller, Bruno, creator. *The Mentalist*. Primrose Hill/Warner Bros, 2008–2015.
———. 1.1, Pilot. 23 September 2008.
———. 1.2, Red Hair and Silver Tape. 30 September 2008.
———. 1.11, Red John's Friends. 6 January 2009.
———. 2.1, Redemption. 24 September 2009.
———. 2.2, The Scarlet Letter. 1 October 2009.
———. 2.6, Black Gold and Red Blood. 5 November 2009.
———. 6.9, My Blue Heaven. 1 December 2013.
Irwin, Stephen M., and Leigh McGrath, creators. *Harrow*. ABC Studios, 2018–.
Kapinos, Tom, deviser. *Lucifer*. Jerry Bruckheimer/Vertigo/Warner Bros., 2016–2018; 2019–.
———. 1.2, Lucifer, Stay. Good Devil. 1 February 2016.
———. 1.5, Sweet Kicks. 22 February 2016.
———. 2.1, Everything's Coming Up Lucifer. 19 September 2016.
———. 2.14, Candy Morningstar. 1 May 2017.
———. 3.1, They're Back, Aren't They? 2 October 2017.
Landis, Max, deviser. *Dirk Gently's Holistic Detective Agency*. AMC Studios, 2016–2017.
———. 2.1, Space Rabbit. 14 October 2017.
———. 2.3, Two Broken Fingers. 28 October 2017.
Larson, Glen A., and Lou Shaw, creators. *Quincy M.E.* Glen A. Larson Productions/Universal Television, 1976–1983.
Lewis, Russell, deviser. *Endeavour*. Mammoth Screen/Masterpiece, 2012–.

Litvinenko, Artyom, creator. *The Sniffer*. FILM.UA, 2013–.
Marlowe, Andrew W., creator. *Castle*. Beacon Pictures/ABC Studios, 2009–2016.
———. 1.1, Flowers For Your Grave. 9 March 2009.
———. 1.2, Nanny McDead. 16 March 2009.
———. 3.1, A Deadly Affair. 20 September 2010.
———. 4.21, Headhunters. 16 April 2012.
———. 4.22, Undead Again. 30 April 2012.
———. 5.5, Probable Cause. 29 October 2012.
———. 6.3, Need to Know. 7 October 2013.
———. 6.4, Number One Fan. 14 October 2013.
———. 7.1, Driven. 29 September 2014.
———. 7.15, Reckoning. 16 February 2015.
McCrery, Nigel, creator. *Silent Witness*. BBC Studios, 1996–.
McGovern, Jimmy, creator. *Cracker*. Granada Television, 1993–1995; 1996; 2006.
Miller, Matt, creator. *Forever*. Warner Bros., 2014–2015.
Morgan, Abi, creator. *River*. Kudos, 2015.
Penhall, Joe, creator. *Mindhunter*. Denver and Delilah Productions, 2017–2019.
Piedfort, Paul, creator. *Professor T*. Channel 4, 2015–2018.
———. *Professor T*. ZDF, 2017–.
Rauch, Michael, deviser. *Instinct*. CBS Television Studios, 2018–2019.
———. 1.1, Pilot. 18 March 2018.
———. 1.2, Wild Game. 25 March 2018.
Rosenfeldt, Hans, creator. *The Bridge*. Nimbus Film, 2011–2018.
Saunders, Cynthia, creator. *Profiler*. NBC Studios, 1996–2000.
Sweeny, Craig, creator. *Limitless*. CBS Television Studios, 2015–2016.
———. 1.1, Pilot. 22 September 2015.
Tamaro, Janet, deviser. *Rizzoli & Isles*. Warner Horizon Television, 2010–2016.
Thompson, Stephen, deviser. *Vienna Blood*. Endor Productions/MR Film, 2019.

Index

L. Andrew and S. Saunders (eds.), *The Detective's Companion in Crime Fiction*, Crime Files, https://doi.org/10.1007/978-3-030-74989-7

Printed by Printforce, United Kingdom